ANOTHER DEAD YEKATERINA...

"What have we got?" Detektiv Alexander Kazakov knelt beside the M.E., Dr. Khalil Khan.

A small brown man with a thick thatch of dark hair and black, slightly slitted eyes, Khan was a Muslim anomaly—a direct decendant of Fergana's historic people in the usually orthodox Christian government machine. He glanced up at Kazakov, then down at the I.D. The victim was lucky to have the little dark man attending. Where most government M.E.s didn't give a damn about their jobs, Khalil Khan was skilled—and he cared.

"That her?" Dr. Khan asked.

"Yekaterina Weber, yes," Kazakov said.

Khan rolled the body over on its side so Kazakov could see the deep lash marks and a puncture wound on her back. He let her slump back down on the grass and her face turned to Kazakov as if to ask him a question.

How long are you going to leave me here? How long before Our Lady Yekaterina rises again? How long before the legends come true?

This was Russia, or what remained of it. Even two hundred years since Empress Yekaterina tried to take the Black Sea's Crimean Peninsula from the Ottomans couldn't erase all the history and yearnings of a people. But then this was a people descended from soldiers, servants, and serfs. Not intelligentsia. Tales of the old hag Baba Yaga, the foolish priest, and glass slippers were still told and perhaps even believed. He'd been raised on such magical fictions. In them Baba Yaga was both the witch who ate children and their savior. A lot like the true Yekaterina. With such creatures, how and whom did one trust?

Dearest Yekaterina, he thought as he studied the girl. *It could take a long time, if it happens at all.*

MYSTERIES BY THE AUTHOR

Detective Kazakov Mysteries
After Yekaterina
Mareson's Arrow
The Tsarina's Mask
Ivan's Wolf

Phoebe Clay Mysteries
Through Dark Water
Beneath Malabar Nets
Within Angkor Shadows (Coming April 2022)

Fantasy Mystery
Death By Effigy
A Death in Passing
Death in Umber

AFTER YEKATERINA

DETECTIVE KAZAKOV MYSTERIES #1

K.L. ABRAHAMSON

After Yekaterina

Published May 2018 by Twisted Root Publishing www.twistedrootpublishing.com

Book and cover design © Twisted Root Publishing Cover image: ©
artfotoss|DepositPhotos.com

ISBN: 978-1-927753-68-2

For more information about Twisted Root Publishing, please visit our website at http://www.twistedrootpublishing.com.

ACKNOWLEDGMENTS

For Kristine Kathryn Rusch whose challenge inspired the story

1

My parents named me Yekaterina after Our Lady.

Yekaterina is my secret name, the one I wear on my heart. To everyone else I am Kadija, after the Prophet's first wife, in case the invaders find us again.

My village has no name. It sits at the base of the Tian Shan mountains like a tick on the neck of a mangy dog. It has always existed, according to the elders, though its population has waxed and waned.

In the night, in the snug warmth of the hide yurt my father's father built outside the village's mud walls, my parents whisper tales of a different day. The days when Our Lady Yekaterina reigned like a goddess in her golden palace, until the heathen Saracen raged through our country. Of how, out of the ashes of Muscovy she rose again and escaped to lead us through pestilence and famine on a march so horrible most of us died in the winters. It was her strength that flowed into our veins, her will that kept us alive and she loved us as if we were her children—until her strength ran out.

It was at her death, when all hope died and the warring captains fought for her simple robe and scepter, that my grandparents fled, for the pestilence had returned and our numbers dwindled further. My grandparents and their friends came here, to the country of Fergana, the promised land.

The tattered history textbook page caught in the wind as Detektiv Alexander Kazakov stood at the edge of the crime scene. The walls of mountains to the south and east were white today, pouring cold air into the wide Fergana Valley, and he pulled the karakul fur collar of his coat tighter around his neck. At four o'clock, the October light was faded. Winter was coming. The aspen and walnut trees had dropped their gilded leaves almost overnight and the golden geese formed *V* phalanxes overhead as if heavy bombers ranged south.

Again.

Except the geese were nigh on silent, just the distant haunting honking as they dared the mountain passes that kept the Chinese if not at bay, at least at a distance. The war between the Ottomans to the west and the Chinese to the east had been going on so long it was almost impossible to imagine a time without war, though the feints and attacks overhead had waned these past few years. History said that the Germans had eaten into the remains of what had once been Holy Russia until they met their allies, the Ottomans. The Anglos and Germans had joined together to overcome the small French general. But Russia was no more—as the old text book bore testament to. And the tiny democracy that was Fergana had grown out of Russia's remains prepared to hold back invaders, but the invaders didn't come.

Not yet, not yet, blew the wind.

The original Yekaterina's aspirations led to her downfall.

"And what did you aspire to that lost you your life, little one?" he said, studying the photo identification in his hand.

The only answer was the rush of traffic from Suvarov Way just beyond the line of trees that blocked the broad boulevards of New Moscow.

He ducked under the police tape and trod the desiccated grass of Potemkin Park, named after the man who had been the original Yekaterina's strength until the Ottomans slew him. The park lay on the eastern edge of the city center amongst three-story walk-ups that were slowly being eaten up as New Moscow's business core grew. In warmer weather the place would be filled with young couples and with mothers besieged by flocks of children.

Now it was almost empty, which accounted for the body only being spotted late this afternoon by an officer on patrol.

The girl lay naked, faceup under the cold October sun with the white-clad M.E. crouched beside her. The blue sky tinged the pallor of her skin. Her eyes were milky white as if she'd been here for some time. A skein of pale hair fanned around her head and twisted around her neck. Her pale pink mouth was half open to the air as if she would drink it in. A northern girl, in police parlance, a true Russian. Not the dark-haired beauties of the area's original Kyrgyz and Uzbek tribes.

He glanced down at her ID locked in a plastic bag. Kazakov had found it in a bundle of carefully folded clothing—slim, gray skirt and a pink fluffy sweater—just inside the police tape along with the history book and a school diary schedule. No one had touched it except him. Yekaterina Weber. German-sounding name. Strange, or perhaps not given the Anglo-German Empire's arrogant citizens apparently had a God-given right to travel wherever they wanted these days. She was sixteen years old.

"What have we got?" He knelt beside the M.E., Dr. Khalil Khan.

A small brown man with a thick thatch of dark hair and black, slightly slitted eyes, Khan was a Muslim anomaly—a direct decendant of Fergana's historic people in the usually orthodox Christian government machine. He glanced up at Kazakov, then down at the I.D. The victim was lucky to have the little dark man attending. Where most government M.E.s didn't give a damn about their jobs, Khalil Khan was skilled—and he cared.

"That her?" Dr. Khan asked.

"Yekaterina Weber, yes," Kazakov said.

Khan rolled the body over on its side so Kazakov could see the deep lash marks and a puncture wound on her back. He let her slump back down on the grass and her face turned to Kazakov as if to ask him a question.

How long are you going to leave me here? How long before Our Lady Yekaterina rises again? How long before the legends come true?

This was Russia, or what remained of it. Even two hundred years since Empress Yekaterina tried to take the Black Sea's Crimean Peninsula from the Ottomans couldn't erase all the history and yearnings of a people. But then this was a people descended from soldiers, servants, and serfs. Not intelligentsia. Tales of the old hag Baba Yaga, the foolish priest, and glass slippers were still told and perhaps even believed. He'd been raised on such magical fictions. In them Baba Yaga was both the witch who ate children and their savior. A lot like the true Yekaterina. With such creatures, how and whom did one trust?

Dearest Yekaterina, he thought as he studied the girl. *It could take a long time, if it happens at all.*

"The lashes look like they were perimortem. Whip, most likely. Done with anger? The puncture wound probably killed her. It was most likely a knife-like instrument. She may not have died here."

Kazakov nodded. "Not enough blood on the ground. Even though the ground's not frozen, there should be some sign of a pool. So, the killing was emotionally motivated. When the whipping wasn't enough, our murderer killed her."

Dr. Khan nodded. "You're learning." He lifted her arm. "By the lack of rigor, I'd say that she'd been here a few hours at most; but it's harder to judge with the cold. It could be as long as twelve hours. You can see the process has started in the tightness of the eyelids and the jut of the jaw." He nodded down at the girl. "Funny how a smile makes all the difference." The girl in the government school ID was dressed in a pink fluffy sweater and her hair was swept back behind her ears. A broad white smile was aimed at the camera.

Khan was right. The smile made her look like a schoolgirl, ready for her future.

But in the grass, she was just another Yekaterina: past tsarina, long dead diarist, they were all just dead on this chill October morning.

I n the cold concrete office of the New Moscow *politseyshiyuchastok*, the police station, Kazakov sat with the girl's schoolbook and identification open before him. The drafty room housed ten detectives, the small city's entire squad, dealing with all forms of crime from drugs to murder in the city center and old city. Other squads, housed elsewhere, dealt with crime in the suburbs, and still another specialty unit dealt with corporate crime. Seven of the room's nine other cold metal desks were unoccupied at the moment. Apparently, most cases had been solved by six o'clock today.

The two other occupied desks held Antonov and Alenin, the A and A team—partners who had worked together the past ten years. Antonov was a granite block of a man with sullen blue eyes and scowling, downturned lips that could turn themselves upright at the blackest of humor. But a frown and a black sense of humor weren't something to be held against him—Kazakov shared them, as did most detectives in New Moscow. Antonov was a fine investigator who had graduated from training a year before Kazakov—and never failed to remind Kazakov of it.

His partner, Alenin, was five years Kazakov's junior and the antithesis of Antonov's body type—tall, with an athelete's broad shoulders and lean muscle slowly gathering the weight of middle age. He had pale blue eyes and a ready smile that offset the dourness of his partner.

Kazakov sighed and inhaled the stink of cold tea and the cheap, unfiltered Ottoman cigarettes preferred by the squad and most of the country. He had quit smoking, or so he told himself, though he still kept a single cigarette in his wallet against emergencies.

"That was a deep sigh, friend," Alenin said, looking up from where he was reading a document over Antonov's shoulder. "Have you finally found a girl who will have you?" He grinned.

It was the same teasing refrain that had hounded Kazakov since he and his wife split up and he hadn't immediately taken another woman.

"I suppose you could say that," Kazakov played along. "Except this one is sixteen years old and dead of stab wounds." He met Alenin's gaze. "Who else will have her?"

"Maudlin bastard," Antonov muttered. "Let him have her, Sergei. We have other fish to fry." The big man gave a small nod to Kazakov. They had worked a few cases together long ago. There was still respect between them, though their outlook on many things had diverged.

Kazakov turned back to his evidence. He sipped his cold, sweet tea as he considered. The schoolbook was one he remembered from his own childhood, a treasured diary of one of the first generations of Russian refugees to make the lush fields of the Fergana Valley their home.

The flood of migrants had come at a price. The traditional Kyrgyz and Uzbek villagers and their animistic beliefs had at first been welcoming, but then had been pushed out by the sheer numbers of displaced people who had come east. Those villagers had taken to the higher mountains, while a Muslim minority had stayed as the desperate Russians settled around them.

The Russians had been starving and dying from the plague that descended on them after the Ottoman war destroyed all infrastructure and food sources. It was on that desperate diaspora following the Tea Road across the continent that blessed Yekaterina gave the devastated remains of her people the gift of democracy for their petty states. For a few of them, like those in Fergana, the gift had held. Yekaterina had always held that Russians were different from all others.

But why was the girl carrying this particular book? It was a two-hundred-year-old book, read to elementary school children; and Yekaterina Weber was certainly older than twelve.

And what was she doing in Potemkin Park? Less than twelve hours dead at most, Khan had said. That would mean that she'd been out before five in the morning. An unusual time for a girl that age. Most teenagers preferred to be up in late morning. And why left there and naked? It was as if the killer was making some point. He would have to wait on Khan's report to know if it was a sex crime, but the lack of clothing suggested it.

First things first. He needed to contact the family, not a job he enjoyed when the news wasn't good. Shoving himself up from his desk, he lumbered over to the small desk in the corner and slumped into the seat. The massive machine was the latest investigative tool provided to their office, courtesy of the city council.

It was a huge, gray, steel-covered block imported from the Germans, almost as tall as a man, with ugly metal on three sides and what looked like a twenty-inch television screen on the front with a keyboard in a small depression beneath the screen.

Bending to look at the keyboard, he typed in Yekaterina Weber, hit the red *send* button, and leaned back in the chair. It groaned under his bulk, for though he had always kept fit through his outdoor activities, he had grown lazy in his exercise these past five years since his fortieth birthday. Not for the first time today, he had the urge to smoke.

Ping.

The machine had things to tell him, like a fairy tale fish or birds that held the secret truth. He hit the blue *receive* button. A list of names appeared with the top name in bold, the most likely match for the requested name. The length of the list surprised him. It seemed there were more German Webers residing in Fergana than he'd realized. For a moment, like a shiver at a memory, the realization made him uncomfortable.

Some said the feeling came when someone walked over your grave.

The home address listed on the government database had been pulled from government school records and existed beyond the large eight-story towers of the business heart of Fergana and beyond the brightly-painted domed concrete replica of Saint Basil's Cathedral in the middle of New Moscow. Beyond the walk-up apartments encircling Potemkin Park, a new area had been planted with young trees at the curb. When the trees were grown, this area would be a paradise compared to the flat, grassland steppes of the countryside.

Neat rows of steep-roofed houses with faux-wood concrete sides were physical echoes of the dacha homes the Russian people had left behind long ago—or at least what they believed them to be. Neat, pocket-sized yards held small vegetable gardens that were now faded and tattered brown with the fall. Here and there, a last wizened tomato blushed forgotten and withered in the cool.

The Weber yard was surrounded by a hip-high concrete block fence like a halfhearted fortress in the midst of the neighborhood. The yard itself was mostly fallow though a few turnips and winter kale grew at the ends of regimented raised beds that looked newly turned. A small stool sat next to the door with a trowel and a set of gardening gloves, the gloves neatly pulled one inside the other. Everything in its place.

The porch was swept, the door newly painted, so slick and shiny red he wondered it didn't come off on his knuckles at his knock. The sounds of footfall echoed within and then the curtain stirred on the window beside the door. There was a moment of hesitation and then the door opened. A woman stood there, slim, with Yekaterina's silken blonde hair darkened slightly by the years. It was twisted back from her face into a precise figure eight. She was tall for a woman, almost five feet nine in her low, boxy heels with the buckles over the instep. She wore a slim-fitting tweed skirt and a brown cardigan—buttoned— over a crisp white blouse buttoned up to her throat.

"Yes?" Her eyes were guarded and she held the door as if she planned to slam it shut at the first sign of danger. As if she did not trust strangers.

"Detektiv Kazakov of the Fergana Politseyshiy." He showed her his identification. "You are Mrs. Weber?"

"Not Weber anymore. It is Bure. My first husband passed away and I remarried." She nodded, but her hand came up to her collar. "Is something wrong? My husband…"

Bure. The name meant something…

"May I come in?" There was something wrong with her response. The cold air of the afternoon swirled around his shoulders. She must feel it, but she seemed frozen where she stood. And no mention of her daughter. Odd.

Finally, she nodded and stepped aside. He ducked his head to enter and found himself inside…history. Wooden floors and walls gleamed as if someone regularly waxed them. The familiar scents of beetroot, tea, and a slight hint of something sweet and spicy. To one side of the door, a small parlor was dominated by a heavy, ornate couch with embroidered cushions and a high, wingback chair covered in crimson damask. A fireplace mantle was filled with old family photos in silver frames that showed Mrs. Bure and a tall, pale man who looked vaguely familiar. Others showed a younger Yekaterina in a frothy white dress that was typical of religious ceremonies, and a much younger version of the blond man with an older version of himself, and an elegant blonde-haired woman who looked strangely similar to Mrs. Bure. His father and mother, maybe.

An antique crucifix hung in a corner, and in a niche in the wall hung what looked like a gold-gilt icon of the Virgin vivid with old paint and gold. It looked old. It looked genuine. It looked like something you would see in the treasury section of the Fergana Museum. For all the middle-class outer trappings of their house, this family clearly had come from old wealth. And had brought it with them. Not a soldier, servant, or serf.

He turned to Mrs. Bure and nodded at the icon. "A lovely piece. It is old, correct?"

She gave a single nod. "It was in my husband's family—all they brought out of old Russia."

He didn't quite believe her, but nodded. "Perhaps you should have a seat. This visit, it is about your daughter."

"Yekaterina?" She perched on the edge of the overwhelming couch and, if anything, her pale skin went almost the color of her dead daughter's flesh. "You've found her, then."

"Found her?"

"My husband reported her missing two days ago."

And that was impossible because, when he entered the girl in the computer, a flag for a missing person's case would have shown against her name.

"Do you know who he spoke to?" Kazakov asked. It was not

unheard of that an officer was slow in entering information in the police information system…

She shook her head and the couch seemed to consume her. "What is this about? What has happened? Is Yekaterina all right?" Finally, she asked the right question. Stranger and stranger.

Why did her concern leap so quickly to her husband when she had a missing daughter? He took a deep breath and took the liberty of sitting down in the chair. "Mrs. Bure, when was the last time you saw your daughter?"

Her gaze fell to her hands. "It was Friday at supper. We were at the table and my husband scolded her. She was acting silly— almost giddy. My husband told her to mind her table manners or she could go to her room." Mrs. Bure bit her lip almost as if she knew what was coming. "She chose her room," she whispered.

These were the times he hated his job. The disaster. The pain that would overwhelm a loved one's eyes. But there was no use in delaying. It had to be done. "Mrs. Bure. I regret to inform you, but we found your daughter's body this morning in Potemkin Park. She had been stabbed. Yekaterina is dead."

"No." She shook her head. "That cannot be."

He reached across a small coffee table and caught her hand. "I am sorry, but it was her. She had her identification."

She went statue still, her face rigid. Then she yanked her hand away and stood. "No. No. Not Yekaterina. No." She paced the floor between the mantel and the door, then stopped abruptly, still dry-eyed. "I must call my husband."

Kazakov stood. "A good idea. While you do, may I examine your daughter's room?"

She met his gaze, her lip quivering almost as if she was angry. "At the top of the stairs. The second door on the right." Then she left him for the back of the house that must be the kitchen.

Kazakov clumped up the stairs, considering. Most mothers would be in tears. Most mothers would be with him right now, sobbing about how their daughter was a good girl, demanding to know how and where and why this had happened and who would do something like this to their child. At the top of the stairs he paused to listen. Silence ticked around him in the darkened hallway, but from downstairs came the sound of harsh whispers. They rose and fell in the staccato of anger. Not grief, but fury.

***

The second room on the right had a closed door, but daylight placed long panels of light on the hall floor through the others. The first room on his left was clearly the parents'. Kazakov ducked his head inside. A double bed with quilted cover in a patchwork of shades of red. A curtained window. Built-in drawers along one wall. A wood heater against the winter cold and another orthodox icon hung on the wall. This one did not have the gold gilt of the one downstairs, but the lustrous paint said it was still old. Neat. Tidy. Well cared for.

He went down the hall to Yekaterina's room and opened the door.

The spice he'd detected at the front door caught him full in the face and he shook himself at the heady scent. It was like catching a face full of church brazier incense. Was the girl very religious? The body hadn't worn a crucifix, but there had been that photo in the white dress.

He stepped inside. A girl's room. Magazine pages of the latest shaggy-headed boy band from Anglia taped to the wall. A narrow bed with a blue bedspread under the window. A desk. A straight-backed spindle chair. A small bookcase filled with books.

Closing the door behind him, he stood there hoping to get a feel for his victim, but from the look of things, Yekaterina Weber was a typical schoolgirl. He opened the drawers of her desk but found only paper and pens—odd in itself. Didn't girls usually stuff odd sundry things into such places? There was nothing that told of Yekaterina or her friendships here.

The closet gave no more clues: a few straight-cut skirts like her mother wore. Blouses. A sweater of navy blue. No pink fluffy sweater. Nothing like that at all. As if the pink sweater next to her body was special? Perhaps something she purchased herself because it made her feel pretty, while these clothes bore the straight-laced, utilitarian stamp of being purchased by her mother?

The bookcase held novels and schoolbooks. There was a slim empty space that he would bet his pay-check had once held the slim diary of Yekaterina of the yurts. He checked each of the remaining books, but found nothing. Where were her school notebooks? The binders teenagers used? She was in school. There had to be something of that kind.

He checked under the bed, but there was nothing there, not even dust. When he stepped out of the room, her mother was waiting.

"My husband will be home in a few minutes. He would like you to wait for him."

He nodded. "She has a very neat room. Unusual in a teenager."

Her chin lifted a little. "I expect my child to have high standards."

"I see." He nodded. "Does she keep a briefcase or a school backpack? I noticed that there are no school notebooks in the room."

Mrs. Bure went still. "She had one. It was a blue courier bag—the latest fashion. We got it for her last Christmas."

"And it is not in the house?" he asked.

"If it is not in her room, then it is not here." Her closed expression did not leave room for more questions.

His footsteps sounded hollow as he went down the stairs after her and soon a black Ziln limousine pulled up at the curb. Kazakov stiffened by the parlor window as a man climbed out of the front and held the door for a passenger. Bure. Kazakov remembered now. Bure was a government functionary who was now being groomed for something greater. The newly formed Reformation Party had great things planned for him. Great enough to command a car and driver to bring him home.

Boris Bure was a man of middle height who seemed to command the hallway as soon as he entered. Perhaps it was his breadth of shoulder. Perhaps it was the rigid way he held his ramrod-straight back and white-haired head. Perhaps it was the metallic scent that came with him when he entered the room, as if he generated an electric charge.

He had pale blue eyes and large white teeth that he exposed almost as a warning as he shook Kazakov's hand.

Even though Bure was a good six inches shorter than Kazakov's six feet two, Bure seemed to look him eye-to-eye. "What's this all about, then? I reported Yekaterina missing two days ago and haven't spoken to a detective since and now you arrive telling my wife her daughter is dead."

Her daughter. Not his.

Kazakov bowed his head. "I am sorry to bring this bad news. Yekaterina's body was found in Potemkin Park this afternoon. She was murdered."

Her mother's hand came to her mouth as if she finally believed. Bure did nothing as if letting the news settle in. Then he nodded. "Terrible news. Terrible."

He caught his wife in a hug. "I know how this must upset you, love." He patted her back as if she might break, but if Kazakov was waiting for emotion in Bure's voice, it wasn't there.

The man made no move to take them back into the parlor either. It was more as if he expected Kazakov to leave.

"Mr. Bure, your wife tells me that you last had dinner with Yekaterina on Friday. Can you tell me about that?"

Bure shrugged, still holding his wife. "We ate. She was being foolish. I told her she could either act like a proper lady or she could go to her room."

Kazakov nodded and made a note of Bure's statement. "Can you tell me what she was doing that was so foolish?"

Bure and his wife looked at each other.

"It was nothing. She was talking nonsense."

"What, precisely, did she say?"

Bure released his wife to turn to Kazakov. "Detektiv, do I look like a man who would remember foolishness? Now my wife has had an awful shock. I would like to tend to her. Perhaps you could leave us in peace in this time of grief."

Bure eased past Kazakov and opened the door, inviting him to leave. Kazakov had gotten as much as he was going to from this odd couple, but it was stranger still that they did not want more from him. Now he just had to determine what this oddity meant.

———

It was at two thirty the next afternoon on his way to an appointment at Yekaterina's school that his radio crackled and he was called to the second body.

This one was on the far side of New Moscow in the old Islamic quarter. Square mud-and-stucco houses leaned together around hidden central courtyards. Once the houses had been the graceful villas of the Muslim caravan merchants, for the Silk and Tea Roads had both wound through Fergana generations ago, but now each house held four or five impoverished families; it seemed the new Russian economy had no place for Muslim employees. Television antennas and clotheslines filled the flat rooftops. Narrow streets barely wide enough for a single car wound through the maze of buildings, the streets still sometimes blocked by a donkey carrying burlap bags of limes or an enterprising businessman who had spread his goods under awnings into the street.

Children scattered through the streets at the sight of his sedan. In this part of town, no police presence was a good thing—in the eyes of the residents. Kazakov came to a stop where the houses ran out and a field of grass ran away toward the mountains.

The roadside was clogged with marked police vehicles and the M.E.'s wagon. Kazakov pulled in behind them near a gathering crowd, but instead of expensive suits like Bure had worn, these men wore dusty trousers and woolen work shirts with their small, white, embroidered felt *ak kalpak* perched on their heads. The women wore scarves, and one ancient grandmother even wore the bright skirts and white, ornately wound *elechek* turban of the Kyrgyz hill tribes like a ghost out of time.

Once, these people and their Uzbek cousins had been the only people in Fergana. Now, after the influx of people and two hundred years of large families amongst the Russians, they were a minority in their own land and becoming more so every year. To the point where some whispered that they sympathized with Fergana's enemies. So far there'd been no trouble, but bad blood festered and there were even rumors of the Krygyz spying in the mountains for the Ottomans against the Chinese.

Kazakov climbed out to the sound of angry murmurs.

Police tape had been set up, roping off an area in the middle of the field. The wind off the eastern Tian Shan Mountains ripped at the tape and its metal poles. It rippled the grass in a sea of violent gold and green and whipped the clothes of the police and the onlookers. Kazakov pulled his karakul collar tighter. It was colder than normal.

Uniformed police officers kept the people at bay. Kazakov waded out into the brittle grass and it rattled and tugged against his pant legs. The earth was hard underfoot and dust rose with each footfall. At the western edge of the old town rose the five peaks of the great Yekaterina's Mountain turned golden in the setting sun.

The body lay tangled in the tall grass with the backdrop of the snow-covered Tian Shan range. His arm was outstretched as if he reached for them, and his legs were tangled as if he'd been running. He wore dark trousers and a plain white shirt— one that looked as if it had been pressed to impress someone. The red bloom of a gunshot wound burned through the center of his back.

Staying to the edge of the police line, Kazakov circled the scene. The victim was young, with that floppy hair the young men were copying from the foreign musicians. His head was turned to one side and his eyes and mouth were open. Beside him knelt Dr. Khan.

"What do we have?" Kazakov asked as he ducked under the tape and knelt beside the M.E.

"Male. Young. I'd say about eighteen. Single shot to the back. By the look of it, I'd say it was a large caliber weapon."

"A fight? A mugging?"

Khan lifted his head from examining a hand. "Nothing under his nails. No bruising of the knuckles. I'd say he was running. By his face, I'd say running for his life. Look at the path he left." He pointed.

It was true. A path of crushed grass led toward the northern edge of the old town. "Any idea who he is?"

"The ID in his wallet says his name's Manas uulu Semetai—Semetai son of Manas."

Semetai Manas, but written in the traditional name structure of the Muslim Kyrgyz. Only the most traditional of the Muslim families held names of that fashion and these were even drawn from the heroes of the great oral epic of the Kyrgyz people. Kazakov nodded, stood, and retraced the victim's path, back toward the old town's weathered, grey-strained walls.

The path led right into the maze of streets, as if the victim might have burst from them before being gunned down. Kazakov reached the narrow dirt street and stepped between the buildings. The sunlight disappeared and so did the worst of the wind, though a scuffle of dust blew around his feet.

The dryness meant that footprints were hard to distinguish. Clearly this was a well-used route because the dusty soil showed many scuff marks. There were no doors in the walls of the buildings here: the doors must give out onto the cross street. No window up above either. Windows would look into the interior courtyards. Inside these buildings were private worlds. Ones that no longer quite meshed with the modern city New Moscow had become. Piles of garbage had been set against the wall to await the irregular pickup. With a foot, he shoved aside the pile of bags and melon rinds and a bright patch of color showed even in the gloom.

Pulling gloves on, Kazakov dug through the sour-sweet rot of melon and the remains of old mutton bones—well chewed by dogs. A blue courier bag lay in the dust and muck, but a sweet spice he recognized cut through the rot. He picked up the bag by its strap and gingerly carried it back the way he'd come. Visiting Yekaterina's school would have to wait.

In the concrete cavern of his office, Kazakov considered his desk and the Weber case's open cardboard evidence box in the center of the top. It held the girl's clothing, including her fluffy pink sweater—

probably something the girl kept for special occasions—her identification, and the schoolbook. Beside it sat the bag he had found near the other murder scene. It fit Yekaterina's mother's description of the girl's notebook bag.

At eight o'clock in the evening the office was empty, though a still-steaming cup of tea on Antonov's desk said that it hadn't been empty long. Crime didn't occur according to schedule.

Beyond the lone window across the room, night had long fallen and the wind flattened a few snowflakes against the glass. He contemplated all the things that needed to be done in this strange case.

Two young people dead, the blue bag a potential connection between them.

Hands encased in thin rubber gloves, he unzipped the bag and rummaged through it. Its contents included a carefully folded white blouse as if the girl had changed into her pink sweater before she died, suggesting that she had some place special that she was going. There were also a small jar of scented cream reminiscent of church incense and school notebooks with the name Yekaterina Weber printed carefully in the center of the inside of each cover. The outside of the covers had the flower and heart doodles and designs of a typical bored student. He could remember doing something similar himself when he was in school, except his doodles had tended more toward airplanes and guns.

Guns like the one that had killed Semetai Manas.

Just what was a school bag belonging to Yekaterina Weber doing in the old town of Fergana? What was it doing so close to a young man's dead body? Multiple murders didn't usually happen within twenty-four hours of each other. Not in New Moscow, though up in the mountains there might be more violence.

He flipped through the pages of the notebooks. Algebra. History: the destruction of an ancient country. The building of Fergana. The tiny new homeland was pressed like a leaf between the Chinese and the Ottomans who, with their sometime allies the Anglo-German, were intent on completing their conquest of China. It would fulfil the Ottomans' centuries-old ambition of dominating the world.

So far Fergana had stood as a neutral space in the Great Game between the two empires. If the Ottomans were victorious, Fergana wouldn't stand a chance.

But that was tomorrow's problem. For today he needed to figure out who had killed two young people and why.

He had tried to interview the Manas family, but in the closed community of the old town, he had wasted three hours before determining that the family had abandoned their last known address. None of their neighbors would talk to him. No one would tell him where they'd gone.

He pulled out Yekaterina's old schoolbook diary found at her murder scene and thumbed through it. Why was it there? Why was her bag at the scene of the boy's murder?

The bag suggested the deaths were connected, but the classroom schedule contained only class assignments. He examined the notes on the day of her death, but there was only mention of a term paper to be researched. In the bottom right corner was a doodle of a heart next to the letter *P*.

He flipped through the pages again and noted the heart repeated many times, while the letter varied between, *P*, *Y* and *PT*. Her body had been found in Potemkin Park. A code of some kind?

He couldn't say, and turned to the history book. It contained only page after page of the old story of the past diarist Yekaterina's escape with her parents and the founding of the Ferganese homeland. It was almost a fable, a creation myth that let people remember there had been another place, another time when they had been a great and noble people under the great Tsarina Yekaterina who had given them freedom. It gave substance to their dreams and to the fables grandmothers told to their grandchildren.

Of course, a child's schoolbook didn't mention how that same Tsarina had brought destruction upon them all by waking the slumbering Ottoman empire with her armies. Or how she had kept her people enslaved as serfs until the extent of the Ottoman destruction was so great that the whole system supporting her kingdom collapsed and she was forced to take refuge with the common people. That was the uncomfortable truth of their democratic freedom that most people failed to remember.

He went to close the book but something caught his eye. The inside back cover held a simple inscription.

For Yekaterina, my heart. Love, Semetai.

There was his connection.

That and a pink sweater that a young, infatuated girl would wear to meet her sweetheart.

A chill ran up his back in the stillness of the room. From beyond the detective office came the sounds of life in the rest of the station. But not here. Here on his desk there was only death and destruction caused by young love.

She'd been giddy, her mother had said. Foolish, in her stepfather's words. All the signs of a schoolgirl crush, an infatuation. It was the kind of thing that a father would tease a daughter about.

But an infatuation between a good Orthodox Catholic Russian girl, stepdaughter of a man on the rise in politics, and a boy named Semetai?

That would be a problem. A problem the family would want to fix.

Both families?

Manas uulu Semetai was a name steeped in tribal traditions and there was no love lost between the tribes and the Russian newcomers—not anymore.

The lashes on the girl's back before she was stabbed. Could that be a scourging by an angry family—angry that she had seduced their boy?

Had the Manas family run because they'd killed the girl? And was that why there was such strangeness in the Bure family? Had they done the same in return?

"I need to understand!" He shoved back from his desk, stood, and then stabbed the desk phone with his finger. It buzzed in his ear and then clicked as someone answered.

"Khan?"

"Yes." The calm voice of the M.E. soothed him over the phone.

The M.E. would be nearing the end of his shift this evening.

"I need to talk to you. Do you have time?"

There was silence a moment and Kazakov heard the smile.

"No. But you will come anyway. I will be here." He hung up.

As Kazakov pulled his coat on, the office door yanked open and Detektiv Chief Inspektor Rostoff pushed into the room. Once they had been friends. They had gone through police training together, but Rostoff had had a free ride because of his family connections. Those same connections had let him rise quickly in rank. Now his large red nose and bleary eyes tracked across the room and settled on Kazakov.

"The others are out? Good. Busy men. Always busy. I like to see that." Rostoff was a bear of a man in the old Russian style, with a heavy coat and fur hat in winter. In the fall it was just the coat that reeked of too much sweat leached into old wool. Rostoff pulled his gloves off and strode through the desks to Kazakov.

"Good man." He scanned the evidence on the desk. "A case. You are busy? Yes?" He pounded Kazakov's shoulder and then hitched a leg over the corner of a neighboring desk and sat.

Rostoff never showed his face in the detective section and certainly not at this hour. He was too busy rubbing shoulders with the bigwigs in the justice department. That he was here now was a worry.

Rostoff grinned a big yellow smile. "My dear Kazakov. Look at the hour."

Kazakov did. Eight forty p.m. He had worked later many times. The question was what or who had brought Rostoff here.

"You are a good man. You work hard, my old friend. Maybe sometimes you work too hard."

Kazakov went cold as Rostoff pointedly scanned the evidence again, then casually picked up the diary, the school schedule, and the bag and dropped them in the cardboard evidence box.

"This case, it has you worried, yes? I can tell by the look in your eyes. Would it surprise you that it has others worried, too? Maybe you should not worry so much. Maybe sometimes you should let things go. Yes?"

His yellow smile broadened as he settled the box top in place. "You see? Not so difficult."

Frozen, Kazakov just looked at him. What could he do that would not bring the weight of Rostoff's sanctions down on him? What could he say?

"It's a double murder. Since when do we let such things go?"

Rostoff said nothing but his thick lips curved in a semblance of a dismissive smile.

Clenching his fists, Kazakov turned his back on the other man and headed for the door.

***

Rostoff might have handed down an official decree, but that didn't mean Kazakov had to listen. It was a double murder. A murder of children. Surely to God, that meant something.

The M.E.'s office sat in the basement of Our Lady Yekaterina Hospital. It was a large, four-story building built with a fountain and garden in the front that briefly in the springtime, could be called beautiful. But summer brought the winds off the mountains that drank the water from the fountain and leached the trees to the color of dust. In October, the fountain was brown with leaves. In November the snow would be falling.

Kazakov left his sedan in the parking lot bathed in amber streetlight and strode through the stand of half-barren, night-bound trees under the half-grown moon. The trees were the tallest in Fergana—maples, while in most of the city it was generally aspen that survived the wind and snow of the winter. The red leaves were a particular treat in a town built mainly of concrete, and he liked the way they shuffled around his feet. Almost like snow, without the cold and the shoveling.

He bypassed the hospital's well-lit main door and went down a shadowed set of concrete stairs to one side of the structure. A metal door was locked, but he knocked and the door buzzed. He pushed inside into the stomach-clenching smells of blood and guts and formaldehyde. The middle-aged receptionist nodded him through.

If Khalil Khan was busy, he had made time for Kazakov. He sat behind a small, scarred wooden desk in a small office as if he was waiting. He had two files closed before him on the desk and nodded

Kazakov into the lone chair across from him. Behind Khan, the wall was lined with books.

"Tell me what I don't know," Kazakov asked.

"The boy was killed with an antique rifle. The bullet was of a type only used for some of the old Chinese makes." He looked at his hands and let the news hang in the air. "It's the kind the Kyrgyz use for hunting. They trade for them at the markets on the other side of the mountains—when the Ottomans and Chinese aren't fighting."

"Any likelihood of a Russian getting their hands on such a weapon?" Given Khan was Kyrgyz, he would have an insight into such things.

Khan pursed his lips and shrugged. "Maybe. It might be possible—from police evidence lockers perhaps—but otherwise unlikely. They aren't licensed and they're kept hidden. The Kyrgyz take their weapons seriously. These things are almost family heirlooms—reminders of a time before the Russians took over and regulated everything."

He said it carefully, no inflection in his voice. It must be difficult for a descendent of those proud tribal people to see how their world had become a Russian country.

"So, what you're saying is that Semetai Manas was likely killed by his own people."

Khan didn't say anything, only met his gaze.

"You know something," Kazakov said softly.

Khan shook his head. "Not know. At least not know-as-evidence know. But there are things in this culture, just as in yours. The sense of proper. The sense of place and the need for continuity of a people. You cannot let anything get in the way of that. Of the blood."

A sick feeling settled in the pit of Kazakov's stomach. Such pride and sense of people ran strong in Russians too. It was bred into them. It was fed by schools with books such as Yekaterina's diary and by the state in the names of hospitals and parks and streets and mountains that bore different names depending on who you spoke to.

"The girl. The lashes."

Khan nodded. "They were deep. Made with rage. There were also deep bruises on her neck and shoulders. I'd say she was throttled in anger, then held down for the lashing before she was stabbed. Whoever did it buried the hilt of the knife deep in her. The edges of the wound were deeply torn."

The air was too close, the stench of death too strong as Kazakov heaved himself up out of the chair.

"One more thing," Khan said. "She was pregnant."

Feeling momentarily drunk, Kazakov nodded. "How far along?"

"First trimester." Khan looked away at his desk and shook his head. "Thank you."

Kazakov left the office feeling old and useless and climbed the stairs to the parking lot.

A gust of mountain wind caught him and he staggered and thought he might be ill. Instead he turned his back on the lights illuminating Yekaterina's mountain and fumbled for the lighter and the lone cigarette he kept in his wallet. Shielding them against the wind, he lit the cigarette and inhaled the warm acrid tar only to let it out in a long belch of smoke.

The wind tore it away and the moonlight caught on the Tian Shan Mountains that loomed white but no longer so high. No longer so remote. With a sigh, he stubbed the cigarette out and headed for his car. He would need to be very careful or he could light a fire that would ignite his country. There was already too much division between Fergana's Russians and the people whose country the Russians had occupied.

War had found a new way across the mountains.

2

It had been one month since Chief Inspektor Rostoff removed Kazakov from major crime investigations and made him the squad's errand boy. Five weeks since the evidence of that most troubling case of Yekaterina had walked out the office door in Rostoff's hands.

The morning wind came out of the west, carrying an acrid scent and a thin haze of red dust from the Ottoman deserts and the fertile Fergana Valley. It placed a veil of pink across the blue morning sky and across the six inches of snow that had fallen overnight to erase the filthy coal dust that had stained the last snowfall—or perhaps it was just the aftermath of too much vodka that placed a bloody hue over everything.

Kazakov rubbed the rough stubble of his beard and blinked up at the November sky. No, there was no such thing as too much vodka—not when he had been ordered to forget a murder case that ate at him and invaded his dreams. Instead of following orders he had tried to quietly interview school officials to continue the investigation, only to have those officials contact Rostoff. Since then, things had not gone well at work—the only good thing coming from it the fact that he had lost weight and found his muscles chopping wood at his dacha. But the tang in the air was the ozone bite of the factories that lay far down the valley sending up their thick smoke to join the dust. The pristine snow would be black soon enough. In Fergana, everything was stained.

Once his people had thought this valley was a Garden of Eden—look at what they had done to it. This morning, on top of his burgeoning resentment, the view just made him angry.

With the Tian Shan and Fergana Ranges to the east and north, and the Pamir Alay range to the south, New Moscow spread around the base of Yekaterina Mountain and besieged the remains of the old Uzbek and Kyrgyz villages and their Silk Road caravanserai that had stood here long before the Russian refugees came. At the base of Yekaterina Mountain along the Potemkin River, the new city was a pathetic sprawl of concrete copies of the glory of St. Basil's Cathedral with its paint-peeled onion domes, the lovingly maintained façade of St. Petersburg's royal palace that covered the concrete bunkers of Ferganese government, and the oozing suburbs of Anglo-German-style cottages gradually devouring the fields and ancient orchards around the city. Broad swaths of timber and minerals had been chewed from the flanks of the mountain ranges, leaving dark wounds. Even Yekaterina Mountain had felt his people's heavy hand with an amusement park bulldozed into the rock at the base of the mountain.

Instead of safeguarding the beauty of the Fergana that was, the people had dreamed only of the greatness of what they wished had been. Holy Russia.

One of the first things the refugee Russians had done when they built their new city as a memorial to the vanished greater Russian Empire was to dedicate Yekaterina Park across the Potemkin River from Potemkin Park, so that the great Tsarina was still comforted by her old lover. At the heart of Yekaterina Park stood a larger-than-life statue of the great Yekaterina, the Tsarina who had raised Russia so high, to its intellectual and military zenith, that it had nowhere to go but to plunge into darkness.

The Great Yekaterina had done that, too. And so Russia vanished and Fergana remained like a crumb left on the table of Asia. So far no one had bothered to sweep it away.

In a way, the statue in the center of the park was fitting. It had been Yekaterina's selfish need for glory that had brought about the great fall.

Sighing, he turned away from the park to the Red Veil. The brothel sat on the eastern side of the park so that the peaks of the Fergana and Tian Shan mountains hung above it like a coronation crown. That seemed somehow fitting this red-stained morning.

Unlike most of New Moscow, this house was of wood and modeled after fashionable Anglo townhouses, or so he'd been told. Its pristine white front rose up three stories, broadening as it went into faux turrets and filigree-adorned gables that crowded the roof so that it appeared to stand on an impossibly narrow base. Each window had curved lintels and each gable had arched eaves. With its low wrought iron fence, it looked like it stood on chicken legs. Its paint glowed strangely virginal considering what the place housed.

Forty years ago, someone had financed this special house and paid off the politicians and the police ever since. The corruption left him sick to his stomach with emotions burbling like an angry stew. A brothel. That was what Rostoff was after: by having Kazakov collect the department bribes he would stain Kazakov's soul, too. Control him and stop his personal investigation into the Weber and Manas murders —or so Rostoff thought.

Kazakov climbed the ten steps to the front door with a weariness that all of Fergana seemed to exude this early morning. The thickly varnished front door was the last barrier before he began what was apparently to become his regular first-of-the-month rounds. He hesitated before knocking, because this time when he stepped through this door he would become a changed man.

The boiling stew of his gut spread outward and frothed in his limbs. Rostoff was wrong if he thought he could blacken Kazskov's ethics. He would find some way around this. Some way to make the whole thing work.

This early in the morning the establishment patrons would be safely gone and Frau Zelinka, the proprietress, whom he had interviewed once before after an assault on one of her clients, would be enjoying a self-congratulatory cup of tea. Gritting his teeth, he knocked once on the thick wooden door and turned away, wishing he could take the knock back.

Across the street waited the snowbound lawns and stately naked trees of the park. All the trees had been planted by hand, for once this space had been mostly grassland with a thin fringe of poplar along the river's edge. According to what he'd learned in high school, this park with its paved paths and lilac bowers was modeled after what his people had left behind. It was as if, after two hundred years had passed, the entire country still carried a ghost branded on its soul.

The door pulled open behind him. "Yes? It is you?"

The girl at the door was Chinese, or perhaps Thai, though with the expansion of the Chinese Empire, was there really much difference? She appeared very young with perfect skin—too young to be working yet—but then what did he know? She wore a simple, chaste housedress of grey silk with a high collar and long sleeves that hid her pale skin like a cloud over the moon. Likely one of Frau Zelinka's imports whose deflowering Frau Zelinka would auction off when it came time to add her to the brothel's delights. Until then the girl would do light duties around the place, serving drinks, making the patrons covetous of her. She bowed gracefully, her palms together by her face, and he noticed that perfection was not quite hers. Her left hand was a twisted, withered thing. But the naturalness of the palm-together gesture marked her upbringing as Thai.

"The mistress waits for you," she said meekly and ushered Kazakov inside after he scuffed the snow off his boots.

The place smelled of frankincense, sweet and spicy. This spoke well of Frau Zelinka's connections with the Ottoman world that she could obtain such a rarity, and of the exotic nature of her goods. But then the good Frau had been here twenty years— long enough to forge links into both the Ottoman and the Chinese sides of the war, as well as the highest ranks of Fergana.

He followed the girl down a wood-paneled hallway. The rooms he passed were draped in blue and green silks and held deep cushions and rich oriental carpets like an ancient caravanserai from the days of the Silk Road. Then tea, spice, and silk traveled by camel and horse across the Tian Shan mountains and across the deserts to Constantinople and places like Paris, Rome, and Barcelona when they could still call themselves the great capitals of Europe.

The girl knocked once on a slickly painted black door and a voice spoke from within. She opened the door and a cloud of acrid- sweet smoke billowed into the hall. Ganja—technically illegal, but then the Red Veil was technically illegal, too, and Kazakov was treading a dangerous gray area.

"Detektiv Kazakov," the girl said and waved Kazakov past her into the smoky room. She closed the door behind him.

"Aah, Detektiv. I was expecting you earlier. But then you are new to this job, yes?" Frau Zilinka peered up at him from her red brocade divan, her silk kimono artfully arranged to expose one long, slim leg. Before her was a red, tufted ottoman that carried a black lacquer tray painted with Chinese dragons and peonies. It held a green celadon tea pot and two cups.

"You're lucky I'm here at all," he said.

One artfully penciled brow arched over a cool gray-green eye. "You must sit with me and tell me of the rumors in this town." She puffed on her ganja cigar and let loose with a string of smoke rings from full pink lips. Even in her fifties she was a beautiful Caucasian woman with long, silver-blonde hair. She had held onto her looks through her career, when so many others had not. Her trajectory to control of the Red Veil was well known. She had been the mistress of Fergana's previous president and a rumored advisor on matters of social and economic policy. The calculation in her gaze as she studied him said she was no fool.

She waved him to a chair beside her. "So tell me, what of your investigations?"

Kazakov remained where he was. "I have none. If I did, I wouldn't be here, would I?"

Again that slight arch of the brow. Then she puffed on her cigar as she studied him. "My, you are an angry one. But no one is angry at the Red Veil. I will not allow it. It is as simple as that." She nodded as if that ended the matter and leaned forward to pat the chair. "Come.

Come. Sit. My sources tell me that it was you who led the investigation into the deaths of those children."

Kazakov stiffened. This was clearly Rostoff asking—he could almost see the detektiv inspektor's hands making her lips move. Was Rostoff truly so clumsy? Was this woman that obvious or did she just not care? Or was this some game Rostoff was playing that Kazakov couldn't yet understand? Perhaps a warning not to continue looking into the case as he was doing?

He shook his head and shrugged. "It is not my case anymore. I believe it is closed."

Frau Zelinka actually pouted. "Come, come. You disappoint me and I so hate to be disappointed. Tell me the story. The Muslim boy, the German girl? Both found one day apart. It was in all the papers along with so much speculation. Surely there is more to such a tragic tale. It is most romantic if what the papers say is true. Of course, it is a warning tale, too. You would be the right man to look into such a sad case, for I think you are a sad man, too." She shook her head. "So dedicated, or so I've been told. Chai? It must be cold outside." She nodded at the tray with the tea pot between them.

Was it as simple as that? She simply wanted to gossip? Could he learn something from this woman who had advised a president? Perhaps there was something other than money that had her doing Rostoff's bidding.

He finally nodded at the offered tea and sat on the edge of the empty chair. She leaned forward in what could only be a practiced maneuver and the folds of her kimono bodice slid open to reveal shadows and curves of creamy flesh. His groin tightened. It had been a very long time since he had been with a woman, but Rostoff was not going to learn anything from him this way.

She filled a cup and offered it to him with a smile. "Well? Tell me a story?"

"There's nothing to tell. It is over. They are dead. At whose hand I don't know."

She pouted at him. "You do not play your part in this little party,

Detektiv. Always you must play your part or the pleasure drains away. There is so little pleasure in the world today."

As if this woman would know. He sipped the tea. Sweet from sugar with the mélange of spice that the body would remember and probably crave on a cold night. With a swallow the warmth began a slow flood through his limbs almost as well as vodka did. He drained the cup.

"Good." He set the cup down and stood, his coat heavy on his shoulders. "I thank you, but I would prefer to simply collect what I came for and leave. I do not play games. Unless you would like to tell me what you know." And he would not discuss a case with this woman —not even a closed one—most especially that one.

Her face stiffened, turning from the flirtatious to the stone-face business woman. "Have it your way, then. I thought perhaps I could share insights with you. I know this town and its people, Detektiv." She shook her head and slid an envelope from beneath a divan pillow and tossed it to the floor at his feet.

Before Kazakov could retrieve it, from the hallway came the sound of running feet and a flat-handed pounding on the door. "Frau! Frau Zilinka!"

It was not the voice of the Thai girl.

"Come," Frau Zelinka said. She glanced at Kazakov as the door burst open. "You may go."

A woman, presumably one of the brothel's girls, pushed into the room bringing with her a scent of lavender. She was raven haired and olive skinned, with the aquiline nose of the Mediterranean regions of the Ottoman and Anglo-German Empires. She wore a colorful robe of patchwork wool as if she was a peasant, and her hair fell in loose curls from the ribbon she had tied it with high on her head. She had the soft look of someone newly woken—except for the fear in her eyes.

"Frau Zelinka!" Her gaze slipped to Kazakov and she stopped. "I am sorry. I am interrupting." She edged back toward the door, but Frau Zelinka waved her forward.

"Come, Maria. Detektiv Kazakov is just leaving."

Maria's eyes widened. "Detektiv!" She turned to him. "It is good you are here. I came to tell Frau Zelinka the police must be called. You see, there is a body…"

Ten minutes later, the envelope forgotten on the brothel floor, Kazakov stood over the body as the city police cars slid into the curb outside the Red Veil. He stood shin-deep in the unseasonably deep snow in Yekaterina Park across the street from the brothel. The woman had apparently seen the dead man from her bedroom window. Before entering the Red Veil, Kazakov had stood all of twenty feet from here, but his view had been blocked by a lone pine tree.

The dead man was a drunk by the reek of him. He wore dust-encrusted trousers and a woolen coat so full of holes and filth it appeared he'd once slept in a pig sty. He had dirty brown hair and the angular face of someone whose use of vodka had burned most of the flesh from his limbs.

Kazakov hauled up his collar against the wind. It had shifted to come off the mountains again and carried the full breath of winter. His fingers were cold even in his thick gloves.

There was something about the dead man that didn't quite work. The man's hair had the pomade of too much sweat and dirt holding it in scarecrow spikes on his head. He had at least five days' growth of grizzled beard. Both fit with the picture of the drunkard. So did the spray of broken blood vessels in the nose that had been broken a time or two in the past, but then half the men in Fergana had such noses.

No, it was something else.

He waved off the uniformed officers to set a perimeter and remained where he was, observing. The man was clearly dead. There was no need to check vitals. The deep brown bloodstain on the victim's chest said that it had happened some time ago.

"So what do we have here?" asked Dr. Khan, coming up beside Kazakov. Kazakov glanced behind him at the street, surprised that he hadn't heard the M.E.'s van arrive.

"You tell me."

The slightly built M.E. looked sideways at him. "Something here bothers you."

"I know what my eyes tell me, but something else gnaws at my brain. I am missing something." Kazakov shook his head. "Tell me what you see and I will know whether it is my imagination."

Khan scanned the earth around the body, then knelt beside it. He pulled out a notebook and began to take notes. "Male, mid-forties perhaps. Approximately a hundred and sixty pounds. Alcohol user by the facial capillary damage, but that's nothing unusual. Strong odor of alcohol."

"Where is the bottle?" Kazakov asked, looking around. "A drunkard would always have his bottle."

Like he had his hip flask tucked inside his coat pocket?

Khan glanced up at him. "Perhaps he finished it and threw it away. Or perhaps it was stolen."

"Or perhaps he never had one." Where that possibility came from, he wasn't sure. It flew in the face of all the external evidence. Besides, there wasn't a Russian male in Fergana who didn't drink. He glanced over his shoulder at the Red Veil, standing virginal white on its chicken legs in the graying snow.

Khan tilted a brow at him and tugged open the man's coat. A half-frozen, half-coagulated mass of dark blood that had been held in by the wool slopped onto the snow. Khan leaned in to examine the wound through a threadbare gray shirt.

"Knife wound by the look of it. Single blow. By the position, it got the heart or a major artery. By the amount of blood, I'd guess the artery. Poor fellow bled out."

The wind gusted and branches rattled in the dry air. Overhead clouds streamed in from the southern mountains, suggesting more snow. From the city came the rumble and blat of morning traffic. Pedestrians had appeared on the sidewalk edging the park and now a few collected like fallen leaves just beyond the yellow police tape.

"I thought you were reassigned," Khan said softly.

"Reassigned. Yes. Still in major crimes where Rostoff can keep an eye on me, but now I commit the crimes—taking bribes on behalf of the team." He shook his head bitterly, then dipped it at the Red Veil where the curtains twitched at each window. "I was visiting. One of the women claimed to see a body from her window."

He shrugged and knelt across the body from Khan. "She was apparently correct. So what is wrong with this picture of a drunk killed for his liquor?"

Khan leaned in to examine the man's face. The eyes were the color of cloudy skies, but darkness underneath the milky surface suggested they were brown. The mouth was open.

Khan frowned. "The teeth are better cared for than I would have expected. See? There is no plaque as one would expect, unless this man is much better at self-care than the usual drunk." The man's arms lay at his sides. Khan lifted one of them.

That was what had bothered Kazakov—the fact that both hands rested so neatly. There was no sign of struggle. No sign of warding off a blow.

Khan turned the hand over. "Compared to the clothes…"

"The hands are clean. So is the wrist."

"And the nails," Khan said, turning the hand back over. "Look at the nails. No grime ground into the cuticle. No stains on the nails. This man did not smoke. Nor did he live outdoors or do manual labor."

He looked up at Kazakov. "The hands look as if they have been washed and the skin cared for more than most men do. Perhaps now would be the time that a person in your position would call in another detective."

"And allow another suspicious death to be written off?" Kazakov glanced over to the uniformed officers standing smoking by their cars. "If I had not been here—if I had not been late making my stop—what would have happened?"

Khan thought a moment, the clouds overhead placing shadows under his eyes. Or perhaps it was everything he had seen in his job. It was not happy work.

He nodded. "They would have called it in as a drunk dead in a knife fight. A detective would have been assigned, but I doubt that I would have ever seen him."

"It would be the perfect way to get rid of a body—in plain sight." He met Khan's dark gaze—until Khan shook his head.

"There are those who would say that you look for trouble, old friend. Isn't that what got you into your predicament? I know it was the murder of two children. I know it catches in a man's craw." His voice faded as if he might say more but thought better of it. Instead he shook his head. "Perhaps this truly is a drunkard killed in a knife fight."

"A drunkard who bathes regularly and who practices good oral hygiene? You disappoint me, Khan."

Khan shook his head. He glanced around again as if afraid someone might be listening. "I only concern myself with your welfare... and mine. Something is happening, old friend. Something that bears keeping your head down. There are those amongst the medical staff who recommend against our friendship and there are watchers everywhere."

Watchers. Kazakov looked up again and caught the twitch of the Red Veil's curtains.

Indeed there were.

3

There was a time twenty-two years ago when Kazakov was a newly minted police officer with a full head of hair and truth was in the air and filled his chest with every breath he breathed.

On this gray November day, seated in his battered government sedan, one of the police fleet of First Autos brought in from China five years ago, it seemed hard to believe. Now the lack of truth constricted his lungs even when he slept. Each morning he felt angry when he woke. And very alone.

The car stank of cigarette smoke from its other drivers, just as Khan's words stank of warning to let this go, even though he was unclear what *this* was. A man killed for some reason, his body supposed to disappear in plain sight. But it was clear that the man wasn't what he appeared. Either he'd disguised himself in a drunkard's clothing to hide, or someone had dressed him in the clothing to hide who he was.

Kazakov tapped his fingers on the steering wheel, trying to decide which way to go. The smart thing would be to simply walk away—not just from the case, but from the whole job, but policing was the only job he had ever had and the thought of doing something else filled him with dread. Dealing with the dead was easier than dealing with the living—his marriage had proved that. And in a country and a city where investigations were sometimes closed for expediency, or where evidence was fabricated to gain a needed conviction, who would search for the truth if he left?

Clearly, Detektiv Chief Inspektor Rostoff had not intended Kazakov to go haring off investigating anything. He wanted Kazakov put in his place and close enough he could be controlled— probably the only reason Kazakov hadn't been fired for his initiative in taking forward the Weber-Manas case. Even being on the scene could warrant a reprimand for assuming control when the responsible one should be the assigned detective. If he was truly following Rostoff's rules, he would have phoned the case in and walked away himself. The way Rostoff wanted it, not the way Kazakov had been trained—not the way any police officer had been trained. But something had changed the department's practice.

So his choice was clear: investigate regardless of Rostoff's direction and take the repercussions when they came, or walk away.

In Yekaterina Park, Khan was standing by as they loaded the body onto a stretcher and wheeled it to the M.E.'s vehicle. One of the uniformed police casually stepped on his cigarette butt and left his car to pull down the police tape. So no one else was coming and they weren't even going to examine the scene more closely for evidence. He gripped the steering wheel and finally couldn't stop himself. He picked up his mobile phone because maybe there was another way.

He called dispatch and said where he was. He asked who the assigned detective was for the case.

Silence greeted him at the end of the phone. "Everyone is busy at the moment. It was only a drunkard. It has not been assigned."

Kazakov inhaled and tapped his fingers on the wheel. Here goes nothing. "I was across the street and brought to the body. It may be best to record that I was on scene. If Rostoff wishes, he can assign it to me."

"I will check," the dispatcher said and hung up.

Kazakov slumped back in his seat. It was done. He had given himself a cover for looking into the case further—at least until Rostoff came sniffing around. If he ever did. Regardless of the dispatcher's last words, in the course of a busy day there was every chance that checking with Rostoff would slip the dispatcher's mind.

For the moment, he could do his job. He climbed out of the car and trudged back up the stairs to the Red Veil. This time his chest did not feel like stones had been piled on it.

At the front door, he knocked as the first snowflakes of the day swirled around his face. The wind had chilled further and he wished that he'd brought his hat from the office. He'd left it there three days before and not reclaimed it. Each time he went into the office it slipped his mind to look for it.

The same sweet-faced Thai girl opened the door.

"I need to speak to Frau Zelinka," he said and bulled his way inside.

"I am sorry, sir. She is in her bath and not taking visitors."

For a moment, he considered simply charging in, but that was an approach best saved for another time. For now, he would be civilized, or as civilized as his job allowed him.

"Tell her that I will be interviewing her girl, Maria, and inspecting Maria's rooms. Where can I find her?"

The Thai girl's inscrutable beauty was marred by a momentary twitch of the eye that spoke of fleeting resentment. Then the moment passed like frost on a spring day. "You will stay here, please, while I advise Frau Zelinka." Then she was gone, disappearing down the hallway like a harem girl apparition in some Ottoman palace lost in space and time.

Kazakov made a point of not staying where he was put. He wandered into the room on his left. Here it was not a Silk Road caravanserai, but something more akin to the saloons portrayed in the American films that were imported from that outpost of independence from the Anglo-German Commonwealth. Bare wooden tables. A wooden bar with cheap glasses against the wall, and peanut shells and sawdust on the floor. Packs of cards sat neatly stacked on a side table and on the wall hung a pair of what looked like antique revolvers. Another one of America's exports.

After achieving their independence, the Americans were being pushed to relinquish their freedom in exchange for the trade they so desperately needed to survive as a string of small city-states along the eastern seaboard of British North America. The saloons that were presented in the films were long ago replaced by Anglo-German parlors after the Americans lost their hold on the far west of the North American continent. So far, according to the news, the Americans still held doggedly onto their independence.

In some ways they were Fergana's brethren, attempting democracy when democracies had fallen from fashion everywhere else. But half a world of oceans and mountains kept them from conferring on their experiences. It was said that democracy could only work for a small country. None of the large ones had allowed it.

He came out of the room as the Thai girl returned. "This way, please."

But she didn't lead him up the stairs. Instead she led him farther down the hallway where the light was dim and, by the dampening of the street noise, he suspected the night noises of the house's business were less audible to this area's occupants.

A soft knock on a narrow misted-glass door and the Thai girl pulled the door open. A cloud of warm spice-scented vapor billowed into the hall. "Frau Zelinka will speak with you."

What now? He stepped into the room and stopped just inside the door. Vapor immediately beaded his skin and hair. It coalesced on the fur on his karakul collar and brought sweat to his face. The room was white tile, poorly lit by veiled lights half-concealed in the corners. They placed a supernatural glow over the mist, and the hard tiles echoed the sound of splashing water.

"You are a difficult man to say no to, Detektiv Kazakov. Did you know that? I do not let just any man into my bath. Only the attractive ones."

He had no illusions about his attractiveness. He was a middle- aged man who, regardless of his recent weight loss, was slowly losing his shape; so what the hell did she want?

The vapors parted to reveal a large, deep copper tub filled to the brim and Frau Zelinka floating there, her face and breasts three perfect mounds in the scented water. Then she sank to the bottom and came up headfirst, sending a tidal wave of water across the floor to slop onto his shoes.

"I need to speak to Maria and any other girl with a room on the park side of the house," he said.

She waved him closer with an arm gone rosy with dewy warmth. "Are you suggesting that my girls had something to do with this horrible event?"

She peered up at him with wide dark eyes, the length and curve of her body too lush and on display in the magnifying water.

Was this a new attempt to control him through this woman?

"If I thought that, I would interview all your girls. At the moment, I simply want to know what they saw. And your doorman. You have one in the evening, I presume. I need his name to speak to him, as well."

In one perfect move, Frau Zelinka came up out of the water, liquid sheeting off her body in a shimmering spray. He took in her attractions and then looked away, committing them to memory.

"A towel," she commanded and gestured at a wooden spindle- back chair set to one side against the white tiled wall.

He complied and she wrapped the towel around her hair, then stepped out of the tub to stand naked beside him. "A hot bath is such a luxurious way to start a day."

He wouldn't know. His days started far earlier than this and at his dacha baths were a matter of heating water on the stove to pour into an aluminum wash tub.

She reached past him for an additional towel and began to pat herself dry.

"You haven't answered my question." Kazakov stood where he was, the warm scent of damp woman caught up his nose. The steam and water droplets placed a pearly glow on her skin and he was sorely tempted to touch her, but temptation was clearly what Rostoff wanted. He was less sure whether the lady actually wanted the touching. "I came to you as a courtesy. I can interview your girls whether you give permission or not."

She stopped patting herself dry to cock her head up at him from under the folds of the towel on her hair.

"You are a very attractive man, Detektiv Kazakov. I think, beyond the dark hair and square jaw, it is the intensity of your eyes—they speak of your passion, but unfortunately it is passion for your job." She tsk-tsked and wrapped the towel around her torso, once more transforming from the temptress to the business woman. "Fine. Go have your interviews, but you will regret rejecting me. Beyond the pleasures I could bring you, there is much a woman like me could do to help you at a time like this. And there is the payment I must give you."

It was as if this woman tried to swallow him down on Rostoff's behalf. Just what was Rostoff so worried about? Kazakov had, to all outward appearances, ceased his investigation into the two young people's murders. Had his surreptitious enquiries come to Rostoff's attention? After Rostoff called him on the carpet the first time, Kazakov had been very careful who he talked to and where. He had gone so far as to drink tea in the restaurant that was the favorite haunt of Yekaterina's schoolmates where he had sought information about Yekaterina, Semetai, and their families. All to no avail.

From a hook on the wall, Frau Zelinka retrieved her silken kimono and strode from the room. "Do what he asks," she commanded the waiting Thai girl before disappearing down the hall toward the rear of the house. Her apartments, Kazakov supposed. Probably as lush as the woman they housed.

He felt like an insect breaking loose of a spider's lair as he followed the Thai girl up the long flight of stairs that led to the second floor. The stairs were thickly carpeted to muffle men's heavy footfalls. The Thai girl's tread he couldn't hear at all, as if she was cast of dreams and air. That probably went for all the girls—part of the illusion Frau Zelinka spun in her house.

The stairs ended in another open lounge with couches and ottomans and more silken curtains that hid walls and ceiling. The carpet was thicker here so he could barely feel the floor, as if he'd been transported to another place, another self where clouds supported him. He could imagine the effect on a man drunk on good Fergana vodka and desire. He would be young again, virile, his tread no longer weighted down with years and unrequited longing.

Beyond the lounge another hall separated rooms at the front and rear of the house. It had pale pink wallpaper and globe wall sconce lights that burned like misty moonlight. At the third door facing the park, the Thai girl stopped. "This is Maria's room."

"Thank you. You can go now." She shook her head no.

Fine. He knocked on the door and heard a soft, "Enter."

He pushed inside, the Thai girl coming in behind him and closing the door. A gentle scent of lavender filled the room. It reminded him of morning gardens, more soothing than the brassy spice of the brothel's madam.

The woman, Maria, lounged on a large, soft-looking bed replete with too many pillows in all shades of red and lurid purple. The colors emphasized her black hair and olive skin. She still wore the thick, multicolored robe that made him think of the biblical Joseph, but this time square, black-framed glasses perched on her nose and, along with a cigarette, she held a thick tome that she quickly slammed shut and stuffed behind her. The glasses she stripped off her nose as she sat up and swung her legs off the bed to sit elegantly with one long leg crossing the other at the knee. She waved her cigarette at him.

"You. You found the body. Who was it? Who killed him?" Her rapid, accented Russian was, for a moment, almost unintelligible.

"Yes, there was a body, but you watched from your window and saw us remove it. I would like to know what else you saw. How did you happen to see him?" He motioned to a claw-foot chair in the corner of the room. "Do you mind if I sit?"

"Sit. Sit, please." She stood up and strode to the window, tugged the curtain aside to peer out into the street, and released a stream of blue cigarette smoke that swirled around her face and shoulders.

"May I have your full name?" he asked.

"Maria. Maria di Maria." The name flowed like water from her tongue, carrying vestiges of her home language. She shook her head. "Frau Zelinka prefers us to sleep in in the morning and she does not like us to have the curtains open. It gives the idea to passersby that they can know our secrets. It suggests to patrons that secrets will escape. So we are trapped behind these curtains and blinds, but every morning I start my day by looking outside at the park and the sky." Another nervous puff of her cigarette. "The girls across the hall claim that they have the best view because they see the mountains, but I know better. I look over New Moscow and Fergana and it is a grand place. My chosen homeland."

She was trying too hard, as if to convince herself as well as him.

"How long have you been here?" he asked. Get her talking and feeling comfortable, then turn her mind to the body.

The curtain fell back over the window and she drew deeply on her cigarette. "Since I was fifteen. My family was very poor. We lived in a tiny village in Abruzza in Italia. When I was seven, there was a terrible earthquake and everyone in my family was killed. A man offered to help me and three other village girls. Eventually he brought me here, but I still remember the scent of the olive groves and the sound of my mother's voice and the way the almond trees shivered in the wind." She sighed. "Looking at the park reminds me of my childhood."

And by her tone, her freedom. Frau Zelinka's girls did not have that luxury.

"What happened this morning?"

Her robe stirred around her as she shrugged. "I woke—as always. I got up. I took my prophylactics."

Said as if her life was an endless string of such days.

She lifted the edge of her curtain again and inhaled from her cigarette, her neck gently arching like a deer's. "I came to the window, sipping tea as I usually do—I am a morning person. The other girls sleep in and are so noisy when they rise. Always laughing and telling jokes about their clients from the night before, though Frau Zelinka does not like it. I prefer the quiet of the early morning and to hold my tongue, for who is to say what would happen if something I said got back to my client." She shook her head. "I looked out and there he was —lying there."

"Describe what you saw." He sat still, with notebook out, taking down what she said.

"It was cold outside, I could tell by the frost on the window. It was a lovely lace that caught the sunlight like prisms. That meant it was harder to see the park for the glare, but I had hoped for new snow. It makes the park so clean and white. My wish had been granted, but somehow the snow was still gray, not like now with the new snow falling. There was a dark blot on the snow that I had not seen before. I looked more closely and, at first, I thought it was someone who had tripped and fallen, but he did not get up. Then I thought it might be Collin, a new client. And when he did not move after five minutes, I realized something was wrong. That was when I came to Frau Zelinka and met you."

She let the curtain fall again and turned back to him, then sought an ashtray on the bedside table and crushed her stub of cigarette. "That was what I saw."

Making a note of "Collin" to pursue, he nodded at the window. "When you looked outside, was there anyone on the street or in the park?"

She thought a moment, but then shook her head. "There rarely is in the early morning. Ordinary people don't live around here. The people who do, travel by car. There are few people from around here that travel through Yekaterina Park."

Frowning, he looked up at her. "Are you saying that the man was not from here?"

She shook her head. "I don't know, do I? I have not seen him up close."

And he would have to bring a photo of the dead man back here. "Who is Collin?" he asked.

Pulling her robe tighter around her neck, she returned to the bed and sat on the edge. "A client. A businessman with the Anglo-German embassy, I think. Leastwise he is Anglo. He boasted that his ancestors helped finance the creation of the Anglo-German Empire and the assassination of Napoleon." She shook her head. "As if the business dealings of his forefathers made him a better man." A better-connected man, at least.

"You are well read," he said, studying her.

"For a whore, you mean?" She reached across the bed and picked up what she'd been reading. "I happen to enjoy world history. Frau Zelinka expects her girls to be educated enough to hold conversations. We are not just pretty faces and warm body parts, Detektiv."

It had not been what he meant. In Fergana's schools, there was an emphasis on his people's history—to the lack of everything else. As he'd aged and the role of Fergana as a buffer between the Chinese Kingdom of Heaven and the might of the Ottoman Empire had become more and more evident, understanding what it meant for his country required the people to better understand the world around them. Unfortunately, the education system did not agree and the children grew from the ignorance of childhood into the blindness of adulthood. He'd often wondered whether it was a conscious government decision. In response, he had become a voracious reader.

Of course, Maria di Maria was not a girl from Fergana. "So what have you learned?" he asked.

She shot him a glance, and by the way she tipped her head, he knew she wanted another cigarette but held herself back. She must limit her smoking because she had no stains on her fingers. An interesting bundle of contradictions and strengths, this woman.

"I think that we live in difficult times, but I suppose each generation says the same." A philosopher, then.

"I would like to bring you a photo of the dead man to look at. Perhaps you may know him."

She shrugged. "Do what you want. I will be here. Reading."

With that she returned to her window and once more peered out. What she must have seen all the years she had been here. As the Thai girl let him out of the room, he wondered what Maria di Maria chose to remember and what she chose to forget.

He interviewed five other girls who had rooms overlooking the park. None had seen anything. None were interested in what happened in the broader world. There was clothing to mend, legs and armpits to wax, hair to be upswept perfectly, and scent to choose for tonight's patrons. They were not interested in him or his questions and shortly he found himself ejected onto the Red Veil's front stairs.

A light snow swirled around him and kissed his face. He thought of Frau Zelinka's pearled flesh, but that melted into Maria's face. She'd been angry at him for putting her down as nothing but a whore, but truly his assumption made sense given the other women he'd spoken to. She was the anomaly, as much as he was for doing his job as a detective. Sighing, he went down the stairs.

He needed the photo of the dead man. Then he could interview the others that worked in the house to see if the man was known. There were the houses that surrounded the Red Veil, too. In the past, he would have had uniformed officers canvass those residents, but now if he wanted to investigate, he would have to do it himself. It would be a lot of work and difficult to hide from Rostoff, but the questioning would bring him back here.

Back to speak to Maria di Maria again.

In his car, he turned the key in the ignition and the engine sputtered to life, a mechanical effigy of his detective career. Oddly, he found himself whistling.

4

The old brown All Auto sedan clunked and fumed down the broad avenue that ran beside Yekaterina Park, trailing a plume of exhaust behind it like a horse's tail. Kazakov turned off at the corner onto the eastern end of Suvarov Way and joined the flow of noontime traffic until its broad four lanes shrank to two. There he turned off toward Our Lady Yekaterina Hospital. The four-story building hunkered down against the snow. Some administrator had decided that preserving parking spots was more important than the park at the hospital entrance.

Chemicals had been spread to keep the paved lot clean and the runoff had flowed over the earth around the shapely, naked maple trees and fountain at the front. Next spring the chemicals would kill the grass, and the small, graceful eden across from the hospital would join the fading glory of the rest of Fergana. He looked away, up to Yekaterina's Mountain looming over the hospital and the city. Today the swirling flakes erased both the distant mountains and the Yekaterina's five peaks that the Muslim Kyrgyz said Mohammed had prayed upon. Fergana existed in a place between—not quite safety, not quite at the heart of everything.

He sighed and inhaled the winter cold. At least ten below freezing, the way the wind stung his cheeks. Much colder than the last time he'd stood here contemplating how conflict and war crept into everything. The young Yekaterina's and Semetai Manas's mysterious deaths. Both of them murdered—executed—though why he thought in those terms he could not say. He shivered and looked again at the mountain that loomed over the city. It was not weather to be out in, even drunkards knew that.

Unless they weren't from around here. That had been Maria's suggestion. His hand went to the coat pocket that once held his smokes, but he pulled it out again. There was an autopsy report to read and a photo to obtain. Perhaps Khan would even offer him a decent cup of tea.

He went down the stairs to the morgue in the bowels of the hospital.

Inside the windowless bunker, the stink of death, decay, and air freshener seemed solidified in the faded-green walls that echoed the rapid clatter of typing. He signed himself in at the reception counter where a young woman hunched over the keys.

"Where's Darya?" he asked, nodding at the new receptionist. She was a sharp-eyed young thing with henna-dyed hair in a bob. A green sweater was buttoned over her breasts and too many bracelets jangled on her wrists.

Darya was the usual receptionist, a matronly woman of forty who had four children, an out-of-work husband and, apparently, a single florid floral dress that she had worn every time Kazakov had ever seen her.

"She quit," the girl said.

"Did she find a better job?" Because Darya had been the queen of the reception desk for far longer than Kazakov had been a police officer.

The girl shrugged. "I never met her. Now what do you want?"

He frowned. "Dr. Khan, please. About the male body brought in this morning."

The girl's lips narrowed slightly. Then she nodded. "I believe he is in his office."

She turned back to her typewriter and Kazakov pushed through the gate into the M.E.'s domain and strode down the poorly lit hall with its old wooden doors and high transoms, waiting for the typing to start behind him. It didn't until he was shutting Kamil Khan's windowed office door behind him.

Khan was seated at his desk and he looked up when Kazakov entered. The air smelled of chai spices and for a moment Kazakov was hopeful that the M.E.'s excellent tea would be forthcoming.

"You have a new receptionist, I see," he said as he slumped into the chair across the battered wooden desk from Khan. Stacks of well-worn books looked about to tumble off the shelves behind the M.E. Khan looked resigned—and exhausted—in his favorite old wood swivel chair. A half-finished cup of cardamom chai sat cooling on the desk before him.

"I tried to get Darya back. She needed this job. Why do this to her? She is at home—and devastated." He rested his fists on his desk. "They said it was time she retired."

Kazakov sighed at the news. It was not uncommon for the son or daughter of a politico to be offered a job that was taken away from a longtime employee, but Khan was clearly upset. The tea would not be offered. "Who is 'they'?"

Khan shrugged. "Who knows? Human Resources. They say there is an election coming and they need to prove that they are cost cutting. They can pay this new girl less than Darya."

"But you do not believe that." Khan shook his head.

"To keep an eye on what happens here?" Kazakov asked softly.

Khan shook his head again, but it was more resignation than denial.

"But why? The people who come through these doors are mostly dead."

Khan's lips curved sadly. "Except you, of course. But then, you have a dead career."

Kazakov managed a smile. "I thank you for that. But I already know. Tell me something I don't."

Shuffling papers on his desk, Khan avoided Kazakov's gaze. "I don't know if I can do this any longer. I also have a family to feed."

"You do your job. That is all that I ask."

"But is that what my employers want?" Khan whispered and finally looked at Kazakov. "Sometimes I fear they wish us to just go through the motions. Imaginary autopsies. Imaginary evidence to build illusions." He shook his head. "Things have changed around here and not just with Darya leaving. I come in, in the morning, and find strange men reviewing my files—not all the files, just those I have worked on. Bodies have disappeared before I could complete my reports. What is happening, Kazakov? This would not bode well for anyone in this job, but for a minority like me…"

Khalil Khan was about the most stoic, philosophical man Kazakov had ever met, but now he was clearly worried. Kazakov shook his head. "Could it be office politics? The hospital administration?"

"They would not take bodies."

"You've done nothing but your job, so you have nothing to fear. Without you, there would be few reliable medical examinations in the city and most likely the country."

"Darya did her job, too, old friend. So do you. Perhaps reliable medical examinations are no longer what's wanted—the kind that has their content controlled are already preferred." Khan sighed and then shook his head. "But there is nothing you can do about it." He took a deep breath. "I finished examining our friend from the park. As you know, there was no identification on him, but he bears very distinct marks."

He flipped open a file on his desk. On the right side was a photo of the dead man, hair still spiked with filth, features still blunted from alcohol and death. A white sheet pulled up to his naked waist. An envelope with Kazakov's name on it rested in the file.

"Photos for you and a copy of the preliminary report. I knew you'd want them."

Frowning, Kazakov picked up the envelope and pulled the file closer. "Strange. Look at his skin. His face, neck, and shoulders are far paler and pinker than his lower chest. It transitions gradually until his belly is faintly sallow looking. Usually it is the other way around."

"A good observation, but that is not all. Our drunk had other surprises beyond the fact that he had no alcohol in his stomach."

Khan sat back in his old wooden desk chair, the joints squealing under him.

Kazakov scanned the file. No tattoos, which was odd given they were almost a rite of passage among the men of Fergana. Kazakov had gotten his first when he was just fifteen—an eagle under a waterfall on his biceps that his father had paid for—much to his mother's horror. He had three others on various parts of his body.

There were, however, scars on the dead man. Small ones around the nose and eyes not atypical of wounds received from fights on the street. He came to the part about the skin and stopped.

"What does this mean?" he asked, tapping the offending paragraph with his finger.

"It means that his face neck, upper torso, and legs—anything that might reasonably be exposed—had probably been subjected to a cosmetic procedure—a bleaching process of some sort." Khan produced a second photo of the body, naked on the autopsy table. The skin across the groin was darker.

Kazakov frowned. "Strange. Are you certain?"

Khan nodded. "There are procedures and creams you can use to keep the skin pale."

Kazakov sat back in his chair. "But why would someone do that? It makes no sense."

Khan huffed and pushed up from his chair. "Why indeed." He studied the books behind his chair and shook his head. "I do not like this, friend. Not at all. You read the file—the marks on the face. The ones around his eyes I checked—they are not often seen in Fergana but they are typical of cosmetic surgery found elsewhere. And then there is the nose. When I did the autopsy, I found a prosthetic."

"A prosthetic?" Kazakov felt like he'd entered a different world with a different language.

Pulling a well-worn, cloth-covered book from the stacks on his shelves, Khan thumped it onto the desk and flipped it open to a page that showed step-by-step photos of the reshaping of a nose, including the insertion of a small piece of plastic bone that made a flat nose suddenly have a high bridge.

"But why do that?" He looked up at Khan.

"A very good question and one you will not like the answer to." Khan resettled himself in his chair and the seat squeaked as if welcoming him. "Someone has gone to a great deal of work to change this man's appearance. They have whitened his skin. They have given him a nose like a Russian or Anglo-German, and they have done work on his eyes."

Kazakov waited. There was something Khan wasn't saying.

Finally, Khan sighed and tapped his face. He was a handsome enough man with the dark hair and slightly oriental eyes of the Kyrgyz. "They have removed the epicanthic folds. Once, this man had East Asian eyes."

Kazakov swallowed, his mind floundering, trying to understand the meaning. "Chinese."

The Chinese Kingdom of Heaven had expanded over southern Asia, only coming to a halt where their mountains abutted the Indian subcontinent. The Anglo-Germans held the Australian continent. The Ottomans controlled the rest of Eurasia and most of northern Africa.

Except Fergana.

He tilted his head toward the mountain ranges he couldn't see at the moment, but that had always loomed over his life. If anything, Fergana existed, on sufferance, as a free market enclave where the Chinese and Ottomans and their allies could meet and plot their subterfuge. The length and breadth of Fergana was a hotbed for spying. Even the upstart Americans had strategists here, when *here* was a world away from the former colony. Was this murder somehow related to all that activity?

"A spy? But why would the Chinese send such a spy to Fergana? I have never heard of such a thing. It would cost a great deal to create such a disguise. And why would a spy dress as a drunkard? That makes no sense."

"Give me a better theory," Khan said.

Kazakov thought about it. "Perhaps he was a businessman who fell on hard times. There are enough Chinese here, buying up the country. They and the Ottomans are like locusts devouring Fergana though we are a sovereign country. But that doesn't explain the need for a spy. Corporate espionage?"

Khan's eyes widened as if he was surprised at the vehemence of Kazakov's opinion. In fact, Kazakov, too, was surprised.

"The Chinese would say that they are threatened by the Ottomans and their influence here. They only seek to have their own point of view heard by our people," Khan said softly. "But then the Ottomans would likely say the same. A spy could help spread such viewpoints."

"You talk as if we know for certain that this man was Chinese. There are men in Fergana with your epicanthic fold from their Mongol ancestors. They have it removed so racial barriers are removed when they do business."

Khan just looked at him. Then he sighed. "There is more. Read the report."

Kazakov rolled his gaze heavenward. Yekaterina preserve him from pig-headed medical examiners.

"If he is a Chinese spy, what does he spy upon? Fergana has nothing—hardly a military since the Ottomans blocked the purchase of military equipment from that Anglo-German company."

Shaking his head, Khan retrieved his book and the file. "You do not usually choose to be blind. Perhaps you should think on this as you conduct your investigation—yes, I know you won't quit. When have you ever? But now I have work to attend to. There are other bodies to be buried in Fergana."

He stood behind his desk and shelved the book. The file he closed and slipped into a drawer.

Kazakov climbed to his feet and stood facing the much smaller M.E. Things had changed between them. In the past Khan had always been there, seeking the truth with him, but this time fear had shrunken the small man's frame.

"I'll try not to bother you so much, old friend. You have a family. I understand." Kazakov let himself out into the hallway and closed the door softly.

Khan's last words floated out at him through the glass transom.

"Be careful, Alexander. Be very careful."

Outside, he climbed into the cold sedan. The car was old enough that its many drivers had sprung the springs in the seat. One of them poked him in the small of his back.

Contrary to the doubts he'd expressed to Khan, he believed in the evidence of the little man. Scientific evidence didn't lie— at least not Khan's. It never had and never would. At least he'd never doubted that it would until now. In future, who was to say if there were threats on Khan's family.

Not that Khan had said outright that his family had been threatened, but it was clear how he felt. Why now? There were many cases they had worked on where the outcome had not been popular with higher-ups.

His breath condensed in the car's cold interior and began to lay a frost on the inside of the windshield that masked the cold landscape of plowed snow and naked maple branches. He started the car against its protests and sat there in the cold air blasting from the air vents, waiting for heat to return.

If it was true that the dead man was Chinese, it raised so many questions. Who was he here? Who was he in China, for there were surely many kinds of spies both corporate and military. Why was he here? Why now? Why was he killed?

He needed to answer all of those questions and he barely knew where to start. He hauled Khan's envelope out of his pocket and unsealed it, pulling out three photos and a typewritten report. Along with the headshot he'd seen on the file, there was a close-up of the man's hands and one of the dead man in the park, his milky gaze peering at the sky as snow gathered on his brows and nose. The park. No one had conducted a thorough search—at least he hadn't, and the uniformed officers had torn down the police tape before anything of that kind had been done.

The car groaned from the cold when he dropped it in gear and the tires crunched over the packed ice and snow as he aimed back toward the city center.

The skyline of Fergana's capital laid dark grey stunted silhouettes across the clouds. For some reason the city hadn't grown the spires and towers of the great cities. Probably because Fergana had nothing in common with those glittering metropolises. Fergana was a backwater, an eddy, compared to Constantinople, Berlin, and London. It was less than a molecule of water compared to the vastness of the ancient Chinese capital of Nanjing and more akin to the photos he'd seen of the modest capital of Charleston that had grown up in the American south. A second-rate capital for a second-rate nation, perhaps. It was enough to give the country an inferiority complex.

And make it hold onto dreams of past glories.

Suvarov Way broadened around him as if welcoming him into the city, but at the moment the city didn't feel safe. There were spies afoot. And now one of them had died.

The sunlight was failing by the time he pulled into the curb at the side of Yekaterina Park again and climbed out of the unmarked sedan. Along the street, the lights came on and the Red Veil had already lit the amber globes flanking its door. Lights shone through the golden curtains over the windows, as Frau Zelinka's establishment readied itself for their evening patrons. But on the second floor a curtain twitched and perhaps that was a pale hand he saw.

Maria.

Of course, it could be his imagination, too.

He turned back to the park. The clouds and the failing light diminished the shadows, and lent a steely cast to the snow. Flakes had drifted into the indentation left behind by the body and his own and the uniformed police's heavy tread. Two knee indentations were all that Khan had left behind. The little M.E. was meticulous at using someone else's footprints to enter a scene. Kazakov trudged through the snow to the body's indentation.

The temperature had dropped farther and now, instead of drifting flakes, the snow had become tiny ice crystals that stung his nose and ears. Again he wished for the hat he'd left behind.

With a gloved hand, he swept away the new snow that had fallen. The snow that had been under the body was pristine except for the blotch where the blood clot had fallen out of the man's coat. Had the heavy wool simply held it all in or had the man been killed elsewhere and moved? But if moved, why here in front of the Red Veil? Surely, with all the parks in Fergana, there had to be a reason.

Like there had to be a reason for Yekaterina's body being moved, too, but that was another case. Another case, another investigation, another story.

In the deepening dusk, he waded through the snow, brushing away the new skiff that had not been present this morning. Thankfully, there was a crust on the previous layer of snow, but there was nothing to find. He reached the bushes that had shielded the body from his view from the door, straining the snow through his fingers.

And came up with a cigarette butt with a pale striped filter. Interesting. Not one of the popular brands smoked in most of Fergana.

A cast-off from the attending police this morning?

But they had stood by their vehicles smoking. He recalled how an officer had stubbed his cigarette out before approaching the body—old training apparently died hard even if the current regime didn't seem to support careful police procedures.

If not the police, then whose was it? Kamil Khan rarely smoked and would never do so at a scene—that was a line he didn't cross. And Kazakov hadn't either.

A passerby after the police had left was a possibility, but whoever it was would have had to come to the site right after he left judging by the depth of snow over his find.

Bagging the cigarette butt, he continued his search through the snow. Nothing else came to light so anything else would have to await the spring to be recovered and by then the dead man would have been forgotten. The snow dragged on his feet as he waded back to the road. The natural light was almost gone. What was left placed a cold, nacreous glow on the evening. The wind picked up, driving the ice crystal snow into his face and eyes. On the stairs to the Red Veil he stomped the snow off his shoes and brushed his pantlegs clean, then climbed the measured stairs to the door again, wondering where the doorman was.

The door opened after the first knock and a whiff of sweet incense was stripped away by the wind. It was the Thai girl again, but this time dressed in traditional Thai silks of rich orange with overlong sleeves to hide her withered hand. Her hair was tied up in a thick coil at the back of her head. Makeup accented her perfect features and the demure gaze that widened just the barest of fractions when she saw him. This one was all about self control. Her mastery of it suggested that she was older than the fifteen or sixteen years that he'd credited her with.

"You should not be here," she said and tried to close the door, but he shoved inside and stood brushing his shoulders free of snow. He hauled the heavy door closed behind him.

"Tell Frau Zelinka that I wish to interview Maria and the staff."

"But...but...this is not the time."

"Go. Now. Tell her."

For an instant he thought he read fury in her black gaze, but then she turned and scurried down the hallway. Her silks whispered like ghosts in the air.

The place had changed; the room lighting had dimmed, no more than candles on tables or thickly veiled light fixtures. The sweet-scented incense lay heavy on the air and classical music rich with the zither, mandolin, and sitar played softly over hidden speakers even in the room designed like an old tavern. In this light, the rows of bottles and glassware glittered as if they were crystal. A few drinks and no one would ever notice the lesser quality. After a long day, this place offered everything a tired man would require to enjoy himself.

"Detektiv. This is most inappropriate." Frau Zilinka strode toward him down the hall, this time dressed as the diva in a low-cut, black silk evening dress that skimmed her body. Her hair was swept up in a loose pile of blonde curls that fell in a sultry disheveled tangle around her face. She wore full warpaint of kohl-lined eyes, defined high cheekbones, and vivid lipstick, reminding him of a windup doll. She stopped in front of him, her hands on her hips. "What are you doing?"

"My job. I'm investigating the death of the man in the park. I told your girl, here, that I need to speak to Maria and to the staff who worked here last night—doormen, security guards, kitchen staff who might have seen something when they left."

Her crimson mouth firmed into a line. "This is not the time. The Red Veil is open. My patrons arrive soon."

He shrugged. "Surely Maria isn't the only girl they ask for. I'll talk to her first and then to the others in between their duties."

She glanced at the Thai girl and gave an adamant headshake. "You cannot. This will not do."

"Frau. This is police business—an investigation. It cannot be stopped because someone comes whoring."

It was as if he had slapped her. Her face went rigid. Beyond her, the Thai girl's inscrutable expression was etched on her features. Frau Zelinka glanced from Kazakov to the girl once more. Did it matter what the girl thought? Or was Kazakov's demand undermining her place with her employees? Frau Zelinka's throat worked and finally she nodded. "You may interview the employees."

She turned and started back along the hallway, her shoulders square and forbidding as a mountain massif.

"And Maria? I need to speak to her first."

At that she turned and looked at him, her gaze at once furious and afraid. "Think about what you are doing, Detektiv. You bring down doom on all of us. As for Maria, she's gone."

"What? Where is she?"

Frau Zelinka raised her hands. "Who am I to say? I am not her keeper. A girl decides to leave. She is gone. Prae went to get her, and her room was empty." She nodded at the Thai girl who must be called Prae.

"Have you checked the house?"

She nodded.

"How could she have left?"

"This house is not a prison, Detektiv."

He could not quite believe her even if Maria had seemed to have accepted her life. When he'd talked to her, she's seemed settled, resigned. He scratched his head. "I want to see her room."

"Fine. Do what you want. Just stay away from the patrons and me.

I shall be busy." Frau Zelinka waved him away and disappeared down her darkened hallway.

Prae led him back up the stairs where the hallway was filled with the bustle of women and the battle of competing perfumes. The subtle silk wallpaper held graceful images of Chinese courtesans, or perhaps they were houri—the not so virginal companions of dead Islamic warriors. The women he saw emulated that look: beautiful, demure, lush as any man could desire. But there was no Maria with her dark horn-rimmed glasses. He opened the door to her room and turned back to the hallway of women.

"Has anybody seen Maria?" he asked no one in particular. No one did more than shake their head and turn away.

But one girl held his gaze for the barest of moments before turning to another doorway.

She was young—barely sixteen by the look of her milky, perfect skin, but he suspected she was at least two years older. She had straight, pale hair that hung in a heavy silken curtain around bare shoulders and deep blue eyes rimmed with thick blonde lashes. A simple blue sheath dress ended just above her slim knees and he was reminded of an image in a magazine he had seen when he was a boy. It was of a young woman picking sunflowers in the paradise of green fields that once was Fergana. As an adult, he had seen the iconic image again only to realize that it was an advertisement for cheek-by-jowl houses in subdivisions that had plowed under the very fields the young beauty had walked in.

He shook his head and fought back the sense of déjà vu.

"You," he said and motioned her closer.

She looked away as if to leave, but he abandoned Prae and went to her. "What do you know of Maria?"

"N-nothing." She shook her head. "She is gone."

"When did she leave?"

The girl shook her head again. "I-I don't know. I saw her this afternoon. She took a call."

"When was this?"

"Perhaps one o'clock?"

"Did she say who it was who called? Did she seem upset?"

"I—I don't know. I hardly knew her. She kept to herself." The girl backed up a step and he realized he was looming over her.

He pulled back and considered. The girl looked almost shaken. "Where did she take this call?"

"She—she was in the washroom. We both were. We each have a mobile phone so that our patrons may call us and tell us about their fantasies so that we can prepare."

"So Maria had a mobile phone."

A nod.

"Where would she keep this phone?"

"The rules are that the phone is to be with you always when the Red Veil is not open," the little blonde told him.

He thanked her and was about to turn away, then stopped and pulled out Khan's envelope. He pulled out the photo of the dead man's face. "Do you recognize this man?"

The girl's blue gaze widened and she looked up at him. "Is it important?"

"Do you recognize him or not?"

She looked back at the photo and swallowed, apparently not liking what she saw. "I'm not sure. There was a patron. An Anglo. I don't remember his name."

Kazakov pondered her. She was at least trying.

"Could the name have been Collin?" he asked, taking a stab in the dark.

"That's it! Collin. How did you know?" And she smiled with such pure pleasure he wanted to keep making her smile. He imagined any man would.

"A guess," he said. "May I have your name?"

"Katya. Katya Faber, but here they call me Yekaterina. Now may I go? I have a patron coming in less than an hour."

He let her go and stood motionless in the flow of women in the hallway. Prae tapped a toe by Maria di Maria's door. Yekaterina. The name kept following him like a flock of crows. A murder, to be exact. This girl even looked something like Yekaterina Weber.

A shiver ran up his back as he turned back to Maria's room and followed Prae inside.

Though it looked much as he recalled, the lavender scent he remembered was faint as praise in his job. The same bed and heaped pillows were somehow lurid without playing off of Maria's olive coloring, the curtain hanging limp over the window somehow more muffling without Maria's honest liveliness twitching it aside. That was it. In this house of veils, she was the one person who had seemed to show herself. A woman with olive skin and horn-rimmed glasses. A woman who set aside the game of her employment in her off-hours. Someone who looked outward instead of in and who had the bravery to say something.

He crossed to the bed. The red spread had been straightened so it no longer showed the imprint of her lounging body. No sign of the book or the ashtray on the bedside table, either. Or the tatty woolen robe. He pulled open the top drawer of the two-drawer bedside table and found the tools of her trade: condoms of all types and sizes, heated oils, dildos, anal beads, handcuffs, alkyl nitrite and other things he didn't recognize. On the top of the sexual aids lay the ashtray—cleaned and washed, likely ready for her customers. No sign of the book or the glasses.

He pulled open the lower drawer and found soft ropes and silken scarves suitable for restraints that would not leave a mark. Nothing more.

Against one wall stood a carved, Persian armoire with an intricate, inlaid wood design of a couple copulating in a verdant green pleasure garden. He pulled the doors open revealing straps and harness he hadn't expected from a woman like Maria even if she was a working girl.

A single drawer lay at the armoire's base.

He pulled it open, releasing a whiff of Maria's lavender and the scent of tobacco. The old robe was stuffed inside unfolded— something his brief meeting with Maria left him unable to imagine her doing. The book he found stuffed underneath along with a pair of plain white underwear, threadbare jeans, and a well-worn, blue t-shirt—the latter two like favorite old friends.

He stood up, his knees creaking, and considered what he'd found and more importantly what was missing.

"Bring Katya Faber here," he said.

Prae hesitated.

"Now."

She went, apparently well trained in taking orders, and soon returned with a protesting Katya in tow.

"My patron is downstairs waiting," Katya said and yanked away from Prae. "He does not like to wait."

"I am sure he will wait a little longer for the likes of you," Kazakov said. His comment seemed to mollify her.

"When Maria was discovered missing, you came into her room, didn't you?" he asked and held her with his gaze.

Her gaze darted to Prae, to the open armoire, and then the closed hall doorway. Finally, she nodded. "I did not believe she was gone."

"And when you entered, what did you see?"

"Her bed was a mess. Her things on the floor."

He nodded. "Did you clean up her things?"

She shook her fine blonde head. "I looked around and left."

He studied her lean lines, the lovely face, so much like Yekaterina Weber except for the hunger in this woman's eyes. "What did you take," he asked softly.

Her eyes grew round as if shocked, but her mouth had tightened. "I took nothing. I am not a thief."

"But why would you be a thief? Maria was gone, her things left behind. What did you take from her abandoned belongings?"

Sighing, her shoulders slumped. "It was not so much. I was her friend. The others would have taken far more. I will show you."

She led him out into the hallway with Prae trailing behind, suddenly gone quiet, the globe wall sconces had dimmed to amber that placed a misty light on the wallpaper as if they walked through a mystical land. From downstairs the volume of music had increased and there was the low rumble of male voices and bursts of women's forced laughter.

Katya's door led to a room much like Maria's—a broad bed, an armoire, a bedside table, a chair—but there the similarity ended, for the room was decorated in misty blues and turquoises that brought out the color of Katya's dress and eyes so she seemed to be a creature moving under water. On the wall was a tapestry of a white castle on a hilltop and a man riding toward it on a white charger right out of a fairy tale. The original decoration of the room or her own addition?

She pulled open the armoire and pulled open the drawer. "Here."

She handed him a carton of cigarettes, not the usual kind one found in local stores. No, these were a brand imported from, of all places, America, and expensive enough that only the wealthiest could afford them.

"An expensive habit. How could she afford them?" he asked.

Katya shook her head.

He gave her a hard look from the tops of his eyes. "Come, Katya. She told you they came from a patron, didn't she? She shared them with you. That was why you went into her room—to retrieve them. They were almost the only thing of value."

Her shoulders slumped and she hung her head. "How do you know these things? Yes, she showed me her treasure. She was so pleased. Why would she leave them behind? Why would she leave this?" She turned back to the drawer and produced a phone, much like Kazakov's, six inches long, two inches thick, and broad enough to fill his palm.

The phone each girl was to carry at all times.

"Why would she not take it with her?" she asked, her voice almost plaintive.

"A very good question," he said softly. He pulled plastic bags from his pocket and bagged the phone and the cigarettes, Katya watching his movements closely. "This is evidence, but when we find Maria, I'll see about returning the cigarettes to you."

She shook her head. "I don't want them. They're Maria's. I'd rather have her back, instead."

He nodded as he wrote the date, time, and provenance on each bag.

"Thank you for your help. I suggest that you tell no one what you've told me." He turned to Prae. "That goes for you, too."

He led Prae back to Maria's room. "Someone searched this room before me. Who was it?"

"I do not know." She shook her head but he wasn't having her denial.

"Yes, you do. You are the hands of Frau Zelinka. You do her bidding. If you didn't search the room yourself, you escorted them here."

The Thai girl kept her gaze averted as if looking away would make his question disappear. When she looked back at him he caught the flash of anger, so she was not the meek little thing he had thought. Frau Zelinka's tool was what she was, not some poor girl traded into servitude.

"So it was you." He looked down at the phone and the cigarettes. "What were you looking for?"

"I say nothing to you." Emotion flared in her eyes and was swiftly smoothed away. "You should leave. You cause only trouble."

"If that's how you want to play it, fine. I want the doorman next. I'll interview him right here." He pulled the chair from Maria's wall and settled himself to wait, knowing that having a police officer on the same floor as the pleasure rooms was bad enough. Interviewing the staff in the middle of the busiest time of the day on that floor was absolutely something to be avoided at all costs.

He leaned back in the chair. "I'm waiting."

"Bastard!" she swore, and in a shimmer of red silk she stormed out of the room. Either she was bringing back the doorman or something would happen. Presumably Rostoff would be called. The Detektiv Chief would not be happy and shit had a bad habit of running downhill straight into Kazakov's lap. He was going to pay, but there was no help for it.

While he waited, he pulled out the bagged items he'd collected. A phone that should not have been left behind. The question was whether she left it behind on her own, or she was taken. The bag of cigarettes he opened and tore open one pack to tap out a single cigarette. The filter was uncommon, a light tan with fine brown lines running up toward the end.

He picked up the other baggie of the filter collected from Yekaterina Park. It, too, was tan and had fine brown lines running its length. He recalled another case where similar filters were evidence and they came from an Ottoman brand that cost at least twice what most Ferganese smokers paid for their habit. Oddly, there was no sign of lipstick on the filter and he could not imagine any woman of the Red Veil stepping out of the house without lipstick on.

He went to the window to peer down into the street. Darkness had fallen and the unseasonable snow was thickly falling, misting everything caught in the yellow glow of the streetlights. Across Yekaterina Park and the river, and beyond the concrete three-story apartment buildings on the other side, in the distance glowed the tragic beauty of the concrete replica of St. Basil's Cathedral. The original, in what had once been Moscow, had been turned into a mosque that had burned down fifty years ago. It proved that nothing was eternal. In the darkness of Yekaterina Park, he sought the spot where a body had been found that might be a Chinese spy named Collin. By the shadows of the trees he thought it might be—there. A greater darkness detached itself from a tree and stepped out of the shadow.

Kazakov froze where he was and allowed the curtain to droop to mask his presence, but still allow him to peer out.

The lone figure appeared to study the front entrance of the Red Veil. Then, through the snow, the figure's head tilted upward and the pale oval of a face was revealed and steadied as if it not only sought and found Maria's window, but the figure went still as if it knew he was here.

Through the snow, he recognized the movement.

Maria.

5

———————

By the time he thundered down the stairs two at a time, shoved past Prae and the once missing and now apparently found doorman, and ran out the front entrance, the figure in Yekaterina Park was gone—if it had ever been there at all. He ran down the front stairs and into the street, wading through the new snow and into the park toward the place he'd thought he'd last seen her.

No one was there.

Deflated, he turned back to the Red Veil and felt the exhaustion of defeat. The door was firmly closed and he could imagine that it would not open for him again. At least not tonight. So much for the interviews he'd planned. The figure could almost have been planned as a means to interrupt his investigation. As he searched the snow for footprints, a sleek limousine purred up to the curb in front of the Red Veil. He stopped what he was doing long enough to watch the passengers disembark. Two large, swarthy men climbed out swathed in thicker furs than any respectable Fergenese would wear in this weather. After all, New Moscow's winters were never as cold or snow-filled as those in the old cities of holy Russia he'd read about. Surviving the usually much milder and drier Ferganese winters was a matter of pride, but these men—they clearly came from a warmer climate.

The third man wore a wool coat similar to Kazakov's, but it had a more expensive cut given the way it hung perfectly from the man's broad shoulders. The man stepped up on the Red Veil's first stair and turned back to his companions. The streetlight caught in his white hair and he grinned at the other men, exposing a set of large, overly-white teeth.

Kazakov slunk back into the shadows, his heart suddenly pounding. He knew the man had pale blue eyes and an assertive air that verged on rudeness. Boris Bure stopped whatever he was saying and peered across the street almost as if he sensed Kazakov's gaze. Could he see Kazakov in the shadows? Would he think Kazakov was here on the matter of Bure's dead daughter? Then Bure turned and led the two men inside as if whatever Kazakov saw didn't matter.

The falling snow stung Kazakov's cheeks and nose. Pings of energy surged through his limbs. Flakes froze in his lashes and the tangle of brown hair on his head before he remembered to move. Yekaterina Weber's stepfather was here and it was as if all of Kazakov's synapses fired at once. He closed his eyes. It suggested that Bure's marriage to Yekaterina's mother was not the happy protective one they had tried to convey. What did that mean for the daughter before she died?

He shook his head. The fact that Boris Bure was a patron of the Red Veil didn't mean anything, even though a tightness in his gut suggested that it did. The task was to determine what.

He wiped the snow off his brow and let the electric charge fill him. The weight he'd been carrying suddenly lifted as he headed for his car. Had Bure noticed it? Had he just not cared, or did he think that most police were on the take?

Boris Bure. If he was a patron of the Red Veil, Kazakov would bet his pension that Maria knew him. He wondered what she knew, what she could tell him that might help him in the Yekaterina case.

When he climbed inside the First Auto sedan, the snow-covered windows were frosted golden by the streetlights. He turned the engine on and the wipers parted the snow layer so that he could see his way ahead. He guided the car toward home even though he wanted to slam the car through the snow and set out on the search for Maria.

But there was too much going on here. Too much he didn't understand. He needed to spend this gift of energy wisely— assessing what he had and then planning, rather than plunging unprepared into dangerous waters.

Then he would find out where a woman named Maria would be hiding.

He lived in a small dacha his father had left him that sat outside the city limits, though the city was now stretching in his direction. The house was small—a summer cottage, really, built of low walls of rough logs and stone that had been pulled from the land the house had been built on. The result was a low, timber-walled and slate-roofed building that looked part of the landscape. When Kazakov was a child, his father had brought the family here often and a young Alexander had walked the hills and fished in the clear stream out of the mountains. In those days the tribal Kyrgyz had still occasionally camped by the stream that ran through one end of the property and Alexander had come to know them and marvel at their horsemanship and how they lived with their herds just as they had done for a thousand years.

Now they came less often or not at all and those who came were poor relations of what he'd seen as young man. The herds were diminished due to government taxation, and the young people were drawn like flies to the heap of New Moscow.

The isolated log and stone house amongst the copse of walnut trees became his permanent home at the end of his marriage—a retreat where he could momentarily forget the world around him.

Before he reached the turn to the dacha, he turned off into an overgrown, narrow lane through the naked aspen, walnut, and snow-laden pines, following a soft glow of lantern light that glimmered through the forest. He pulled to a stop before an ancient dacha that looked more like it was part of the forest floor than a house. The builder of the house had long ago built up soil and stone around the house's walls so that the light through the windows appeared to gleam out of a mound of earth. The snow was a white veil across the darkness as Kazakov climbed out of the sedan, carrying a small shopping bag.

He waded up the snow-covered stairs and knocked at the low, wooden door.

"Just a minute. Just a minute." Agafya Ryabkov pulled the door open and looked up at him with eternal suspicion on her face. "What do you want?"

Kazakov held up the bag. "I went to the store and picked you up some things."

She still blocked the door to him. Her memory was clearly getting worse.

"Remember? You said that if I was near a store, you could use some more flour and tea? And I brought you a bottle of vodka as well."

"Vodka." Her small black eyes gleamed. "I didn't ask for vodka. I won't pay you for things I didn't ask for."

He smiled down at her. She hadn't actually asked for anything, but this was the only way he could check on her. She was the fiercest woman he'd ever known, a tiny Kyrgyz woman dressed in thick, felted skirt and leggings, with a dowager's hump and the last few strands of her fine gray hair braided and wound around the crown of her head. Through some chance of fortune or fate, she had done the unthinkable and fallen in love with a Russian. The two had married against their parents' wishes and they had spent their lives here together, scraping a life out of their gardens and Joseph's hunting skills. Joseph had died five years past and Agafya had become more reclusive with each passing year since then. Still, Kazakov tried to look out for her.

"Shall I help you put these things away?" He held up the bag again and finally she relented, allowing him to duck through the doorway into the snug one-room cabin that was her home. He toed off his boots and then unloaded the bag onto the scrubbed top of the board table her husband had built for her. Flour. Tea. A few apples. A bunch of twisted winter kale. A package of sausage. The clear bottle of vodka.

Her bird gaze pecked amongst the items and landed on the bottle. Her expression made it clear that she wanted it, but the cost was the issue. She shuffled over to a desk on one wall and pulled a small purse out of the top drawer, digging through the contents. She pulled out coin after coin; little enough, but all she had. Kazakov had been subsidizing her grocery bill since her husband died.

"Enough." He waved her purse away and picked up a few coins. "There was a sale today. And the vodka—consider it a gift." She eyed him as if she would argue, but then seemed to think better of it. Her creased face managed a gap-toothed smile. "My Joseph said you were a good boy. I suppose I should listen to him."

Kazakov took the compliment with a smile and glanced around the room. Wood was stacked near the woodstove and the place was warm. "The water is still running?"

He had made sure its insulation was adequate earlier this fall, before the first snow. "It runs."

"Then I will leave you to your evening, but one of these days I am going to come over and ask you to sing for me. Okay?"

The suspicion in her eyes slowly faded. Singing the old songs was something she loved and it was something he loved to hear. The old tribal songs reminded him of his childhood—a time when the world still seemed good and pure.

She nodded and Kazakov let himself out as Agafya began humming to herself as she sorted through the groceries. He had no idea what she usually survived on. The woman was mainly sinew and bone from what he could tell. But for a few days at least he could take comfort in her having adequate food.

He climbed into the sedan and returned to the road for the short distance to the turn to his home.

The dirt lane into the dacha wound through the darkness under the shelter of poplar, aspen, and blue spruce. The lane ended in the clearing where the house stood like a hunkered old man against the snow. He could imagine that the rest of Fergana did not exist. Or perhaps that was his wishful thinking. Through the thin layer of snow, the tires crunched on the hidden stones and potholes as he pulled the car to a stop at the rear of the house. Technically the government vehicle should not come home with him, but on the scale of infractions he'd engaged in today, it was small change.

He turned the vehicle off and stepped out into silence except for the ticking of the cooling engine. The snow fell heavier here at the slightly higher elevation. The dacha was situated on a slight bluff in the hills to the east of New Moscow so that the lights of the city spread across the plain in the distance and placed a glow on the lowering clouds through the barren walnut trees. Once it had seemed like he was the only person in the world out here. Now, as the wealthy of Fergana sought retreats from the summer heat of the city, they and the rest of the world threatened his and Agafya's small bastions of comfort.

He waded through the six inches of new snow and up the three steps to the porch of the small house. Inside, it was cold and dark and smelled of garlic, wood smoke and the cedar shavings in his cat's litter box. He fumbled matches and lit a lantern, then lit the iron stove in the corner for heat. The dacha was one room, the walls rough stone and timbers decorated in the corner kitchen with wooden shelves that seemed to grow directly from the walls. The kitchen table sat near the door and two small windows flanked the door and reflected the lantern light back at him. During the day they let in the sun. He tugged their flowered curtains closed.

Koshka, his rebellious female black cat, stood and stretched and leapt down from her favorite perch to butt his leg for a head scratch and a leg rub in the hopes of dinner as he settled onto a chair at the scarred wooden table and pulled off his boots. He slid his feet into worn leather slippers as he slipped off his coat and his chest holster and hung them on a wood peg set into a timber by the door. His cell phone he tossed on the small kitchen table. A tattered burgundy sweater completed his ensemble against the chill in the room.

The rest of the room was functional and Spartan. An old battered couch with sprung springs in faded burgundy against one wall; the small, square kitchen table and four chairs that his father had made in the center of the room by the door, the top smoothed by years of use; a bed against the back wall.

Once there had been two beds, but he had removed one and replaced it with a second wooden table that served as a desk beside the wood stove. Above the desk, the wall was filled with everything he knew and suspected about the Weber-Manas murder. A single shelf above the bed held the vacant spot where Koshka usually laid, and a small, heavily-insulated flap door at the rear of the kitchen provided the little cat with the opportunity to go out hunting whenever she pleased. It also meant that he frequently found small dead gifts she had brought for him.

He put a kettle on the stove to boil and filled a tea bulb with loose tea, then fed Koshka before settling at the desk in his old wooden chair to stare up at the evidence wall. He was not supposed to have any of it, but he'd had the foresight early in the case to make copies of most of the documents before Rostoff had confiscated everything and, in the month since the murders, he'd learned a lot more about Yekaterina Weber and Semetai Manas. Quietly, he'd spoken to Yekaterina's friends, first at the restaurant and then catching them alone. He had stayed away from Yekaterina's funeral so as not to arouse Boris Bure's ire and to keep news of his questions from Rostoff.

Yekaterina had been a first-class student with a passion for music and song. She had met Semetai through a music conference that had brought together Russian, Kyrgyz, and Uzbek students from across New Moscow and beyond—the only time such an inclusive conference had been held.

Plans to annualize the event had been canceled after the murders.

Her girlfriends said the romance was a secret at first, but had bloomed so bright that everyone noticed and Yekaterina came to a point where she didn't care. She hadn't even cared that her parents knew and that the scandal had been a point of serious contention, but for the girl in the pink fluffy sweater in the picture on his wall, this had been important enough to stand up to her parents. Her best friend had revealed that there had been terrible fights and that Yekaterina had come to school with bruises. Of course, given the prominence of her family, no one had done anything.

The kettle whistled and he stumbled up out of his chair and poured hot water into his teapot. Three cubes of sugar in his chipped china cup awaited until he poured the deep brown liquid. Slowly the sugar cubes melted away and he stirred, took a sip, and sighed. It was not quite the smoky flavored water from the new-fangled samovars that had been imported from the Crimea, but it was his old standard—better than vodka for thinking, too.

Semetai Manas had been in his final year at the Muslim high school that lay at the edge of the old part of the city. Once the old town had been the only town, a sprawling ancient city that had gone by a different name and had resisted the brutalization of the most recent despot in a region where too many successive empires had risen and fallen. When the Russians arrived, they found a proud people in a city of gardens who had taken pity on the survivors who had lost their homeland to war.

That welcome had long ago worn away under the friction of a Russian people determined to remake their new country in the image of the old. Very quickly the Russian immigrants had built businesses that only served Russians. At first it had been because what they served only appealed to the Russians. Gradually it changed to exclude those local people who had not assumed Russian ways and then to where it was now—non-Russians excluded because of their race.

Except for a few stubborn souls like Khalil Khan who had been too good at their profession to be turned away.

Had falling in love with a Russian girl been so heinous it required Semetai's death?

Kazakov shook his head. To a traditional family of a culture that had lost so much, what could be worse than falling in love with a Russian girl?

But then Agafya and Joseph had done it. As a result, they had spent most of their married life hidden here in the forested foothills.

Seduction? Clearly Semetai had slept with her given her pregnancy —unless the girl had a secret lover and none of her friends had reported any suspicion of such a thing. Fathers were known to do terrible things to the youngster who deflowered their daughters prior to marriage. But Boris Bure was not the girl's father. Why kill the girl, too?

Kazakov leaned back in his chair. Yekaterina and Semetai were questions that he could not answer and there was another murder to solve. What had led to the death of a man who might be a Chinese spy who had gone by the Anglo name of Collin?

Kazakov sipped his tea feeling, oddly, the absence of his ex-wife though she was seven years gone and apparently happily married to a businessman of substance and successfully climbing her way up the government communications ladder.

This place needed a woman to make it complete, but Annushka had never been happy here. Too far from her friends in the city, she'd said when they first got married and he'd brought her to his favorite place. They'd gotten an apartment in the city and she'd never come back, though Kazakov had—more frequently as the marriage failed. In the divorce, his name and the dacha were the only things he'd retained as his own.

Scanning the low beams of the ceiling, he supposed the dacha was a good place to hide from the world. The original Russian dacha had been gifts from the original Yekaterina to her favored nobles. Now they were mainly escapes.

Had Maria di Maria escaped somewhere similar?

He thought of her warming those long-fingered hands of hers by a fire like his. The light would catch in her raven hair and her eyes would glimmer. But a foreign girl who worked in the Red Veil would not have many allies. If she had some knowledge of Collin's death and it involved the Red Veil, and if she had truly left on her own and not been taken, then he doubted she would have somewhere like this to hide. She would not trust anyone she knew from the Red Veil. She could not afford to. She either knew something about the murder or someone thought she did and she'd been smart enough to go to ground.

And the fact that she had run would tell whoever had come for her that she did, indeed, know something.

"*Derr 'mo!*" he sat up straight and barked his knees on the support under the table. What was he thinking! He was an idiot! His brain had turned off when he thought he'd been shocked awake by the presence of Boris Bure at the Red Veil. Boris Bure was not the issue at the moment, though Kazakov had taken an instant dislike to the man. Maria di Maria was out there alone and there was no question that they —whoever *they* were—would be looking for her.

He should have done more to find her—followed what he thought were her tracks in the snow.

Quickly he set the teapot and cup in the sink and then dampened the fire to slow the flame. He hauled on his boots, holster, and coat again, grabbed his phone, and stepped out into the cold night. The snow fell more thickly now, the wind hauling it off the mountains in thick, driving white flakes. Already his footsteps from the car to the door were half filled and the dark tree branches sagged under the weight as he trundled around the house to the car. Winter had come far earlier this year and was bringing far more snow than usual.

The old sedan roared to life and he aimed the vehicle toward the dark space between the trees that was all that he could see of the lane in the blindness of the snow glare in headlights. The tires squeaked on the snow. The undercarriage grated until he reached the partial shelter of the trees. He picked up speed, still berating himself as a fool and idiot. The woman had nowhere to go. Why else would she make sure he saw her? Why else be so circumspect when he questioned her, other than she knew something and she could not let Prae know. The Thai woman was quickly becoming something far more than what she seemed, but that should not surprise him. Nothing in this case was what it seemed.

He came out of the trees into drifts of snow blowing across the road. The wind came from the mountains to the southeast and seemed intent on drifting the snow over the road and erasing the scars on Fergana. There were legends whispered in the old town that said the hills were full of the ghosts of all those displaced by the Russians, and that one day Kurmanjan Datka, the legendary female leader who had led her people to freedom from the brutal Kokand khanate, would rise to lead them to take back their land. Most Russians took it as old men's wishful thinking. These days Kazakov found himself not so sure. At least the Kyrgyz were looking forward—unlike their Russian brethren.

By the time he had driven the long road downhill and arrived at the end of the long line of houses that had spread like mushrooms up into the hills, the snow fell heavier and seemed to form a wall around them, as if intent on keeping more people out of the hills. He eased the gas pedal down and made better time, sliding around the corners down toward central New Moscow and the five hidden peaks of Yekaterina Mountain.

The stucco and glass apartment blocks rose out of the swirl of snow like mounds of dirty gray boulders. He skirted the narrow roads that ran into the remains of the old oasis town and came onto the broad back of Suvarov Way that ran north-south along the river.

Maria was smart, that was clear. Both from her reading material and the fact that she had known to get clear of the Red Veil. Perhaps even leaving her phone behind was good, because he'd heard rumors that the government had the technology to track a person through their mobile. He pulled his out of his pocket and considered. Surely no one would be tracking him—at least not yet—and if they were, it would mean that he'd fallen into a case far bigger than he'd thought.

Deep enough it could involve a Chinese man altered to look like something else?

He shivered though the little sedan's heater pumped out more exhaust-stained warmth.

So where would a smart woman go in the city? She dared not go to the train station. That would surely be watched. So would the buses. A hotel? She might have the money, but even that might be chancy given the need to show ID when she registered. Initially she might have stayed in the park, thinking that they could connect there, but he had gone inside too quickly and then there had been the limousine and Bure, so if she'd been there she'd had no chance to connect.

If a connection was what she'd been seeking.

He slowed the sedan. Why had she left? If she was looking to connect with him, why hadn't she stayed? Did she suspect that he was not her friend? Either way, if he was her and with the snow falling in an unfriendly city, he wouldn't have hung around.

Now that he considered, there was only one place in all of New Moscow that she might go to ground with some sense that she might not be found. He slowed the car and checked the rearview mirror. There were no other cars about at this hour.

He turned the car around and cruised back the way he'd come, turning off Suvarov into the narrow streets of the old city.

The old city was named that for a reason. It had been there two hundred and fifty years ago when Fergana was established and its presence stretched millennia farther back. It had stood waiting for them like an Eden when the weak, the ill, and the exhausted had staggered out of the northern mountains into Fergana. The yurt-dwelling nomads who had taken in too many refugees had brought them here and deposited them, probably glad to be rid of so many extra mouths and so many angry young men. It had probably looked the same then, with its stone and mud walls, high windows, and lonely doors that gave onto the street. Its stout walls, like egg shells, holding the life inside.

He had been inside a house or two and they had always surprised him with the light and tile and garden-filled courtyard even though what had once been a stately family home now was a ghetto of three, four, and sometimes five or six families crowded into apartments that had once been single bedrooms. With the arrival of the Russians and the diminishment of the Silk Road, the fortunes of the trading families who had lived here had faded.

There was a tea house he knew of that might help him. Men met there in the evenings to drink their tea and their vodka. He'd arrested men there a time or two. He drove slowly through the winding, narrow streets that pressed in at the vehicle and finally parked the car and climbed out. Ahead the street became too narrow.

Snow swirled into his face, but the wind was less here. Flakes melted on his hair and water ran down his scalp as he paused, then pulled his phone from his pocket and tossed it under the seat of the car. If they could track his phone this far, well, tracking him in the maze of streets that made up the old city would still be daunting, especially in this weather. Head down against the flakes, he struck out through the ankle-deep snow.

The Blue Corner Tea House sat a junction of five streets, each no wider than two donkey carts could comfortably pass. Where the streets met, they formed a small community square where a trickling fountain on one wall provided water for the local houses. The Blue Corner Tea House filled one odd-angled building that stuck out into the square. During the day in the summer, a bright striped awning spread shade to small tables, but at night the awning was furled and a sturdy blue door marked the entrance. The scent of burning charcoal and wood filled the chill air.

Kazakov pushed inside into firelight, dragging snow and a gust of cold into wood-fire warmth. He stomped his feet at the door and knocked the snow off his shoulders, then looked up into silence. Twenty men in worn trousers and woolen work shirts with small white embroidered skull caps perched on their heads sat on three-legged stools around small wooden tables in the narrow room. The place had blue-washed walls that gleamed like clear water and would give a sense of cool in the hot summers. Benches sat along the walls covered in woven and felted pillows in faded colors. The men all looked at him, their expressions unfriendly. The owner, he knew from a previous case, was a bull of a man with a thick dark beard. He stood at the back of the place beside the fireplace stacking cheap glasses beside a large teapot on a table beside the fire. A blackened kettle hung in the hearth.

Ignoring the men at the tables, Kazakov crossed to the owner and pulled out his badge.

The owner waved his identification away.

"I know who you are. I remember." He turned away to adjust the wood on the small fire. Low conversation started behind them as the owner straightened. "What do you want?" He mumbled something unintelligible in Kyrgyz under his breath.

"I'm investigating the death of Semetai Manas," Kazakov said, stretching the truth slightly.

The room went still behind him.

The bullish owner turreted back to him. "The case is closed with no suspects. That is what the family has been told. The police have moved on."

And the family had moved away was what his investigation had told him at the time. Kazakov stepped in closer.

"Is there somewhere else we can speak?" He nodded at the other men. They eyed him closely and he wished that he'd not said what he had. If there were Chinese men who looked western, how easy would it be to have spies in a place like the Blue Corner? The bullish man must have read his urgency. He wiped his hands and tossed his rag on the counter before leading Kazakov through a narrow, unpainted door at the rear of the room. Kazakov found himself in a storeroom that might have been a hallway, for at the far end a curtain held back electric lights and the noise of a distant radio.

"I repeat. What do you want?" The bullish man seemed to fill the space, and though Kazakov was a big man, the bearded owner towered over him. He must have Uzbek blood in his anscestry. They were bigger men than the more slightly built Kygyz.

"And I repeat, I am looking into Semetai Manas's murder. It is unofficial. My superior has closed the case, but I believe the culprit may still be identified and caught."

The man's black eyes bored into Kazakov, but Kazakov held his ground. Finally, the man nodded. "I am Dasten Abdulin. I am Semetai's uncle."

"His uncle." Kazakov considered the unlikely coincidence.

Abdulin shrugged. "His father and I were friends, as were our parents before us and their parents before them."

An uncle, not by blood but by the extended clan connections of his people. Kazakov nodded.

"His death broke his mother's heart. It killed his father. Semetai was a good boy—the first in his family to be accepted into the university. How can I help?"

"Thank you." Kazokov studied the man. "May I ask why did you not come forward when I was asking questions before the case was closed?"

Dastan Abdulin's gaze dropped to the floor. "Perhaps consider the situation. We are Muslim. We were certain we would be accused of the death. It has happened before. Always we are blamed."

It was a truth Kazakov could not deny. He nodded. "Then what has changed now?"

Abdulin shrugged. "Time, perhaps. You are the first person who has shown any interest in Semetai's death."

And that was probably the truth as well, though Kazakov had mentioned Semetai Manas only as a ruse to get information about the woman. Kazakov checked over his shoulder. The door was closed. He had stretched the truth to get this far. Now he would stretch if further. "I am looking for a woman. She has information that I believe will help to solve Semetai's murder."

It was a very slim chance, one he did not quite believe in himself.

But Dastan Abdulin's apparent willingness to help suggested that Kazakov might have to reconsider his first suspicion that Semetai Manas's family had murdered the boy because of his involvement with Yekaterina Weber.

"The woman is on the run," said Kazakov. "She has no friends or family in the city. I thought that, given she does not trust the authorities, she might have come to the old city."

Abdulin's dark gaze was unreadable. He began to straighten canned food on a shelf. "Why would I know if such a one came to the Islamic part of town? I am not an Imam or one of your psychics."

"Aah, but many people pass through your doors and if they do not speak directly to you, they speak within your hearing. If something odd happened, you would know of it."

Abdulin's beard rose and fell as if he swallowed. "Perhaps that is true, but why would I tell such as you? If such a girl existed, would she not be afraid of police?"

"I'm trying to save this woman's life. I believe she ran from someone. I don't know who. I think she knows that if they find her, they will kill her."

The bullish man turned to him then. "Then perhaps it is best if she is not found by anyone."

Kazakov had to nod. "There is that. But I thought that she may wish to help bring a killer to justice. Perhaps—perhaps you might know a way to get a message to her, to tell her that I will help her. Tell her my name and that I, too, like to look beyond curtains."

The beard rose and fell once more. Then the café owner shrugged. "If there were such a woman, it would be interesting to know what she thought. But then, I have no way of knowing."

Kazakov dug in his pockets and pulled out his battered hand-stitched wallet. From this he extracted a card. "If you should come across anyone who has seen her, perhaps you could pass along my contact information." He reached into his breast pocket and came out with a pen and scratched out his office number, replacing it with his mobile phone number. "She should not identify herself. Tell her to say she is my cousin, visiting from out of town. Do you understand?"

The owner nodded. "I understand you are a man with a vast imagination. Some would say you must be drunk. I think you are a lost soul blown in by the storm and now I must send you out again."

He reached across Kazakov's shoulder and shoved open the door to the Blue Corner. The place was empty now; only one man remained, wiping a table with Abdulin's cloth.

Kazakov preceded the owner out of the storeroom. "My apologies for interrupting your business," he said.

The owner cocked an ear to the rising sound of the wind and shrugged. "There is a storm settling over us. It is best for a man to be home."

With no other ideas of where Maria would take cover, Kazakov drove once around New Moscow, skirting Saint Basil's domed cathedral, the behemoth government buildings, and the ramshackle structures that made up the ancient open-air market—all darkened in the night snow—then took Dastan Abdulin's advice and returned through the deepening snow to the dacha. He hoped Maria had truly found shelter from the storm.

The sedan, for all its age and battered fenders, had the weight to plow its way back to its resting place behind the dwelling. Kazakov stumbled out and through the snow, stamping his feet up the half-covered front stairs and inside to warmth, where snow fell off his boots, hair, and shoulders to puddle on the floor by the door. He once more lit the lantern and divested himself of coat, mobile phone, and weapon. Koshka uncurled and stretched her lean length on the bed before leaping down and padding across to him. She sniffed disdainfully at the melt water and mewed up at him.

"You've been fed, cat. I haven't forgotten." But out of habit he found the tin and spooned a little more into her dish. The room filled with happy cat licks.

Fortunately, the fire that he had banked still had embers. He stirred them to life and added more wood. When the flames caught and crackled, he reheated his half-finished tea on the top of the wood stove and settled back in his desk chair.

He had learned nothing for certain, but he had left a message for Maria. Hopefully it would get to her. He placed his mobile on the center of his desk and closed his eyes. Behind his eyelids, dark men trudged through the darkness and the snow to take the message to her. At least he hoped that they were taking her the message.

They could just as well be going to kill her.

6

It was a Baba Yaga dream like one he once had as a child. He was small and searching for something in a darkened forest.

He had come upon a small house in the woods and the building was built of odd angles and danced on chicken legs in its yard. When he knocked at the door, a misshapen crone answered. She lay across her iron stove and when he asked for her help to find what was lost, she only laughed. It was shrill and biting and sent him stumbling back into the forest, her laughter taunting him.

Kazakov woke with a start to a shrilling sound and the undeniable sense that he had forgotten something. He stumbled up from his desk into the lantern-lit dacha, upsetting Koshka from his lap, into a squalling fur ball onto the plank floor. Not a forest, the dacha. He was at home. The fire had burned low—he'd forgotten to dampen the flue —and the room was cold. On his desk was a stone-cold cup of tea and the infernal, squawking, mobile phone.

He grabbed it up. "Hello?"

For a moment, he felt like he was asking the question across worlds, as if he'd be answered by Yekaterina Weber or the great tsarina herself.

"Kazakov?"

He settled back into the chair, recognizing the voice and looking at the phone. Khalil Khan almost never phoned him.

"Yes?" he answered.

"Where are you?" the M.E. asked. His voice was as cool as Kazakov had ever heard it—as if this was the coldest of professional calls.

"At home, of course." He checked the small alarm clock on a shelf above the bed. "It's the middle of night." Three o'clock the clock said.

"I just got the results of some of the tests on our body. I thought you might want to come down and see."

Kazakov stood and staggered to the window, both of his legs half asleep with pins and needles. Through the frost on the windows, in the darkness outside, the snow was still falling. He couldn't see his front stairs anymore. "I'm not a hundred percent certain that's possible at the moment."

There was silence on the phone a moment, then: "If it is possible, you should make it happen."

The line clicked and went dead from Khan's end and Kazakov swore. He set the phone down and worked his neck, stiff from sleeping in the chair, then went to the sink and shocked himself awake with a palmful of cold water in his face. Koshka was awake and threading his legs for breakfast. He scooped her up.

"You will have to wait just like I must." He stroked her soft black fur and settled her on the floor where she head-butted him once and then paced over to the bed, leapt up to her shelf, and curled up on her cushion to stare at him with disapproval. Such were the females in his life. Not one had approved of him in the long run.

He was tired enough he would have liked to join her on the bed, but instead he gulped down his cold tea, shuddered at the taste, then rebuilt the fire and dampened the flue. He pulled on his coat, a patchy, old, black fur hat, his boots, and his gloves; blew out the lantern; and stepped outside.

Cold slammed into him as he waded into the pine-scented night. He wrestled the dacha door closed against the snow that sifted in when the door was opened. A foot of snow covered his stairs and he used the shovel he kept beside the door to clear them and then a pathway around the side of the house to the vehicle. Fortunately, the shelter of the house had kept the worst of the blowing snow off the sedan, but it still looked like a snowdrift under six inches of snow. He used his arm to brush it off and then climbed in and started the engine. Back outside, he shoveled the route across the dacha's clearing to the trees, tossed the shovel in the back seat, and climbed in.

The heavy old sedan rumbled over the snow and as he picked up speed under the trees, its tires thumped from the shape they'd frozen into. Luckily, the snow had lessened and provided only a lace curtain as he passed Agafya Ryabkov's lane and came around a curve to the open and the view of the lights of New Moscow.

Thirty minutes later the sedan sent up almost blinding clouds of snow as it bulldozed its way through the silent streets. On Suvarov he saw his first sign of life—a lone plow futilely trying to clear the major thoroughfare. Typical Fergana—prepared to only scrape futilely at the surface. At times, he thought the entire country was no more than a patina of Russia layered onto something far older. Now the patina was wearing off, leaving a vacuum in its place. Fergana could never be the Russia that was, just as there would never be another tsarina or another Yekaterina clad in a pink fluffy sweater and the hope of her youth.

There was only Fergana, but what Fergana was had never been determined. It was an agglomeration of people with a Russian overlay and something rotten at the heart of it.

The fact that only he seemed to care about the deaths of the two young people and now the death of the spy seemed to prove it.

The hospital parking lot had not yet been plowed, and parked cars had become abandoned snowdrifts caught in the amber lights of the lot. Khan's M.E. van sat pulled to the side of the building with a cleared front window and conspicuously less snow on its rooftop. Kazakov pulled the sedan in behind the van and climbed out into the amber-stained snow and waded to the stairs and down to the M.E.'s reception office. He stepped inside to the perennial stink of chemical air freshener and formaldehyde, pulled his threadbare hat off, and stomped off the snow.

The blue fluorescent glow of the lights flickered over pale green walls and the brown vinyl tile floor. The reception desk was empty, but that was normal at this hour and frankly, the last thing he needed was someone keeping track of his movements. The hallway leading back to the exam rooms was dimly lit. There was no sound, no movement except the fetid circulating air.

"Khan?" he called softly. There was no answer.

He headed toward the M.E.'s office and heard voices. Light spilled out the transom above Khan's barely open door. He eased along the hall and kept to the shadows while he peeked into the room. Khan at his desk, a person hunched in a heavy man's coat and hat sitting across from him, both now silent.

What the hell was Khan up to? The M.E. didn't look happy—at all. Did he have another late-night visitor, or was this something more? Kazakov had two choices: go in and find out, or ease away from the door and let Khan think that he hadn't been able to make it through the snow.

One way was a coward's way—the way the unsuccessful hero acted in a fairy tale. One way he'd be walking away from the case just like Rostoff would want him to—if Rostoff even knew about the dead body in the park. He pushed open the door and stepped inside into the scent of warm wool and—lavender?

Khan looked up, startled, as Kazakov crossed to the desk and Khan's companion.

Maria di Maria looked up at him, her brown eyes gone the color of honey in the blue fluorescent light.

"Detektiv Kazakov," she said and bowed her head.

"How?" He turned to Khan with his question. Khan did not look happy to see him even though the M.E. had called him.

Khan pushed up from his desk chair. "How does not matter. You are here. Let's just say that a friend of a friend of a friend asked me to bring her here and get in touch with you." He held up his hand before Kazakov could speak. "I don't wish to know anything. There is a file here on my desk that you may wish to read. Now I am going home.

Please ensure the door is locked when you leave and don't ask for my help again."

Khan stalked toward the office door where he pulled on a heavy coat and a traditional tall Kygyz fur hat that Kzakov had never seen him wear before.

"I didn't ask for you to be involved," Kazakov said.

"And for that my wife and children thank you, but I fear it may already be too late."

Kazakov crossed to him. "What's going on, Khan? We've worked well together all these years. You're the one man I trust."

Khan met his gaze, then sadly shook his head. "The world changes, old friend. Everything does, and you seem to be the only one who does not see it." He pulled the door open and left, trudging down the hall toward the entrance.

Kazakov watched him go. He knew the world changed; he just wondered what it was changing into and how to make sure the change was for the better. He turned sadly back to Maria, who was still sitting.

Not better when he lost a friend.

"He's a worthy man. How did you get to him?"

Her faint, enchanting scent stuck in his nose reminding him of something sweet, perhaps from the happier times of his childhood. He hooked his hip over the side of the desk. She had stuffed her hair inside the hat so that, with her height, until you saw her face, she might almost pass as a man.

"I went to the old Islamic town. Given what I had learned inside the Red Veil, I thought that place might be safer. An old woman took pity on me because of the snow and she took me to her son. Apparently, word of a foreigner in their midst travels quickly. The next thing I knew I was bundled into a black van and transported here to wait for you." She brushed a nonexistent hair back off her face with an elegant white hand.

She smiled up at him, lighting those honey eyes like sunlight through a brown bottle.

"You waited for me at Yekaterina Park."

The smile brightened. "I did. But you left me there." Her gaze met his matter-of-factly.

"You disappeared. I couldn't find you."

He shook his head and rounded the desk, its bulk more comfortable between them though her hands looked so soft. He settled into Khan's chair.

"Why did you leave the Red Veil?" he asked, lacing his fingers before him on the file Khan had left. He would look at it later.

She blew out a sigh. "After you left, Frau Zelinka called me downstairs to find out what you'd wanted. I told her what I'd told you —almost nothing at all, I'm sorry to say." Her hands shook and she looked like she wanted to smoke. "You see, there was more to it. I am sure I know who the dead man was."

She lifted her chin like a smoker and met his gaze. "I mentioned him this morning—yesterday morning—the one called Collin. Collin Archer he said his name was. He had been to visit me weekly in the past three months. Before that, for about six months he had come once a month. He was about five feet ten and slim, with the broken veins of a drinker—which is odd given every time he came to see me he only drank water. He was a nicer man than most. He liked to talk about the world and actually made me use the book knowledge that I had instead of simply being someone to fuck."

She looked at him sideways—to see if he was shocked at her language? Still not beyond a whore's games, then.

"Collin visited the night before last. He seemed distracted when we were together. I'd seen him talking to Prae when I came down the stairs to him. At the time, I thought she only offered him refreshments. Now I am not so sure. You see, after we were done it was quite late." She eyed him again as if for a reaction. "The house was quiet and I let him out of my room. He said I need not escort him down the stairs—it made him feel ungentlemanly forcing a lady out of her boudoir."

She smiled and brushed again at that absent hair. He found himself wondering once more what her hand would feel like on his skin.

"I stayed in the room but then realized that he had left a scarf behind. I left my room and went to the stairs but something made me stop—a thump, a gurgle—I can't be sure, but all the hairs on the back of my neck stood on end and I tiptoed back to my room. I thought that was the end of it, but after you left, Prae came back to my room. She went to my window and looked out. She asked me, "How could you know if it was Collin?" and suddenly I felt like it was a warning. I thought of what I'd heard the night before and I was sure. I knew I had to get out of there or I was going to disappear or at least be found dead somewhere. So I ran."

Her faint perfume overlaid the dry heat of the building's radiator. He leaned back in the chair and swiveled it sideways but watched carefully from the side. "That does not seem like a lot to throw your— career—away? Barely a suspicion, really. I don't understand why you would fear for your life."

She went still as if she'd joined the ranks of cadavers in this dead place. Then she stood up abruptly. "I thank you for coming, detektiv. I am sorry to have wasted your time."

Stiff shouldered, she swung out the office door and marched toward the exit. He scrambled out of the chair and sprinted to catch up. He caught her hand. Her skin was softer than he'd imagined. "I don't doubt your story, Maria." He stopped her from pulling away. "I just don't understand why he would be killed in the Red Veil. Can you explain it to me?"

"Why should I? You are just like all the rest. All the men who think they're better than me."

He released her hand and stepped away. "It may surprise you, but that is not how I feel at all. You—puzzle me—and I am a man who lives always with puzzles. I think there must be other things happening at the Red Veil that have concerned you, for you *are* an intelligent woman. I need to know everything." He thought for a moment of the tingling that had filled him when he'd spotted Boris Bure on the stairs to the Red Veil. "There may be a link between the Red Veil and a pair of murders that I have been ordered not to investigate. I want to know why. I want to know whether Collin Archer's murder is somehow connected."

Her lovely face frowned as she crossed her arms over her chest and looked him up and down. "Then perhaps we can help each other to understand what happened—to Collin and to your other victims." Turning on her heel, she returned to the office. "I will help you."

He settled behind the desk again and pulled Khan's original manila envelope from his coat breast pocket and pulled out the photo of the dead man. "Is this Collin?" he asked as he slid the photo across to her on the desktop.

She did not touch it, simply leaned forward from the edge of her chair to study the face in the image. "It is him. Strange how the lack of life leaves a man… empty. Soulless. Something that was, will never be again." She touched the photo then, gently, as if it was a fragile flower. "I remember when I was a child. Abruzza— the destroyed village—she looked the same way."

Sighing, she sat back in her chair. "Of course, better like this than a living man without a soul. I have known a few of those. It is the empty eyes that betray them."

She glanced at him as if checking. She looked sad and tired, but there were too many things he had to know. He glanced up at the clock on the wall. It was almost six in the morning. The M.E.'s staff would be arriving soon. Khalil Khan would return as well, and Kazakov knew the M.E. would not appreciate finding Kazakov still here.

"I need you to tell me everything you know about Collin Archer, but not here. We need to get you some place that they won't look for you." He stood up and flipped open the file on Khan's desk, scanning down past the things he already knew. But the file was not the originals; Khan had copied everything for him as if he knew they might not have such a chance again. *Thank you, old friend. You've taken risk enough.*

He flipped the file closed and, with it in hand, led Maria to the morgue entrance, opened the door, and peered out into the gray of early dawn. The snow had stopped falling but the clouds streaming overhead from the Tian Shan and Fergana Mountains said that more was on the way, even though they had already received more than they usually received in November. Nodding at her to follow, he flipped the lock on the door and waded out into the snow, leading her to the car. Their path was clear in the snow and there wasn't a damn thing he could do about it. Whoever arrived would see that someone had been here when no one should have been. He held the passenger door for Maria and then made a point of walking over their path a few times to make it less obvious how many people had been here. Then he climbed in beside Maria and started the car.

For an old beast of a vehicle, the engine roared to life and he only needed to rock the sedan once to get it plowing through the snowdrift that had settled around it. They crunched and rumbled out of the parking lot and into the street. They were the only traffic, which was a concern, for anyone with two eyes could follow them. He needed to get them amongst other vehicles so that their trail would be, if not lost, at least less clear.

"Tell me about Collin Archer," he asked as he steered slowly toward downtown New Moscow seeking more traffic. The architecture grew more modern, the bungalow-style housing and Islamic quarter abandoned in showy glass and steel that surrounded the huge plaza where the ornate eight-hundred-foot-long façade of the Winter Palace was pasted on a vast bunker of government offices. Facing it was the garish façade of Saint Basil's cathedral. Like Maria's comment about Collin's body, the cadaver of the ancient palace and church now seemed soulless, the originals long ago remade by the defiling Ottomans.

"He was—a cold man. Many who came to me were. It was as if the sex were obligatory or a physical expression of power. He was strange, both pale and not. He did not like to take off his clothes, preferring to take me from behind while still dressed."

He glanced at her and she sat stone-faced as gradually traffic increased on half-plowed roads. He drove them around until he was satisfied they weren't being followed and then turned them toward the hills. Did he dare take Maria back to his dacha or should he find another place? At the moment, he could not think of an alternative that could provide as much safety. Besides, he needed Maria close so that he could mine her information. He turned onto Suvarov toward home.

"He often spoke of England—its green fields and tall trees and how he missed them. He was good at languages, too. He spoke English and German and Russian and once we were passing Prae and she was talking to another Thai girl. I don't know what they were saying, but I think Collin did for he shook his head as if he knew what they were talking about."

"What was he wearing the last time you saw him?" he asked as the central part of the city was left behind.

"Dark gray wool trousers—expensive looking. A camel-colored Kashmir sweater. A scarf to match and his coat was navy wool, cut closer to the body than most men's. It made him look taller, I think. I think that was important to him."

Frowning, she looked out the window as they left the downtown, skirted the Islamic old city, and entered the wilderness of suburban sprawl. "Where are we going?"

"Some place safe," Kazakov said, keeping his eyes on the road, for the unplowed snow made the driving treacherous. "What more can you remember about the man?"

She thought for a few minutes. "He was a loner. He never came with friends, unlike the others from the Anglo-German Embassy. The others often asked for English girls—I guess they missed home—but he never did. When other English were at the Red Veil, he wanted nothing to do with them." She frowned. "When I think of it now, it is strange. It didn't feel so at the time. Perhaps my memory fails me."

She turned to him. "Perhaps I am unreliable?"

At that he did glance at her serious face. "Somehow, I doubt it." He looked back to the road. The houses were ending and ahead the world was a field of white turned gray by the heavy clouds. On the slopes above them the land undulated with narrow stream channels. There, hidden among the trees above one such channel, was his home. But the road through the field of white was cut by a set of deep ruts. Someone had driven this way before him. Beyond Agafya Ryabkov's place and his dacha, there were few other hardy souls who lived up here all year. Most of those homes were owned by wealthy people who had winterized larger, more expensive homes than his. Perhaps they had driven into town for work early this morning.

His uneasiness turned to concern when he reached his turn and the tire tracks turned ahead of him. He slowed to a stop.

"What is the problem?" Maria asked.

Kazakov inhaled. "I'm not sure whether there is a problem or not, but someone is here." He put the vehicle in park. "Stay here." Cautiously, he climbed out of the car. The snow sifted down around him. The cold froze his cheeks and he was thankful that he'd thought to bring his old hat.

Keeping to the edge of the trees, he followed the tracks up his laneway. The snow lay less deep under the trees and the other tire tracks were clear, as was the black police sedan sitting by his front door.

He stood there, considering. Rostoff took kickbacks from the New Moscow brothels, but Kazakov couldn't believe that the man he knew would countenance murder. Though Kazakov had a sinking feeling about the evidence displayed in the dacha, police weren't going to hurt Maria. In fact, depending on who was here, they might be of assistance in protecting a witness.

Still… He would proceed with caution. Besides, where else was there to go?

He returned to the car and climbed in. "There are police at my house. I suspect that they will want to talk about another case—one that does not involve you. Stay out of any conversation about it. Depending on the situation they may be able to help us, but when we arrive we will say that you are my mother's sister's daughter. Her name is Alina and she comes from Kokand. Do you understand? Do not talk unless they ask you a question."

Maria cocked a brow at him. "Will that not be suspicious if I don't talk? A normal woman would chatter about her cousin, would she not?"

"This isn't a game, Maria."

She shook her head. "I am not playing one."

He dropped the sedan in gear and drove up the lane to park behind the house. Maria pushed open her door and climbed out, rubbing at the makeup on her face until most of it was smudged as if she'd slept with it on—perhaps on a bus.

Kazakov retrieved the shovel from the sedan and led the way around the house, a smile pasted on his face.

"It is beautiful here, after the snow," Maria/Alina said brightly as they stomped up the steps to the door. "So lovely on the trees. We have not so many in Kokand. So wide open, you know?"

Kazakov nodded and steeled himself as he pushed open the door. "So who is it who disturbs us on such a fine day?" he said, trying to be stern but friendly.

The single person in the room stood with his back to the door. Chief Inspector Rostoff apparently studied Kazakov's evidence wall. When he turned to them, Rostoff's flushed face was far from smiling.

7

Kazakov's heart sank as Rostoff's furious scowl chilled the dacha even though the man had taken the time to stir a fire to life. In the columns of morning light through the frosty windows, Koshka crouched in the bed's furthest corner, her pupils dilated, fur fuzzed, and tail twitching unhappily—about as happy as Kazakov felt.

"Rostoff." Kazakov tipped his head hello and removed his hat. "To what do I owe this visit?" He made a show of helping Maria/ Alina out of her coat and removed his own. Rostoff still wore his and his heavy fur hat. "You recall my cousin Alina from Kokand? She's here for a visit. I was just in town picking her up. The roads are not good, eh?" He shook his head.

Rostoff looked from one to the other, his heavy features going through permutations of fury at the fact that someone else was here and he could not simply explode at Kazakov.

Rostoff bowed his head in polite greeting. "Madam—it could not be Miss?"

Maria/Alina played her part and actually laughed. "Please. It is Miss because no one will have a strong woman these days." She shook her head. "Come. We will have tea. Take off your coat. This one must be a better host." She sniffed womanly disdain in Kazakov's direction.

Rostoff glanced at the evidence on the wall. "I think not. I must be on my way. I was simply looking for a pencil and paper to leave Detektiv Kazakov a note to call me, but now the note is delivered in person." He shuffled heavy-footed toward the door. "Join me a moment, Detektiv." He held open the door and motioned Kazakov outside.

Obediently, Kazakov stepped out onto the stair. Rostoff pulled the door closed behind them with a nod to Maria/Alina. Then he caught Kazakov's shoulder and shoved him against the wall. Snow from the roof sifted down over both of them as Rostoff glared.

Kazakov waited for Rostoff's fist, but instead of punching Kazakov, Rostoff hauled him in close by the collar.

"What the hell are you doing?" Rostoff growled. "You were told that investigation was over. You were given a task that surely even you could not fuck up, and then I learn that you have taken it upon yourself to waste resources investigating a drunkard's death. What am I to do with you, Kazakov? Tell me and convince me, because otherwise I know what I am sorely tempted to do." He let the threat hang chillingly undefined in the air.

"I thought I was a police detective. I was doing my job." Kazakov stiffened, holding his anger in check. This was no time to end up on charges for attacking a senior officer, though he was sorely tempted.

"Yes. Yes. A body. I know." Rostoff waved his words away as if they meant nothing. "I cannot afford a problem right now," Rostoff continued. "Nor can you. Least of all you. There is an election coming and there are people who do not want trouble. Do you understand? If you want to keep your job, keep your dacha, keep that 'cousin' of yours, I suggest you reconsider your actions. Do you understand?"

"So, to be clear, you are ordering me not to do my job."

Rostoff's face darkened. He leaned in close. "You listen to me, Detektiv. I am all that stands between you and being tossed out on your ass. Do you understand? Keep me happy and you just might have a job tomorrow."

Kazakov met his glare like he would the glare of a suspect. Rostoff had placed too many questions in his head. He waited until Rostoff finally released him and brushed snow off of his coat before starting down the stairs. Kazakov watched him to the car, assessing Rostoff's actions. This corrupt *mu'dak,* this ass hole, was the source of the problems. Rostoff was the reason Yekaterina's and Semetai's deaths went unsolved, just like countless other cases—because no one in the squad gave a damn anymore.

But Rostoff had said that because of the election he could not afford the problem posed by Kazakov. That suggested something more was going on and that someone else was pulling strings… Like Bure?

Rostoff circled his car and opened the door. Over the roof he peered back at Kazakov in his shirtsleeves in the freezing cold. "I expect that material from your wall in a box on my desk this afternoon along with your collections from the brothels."

His gaze carried an earnestness Kazakov couldn't quite believe.

Their friendship had ended years before.

"Understand, Alexander," Rostoff said softly. "I am risking things to do you a favor. The alternative is not good for your health—or mine. Now get inside, old friend. You'll catch your death of cold out here like that."

Rostoff seemed to dimish a little. Then he shook his head and slipped into the car. It purred to life, then shouldered its way through the snow in the yard right over Kazakov's garden plot hidden under the snow. Rostoff's vehicle disappeared down the lane beneath the arbor of trees.

The rumble of the car's engine gradually faded, leaving the silence and the thump of snow falling off branches from deep in the trees. Usually, on winter days like this, he enjoyed the silence and the peace of his dacha. Feeling the sting of the cold on his skin, he blew a breath out as he turned to the door.

What the hell had that been all about? For a moment Rostoff had looked like a beaten man. Kazakov pushed inside into the warmth of Rostoff's fire and Maria's scent of lavender.

The way Rostoff had acted in the place, Kazakov wondered how many times the man had visited before while Kazakov was away. He looked around his home and nothing looked the same, just as Rostoff had changed during their conversation. The old tingling sensation burbled again in his gut. Something big *was* happening, but what?

Maria sat on the couch, Koshka at her feet sniffing her hand. It was a peaceful scene. One he could grow to like, but there was no sense of peace in the dacha anymore—only defilement.

"That is done," he said simply and went to the evidence on the wall. The photo of Yekaterina in her pink sweater stared, pleading, out at him. He tugged it from the small tack on the wall and the tack—like his dignity—tumbled to the floor down behind his desk.

"Are you okay?" Maria asked.

What could he say? That he'd failed and they'd found him out— whoever *they* were? That he was an old fool for ever thinking that he could go behind the backs of men like Rostoff or Bure to do what was right? That the investigation was over? But then why should Maria care about it at all? It had nothing to do with her— unless it did.

He looked down at Yekaterina's face. She had been so young. As young as the Yekaterina who had written her diary, exposing her heart on the page. This Yekaterina had exposed her heart to Semetai Manas and someone had killed her for it.

"Who is she?" Maria asked, coming up beside him. "She affects you so."

He sighed. "Just a schoolgirl who died. Someone left her body in Potemkin Park, naked and beaten."And yet her clothes had been folded and left beside her as if someone had cared about her. He nodded at the school photo of a smiling, handsome, dark-haired Semetai and pulled it loose from the wall. "She loved this boy. He was from the old town. Muslim. Someone killed him, too. He was shot as he ran from the town and no one is saying anything—not her parents, and his parents left town."

"And you are determined to find who killed them just as you want to find Collin's killer. I think you are a good man, Detektiv Kazakov." One hand clasped his arm as she handed him a cup of newly brewed tea with milk. Steam curled up over its rim, carrying the heavy, earthy scent of oolong tea. "Drink this. It will warm you up and give you energy. I put three sugars in it."

Three sugars—his regular amount. How could she know that? He sipped and nodded. "Thank you. But it seems that the case must truly close—according to Rostoff and whoever gives him orders. He wants the evidence in his office—and probably destroyed."

He began pulling the papers off his wall and Maria helped him. Autopsy reports. Witness statements, scene photos. Photos of the bodies. He pulled open his desk drawer and withdrew his working file complete with the information he had quietly been gathering about the families. The Manas family had been merchants and well to do by the standards of those who lived in the old city. The import business had been handed down through generations and had stood the test of time and of the influx of Chinese traders who seemed to be muscling out much of their competition. The disappearance of the Manas family had left a void in the import sector that was quickly being filled by various Chinese newcomers. It had also left a number of the Muslim truckers and laborers out of work. Though it had only been a month since the family left and the father died, a few of the truckers had banded together to try to recreate the company, but their lack of acumen made their success doubtful.

On the other hand, the Weber-Bure family had gone on almost as if Yekaterina's death had not happened. Yes, there had been a funeral and the news had carried Boris and Natania Bure's sorrow in its broadcasts. After all, Boris Bure was becoming more and more of a public figure. He would run for the fledgling Reformation Party in the spring election. According to the neighbors, the already reclusive Natania Bure had not been seen since the funeral, but Boris Bure—well, aside from time off to attend the funeral and the subsequent reception, Boris Bure had proven himself a dedicated public servant and had not missed another day of work or electioneering. And now Kazakov had seen him at the Red Veil.

Kazakov glanced at Maria, who was peering over his shoulder at the file. He flipped it closed and tapped Yekaterina's photo. "You may know her stepfather—Boris Bure?"

Her eyes widened slightly and she returned to the couch to perch on its edge. She clutched her tea cup in both hands as she sipped.

Finally, she nodded. "I know him—I've seen him. He was—is—an important man. Frau Zelinka always makes sure that he gets what he wants—and then cleans up after him. He is not kind to women. I was fortunate that I was not his type—it was usually the pale northern girls he preferred."

Kazakov leaned on the desk and watched her. She was a lovely, graceful woman, with a swan neck and long slim limbs that belied her curves. Her long dark hair flowed across the shoulders of the simple woolen workman's shirt she wore tucked into the waist of sturdy workmen's trousers. Her long feet were enclosed in thick, hand-knit socks and she'd worn thick-soled boots. Either she'd been prepared to run for a long while or someone had helped outfit her.

Still, unfortunately, he didn't quite trust her.

"How often did he come to the Red Veil?" he asked.

She thought a moment, her head tilting as if she would shake a memory loose. "It was about once a month. Then lately he has come more frequently—about once a week, I think."

"How long has he been coming once a week?"

She thought a few minutes. "I think about three months."

So before his stepdaughter died. His visits to a brothel were not because of Yekaterina's death.

"And how long had he been coming to the Red Veil before that?" Years, most likely. Men who liked brothels were long-term patrons and a man who came weekly was definitely a long-term patron.

"Nine months. I am fairly sure. I remember the first time I saw him. It was my birthday and he was such a good-looking man that I joked that he was my birthday present. Of course, he didn't take me." She smiled up at him.

He thought about the information. Maria had told him that Collin Archer had also been coming to the Red Veil for about nine months. Was it simply coincidence that Bure showed up at the same time? Simply chance that Bure was there just after another body was found? Kazakov thought about the man's ice-blue eyes and the hardness behind them. Was his willingness to find a connection between the two cases only because he did not like the man?

"Did Bure and Collin Archer ever meet? Were they at the Red Veil at the same time?"

She studied the dacha ceiling, the old wood beams complete with cobwebs that, as usual, he had neglected to sweep away for some time.

"I don't think they ever spoke in my presence. I remember being with Collin one night when Bure swaggered in." She glanced up at Kazakov. "Sorry. I did not care for Bure by then. He had already beaten three girls.

"Collin and I were having a drink and he had just stood up to visit the men's room. Bure swanned in and acted like he was a king. Collin sat down as if he'd forgotten his need to relieve himself."

As if perhaps Collin was meeting someone but dared not with Bure present?

"Who else was there, do you remember?" he asked.

"I recall there were two other girls and their dates in the room. They were Leskov and Polunin. Leskov is a businessman."

"In railways, yes. I know. And Polunin is a bureaucrat in charge of what passes for security in Fergana. Important men." With a possible spy at the next table with them.

"And Prae had just come to check that everything was fine in the room. But she only stuck her head in and left again."

"Was this before or after Bure came in?"

Maria frowned. "Before, I think. Is it important?"

Sighing, he shook his head. "I'm not certain. But there is something there." And it filled him with disquiet. Something was clearly wrong and Bure was somehow involved in all of it. It might seem tenuous, but the two cases were somehow connected by more than his imagination.

He set down his cup and scooped the documents and photos into a file, then headed for his coat. "You stay here. There is somewhere I must go. I should be back in a few hours."

By midmorning, New Moscow's few plows had been hard at work and traffic was moving in the city again. Kazakov's sedan plowed down as far as the houses and then had clear sailing—almost as clear as the wisps of clouds in the blue sky. They were fools' clouds, there to fool the unwary into thinking the storm was over, when really they were harbingers of things to come.

He glanced down at the file and the photos. Rostoff could have them. He would make his own archive—again. At the old town he pulled off and found a printer's shop on a side street that he'd recalled from a prior counterfeiting case.

He walked in to the sound of a bell overhead and the scent of ink and dusty paper. The place was poorly lit in the front, but a beam of light came from the backroom. Someone scuffed their feet, presumably in reaction to the sound of the bell. Then a thin, short man in a long-sleeved, white shirt and black trousers came into the shop.

"May I help you?" he asked. His white shirt had blue-stained cuffs that matched the blue skull cap he wore.

"I need the use of your photocopier."

The thin man pursed his lips and then shook his head. "I know you —polizia. Don't think I don't know your tricks. I let you in and then you plant evidence so that you can arrest me later."

Kazakov closed his eyes. He'd heard tell of such tactics when the department was under scrutiny for too few successful arrests and prosecutions. For a moment he wondered if such had been the case with the old counterfeiting file.

"Is your photocopier available or not? It may help solve the murder of Semetai Manas."

There. He knew that exposing his purpose could be dangerous, but in the old city he had to think that such information might also lead people to help him. The elderly printer's gaze narrowed, his lips thinning to a line.

"I do not want to see what you are doing," the printer said, looking Kazakov up and down. "I was there when the police came. I remember you, now. You—you are the one who is friends with Khalil."

The printer's knowledge surprised Kazakov a little. To be known as a friend was an honor amongst these people. Nodding, he held up the file. "I am—at least I try to be. Please help."

The printer nodded him back behind the counter and into the brightly lit back room. The printer left Kazakov to quickly copy the documents. When it was done, the little man refused Kazakov's money.

"Just find those who killed the boy. Please. The old town. It is not like it used to be. Now people are afraid. There are things happening." He looked over his shoulder in a motion Kazakov recognized as something he did himself—looking to the mountains.

"Things have changed," Kazakov said.

The little man nodded. "Many of us have family who did not settle when the Russians came. They make their livelihood with their herds and bringing goods over the mountains. But many families should have traded this year before returning to their winter places in the lower mountains. So far, they have not come and the passes are closing. There are whispers that something is stirring. People are worried that the war between the Chinese and Ottomans is returning and this time Fergana will no longer be a buffer."

Kazakov checked his watch and looked to the door. Tribal legends and rumors of war were not, at the moment, his problem. "Listen, I have other business to attend to and I must get these files to the man who demands them. But if people would be willing to talk to me about Semetai Manas, I would be willing to speak with them. Ask around. Tell them I will check back here at about noon tomorrow. Will that work?"

Meeting Kazakov's gaze, the little man nodded. "If this hurts these people, I will find men to kill you. It is too long we have allowed your people to take, take, take from us and our families."

Kazakov bowed his head. "We have all lost something. For your people it was your land. For us? I fear Baba Yaga has swallowed our soul. Thank you, friend. I will be here tomorrow."

He left in the milky sunlight of late morning, the wispy clouds having joined hands to form a haze over the sun. The temperature had fallen, too, and the wind came from the eastern mountains. It smelled of snow and he wondered again what had brought this unseasonable winter upon them. It was as if the world was intent in weighing them under.

In the car, he realized that he was hungry. It was many hours since he'd had tea the night before. At the edge of the old city he availed himself of a small restaurant run by a proprietor who looked like he might be of mixed Russian and Kyrgyz blood.

Kazakov ordered a thick noodle soup that came mixed with minced carrots and potatoes and small chunks of lamb redolent with grease. He slurped it up under the less-than-friendly gaze of the proprietor whose lunchtime trade vanished as soon as Kazakov walked in. With the soup came a round of what Russian's insultingly called tribesmen's shingles —flat bread baked on the side of a brick oven with succulent, chewy crust that he soaked in his soup broth. When he was done, he paid and tipped the owner handsomely for his trouble before returning outside to the snow and wind. With his belly full, he no longer felt quite so cold.

He steered the old police sedan back to the Red Veil's location and climbed out. Sighing, he trudged up the stairs and knocked on the red door dreading more of Frau Zelinka's games. Instead, Prae must have seen him coming, for when the door yanked open she held a small tray of inscribed silver.

"Frau Zelinka says I must give this to you, but I am not to let you in."

On the small silver tray rested the same brown envelope he had avoided in Frau Zelinka's boudoir. Even through his leather gloves, his fingers felt soiled when he picked it up and silently slid it into his pocket. Rostoff's retirement plan burned like a hot coal against his chest, and there were other establishments in the area to visit. He turned and returned back down the stairs, waiting for the sound of the door closing behind him. It came when he stepped out onto the sidewalk.

Head down against the wind for his old hat's patchy fur allowed in the cold, he made the rounds of three lesser brothels. At each he casually asked about Frau Zelinka and the Red Veil and learned that she had long been feared for her connections to the country's most powerful men. She had apparently had a meteoric rise from whore to brothel owner that no one could fully explain except that she had quickly filled the void when the brothel's previous owner had died under mysterious circumstances. None of these other brothels served the upper echelons of government or foreign embassies like the Veil. At each one he asked a follow-up question: "Have you lost many customers to the Veil over the years?"

Two owners handed over their envelopes of cash with a shake of the head. The third, a thin, wizened woman named Zelda, narrowed her gaze at him. She had penciled eyebrows so rigidly arched that she seemed eternally surprised.

"Is this about him, then? Bure?" She sat beside a small, scroll-topped desk in a room of dark wood paneling that drank in the light from the small lamp above the desk. Through the dim light, shadows veiled paintings of naked men and women on the walls.

"Bure? What are you talking about?"

The woman's gaze turned cagey, the light catching the angles of her face to show her age. "You know who I'm talking about. Boris Bure. That bastard had that bitch Zelinka steal my girl Katya. I'd just brought her in when Bure decided he was too big for us and started going to the Veil. The next thing I know, two men are here. They drop a few thousand dollars on my desk and then bundle her off. I know it was Bure behind it. He always liked the youngest girls."

It took a moment to process this information. Then he frowned at the woman. "How long had Bure been coming here?"

The woman's smile was yellowed from too many years of strong tea and tobacco. "What is this information worth to you? You want the dirt on Bure? I have photos."

Kazakov shook his head. "If you had photos, you would have used them by now." And if he paid her, he had no doubt she'd probably sell that fact to Bure himself.

"A pity." She shook her head. "I always wanted to pull him down a peg. He thought he was so much better than us—a descendent of the great Yekaterina, no less." She looked up at him. "Well? What are you waiting for? You've got your money for the month. You stay here too long and that bitch Zelinka will have her lads after me again."

She turned back to her desk as if he wasn't even there. The envelopes in his pocket were heavy—just what did Rostoff charge for protection?

The weight of Kazakov's new knowledge was heavier. Katya.

The young blonde girl who'd taken Maria's cigarettes.

The one who reminded him of Yekaterina.

Instead of returning to the sedan, he stood on the sidewalk outside the brothel feeling sick to his stomach and looked up the street. The Red Veil stood like a central jewel in a tiara of graceful houses that curved along the street edging the park. To either side of the Veil, some of the buildings had been turned into offices when families objected to the Red Veil in their midst. Kazakov trudged up the street toward them. He would have liked to have finished his interviews at the Red Veil but that was apparently beyond him given Rostoff's words.

The Detektiv Chief Inspektor would surely have a stronger reaction if he knew what Kazakov was about to do. He came to the house just past the Veil and climbed the stairs. There were no signs or brass placards indicating this was a business, so it must still be a personal home. The small alcove by the door was framed with white pillars that gleamed against the building's gray stone. White sills framed the windows and graceful lace curtains masked what lay inside.

He knocked on the door and soon heard crisp footsteps. The door opened to reveal a woman in a blue, silk suit with lushly embroidered lapels that reminded him of a sari's veil over her broad shoulders. The woman herself had high Slavic cheekbones and rich golden hair that had been tamed into a tight coil behind her head. The white blouse she wore open at the collar to expose a plunging décolletage that left no doubts as to her lusher attributes.

"Yes? May I help you?" Her bright blue gaze met his, but it was guarded.

He introduced himself and produced his badge. "I am investigating the man found dead in the park yesterday morning. I wanted to ask whether those who live here saw or heard anything."

"I am sorry. I am the housekeeper. I come in only in the morning." She went to swing the door closed, but Kazakov got his hand in the doorway. There was no way this woman was a housekeeper.

"And the owner, those who live here?"

She shook her head, those precious gold locks bouncing on her head. "Mr. Enver is not here."

"Enver?" he asked?

"Enver Pasha." She nodded.

For a moment he didn't know what to say. For someone named Enver Pasha—clearly an Ottoman name and with an honorary title most often used for military and political dignitaries—to own a house next door to a brothel was unusual on so many levels. "And who is Mr. Enver?"

This time she gave an impatient toss of her head. "Mr. Enver is a businessman from Constantinople."

Interesting. "What kind of business is he in?"

"Why all these questions? He is not here. Ask them of him when he is back."

He bowed his head respectfully, for this woman would certainly report this meeting to her employer and the Ottomans were known to be quick to take offence. "When do you expect his return?"

Her sigh was deep as she looked back toward the depths of the house. "I don't know. It could be a few days or a few weeks. He is in the mountains. He goes there for the waters."

Odd, given the "waters" would be freezing.

The woman checked over her shoulder again as if someone or something was waiting.

"Mr. Enver lives here alone?"

She nodded. "Except when he has guests, yes."

"And you are here alone, now?"

Her lips pressed into a line. "I said I was. I am. I have work to attend to."

Kazakov held up his hands to placate her. "Then one last question. When did Mr. Enver leave for the mountains?"

Another deep sigh. "It was yesterday. Yesterday very early in the morning. He had not expected to go, but something called him away."

So it was not just a trip for the waters. He thanked her and the door thudded closed behind him as he started down the stairs. At the street he looked up at the house and a curtain stirred. She was watching him leave, and if he was any judge of character, she would be on the phone to her employer soon.

Why he was bothered by the conversation he wasn't sure, but something didn't sit right, beyond the fact that Enver Pasha had apparently left home just after the time Collin Archer was killed— at least according to Khan's estimate of time of death. Had he seen something and, like Maria, decided it was time to run? Could Enver Pasha feel himself at risk even if he was Ottoman? Kazakov added interviewing Enver Pasha to his list of things to do.

He checked at the homes on the other side of the Red Veil but no one had seen anything or, if they had, they weren't telling. Not unexpected when an establishment like the Red Veil had the influence to make any troublesome neighbor simply go away.

He waded through the snow to the place Collin Archer's body had been found and looked up at the Red Veil and Enver Pasha's house beside it. The two were built close together, and the way their eaves and dormers reached across their upper stories, they appeared to lean toward each other. Like sisters. Or perhaps they had been built by the same builder. He looked from the houses back to the spot where he stood and back to the houses again. Odd. He'd thought Archer was found in front of the Red Veil, but now that he considered the curve of the street, the body's position could just as easily be in front of Enver Pasha's house.

Considering what this might mean—to incriminate the Ottoman? Intimidate him?—he returned to the sedan. Either reason could lead Enver Pasha to leave the city. Of course, so could responsibility for the murder.

Kazakov headed to the low, bunker-style, politseyshiy headquarters. It was only three stories compared to the steel and concrete towers that had sprung up around it. The square that it faced housed a twice-life-sized statue of the original Yekaterina clad in a long, ornate dress and fur cloak, an extra shawl around her torso. The statue's hair was spun around her shoulders by a harsh wind as she held up a lantern and peered eastward— presumably through snow. That was what the great tsarina was beloved for—leading her people through the wilderness like Moses. But instead of desert, it was the frozen wastes of Siberia. Like Moses, she had died before she arrived in the promised land. The stories told how she had shared her shawl and coat with women and children, and it was that generosity that had killed her with pneumonia—but not before the people promised to do her will and find safety.

He chuckled. As if there was safety for anyone trapped as Fergana was between the Chinese anvil and the Ottoman hammer. He parked the car in the police garage and, original Weber/Manas file in hand, strode into the building. The front reception was a cavernous space of glass complaint kiosks along the rear wall that were staffed by junior officers. It was an onerous task, one every officer had to endure. He had hated his time there, preferring to be on the streets where the real police work was.

Except it had turned out that wasn't the case. Not in Fergana.

Once through the reception area, the place was a warren of offices connected by hallways and elevators that led up to the officers' floor and down to cells in the basement. The one unique place in the building was on this floor—the central dispatch filled the center of the building with its radio equipment that reached out to all police in Fergana.

This afternoon most of the kiosks were empty and one harried looking uniformed female officer dealt with a lineup ten citizens deep. The air was chill and smelled of wet wool as he nodded at the people in line and crossed to a lone door at one side of the room. He knocked and was permitted into the hallway that ran in front of the dispatch center next to the bank of elevators and a stairwell. The duty officer, a dour older Russian uniformed officer named Tsitnikov, with the bulbous nose of the heavy drinker, looked him up and down.

"Haven't seen you in a while, Kazakov." His voice rumbled down deep in his throat and he stood close enough for Kazakov to smell the vodka Tsitnikov had snuck at his break.

"I've been busy," Kazakov went to step past him.

Tsitnikov stepped sideways to block his path. "So I've been hearing."

Kazakov was tall and solidly built even if the years had shifted his weight slightly earthward, but Tsitnikov was bulkier.

Kazakov met his gaze mildly, assessing the other man's challenge. "Then you'll know I've got better things to do than argue with a glorified doorman." He shoved past the bigger man and stepped into the open elevator. The doors slid closed and he exhaled. Prisoners had been beaten in enclosed spaces like this. He would not put it past it happening to officers who stepped out of line. In the past, he had been viewed as an asset because of the cases he cleared. Besides, his clearance rates, and those of officers like Antonov and Alenin, took the heat off the others to perform.

But something had changed with the Weber/Manas case.

The elevator doors slid open on the third-floor detective squad room. A stink of harsh cigarette smoke, wet wool, and cold tea slapped him in the face. He stepped out of the elevator and the room went almost as quiet as the Blue Corner café had been. Eight officers sat or leaned on desks, tea cups in hand, cigarettes at their lips. One man, Pavel Chelomeyev—the youngest man on the squad, who had once aided Kazakov on a difficult murder case when Chelomeyev's partner Sherepov was ill—actually resumed typing as Kazakov wound through the sea of desks to his own. Detektivs Razin and Pogolin nodded hello. Might as well reclaim his hat while he was here. It didn't look as though the snow was going to stop any time soon.

The top of his desk was clear, as he usually left it, except for a single piece of paper that sat in the center. On it was a crude drawing of a bullet. A warning or a request—either way, something to rid the squad of a problem. He felt the heat of the gazes of the other officers in the squad. Were they all in on it? Someone snickered. Probably Sherkov—he had always been a weaselly *khu i*—a dick. Young

Chelomeyev studiously typed out a report. The kid had shown promise. It was a shame he was partnered as he was.

Kazakov slid the paper off into the wastebin beside his desk.

Razin and Pogolin looked away as if they'd rather not see.

Antonov looked up from the file he'd been reading, possibly catching a glimpse of the image. He heaved himself up. "Fuck. What fucking imbecile thought that was a joke? The man's just been trying to do his job."

Unaccustomed to feeling gratitude, Kazakov retreated to the break room.

"This is not the Fergana it once was—nor the police force I joined," Antonov said softly from the doorway.

"You think I don't know that?" Kazakov said as he poured himself a cup of steaming black tea.

Antonov shrugged. "I think you fail to see what it means for you. We all must do what's best for Fergana. You've been a good officer, Kazakov…"

The unspoken "but" seemed to hang in the air. Kazakov added three sugars and tasted, but the cup was as bitter as the situation. He abandoned it on the counter.

Was he out of date? Out of touch? An anachronism in the police force? Was Antonov, who was his senior, suggesting he quit—or worse, retire?

"I am what I was hired to be all those years ago," he allowed.

"A self-righteous, pig-headed, asshole?"

Kazakov smiled remembering days when they had laughed together. "Not going to change any time soon. Consider it part of my charm." He pushed past Antonov back into the room.

Across the desks, Alenin leaned against the wall with his arms crossed, as if a disinterested observer to the scene.

Kazakov turned to Chelomeyev, young, blond, ambitious, and trying his best to fit into the office. "Is Rostoff in?"

The baby-faced detektiv nodded. "I—I think he waits for you."

Kazakov nodded and dug in his desk's bottom drawer for his hat. He'd left it there the last time he was here.

The lynx and ermine hat with the earflaps wasn't there. Frowning, he looked up at the officers who had once been—if not his friends, at least his police comrades. Most were studiously looking anywhere but at him. Even Antonov, but then perhaps someone even older than Kazakov had to work to fit in.

Just how far had he fallen out of favor? If this was any indication, it was very far indeed.

He shoved the drawer closed with his foot and headed for Rostoff's office.

It lay beyond the elevator and down the hall in the direction of officer territory. He nodded once at Rostoff's secretary, Dabria Smirnova, a smooth-skinned officer as pale as Arctic ice whose uniform could not conceal her curves, and knocked on Rostoff's door. She shook her head slightly: Rostoff was in his usual foul mood.

"Come," Rostoff's rough voice sounded through the door.

Kazakov shoved the door open and blue smoke met him. This was not the typical harsh smoke of local cigarettes. No, these—these were similar to those Maria smoked. He closed the door behind him.

"What took you so long?" Rostoff growled.

"I brought the file as you requested. And I brought the envelopes you asked me to pick up." He said it clearly, for there was every possibility their conversation would be recorded and used against him.

Rostoff's office was the only one delegated to the detective squad and though it did not sit anywhere close to a corner of the building— those offices being reserved for the Chief of Police and the senior officers—it still had the much sought-after view of the haunting statue of Yekaterina. Did it inspire Rostoff? Encourage him to care? Judging by the photos filling the white office walls— all of Rostoff shaking hands with various dignitaries—the only thing Rostoff cared for was himself.

Behind a desk of smooth dark wood, the man himself leaned back in a high-backed, black leather chair. A cup of tea in a fine china cup and saucer with golden edges sat steaming on his desk. A small version of the new-fangled electric samovar sat on a table in the corner, its sides glazed in china covered in scenes of the Russian diaspora. The machine was likely made somewhere in the Ottoman empire, but the irony was obviously lost on Rostoff.

Kazakov crossed to the desk and deposited the file and the envelopes.

"Open them," Rostoff ordered.

Kazakov flipped open the file. Yekaterina Weber and her pink sweater gazed up at him with her beseeching smile.

"Not the file, idiot. The envelopes."

Kazakov shook his head and stepped back from the desk. "You asked me to pick them up. You asked me to bring them to you. I will not touch what is inside those envelopes."

Rostoff's fleshy face reddened. He grabbed the edge of his desk. "And just what do you think is inside these envelopes?"

Lord, let him out of here. He did not want to play these games of cat and mouse. At forty-five, surely he was too old. He deserved respect—not that garbage on his desk.

He steeled himself, but the question was asked. Now his task was not to incriminate himself. "I do not know for sure. I believe there is money extorted from illicit businesses in New Moscow in exchange for police protection. But given I believe that the higher echelons of the police force arranged such a thing, I do not wish to know for sure, because I cannot countenance such a thing."

Rostoff's ruddy face darkened and a vein stood out on his forehead. Finally he gave a nod and Kazakov turned and left. He pulled the door shut behind him, but not before he heard the shatter of china. He would bet the china cup no longer existed.

He left the building after checking for any messages and went down to the garage to reclaim his own vehicle—a five-year-old Perseus import, a German brand manufactured in Tashkent. He'd bought the vehicle because he liked its sleek lines and had appreciated the fact it was four-wheel drive. He climbed into the black cloth interior and inhaled. A faint scent of cigarette and vodka lay on the air and the hairs of the back of his neck stood on end. He neither smoked nor drank in the Perseus.

He scanned the front and back seat. There was nothing to see. Plain black seats. Floormats mostly bare. He liked the car enough that he had taken great care to keep it clean.

Someone else had been here. Searching his vehicle? At least they would not have found anything.

But someone wanted to know what he was doing. Rostoff? But the man already had a good idea what Kazakov was doing and didn't give a damn as long as Kazakov left the Weber case alone and picked up Rostoff's payments. So who? Whoever it was had access to the police parking garage.

So there might be another player in the mix, but either way he preferred the Perseus.

He started the vehicle and it purred like a contented Kochka. Satisfied, he backed out of his parking spot and drove out to the street. The streetlights came on in the dusk that came ever earlier each day. It was four o'clock.

The wind grabbed the few falling flakes and whipped them into a frenzy in the fading light. It was going to be a miserable night. He turned the car toward Suvarov Way and followed the road to the edge of the city as the heavy clouds drained the light from the sky. The snow turned to huge flakes that clogged headlights and windshield wipers, forcing him to stop twice to clear them.

When he reached the edge of the housing sprawl, the road that rose upward toward the foothills had disappeared and so had the light, so he drove forward into a swirling tunnel that had no beginning or end.

The Perseus's heater churned out heat that dried his woolen coat and melted the snow he'd brought in on his boots. The wind buffeted the large car and howled over the hood, so he was surprised when the wail suddenly stopped. He peered out the window and realized he'd reached the trees on the mountain slopes and they blocked the worst of the wind. Ragged flakes still swirled into his windscreen.

The snowdrifts had to be almost headlight high and the tires strained to keep contact with the dirt road. It was an unusual amount of snow. An inky void marked the turn to Agafya Ryabkov's dacha. The Perseus plowed past and he squinted to make out the turn to his house. The car's rear end slewed sideways when he turned.

The snow lessened under the awning of barren branches and he followed the ghostly line of hoary walnut trunks, here and there pine branches bowed almost to the ground. Ahead a faint light through the dacha windows glowed like a beacon and he touched the accelerator just before the Perseus entered the clearing so that the car had enough momentum to take him up and around the house to the semi-shelter behind.

When he turned off the engine, the metal ticked around him as the cold stole the warmth. He climbed out into frigid wind and stinging flakes and, with his collar up and head down, he waded to the front stairs and the door.

He stepped into the aroma of onions and garlic and was immediately transported years past to the days when Annushka cooked for him—before her betrayal. Before she left him.

Maria sat on a chair at the table, an open book in front of her— probably his. She still wore her men's work shirt and trousers, but she'd braided her hair at the back of her head and had washed off her makeup so she looked like she could be anyone's wife—or a cousin— certainly not a high-priced whore.

She smiled up at him, but he looked away and took off his coat, plucking the copied file information from his coat pocket. The thought was unkind, but he resented the reminder of who and what he'd lost. Once, he'd thought he'd have a family, but like much in Fergana, it had been an empty dream.

"I started dinner," she said.

He nodded and hung up his coat and gun holster on their peg.

"I didn't know when you'd be back, so I didn't finish cooking it."

That was unusual. Annushka had always cooked the meal and become furious when he wasn't there to eat it as and when she had planned. Another nod as he crossed to his desk and thumped his newly copied file on the top. He flipped it open and Yekaterina, no longer on glossy photographic paper, stared up at him. Perhaps it was fitting that the paper was dull. Apparently so was her memory to those who should remember—her family.

"I thought you had to turn those in," she said, coming up beside him. He could smell the fragrance of her newly washed skin. It was a memory he hadn't realized he yearned for.

"I did. I made copies."

Her perfectly arched brows rose. "Clever of you, but isn't that breaking the rules?"

"Probably." He considered what Rostoff would do if he found out what Kazakov had done. But regardless of all the instructions to the contrary, he was going to continue his investigation. This was a case that needed solving. He stabbed a tack through the photo of Yekaterina and tacked it back to the log wall. The rest of it followed. Let the rest of the world see it.

Maria started to help him, but he stopped her from handling the papers. For all intents and purposes, she was no more than another source of evidence. She had no right to touch the remains of Yekaterina and Semetai. Hell, she wasn't even Russian.

And just where had that bigotry come from?

She stepped back to watch him, then went to the kitchen. "I'll finish dinner."

"Don't do it for me. I'm not hungry." But his growling stomach called him a liar and he wondered what had brought this mood and such ugly thoughts into his head.

Still, pots clanked and spoons clattered. Beef that he'd had in the cold box sent a luscious scent into the air as he pondered the evidence.

How could the deaths of two teenagers on opposite sides of town relate to the death of a Chinese spy at a park in the city center? The only connection he could see between them was Yekaterina's stepfather.

He opened Khan's envelope and flipped the file open. All he'd had time to review was the photo. He pulled the small sheaf of documents free and spread them on his desk. Copies of the autopsy report and photo. X-rays. Lab test results.

He sat down to read, tuning out whatever Maria was doing in the kitchen.

Collin Archer had been a healthy male of about thirty-five to forty, contrary to the older countenance of his face. He had been of good health, though his skeleton showed slight signs of rickets—a common enough childhood condition in poorer families in China, from what Khan said in the report. Differences in hip geometry confirmed the suspicion of Asian ancestry—probably Chinese.

So in addition to the scarring from cosmetic surgery and the skin bleaching that covered his limbs and most of his chest and torso, there were skeletal differences that would be impossible to alter. Collin Archer was most definitely not born with the name that went with his renovated face.

He scanned through the rest of the report, but stopped when he came to the last paragraph. On the man's left hip, a small, unnatural flap of skin had been found that created a small pouch about an inch wide and three inches long.

Kazakov sat back in his chair, ignoring the wonderful aromas and the sound of his piecemeal china clattering.

A pouch like that was no accident. It was perfect for transporting something small and very, very precious. Once upon a time, traders from the east had risked their lives to bring out silkworm larva and the mulberry bush upon which they fed. Others had risked everything to bring out the source of spices and the seed. All had passed through the Fergana valley on their way to the west.

So what was so precious these days?

"You look very deep in thought, but dinner is ready."

Maria stood over him, an old blue dishcloth tucked into her trouser waist band. She brushed a stray hair off her face with a floury hand leaving a charming, pale streak on her cheek. Beyond her, Koshka was happily lapping up milk with her evening meal of crunchies. Clearly the cat and the woman had bonded.

"Milk is not good for cats. You should not have fed it to her." He stood and confiscated the little black cat's treasure. She mewed piteously at him. "Look what you've done!" he said and rounded on Maria. "She never begged before." Which wasn't exactly true.

"Perhaps because she did not know there was something better," she said stone-faced. "What is the matter with you? You are sour as old milk and have been since you returned. I had thought you a decent sort."

Was he sour? He felt it—sour and angry with everything curdled inside him in frustration at this case. Why was that? He'd had difficult cases before—and why take it out on Maria and Koshka? He glanced at her, for it was about the longest speech she had made aside from answering his questions.

"I'm no longer used to having people in my space. I don't like it." He ended lamely, even to his ears.

She settled her hands on her hips so much like his ex-wife he had to look away. "It was you who brought me here—to a place of safety and peace, I thought. Do whatever you want, but I am having dinner while it's hot."

She turned and left him and he heard the grate of china and the clatter of cutlery as he looked back at the file. Just why was he being this way? Maria had done nothing but make him a meal. Frustration was part of it, but only part. It was as if the whole world was getting under his skin—the job, the people. The damnable investigation that had no leads and made no sense. Why was he so damned determined to investigate in the face of this? Especially when everyone and everything seemed determined to discourage him. Even Antonov suggested that Kazakov should consider changing.

Changing into what was the question.

He had no idea. All he knew was that a girl in a pink fluffy sweater stared out at him whenever he closed his eyes. Her beseeching gaze seemed to suck him in so that he saw back through her to other Yekaterinas—all pleading for things to be different. A country saved. A people preserved. A life not lost in vain.

It all sat like a heavy weight on his shoulders, but there was nothing more that he could do at the moment. The snow held him here, and in truth he wasn't quite sure where to go with his investigation other than keeping his appointment at the printer's shop tomorrow.

He shoved back from the desk and went to the table—so different than Annushka would have done. Annushka had always been in a hurry. Food was slapped on the table so that they could quickly eat and she could get back to her studies. She had been working on her graduate degree in business communications and had finished it just before their relationship had finally shattered. From what he'd heard, along with a new husband she had completed further studies at a university in Nanjing and was now a senior official in the government communications office. It felt odd to even think of her after so many years. Maria had stirred the memories up in him.

He was not sure that he liked it.

Maria's table didn't have the jar of cutlery in the center that Annushka had preferred. Instead two place settings were set complete with dishcloths folded like napkins beside each place. In the center of the table, one bowl held mashed potatoes and another a steaming savory meat gravy that made his mouth water. She took his plate and spooned potatoes onto it, then ladled the meat and gravy over. The room was filled with the spice of dill, garlic, and paprika. She handed him his plate and filled her own, then produced a rich red wine that he recognized as one that he had squirreled in the cupboard in another epoch when Annushka had just left. She poured two glasses, then sat looking at him.

"A blessing? Do you know one? It is your home."

A blessing? When was the last time he had something to bless? He shook his head and she bowed hers and spoke swiftly in what must be her native language, then looked shyly up at him.

"I thanked God for bringing you to find me. I truly did not know what I was going to do."

A charming woman. Almost too much so, like a trap for his feelings. Nodding, he forked up a mouthful and tasted the bouquet of onions and spices overlaid on the light char of the strips of meat, in the smoothness of the gravy that mixed perfectly with the smoothly mashed potatoes. Another forkful found its way to his mouth before he even knew he had done it.

He felt her watching him and finally met her gaze. "Good. Very good, in fact. And I apologize for being sour as old milk. How did you do this? There was almost nothing in the house."

Maria shrugged. "I snooped and poked into all your secret corners and this is what I found."

Snooping was not something he needed in his home, though apparently he should get used to it given Rostoff's presence this morning.

She held up her hand at his alarm and smiled again. "Don't fret. I kept my snooping to the kitchen and your library." She waved at his low bookshelves beside the door and by the bed. "It was a pleasure to cook and a pleasure to read something Frau Zelinka did not require to stimulate conversation with our patrons."

"Apparently I had forgotten my secret supplies," he said and sipped the red wine rich with tannins and berry. He looked at the bottle and went still. It had been bought years before at a small winery in the foothills of the mountains on the way to a resort where he and Annushka had celebrated their honeymoon and later tried to save their marriage. The bottle had been packed away against another, bigger celebration that would never come.

It was sad, and yet Maria was the first woman who had come here since Annushka. Perhaps it was time.

He raised his glass. "To the cook." He clinked her glass and drank of the full-bodied memories.

"To saviors and safety. Thank you for bringing me here," she said and reached across to touch his wrist with her free hand.

It was the lightest of touches, barely a glance, but an electroshock ran through him and he yanked his hand back. She might be attractive, but the last thing he needed was a woman in his life and all the drama she would bring. This woman least of all.

Maria had gone still and watchful as if his reaction surprised her and she was not used to being surprised when her livelihood depended on reading men. Her gaze grew sad—and resigned. For her or for him?

"Collin Archer," he said. "When you were with him, did you ever notice anything odd about him physically?"

She sipped her wine and shook her head. "As I told you before, he did not take his clothes off. It was strange, but not the oddest thing I've dealt with."

Picking up her fork, she began eating again, gaze averted as if she sensed things had changed between them again.

"Did he have regular appointments?"

She shook her head. "I would know perhaps an hour or two ahead. Sometimes it would be difficult if I was with another patron. He always insisted on me, though. Sometimes he would change his time a little. Sometimes they would reschedule my other appointment with another girl."

He thought about it. Clearly it was important that Archer be with Maria. The question was why. Or else this woman was not the innocent she claimed to be. Had she not truly run, but been sent to spy on him and his investigations? Telling him these things could be a strategic way to gain his trust. To gain insight into what he was doing with Manas/Weber case?

"Tell me about the Red Veil."

Her brow rose. "What do you want to know?"

"Everything. How it works. Who does what? How do the girls come here? Everything. What is a day like?"

She chewed her food slowly as she thought. Then she nodded. "The girls come from all over Europe and Asia. There is even one who claims to be from America, but I believe she is Ottoman Greek and has just put on an act. That is part of Frau Zelinka's fame, that she has drawn girls from so far and wide. In fact, many of us were not drawn, we were sold. It is a hard life in many corners of the world. Wars, disasters, poverty. Frau Zelinka's chosen business takes advantage and we are brought here. When we are very young, they teach us things like the ancient courtesans were taught, so that when we enter the business we can properly please a man. We are taught how to dress, how to smile, how to touch, what to say." She shrugged. "It is a business. Our comforts and our bodies are our trade. We learn it well or we do not stay—sold again, to a lesser house far from Fergana. Frau Zelinka does not like her failures waving at her from the street."

Kazakov dipped his head, feeling guilt that such slavery existed. While slavery remained embedded in Ottoman and Chinese cultures, the Ferganese preferred not to think it existed in their past, even though the serfdom that had supported the great Yekaterina's world had been nothing more than a different form of slavery. And here Maria described how it existed in Fergana today and it was likely that many of the self-righteous politicians were patrons of the very girls who lacked freedom. So much for Ferganese pride at their enlightenment.

But that was not the issue—or at least not the issue now. "Does she take older girls as well?" Kazakov thought about how the girl named Katya had been forcibly "bought" from her brothel for a patron who had shifted to the Red Veil.

Maria shook her head as she took another bite of food.

"Odd. I was told today that Katya was brought to the Red Veilat the request of a patron."

Putting down her fork, Maria looked at him. She nodded. "That is true. But she was only thirteen when she was brought in." With her makeup on, Kazakov had thought Katya was sixteen.

This new information said she was at most fourteen and more likely still thirteen and yet she was working. Rented out to any man who wanted her—like Boris Bure.

He no longer felt hungry, yet what was the difference between thirteen and sixteen? Yes, Katya was no more than a child, but all these women had been that young once and were still enslaved today. It was not right. He scrubbed his face, the stubble of his beard making him feel far too old to be suddenly questioning everything about his society.

"It is not so bad—our life. I began at fourteen. The man was gentle —Frau Zelinka makes sure of it. She keeps us safe."

He looked up and Maria must have read the revulsion and pity on his face. And she was justifying Frau Zelinka's use of children?

"You—this Katya—you were children. That is not right."

She sat back in her chair. "There are 'children' married with children of their own in some parts of the world, Detektiv. Some in these very mountains."

It was true, but that did not make the enslavement and prostitution of children and women right. "And yet you did not feel safe remaining there."

Sighing, she abandoned her food and sipped her wine while he ate in silence. "The youngsters bring us water and tidy our rooms. They sometimes watch what happens through closed-circuit television so they know what to expect, and Frau Zelinka will bring in a trusted patron to break them in. After all, she will, by that time, have invested greatly in us," she ended sadly.

"And who 'broke in' Katya?" The words tasted vile in his mouth.

She frowned over her wine glass, the lantern light flickering over her lovely features and catching in the darkness of her lashes. "I am not sure. It would have happened before she joined the Red Veil. When she came, Katya was happy—giddy even—like a schoolgirl. Her heroic, blonde, first patron had brought her a present. She went on about him endlessly."

Kazakov stiffened. Boris Bure. It had to be. Madam Zelda at Katya's original brothel had said Bure had had Katya taken to the Red Veil. But the description of Katya as giddy reminded him too much of the description of Yekaterina Weber before she died. It sent a shiver up his spine.

"Tell me how the Red Veil operates."

She drained her glass and refilled both his and hers, then nursed hers again, her elbows resting on the table. "The mornings are easy. There are no patrons until eleven o'clock, so we can relax. We bathe. Some do exercises. A few go out for a walk. Some practice musical instruments or paint and some even garden in the back of the house. We are normal women with normal interests. The mornings are the time for that. There are also fittings—Frau Zelinka has clothing brought in for us that fits the fantasies of her patrons. Sometimes they must be resized. There is breakfast from the main kitchen, usually eggs —and tea, of course. And doctor's visits—we must, at all costs, be healthy. At eleven we are all dressed and ready. Lunchtime patrons arrive and are served a meal and perhaps given a massage or whatever they need to relax to get through the rest of the day. And the sex of course. And in the evening there is more of the same, though massages are less and sex is more and it is a light dinner that is served. Behind it all there are the cooks and cleaners and the workmen who unload shipments and who do repairs, but most of them have their lives elsewhere and serve Frau Zelinka for a wage."

Shrugging, she sat back as if she'd done her job, but it still didn't tell him what he needed to know.

Kazakov looked down at his near-empty plate. With his fork tines he had shredded the remaining potatoes into futile tic-tac- toe designs —a game where nobody wins. "So as a patron I arrive in my Ziln at the front stairs of the Red Veil. What happens?"

She pursed her full lips. "I suppose if the place is open, Sergei, the doorman, greets you and ushers you up the stairs. He would also make sure the stairs are free of snow. He will hold the door for you and usher you into the arms of whoever is assigned to answer the door."

"So it is not Frau Zelinka who welcomes patrons?"

Maria shook her head. "Almost never unless it is a very prestigious client. Usually it is Prae."

"Never you?"

She smiled. "I have not the talent. As you have seen, I can be abrupt and pushy sometimes. That is not the face that Frau Zelinksi wants for the Red Veil. Besides, I am not exotic enough. Nearly as plain as a Russian girl. So that honor goes to the others."

He thought of Collin Archer going into the Red Veil. "Do you know who greeted Collin Archer when he visited?"

She shook her head. "This last time it was Prae, but I can't recall the other times."

And it was something he doubted could be checked.

"So I have come in the door. What do they do besides closing the door behind me?"

She frowned. "I don't understand. What does this have to do with Collin Archer's death?"

"It is important that I understand all the people he could have come in contact with." He would not say more than that.

Her expression firmed. "His coat and hat would be taken and hung away. The same girl on the door would lead him into the dining room where waiters would bring in the food, but his date would serve him and sit with him through the meal. He might also arrange for a single dining room, but Collin never did. I think he liked to see everyone around."

For a spy, that made sense.

"After the meal they could adjourn to the parlor where there was music and they could enjoy a smoke. Some of the men might speak together, but Collin rarely did. Usually we retired up to my rooms."

"And when you got there?"

She looked him squarely in the eye and her expression hardened. "We fucked, or course. You want to know the position?"

He ignored her barb. "Did he have rituals? Did he give you gifts or things to give to anyone else? What did you talk about?"

She shoved away from the table so hard the dishes clattered, and she crossed to the window to peer out into the darkness and snow.

"Why do you treat me like—like a criminal? I've told you everything I know. He would come in. He would have me over the edge of the bed with our clothes still on as if he was in a hurry to get it over with. Then he would sit on the bed and smoke and talk about history. That is all I know." She crossed to the package of cigarettes he had returned to her and dug out a smoke with shaky fingers.

"Did Collin ever say who he worked for?" he asked.

She glanced at him and shook her head. "I've no idea." She lit the cigarette with shaky fingers and inhaled. Held and then released a blue tendril of smoke that rose up to circle the ceiling.

"Why does this upset you so much?" he asked from his chair.

"I have no idea about that either," she said, looking away to the reflective window. "Or perhaps I do and I do not like the reason."

8

Kazakov lay awake too long, the plank floor too hard under his shoulder, even with a blanket under him and another pulled over top. Initially, he had tried to sleep on the sofa, but the piece of furniture had been too short and uncomfortable for his length, so he'd shifted to the floor and stretched out. But now the sounds of another person were too loud in the dacha. A sigh. A breath. The soft, rhythmic thump of the wind bumping a tree branch against the wall that could just as easily be Maria's heartbeat. Or the stump and groan of Baba Yaga. The dacha was almost the perfect image of the old crone's lair— a small house in the forest just waiting for some young nobleman or a foolish princess with raven hair. Both would fall into her clutches and only the wisest, with the help of magic, would escape her dungeons. The odd thing with Baba Yaga was that, according to the old stories, the old witch could sometimes be an ally, help bring the prince and the princess together, or help them escape evil pursuers.

An enigma, that's what the old woman was. No matter how well you knew her, you didn't.

Just like Yekaterina—all of them.

He groaned and rolled over onto his back, beat his pillow into a new shape, and pulled the blanket around his shoulders. The floor was the coldest part of the house, though he had laid out close to the wood-burning stove. But hours had passed and the huge log he had placed in the burner to hold the fire overnight had long since settled into ash and embers that would sputter and glow until morning. He should get up to feed the stove, but did not want to disturb Maria.

"You have not slept at all, have you?" Maria's soft voice came from his bed.

Blankets rustled and then a slim white shape clad in his shapeless t-shirt stood over him in the darkness.

"Come to bed. It is cold on the floor and it is not fair that I steal sleep from you." She caught his hand and again there was that tingle that threatened to awaken feelings long locked away in a dungeon like Baba Yaga's prisoners. Attraction to a woman was not something he had room for in his life. They needed too much of him that was already consumed by his job. Attraction to this woman was even less acceptable. She was a witness. She was a victim.

She was a whore.

He could already hear Rostoff and Antonov laughing.

"I'm fine here." He tugged his hand away, pulled the blanket higher. He didn't want her and her lavender fragrant hair or her smooth skin. He'd given up that kind of pleasure long ago. Annushka had burned the desire out of him.

"You will not be able to think if you are tired, and you must be able to think if you are to solve this thing." She stood with her hands on her hips above him. "Take the bed for what remains of the night. I have slept. I will doze on the sofa."

She stripped the blanket off of him and curled up on the small sofa as he came up off the floor protesting in his skivvies and t-shirt. She waved him away.

His bed was there and the need for sleep weighed heavy on him.

"Fine." He stumbled to the bed.

He climbed in to be confronted by the cocoon of her warmth and her lavender scenting the sheets.

He lay like a board on his side, his back to her, but still felt her gaze on him through the darkness. The dark fall of her hair like a wave.

The graceful way she moved. He could picture it even when his back was turned.

"*Eto piz'dets,*" he muttered. This was so fucked up. He wanted her, but he should not. He could probably have her with just the flick of a finger, but he would focus on the case and solving it. He knew so little about this Collin Archer.

The man was an enigma, too. Kazakov knew nothing of his life. Where did he live? Where did he work? What was he doing in Fergana —at least on the surface. If he could identify the surface, perhaps he could peel it back to find out what was underneath. He needed to go into the office to gain access to the computer. He should have done it yesterday, but the extortion money had burned in his pocket and he had wanted to get back to Maria.

It was like this woman and Yekaterina had destroyed his mind, his logic. It was the first rule of investigation: know your victim and you will be that much closer to finding the killer. Instead of gaining that knowledge, he'd spent yesterday copying files and collecting bribes.

He groaned and rolled over to find Maria standing over him. Her white skin seemed to glow through the t-shirt. She sat down on the bedside and stroked his hair back from his forehead, stroked his cheek and leaned down and kissed him there.

Her gentle touch froze him. He couldn't move. Wanted to move. Wanted to tell her to get the hell away from him. He did not need distractions. Was that why she was here? To distract him?

But he had brought her here.

Had that somehow been a trick, too?

"Is this what they teach you?" he said harshly and felt her wince.

"Yes. It is," she said with a grace he would not have thought possible. "We bring comfort and relief. Now close your eyes. Sleep."

Her hand stroked his head as his mother had done, so many years ago it was almost a legend. He obeyed and his breath escaped him in a long sigh. The bed shifted under him and her long slim shape stretched beside him. Her hand stroked his head, his shoulder, his back. Her lavender scent filled his lungs with her presence.

The image of young Yekaterina stroking Manas's hair came into his head. They were on a blanket spread on a vivid green lawn. Walnut tree shadows dappled their skin as they lay side-by-side facing each other. They were talking—about love, about leaving, but something else, too. Though Yekaterina's touch was soothing, there was a rapid beat to her heart. Yekaterina was afraid.

So was he.

———

Kazakov woke with a start, as if he just now remembered to breathe. The dim, pale light of morning snuck past the floral curtains covering the dacha windows. Koshka's furry form lay warm behind his knees, while Maria pressed her warmth against the front of him. She lay outside the bed covers, with his thin blanket pulled over top. One bare shoulder had goosebumps while he was toasty warm.

He needed to get up. Let her have the covers, the bed. He had things to do this morning, not the least of which was visiting the printer's shop again.

He first tried to shift Koshka and the black cat mewed in protest and refused to budge. He shoved her out of the way and slid away from Maria toward the wall.

She moaned and rolled over, snaking one long, smooth arm over him. Her face was too close, her breath too hot in his face. He eased away, intent on climbing out over her.

But she tugged him in closer and her eyes flashed open. She smiled. "Good morning, Detektiv." Then she kissed him.

It was a shockingly sweet, chaste kiss—to start. But it lingered and morning breath dissolved in desire. Her lips and tongue played over his mouth and he couldn't move. No. He wanted it, was hungry for it. Starving.

His hands snaked up and caught her hair, her head, and he kissed her back. His hands sleeked her hair, her shoulder, her breast.

What the hell was he doing? She was distracting him again! This was exactly what Rostoff would want in order to compromise him! He shoved her away and rolled off the bed, leaving her huddled in sheets and blankets. He should be starving for answers to this case. That was where he should be focused.

She looked up at him, her hair and gaze tangled with sleep.

"You do not need to stop. I would have welcomed you."

"Would you? As payment? Or a job? I keep you safe, you pay me in kind? Or perhaps there is another reason for you being here that you've not told me? Perhaps someone else pays you?"

She blinked as if he'd struck her, the sleepy languor faded away. "I wanted to be with you. You are kind, but oh, so lonely. I wanted to take the loneliness away—at least for a little while. Is that so bad?"

He snorted.

"I do not kiss just anyone."

"Aah. The myth of the whore who keeps her kisses sacred." He stepped into the water closet that occupied a small shed he'd added to one end of the kitchen for Annushka when she complained about using the dacha's outhouse. The unheated room also held a metal tub he could haul into the kitchen for his weekly bath. Sometime in the future, he really should build a proper bathroom.

Back in the kitchen he doused his face and brushed his teeth in the kitchen sink, then pulled on the trousers and shirt that he'd hung on the back of a kitchen chair last night. He pulled clean socks from a bin under the bed and pulled on his boots, gun holster, jacket, coat, and old fur hat. "I have work to do. I'll be back."

He shoved out the door into—cold.

Sometime last night the snow had stopped and the sky had cleared, leaving a scraped-clean bowl of blue overhead. His breath steamed in the air. His cheeks, nose, and ears stung. There was no wind and the trees around the clearing were a lace of black limbs and glistening white, the boughs weighed almost to breaking with their load of snow. In the silence, a cr-r-a-ac-ck in the forest said a branch had given way under the load. A trace of smoke and the smell of burning wood filled the clearing from the dacha's chimney, telling him that Maria had risen and stirred the fire to life. Her choice. She could read or do whatever women do. She was safe and she owed him nothing.

It was a bad idea bringing her here, but what was done, was done.

With some regret he left a trail in the pristine snow and climbed into the frigid vehicle to turn the key. The engine complained and then roared to life. He climbed out and scraped the windshield clear, then eased the resistant clutch into gear and backed out, surprised the vehicle could handle snow deep enough that he really should shovel. He aimed for the tunnel through the trees that marked the lane and the Perseus rumbled forward. In the rearview mirror, Maria stood at a frosted window.

Was that how she lived her life? Always looking out, hopeful? He hated to tell her, but there was nothing better outside.

Perhaps there was no such thing as freedom.

The drive in was uneventful, the roads mostly unplowed this early in the morning, though a lone behemoth plow prowled the main street sending up a huge stream of snow onto the sidewalks. No one would care. Anyone who was anyone drove.

At the police station he drove around the block until he found a side street that hadn't been cleared. He pulled into the curb, regardless of the fact that he would likely find the Perseus covered in snow upon his return. Clearing snow was preferable to once more finding his vehicle searched or tampered with. He waded through the frigid morning, his ears and nose freezing regardless of the old hat he wore. He was going to have to replace his missing one.

At the station, it was as he suspected—no one was in the detective squad room at this hour. It was too early. Only the aroma of old cigarettes and cold tea from the unwashed cups on the desks greeted him. He left his coat on his desk and went to the data machine in the corner. There he prepared a search for Collin Archer and fed it into the machine.

He sat back waiting, keeping an ear open for the sound of voices approaching as the machine's lights flashed. No one came. The green light blinked and the screen lit up. He stabbed for a printout and the busy rat-a-tat of the keys filled the room. Then the page fell down into the basket for his collection.

He returned to his desk and started reading.

Collin Archer. Age forty-one, so Khan had been right that he was younger than his face. Arrived in Fergana six months ago on a business visa. His documents said he was an executive for the Anglo-German company, AngloTec, and had an apartment in a quiet part of the city.

Kazakov frowned. AngloTec had arrived in Fergana with much fanfare four years before. They had planned to build a large factory that would specialize in miniaturized communications equipment— going head-to-head with Ankara, the largest Ottoman company, and with ShenZhen out of China. The factory had gone up quickly, most of it built in pieces in Europe and then carried by train across Eurasia because, the news reports had said, the Anglo-German consortium that owned AngoTec had been concerned about building quality in a backwater like Fergana. It had caused a firestorm of resentment, but that hadn't stopped Fergana's best and brightest from flocking to the relatively well- paying job opportunities at the company.

If Archer was an executive for the company, why hadn't he been reported missing? It didn't make sense for the disappearance of an important man to go unremarked. Were the Anglos aware they had a spy in their midst? And spying on what? Corporate espionage? That would make sense. Neither Ankara nor ShenZhen would be happy about the competition.

He frowned. Perhaps he was wrong to think that there was a link between Archer's death and that of the two teenagers.

What did he have to pin them together other than Boris Bure's presence at the Red Veil?

He needed to know more about Bure, too. But running a name like Bure on the police computer was likely to set off a few alarms somewhere. For all the democracy that the original Yekaterina had bestowed on them, the rumblings of war between the two empires and awareness that Fergana was awash in spies meant that the government was keeping a closer watch on everyone these days.

Was that why Maria was with him? Sent to keep track of him? Did she have a phone he hadn't seen? He hadn't searched her or her belongings.

A part of him resented his suspicions, for there was no question that something about Maria attracted him. He could still feel the smoothness of her skin, could taste her lips and smell her infernal lavender scent as if those transitory sensations were branded on him.

He grabbed his cup with a three-day sludge of tea at the bottom and went into the kitchen to run a glass of water. Cleanse his mouth. Find something to eat and bury her taste. But her lavender scent was on his skin, his face, his hands. He washed again, in the office washroom, but her scent didn't come off. He washed again. And again.

But apparently only time would rub her off. That and getting her out of his house.

The folded Archer printout in his pocket, he headed out the door and outside. The three-story main library was only three blocks away. His karakul collar up against the cold, he waded through the heavy snow, stepping into the street where it was plowed until he reached the library.

At eight thirty in the morning the place was still closed, so he retreated to a café with a lone sad-faced waitress, six small metal tables and chairs, and a grease-spattered kitchen. On the wall hung a painting of the original Yekaterina's palace gaudily painted to fit the painter's vision. Fireworks darkened the sky behind the building—or perhaps it was cannon fire.

As the lone patron, he listened as the radio droned on with news stories about the mounting tension between the Ottoman regime and the Chinese Empire. Both were saber rattling again and demanding that the other reduce their strategic build-up of arms along the border between the two powerhouse nations. The Union of American Nations, a coterie of small states from South and Central America along with the United States, had joined with the Anglo-German Empire to urge calmer heads to the table. Of course, Fergana sat in the middle of this hot spot, armies crowding her borders, but a point of calm reason between the two fractious nations like the eye of a growing typhoon. The international community was suggesting mediation.

A further story spoke of government corruption in the lease of mineral rights in the Fergana mountains. The opposition party was screaming that the president should step down. Pundits were interviewed about the heir apparent to replace him. They mentioned Boris Bure and the Reformation Party.

In other news, two children were rescued from a collapsed well in Kokand. In America, the latest president of the eastern seaboard country refused to give into Anglo-German pressure to stop slavery and more sabers were rattling on that continent over Anglo-German North America refusing to return runaway slaves. The Anglo-German empire had demanded that independent African states cease their human traffic, though Ottoman North Africa still continued shipments. The Anglo-German navy had had skirmishes with the Ottomans when they tried to cut off shipments. As a result, America was implementing a government breeding program to "produce superior workers to support domestic industry."

Kazakov shuddered and let the drone of the announcer sweep over him. The shipment of human cargo. Wasn't that what had brought Maria here, too? For all the self-righteous posturing of the Anglo-Germans, slavery was happening right in their own backyard. It must not have been easy for Maria and the others like her. Perhaps she had tried to thank him in the only way she knew how.

Perhaps he had been too hard.

Considering this, he sipped sweet milk tea and feasted on a simple breakfast of heavy rye bread, fresh butter, and piping hot sausage that leaked warm grease into the bread. The sausage popped with each bite and the bread required good teeth, just as this case required much thinking. He needed to visit AngloTec Industries to gain further insight into Collin Archer. Perhaps the man was on holidays so he had not been missed. He needed to visit Archer's apartment, too.

Beyond the frosted front windows, the city slowly woke, cars droning down the plowed street while shop owners arrived and slowly shoveled a trail through the snowbanks that the plows had created.

He nursed his meal and his tea until nine thirty and then paid his bill before shoving out the door. Across the street, the library had just opened and he headed to the entrance, following behind another patron, a woman, bundled against the cold. He pushed inside behind her as she pulled her scarf from her hair. Blonde. Slim.

Then he caught her profile. Natania Bure stood in front of him, unaware of who had followed her in the door.

He hung back with the draft by the door, surprised that she could be here.

Logic said he should leave her alone. Bure had the power to make Kazakov's life hell for bothering Bure's wife. But a coincidence like this was too good to be ignored. It was as if the universe had brought her to him. It was his chance to talk to her again. To gain a better understanding of what had happened within the family and perhaps of who had killed Yekaterina. Instead of heading to the periodicals section, he hung back and followed her inside.

Natania Bure opened her coat and threaded through the lines of book shelves as if she knew exactly where she was going. Though she had a book bag in her hand, she neither returned a book nor picked anything up from the shelves. At the rear of the library she settled at one of the tables, pulled a magazine out of her bag, and began to read. Her face, never fleshy, looked gaunter than when he'd last seen her and, though she had not been a big woman before, now her sweater set hung from her shoulders and her no-nonsense black boots were scuffed. Even her tightly coiffed hair seemed to have loosened, letting fly-away hair escape around her face.

The past month had not been kind to Natania Bure.

Kazakov picked up a random book from a shelf and found a chair where he could pretend to read while watching. For fifteen minutes the woman neither looked up nor checked her watch as if she was waiting. No, this was more the look of a woman who was, for a few minutes at least, escaping into a place that was purely hers. Interesting. Perhaps her home life was not the perfect place she attempted to present to the world.

When he finally decided that no one was joining her, he sauntered over, stood across the table, and waited.

Three beats of his heart and she raised her gaze to his. Her eyes widened and her lips moved.

"You," she mouthed, but her voice was silent. She closed her magazine.

"Mrs. Bure," he said, keeping his voice pleasant. "Such a pleasant chance this is. How have you been?"

Her mouth moved again and finally words came out. "How do you expect after the loss of a child?"

Now, finally, she sounded more like a bereaved mother. He looked down at the table and chair between them. "Do you mind?" he asked as he pulled out the chair and slid in to face her. "I expect you must miss Yekaterina terribly. She was, after all, your only child. I am still sorry for your loss."

As she met his sympathetic gaze her fingers white-knuckled her magazine into a cylinder as if he was a fly she would smash.

"What do you want?" she asked. "My daughter is dead."

"I know," he said. "And I don't go through a day without thinking of Yekaterina. I wake at night wishing I'd found the culprit. Don't you wonder who did it? Don't you wish he was caught?"

Her gaze slid away from him down to the magazine and she made a show of flattening it out on the table. A simple magazine of Russian crafts. A typical magazine found in many Russian homes.

Finally she nodded. "Every day."

It was what he'd hoped to hear and he leaned forward. "Then help me. Talk to me and tell me what you know. What happened that last night at home? What was going on between her and Semetai Manas? What do you know about the murdered boy?"

It was wrong—wrong to inundate her with so many questions, but it was as if a flood gate opened and the questions spewed through the spillway of his mouth to crash over Natania Bure. Her gaze, tentative at first, turned frightened and she looked around as if seeking rescue.

Then she folded the magazine again and stuffed it into her bag. "I can't speak to you. I need to go."

Kazakov caught himself. "Why can't you speak to me? Has someone told you not to?"

She hesitated and looked at him. Shook her head and buckled the book bag closed.

"You know I'm still searching for her killer. I will find the truth for you."

The bookbag slammed onto the tabletop, and she leaned forward, her face skeletal, her expression as ferocious as a mother protecting her child. "Don't. Just don't. There are some truths that should not see the light of the world. Do you understand? Don't help me. God help me, don't look any further—not if you truly care for Yekaterina."

She yanked on her coat and he knew he only had a moment.

One more question. One more chance.

"Have you ever met a man named Collin Archer?" he asked, watching her face for signs.

Hat and bookbag in hand, she glanced at him one last time. "Do not follow me again, Detektiv."

Then she was gone—almost running toward the door.

Kazakov sank back in his chair. He had not meant for it to go like that. He certainly hadn't meant to spook her or cause more pain. He should have spent time enquiring as to her health and welfare. He should have asked her about crafts she enjoyed—anything to build rapport. Instead he had done what even the most rookie investigator knew not to do—he had gone for the jugular and elicited a reaction. Clearly her daughter's death caused Natania Bure significant concern. He did not understand what had her too afraid to help find her daughter's murderer. It made no sense. He tilted his head back and closed his eyes. But he had the answer at least to his final question. He'd seen the flare of recognition in her gaze.

He'd found a connection between the cases.

When he left Natania's table, he returned to the front of the library and the quiet bustle of kiosks opening and the calming scent of dust and old paper. He inhaled the scent that had been so much of his childhood. His father had never had time for a child after Kazakov's mother had died. So Kazakov spent his free hours here or with books borrowed from the library, burying himself in fairy tales as a child and in adventure fiction as he got older. Even at the dacha he had often preferred to read rather than accompany his father when hunting.

He went through the archway to the newspaper archive section. Gradually the Fergana State Library was following the example of the great libraries of Europe and Asia by saving the newpapers electronically to reduce the space they took, but in Fergana—often a late adopter of new technology—they were just at the beginning of the process.

The newsprint archive was a separate room at one end of the huge block building. The room was a cavernous hall under low ceilings with flickering fluorescent lighting, filled with long rows of shelves hung with yellowing copies of newspapers like so many parchment bodies. He found the librarian, an ancient, wizened man with bent back and head almost devoid of hair save for dense sproutings out of both ears and a ring of gossamer white around the back and sides of his skull. He wore a dusty-looking, green cardigan and shiny, baggy gray trousers.

"I'm looking for articles on a company called AngloTec," Kazakov said."Can you tell me where I might find them?"

For all his age, the librarian's gaze was particularly sharp. "Anything in particular?"

"No." Kazakov shook his head. "I'd like to look at everything."

The librarian pursed his lips. "That's a lot of reading."

Kazakov considered the man. There was something about him that was vaguely familiar. "I'm looking for articles that give me some insight into the company and in particular for information about its executive team."

The librarian thought a moment. "Take a seat. I will be right back."

He shuffled off into the dusty rows of yellowing paper and the reek of printer's ink and Kazakov settled into an old straight- backed chair at a scarred table. Soon the librarian shuffled back, his dragging feet on the concrete floors sounding like he walked though old leaves. He dumped a heavy pile of yellow newspaper sheaves on the table.

"Start with these. If you narrow your search, ask."

He walked away, his work done, and settled behind a desk in the corner. He picked up a book, but slowly his head began to nod, his chin slipping lower until is hit his chest. The fluorescent lights glimmered on his smooth head.

Kazakov turned back to the stack of papers and began flipping through. In a paper dating back about five years, he found the first excited announcement that AngloTec was building its factory. It was a government press release speaking of the many jobs the corporation would provide to Fergana's economy and how the brain-drain to the world's scientific hubs of Constantinople, Nanjing, London, and Berlin would stop.

He flipped through more papers. More announcements. More background on AngloTec as a foremost research center and producer of domestic and military technology. Status reports on the selection of the factory site. Then came the big announcement of the ground breaking. There was an artist's rendition of what the factory park would look like —a spacious, low slung building surrounded by mature leafed trees and actual parks for the neighboring town to use. This was followed, about a year ago, by a front-page article about the grand opening. It included photos of the people attending the ribbon cutting.

There, smiling up at him from the middle of the group of dignitaries, was Collin Archer, looking far different than the corpse in the morgue. Two men over stood another familiar figure. Boris Bure glared at the camera over a crescent of too-large, bared teeth.

Kazakov sat back. So Archer had obviously been in Fergana before receiving the visa that brought him here six months ago. Interesting. How long had he been traveling to Fergana and for how long had AngloTec had a Chinese spy working for them? Did they know? Was that what his murder was about?

The photo also confirmed what Natania Bure had revealed. Bure and Archer knew each other. The question was how well and for what purpose. Of course, at an event like this there would be many people in attendance, swirling around, trying to catch the opportunity for brief conversations with important men. Bure could have been there in that capacity—or as the up-and-comer that others wanted to know and be noticed by. Bure didn't have to know Archer—simply be aware of him. A photo like this didn't mean they were friends, just that they might have met each other. But there had been Natania's reaction. That would seem to indicate more.

And there was the Red Veil connection. Coincidence?

He set the newspaper article aside to copy and kept reading.

There was nothing else there.

Easing his back, he realized he'd been there two hours already. He went to the librarian's desk, and the old man stirred as if he was an automaton with a movement sensor like those found in the cheap dioramas of the Russian Museum. He blinked up at Kazakov as if he didn't know him, but then his rheumy gaze cleared.

"Yes? You found what you wanted?"

Kazakov laid the newspaper with the photo on the desk. "I have found something, but I don't know what. What can you find me about these men? Do they know each other beyond this event?" He tapped the group photo without singling out either Archer or Bure, but the old librarian's eyes widened.

"I—I'll see what I can find." He rose, his knees crackling, and shuffled off again, his trouser bottoms dragging as he disappeared into the rows of paper.

Kazakov made a photocopy of the photo and set the newspapers aside for filing. The old man's shuffle slowly returned and he appeared carrying an armload of newspapers that looked precariously close to toppling. Kazakov hurried to help him.

After depositing his gleanings on the scarred table, the librarian dusted off his clothing and looked over his shoulder as Kazakov settled back in his chair. The old man leaned in and flipped the top newspaper open to a business page that provided an executive profile. Collin Archer smiled out from a photo that was clearly professionally done outside of Fergana, for it showed the blurred background of an Anglo garden behind him. "Here he is. There are similar articles on all but one of the others."

The librarian leaned in close enough that the dusty scent of unwashed old skin filled Kazakov's nose. "Have a care. The other one is not anyone's friend."

Then the old man was gone, shuffling to his desk again as if nothing had been said.

Kazakov looked from the paper to the old man. Was he right to think the old man was talking of Bure? Surely he was a known entity? A government executive become politician. His biography should be on file; the media would demand it. And with the rumors of grooming for political roles, wouldn't that be doubly important?

He read through the ten-month-old article on Archer. Born of an old Anglo family in a place named Devon, schooled at a place called Oxford. He had graduated with a degree in science and had a higher degree in technology before being recruited away by a headhunter from AngloTec. At least that was the story the newspaper told. An eligible bachelor, patron of the arts, skilled marksman and horseman and practitioner of the ancient art of fencing, he had purchased a penthouse apartment in downtown New Moscow. The quote from Archer said the usual pap about being impressed with the lovely city of New Moscow and its historic past.

Kazakov flipped through the papers. There were small articles here and there that mentioned Collin Archer and similar profiles of the other men in the photo. All except Bure. There were mentions of Bure's presence at gallery openings or during government announcements. There was nothing placing them together or even running in the same circles until he came to an article in a newspaper dated six months ago that the old librarian had marked with a dog-eared page corner.

The sports page showed photos of a charity polo event, a mass of horses and riders slashing mallets at a dying goat as the game had originally been played. Beneath the photo, the article talked about the charity—an event to fund ongoing conferences that would bring together gifted musical students from across New Moscow. The article said nothing more of the event, but listed the players. Because of their last names, two names stood out together at the top of the list: Collin Archer and Boris Bure. They both played for the same team funded by AngloTec. He scanned down the list and noted another name he'd heard before: Enver Pasha, the Red Veil's neighbor.

Kazakov sat back in his chair, feeling breathless. Was this event related to the conference where Yekaterina and Semetai met? He glanced at the old man who once more appeared to doze in his chair. There was more going on there, Kazakov was sure, but what would an Ottoman functionary, a Chinese spy, and a Ferganese government official have in common aside from polo? Could Yekaterina Weber and Semetai Manas have even been there? He could imagine that potential patrons might want to meet some of the students they would be helping. Could the two youngsters have seen or heard something that led to their deaths?

He left the reviewed newspapers on the table and photocopied the sports article, then approached the old man.

Again, those rheumy eyes flashed open, the intelligence unmasked in calculation.

Kazakov placed the sports article before the old man. "This event. Was there anything more reported? Perhaps from the arts and culture side of things?"

"Arts and culture? Perhaps a small piece. Let me check." The old librarian stood slowly and shuffled off, but this time Kazakov followed. The old man led down a canyon of head-high wooden racks hung with yellowed newspaper. With each step down the canyon, the yellowing of the paper increased as if they stepped back in time itself.

The librarian stopped and riffled through the papers hung on the left side of the canyon. Then he harrumphed in satisfaction and slid a sheaf of newspaper off the wall. When he turned his eyes widened as if surprised to see Kazakov beside him. "You should not be here. Only staff can remove the papers."

Kazakov nodded. "But as you see, I haven't touched them." He looked at the papers in the old man's hands.

"Arts and culture," the old man said, his face oddly noncommittal like a suspect only admitting what he knew the police already knew.

Kazakov sighed, because nothing was ever easy.

"Is there anything else about that event? Something not in the sports or arts and culture sections?"

A twinkle seemed to catch in the old man's gaze as if he was a teacher pleased with a bright pupil. "In fact, I think there is." He turned back to the wall of papers and pulled another newspaper section loose, then stepped past Kazakov to lead him back to the reading table. He set the papers down and left Kazakov to read again.

Settling back into a chair, Kazakov flipped the paper open.

The arts and culture article was small, most likely overwhelmed by the much larger article about the marriage of the daughter of Fergana's president. There were photos of flowers and women in flowing dresses that framed around a small article about the charity event. The two paragraphs told about the event being held at a nearby polo field and of the many dignitaries attending along with a sampling of youth musicians as ambassadors for the program. Over twenty thousand dollars was raised for next year's conference.

If young people were there, there was a good chance Yekaterina and Semetai were, too. It was something he could likely check. He set the article aside and pulled the other section to him. It was the news section.

Frowning, he scanned the first page and flipped it open. Nothing on the second page either. He flipped the pages and finally found what he was looking for sandwiched between advertisements for a new model First Auto and one for modern apartment homes in a new building located at the base of Yekaterina Mountain. They were calling the complex Yekaterina Gate.

The article, dating back to last spring, was six paragraphs long and detailed an altercation that occurred at the reception held in the evening of the charity polo event between adult attendees and an uninvited "tribal" youth. The police were called, but the youth left before they arrived. Apparently one of the guests had his nose bloodied. The youth was being sought for assault.

Kazakov sat back in his chair wondering just whose nose was bloodied. An uninvited tribal youth. He'd bet money on it being Semetai. Events like this probably wouldn't include a Muslim youth on their guest list, but he could see Semetai showing up anyway if it gave him a chance to be with Yekaterina. Hell, she probably encouraged him. So, would the altercation have been with Boris Bure? If so, what did that have to do with Collin Archer?

Damn it, this raised more questions than answers!

He shoved up from the table and leaned on the snoozing librarian's desk. "Thank you for your time. Your suggestion was appreciated. May I ask, just how do you come to your conclusions about the items I will need? It seems a momentous task to remember everything."

The librarian's thin lips quivered into a grin. He tapped the side of his head with a bone-thin finger. "Old man. Long memories, and mine is particularly long. That is why they allow me to keep my job until the electronic filing is done. No one has a memory longer than mine." He cocked his head. "There are things from the past that remain unwritten, but people remember. I remember." He cocked his head. "Like I remember you, Alexander Kazakov. I remember your mother, too."

Kazakov stumbled back a step. "You know me?"

The old man smiled sadly, revealing the stubs of broken teeth. "Once I lived beside you, but you were very young. You used to play outside on a swing. Your mother would push you."

The swing was a hazy memory of air past his cheeks, green swaying overhead, and his mother's laughter as she held him on her lap. It had been—over thirty-five years? Forty? The years were like mist over the memory, but there was no wizened man next door there, though he might remember a young friend and his parents. Maybe.

He shook his head. "I'm sorry, I don't remember. How could you know it was me?"

"I remember the name. I have followed your police career in the newspaper." The librarian waved his answer away as if he didn't matter.

"May I have your name? I am at a disadvantage."

The old man thought a moment. "Your parents knew me as Artyom Shepovalov. These days I am simply Old Man—meant in the most affectionate way, of course." He shrugged in his chair. "Now you had best be on your way. There are those who would not be happy at where you are looking."

Kazakov leaned in over the desk. "You say things like that— what do you know? Tell me?"

Shepovalov shook his head. "I've said enough. These are an old man's words. An old man's suspicions. At my age you have time to fully read all these articles and remember them. You can put pieces of what is said and unsaid together. But they are only suspicions nurtured over the years. It takes a young man like you to prove anything. Unfortunately, few young men come asking."

He stood up and shuffled to the table to reclaim Kazakov's detritus and disappeared back into the stacks, his fading footsteps putting Kazakov in mind of a mythical creature dragging itself away from Baba Yaga into the western deserts to die.

He took his papers and his suspicions and returned out to the street. He was surprised that the day had swallowed the morning and noontime was here, filling the streets with fur-clad people hurrying to midday meals. The wind had died, but the temperature had dropped precipitously so that his breath seemed to freeze before it could be exhaled and ears and nose were painful. Gloved hands over his ears and his collar up, the soft fur protecting his neck, he hurried down the now-shoveled path on the sidewalk back to his car. Inside, he sat shivering with the heater turned on full. It was no time to be outside. It was a wonder the Perseus started. The rubber tires thumped as he drove, the rubber already frozen flat on one side as he headed for the printer's shop in the old town for his appointed meeting.

Again, he did not chance parking near the shop but parked outside the narrow streets of the Islamic quarter and trudged inside on foot, following ragged trails through the heavy snow. There were no plowed streets here, only the occasional doorway or shop entrance where the worst of the snow had been cleared away.

The printer's shop was one such place, its cleared doorway masking how many might have passed this way. Kazakov climbed the single stone stair and stepped inside into blessed warmth. Somewhere unseen a wood-burning stove was working, its natural warmth far more pleasing than the electric heat that chugged out of the vents in the squad room or the newspaper archive. The small silver bell jingled over his head and the same proprietor stuck his head through the curtain from the rear of the shop.

"You came. In this snow, I thought you might not." He stepped through the curtain and came to the door, checking outside before locking it and turning the open sign to closed. "Come. This way. There are others waiting."

He led Kazakov through the curtain into a storeroom and, like the Blue Corner, beyond the storeroom into modest living quarters.

The room was a kitchen with a low ceiling and a soot-blackened clay hearth against one wall. A great black kettle hung from an iron hook over the fire in the hearth and wood shelves were set into stucco walls. They stepped through another curtain and he found himself in a sitting room with worn carpets over the floor and low seating platforms built along the walls, now covered in faded embroidered cushions. Age-silvered beams held up the ceiling and an electric heater sat against one wall, humming out its warmth. Seven men and five women sat on opposite sides of the room, the men dressed in workmen's stout trousers and woolen shirts, the women in a variety of dress—four in house dresses and one younger woman in trousers. All the women wore headscarves and the men had the small white *taqiyah* perched on their heads. They all watched him with silent dark eyes as the shop owner produced a chair from somewhere and placed it on the floor in the center of the room as if a detective would not deign to sit with them in their customary way.

"For you," he said and motioned Kazakov to the chair.

"Thank you, but I've no need for such a thing." He shifted the chair next to the wall and awkwardly settled cross-legged to the floor. It was a long time since he had done such a thing, though as a lad he had sat with the tribal visitors near the dacha many times. His heavy coat spread around him and formed an uncomfortable lump under his bum.

"Thank you for inviting me," he said to his host. He looked around the room. "And for coming today. I am Detektiv Alexander Kazakov with the New Moscow *Politseyshiy,* the police department. I appreciate your trust in me."

"He investigates Semetai's death," said his host.

Kazakov nodded and scanned the waiting faces. "What can you tell me of Semetai Manas, the young man?"

The men looked at each other, apparently each waiting for someone else to start.

"He was a good boy. The best. But he fell in love—with that girl!" spat the younger woman in trousers.

Kazakov looked at her mildly, encouraging.

"I am his aunt. I should know. He looked up to me because I have found a way to walk in both your world and ours. He was smart. He was funny. He was devout to the faith."

Her words were the typical litany of the bereaved and not particularly helpful. "Devout enough that he fell in love with a Russian girl."

"He thought she had connections that could help him," one of the other women said, her hair hidden under a floral scarf, her dress so faded he could almost not make out the floral design.

"No," said a thin woman who huddled in the middle of the five as if she was ill. "He loved her. Do not speak ill of the dead. I may not have approved, but my boy loved her. She loved him back. She even came to my home and she was a charming girl—always willing to help. He was devoted to her."

She had large, faded brown eyes that pooled with tears and Kazakov inhaled. Semetai's missing mother was here in the room.

"I miss him," the woman said. "But she would mourn him, too."

The line of men nodded.

"I knew Semetai. He was my friend," said a young man with dark hair and eyes who looked to be of an age with the dead youth. He looked to the shop proprietor, who nodded. "He cared for Yekaterina very much. He spoke of marriage."

There was a tsking amongst the women.

"He did!" the youngster said. "When they were together, he was truly happy. He could see a future for himself." He shook his head bitterly. "Not like most of us."

The youth fell silent and so did the others. Kazakov hauled his notebook and pen from his coat pocket. "Semetai's body was found in a field outside of the old quarter. Yekaterina was found dead in Potemkin Park. What can you tell me about that?"

More looks and an uneasiness stirred through them as if they were stalks of grass in the wind.

"He was supposed to be home," volunteered the thin woman who was Manas's mother. "He had gone to see Yekaterina. He was upset about something but would not discuss it. Always he went to see her. I suppose you can talk to the one who has stolen your heart, but he was supposed to be home by then. He was always home on time." She shook her head and swallowed—to hold back more tears, Kazakov supposed.

"I heard a shout." A man who had not spoken previously lifted large, grease-blackened hand off his lap as if to wave his story into being. "It was closing time. I own a mechanic shop at the edge of the new city. I heard a shout and then footsteps running. It is usually quiet at that hour so something made me go to the window. Three men ran past, into the old city."

Kazakov made a note of it. "Tell me more, please."

The man's trousers were stained with grease, his shirt as well, and yet both bore the creases of fresh laundering. His face was newly shaven and his hair neatly combed. This was apparently an important meeting.

"They came from the direction of the new city. Perhaps down Peter Street. They looked as if they pursued someone, but I did not see who. They entered the street at the end of my block and I did not see them again, for I closed my shop and went home. I did not think of it again until I heard what had happened."

"Did you tell the police?" Kazakov asked and received a shake of the man's head.

"What did they look like?" Kazakov tried again.

The big man stirred uneasily. "They wore black coats and fur hats…"

He paused, and Kazakov nodded encouragement.

The man closed his eyes. "They wore black coats and fur hats like *ofitser politsii.*"

The room went silent and Kazakov felt thirteen sets of eyes on him. He exhaled and nodded. "All of them?"

The man nodded. "At least two."

"Were they Russian, too?"

The man nodded. "I think so."

Kazakov straightened to ease his back and reevaluated what he'd previously thought. He'd concluded that the community had probably killed the son. He'd thought that they had rejected Semetai because of Yekaterina and her parents had killed the girl for the same reason. Natania Bure's plea not to investigate fit with that story. What the hell was going on and what did it mean?

"Can you tell me anything distinctive about these men?"

The man shook his head. "I saw them only for an instant as they ran past and then only from the back."

"Did they see you?"

The man frowned. "I—I don't think so."

That was something. "Good. Do not speak to anyone else about this."

Kazakov looked around the room. "There are other voices here. What do you know? Help me find Semetai's killer. Please."

"We saw them," one of the other women said. She was older, with strands of steel-gray hair straying out from under her kerchief. She clutched the hand of the woman next to her, a young woman, not much more than a girl but already clad in drab colors and, peeking out from her scarf, her rich chestnut hair had gone dull. The younger woman swallowed, nodded.

"Tell me what happened?"

The younger girl's knuckles were white where she gripped the older woman's fingers. "We were coming home from visiting friends. It was time to make dinner for my husband."

She lifted her chin as if she took power from the fact that she was married so young. Some of the Muslim families held to older, tribal ways and believed that their daughters were best married at sixteen. Once it had been younger, but laws had been passed limiting the age.

"We came around a corner and Semetai crashed into us. Mother fell. I was pushed against the wall. He looked at me as if he did not see me, then turned and ran. I never saw him again. I helped mother stand, but three men came around the corner. One produced a badge and said they were seeking a criminal. They asked if we had seen anyone. We both said 'no,' but I don't think they believed us. We went right home and only later heard that Semetai had been killed."

Kazakov wrote it down. "Can you describe these men?"

The girl looked at her hand intertwined with her mother's. "Big, like you. Two had brown hair. One had much lighter hair. One had big teeth. One man had a gun drawn. After they left us, we hurried home. We are afraid to go outside again, for they know what we look like."

The men nodded.

The print shop owner nodded, too. "There are strangers in the old town. I have seen them myself. They dress in workmen's clothing and drink tea in our tearooms, but they are not of us. They come from the city." He lifted his chin and it was if all of New Moscow was a foreign land to them.

"I am afraid to speak to my friends in public," said the young man who had spoken earlier. "These newcomers watch us and they are everywhere. My brother worked for a time across the mountains in China and he said it was like that there—watching, always watching. I told him he should not stay there, but he said there is work."

He shook his head.

"You are police. Who are these men?" asked the old woman.

All eyes turned to Kazakov as he shook his head. "I wish I knew."

But his mind was racing. Watchers infiltrating the town. That was news to him. And men with badges pursuing Semetai Manas. Men dressed much like him. Could the police be involved? He thought of Rostoff's determination that Kazakov not investigate. It made too much troubling sense and meant that he was going to have to be very careful, indeed.

"Did anyone see Semetai Manas again?" he asked.

Again, the troubled stirring. No one said a word until finally the shopkeeper rose and crossed to the oldest grandfather present. The man's face was wizened with the squint lines that came of years in the mountains peering into the distant, glaring snows. He wore the same trousers and work shirt as the others but puddled around him was a thick fur coat and beside him sat one of the tall, traditional fur hats worn by the tribal people. A mark across his brow showed where the hat usually sat.

"You must tell him what you saw."

"I must do nothing. I do not trust his kind." He shook his head.

"He asks much and tells nothing, like all his kind."

Did he mean police, or Russians? Probably both. It was a sad insight.

"What do you want to know?" Kazakov asked and the old man turned a gaze on him faded almost white. Blind?

"Who would do that to our Semetai? What kind of men would kill a harmless boy who loved only music and a girl?" the old man asked.

"The answer is that I do not know. But I've learned that Semetai may have been involved in an altercation at a charity polo game, does anyone know anything about this?"

"Polo?" asked Semetai's mother. "Why would my boy have gone to a Russian polo game? This is not *kok boru*. Not a true Kyrgyz game." She set her jaw firmly against any such possibility.

Kazakov nodded. "But this game was modeled after the old game." The barbaric game, but he dared not show what he thought. "It was raising money to host another student music conference like the one where Semetai and Yekaterina met. Perhaps he was invited to attend? Or not?"

He scanned the men and women on both sides of the room, but the place had gone stony with silence.

"I am not trying to blame Semetai for anything. I simply need to know whether it was him that became involved in an altercation. Whatever happened, if something did, it could be the reason Semetai was killed."

There was only more silence so, clearly, he was not going to gain those answers here. He needed to change the direction of his enquiries or he was going to get nothing more from this group.

"You have given me much information that I did not know." He sighed. "When Semetai died, I found Yekaterina's school bag in the alley. She had been found earlier the day before. I don't know who killed her, either, but at the time, the condition of her body and the way Semetai was found suggested that they may have been killed by their families. It was plausible given how horrified people were that they were seeing each other."

The old woman hissed. The mother covered her face. The men started talking over each other until the print shop owner waved everyone to silence. "You see how important it was for us to meet with him? He could actually accuse one of us of killing our own if we did not talk to him. They would use our silence to say we hide our guilt from them."

Kazakov shook his head. "That is not the only problem. In the police department—it seems there is not to be an investigation. All my evidence was taken."

"By whom?" the print shop owner asked, his role as a leader in the old city becoming clearer by the moment.

"I don't know where the direction comes from," Kazakov said placing his hands on his knees. "Rostoff, my boss, took the file away from me and was not pleased when he discovered that I investigated on my own. But there may be other parties, other forces at work." He would not tell them of Collin Archer's death.

On impulse he pulled out the newspaper article photocopies he had made this morning and spread them on the floor in front of him. "Do you recognize any of these men?"

The men passed the photos around, then handed them to the women to inspect. The young girl and her mother both hissed when the photocopies came into their hands.

"This one. I remember this one," the old woman said holding the photo of the plant opening close to her face.

"Which one, Mama? Let me see." The younger woman eased the photo from her mother's clutch and studied the image. Finally she nodded. "It is him." She leaned forward, tapping the image, and Kazakov took it from her, checking where she'd touched.

Collin Archer peered out at him. Only then did Kazakov notice that, like Boris Bure, the dead man had predatory, overlarge teeth.

9

The dusk of a short winter day had gathered by the time he crept out of the old city to his vehicle. The community information had been a lot to take in and it filled him with concern on many levels, not least of which was the trust they had placed in him. How had he been so wrong as to think that they could have killed their own? But then killers lurked in unexpected places. A jilted fiancee's father, a long-time friend suddenly jealous over a scholarship, an unsuccessful businessman seeking revenge on a successful one. In each case you found the motivation, the emotion, and you would find the killer. Usually it was someone close to the dead person. This time, aside from the two young people being lovers, he was not so sure. What if he failed to find Semetai's and Yekaterina's killers? What if these people did not like the results?

Walking through the winter streets, he felt as if he burrowed through darkness like some worm or mole. But it was always like that in winter. The shorter days took their toll on people. In the west there was a line of clear sky far out over the lowlands of the eastern Ottoman Empire and it allowed the horizon to burn while New Moscow and the mountains were buried under the threat of clouds burdened with more snow. He opened the Perseus's door and sniffed the air. Just the scent of his wool and the soap he used greeted him, so it seemed that no one else had been there. He climbed in, started the engine, and cruised past Potemkin Park to the far side of the city.

Collin Archer's apartment sat in an area of New Moscow plentiful with gardens.

In the summer.

At this time of year, the open plantings that were maintained by community gardeners were usually dry stalks in winter-burned earth. Today they were buried under the drifting snow, with only the sad remains of sunflowers and cold-blackened tomato plants poking through. Interspersed with the lifeless gardens were the stone outcroppings of the buildings. Most were expensive stone-and-wood homes that hunkered down around twin ten-story towers of glass and steel that had been heralded as New Moscow's most modern living environments. Collin Archer's building had a view over the rooftops of the old city to the crags of Yekaterina's Mountain.

He parked the Perseus in the lone visitor's parking stall— apparently anyone worth talking to already lived here—and went to the well-lit main door. Inside, white marble-tiled floors gleamed under a thick Bukhara carpet of reds and blues. Dark blue couches faced an electric fireplace that demarked a visitor waiting area away from the elevators. An aging security officer in a crisply pressed blue uniform sat at a white-tiled desk near the door. He watched Kazakov try the locked entry, but buzzed him in after Kazakov pressed his badge to the glass.

Kazakov made his request to access Archer's apartment.

The security officer shook his head. He was about ten years Kazakov's senior, with a balding head and shoulders sloped as if he bore the weight of Yekaterina's Mountain on his back. "Mr. Archer left instructions that no one is to go in without him."

Kazakov sighed. "I hate to be the bearer of bad news, but Mr. Archer will not be coming back. Mr. Archer is dead. I am investigating his death. Now let me in or I will be forced to obtain a court order and the culprit will have time to escape." He was being more than a little melodramatic given he had no chance of obtaining such an order.

The old fellow hesitated, but then produced a set of keys.

"I'll—I'll go up with you. See you don't disturb anything."

Which was exactly what Kazakov intended to do. He smiled. "And who will watch the door for you? I would hate for this to cause you a problem."

The old man stopped and looked to the door. Clearly, opening it for people and checking them in was an important part of the job.

"When was the last time you saw Mr. Archer?" Kazakov asked.

The older man frowned. "Three nights ago. I think. He goes out every Wednesday night. I think he has a regular date."

Kazakov filed that bit of information away. It fit with Archer attending the Red Veil at least one night a month. Where he was the other Wednesday nights was anyone's guess.

"Has anyone else been to see Mr. Archer in the past three days?"

The guard's open gaze grew shuttered. "Not that I can recall."

Of course, recollection could be a selective thing.

"Perhaps you could try a little harder. Did Mr. Archer have visitors?"

The aging guard's lips firmed, but his gaze turned pleading. "You have to understand. I am paid to have discretion. I tell stories and I lose my job."

"Just tell me whether someone was here these past three days?"

"I'm sorry. No." The guard shook his head.

Kazakov slipped the keys from the old man's fingers. "Then I will take that as a yes. I will not cause any harm. Now which apartment is it?"

The old security man's gaze flipped from the building entry to the keys to the bank of elevators beyond the fireplace. Then he sighed and nodded and sank down on his chair. "I guess a man can't be everywhere. And you are the police. It's apartment 9B. A nice view from up there."

Kazakov took the elevator up the nine floors—not quite to the top, but damn close—and stepped out into a vestibule of thick pile carpet the gold of old wheat and paler velvet wallpaper. The heat was on high and so dry that he felt as if he had fallen into a silo of chaff. The walls to either side were blank, but there were two doors facing him with plain gold lettering: 9A and 9B. There were no other apartments on the floor.

Fewer chances of witnesses?

He used his borrowed keys and let himself inside Collin Archer's apartment.

The first thing he noticed in the darkness was cold. He toggled on electric lights and found himself in another foyer. This one gave onto a dining room to his right with high coffered ceilings and burgundy walls with ornate white crown moldings. A dark wood table complete with candelabra gleamed in a chandelier's light.

He abandoned the foyer and ventured into the other room, a grand parlor complete with huge windows that overlooked the gleaming lights of New Moscow skirting around the five-peaked mountain. The windows radiated cold. For all the heaters in the elevator foyer, they could not compete with this colder than normal winter. Kazakov held his hand over a heating vent. Cold. Apparently, Collin Archer depended upon the ambient heat of the building to heat the place. Or turned everything off when he left to go out.

The room held two large, pale gray, leather sofas facing each other over a large glass coffee table that bore a simple, low, square vase and the twisted limbs of a bonsai. On the room's three other walls hung artwork. Kazakov frowned. He might not know art, but this looked like the real thing, not the usual kitschy painting of Saint Basil's Cathedral or dreamscape images of Russia remembered. These were minimalist depictions of mountains and birds, but instead of Chinese karsk landscapes of steepsided limestone mountains, these had a bucolic Anglo flavor to them with brief blue strokes of rivers winding between sweeps of green fields. Still, there was something of the oriental in them. He leaned in to read the artist's signature. *A. Bruce*. Could be from anywhere. Perhaps the artist simply mimicked the ancient Chinese style. After all, the Anglo-Germans were in league with the American states trying to broker a peace between the two empires.

Kazakov smiled at the similarity of style. Collin Archer had had his features transformed, but not his taste. Perhaps he wasn't a very good spy at all. Odd, given the painstaking changes that had been made to his body. What made more sense was that as a pseudo-Anglo-German he chose this style for a reason. Perhaps it was in vogue in that Empire. He seemed to recall seeing something about cross-cultural art being in vogue. It was something else to check.

Shelves and drawers were built in under the paintings and he set about his search. The drawers were mostly empty. When he finished his cursory look, he eased his back. Collin Archer might have rented this place, he might have resided here, but this room might as well be empty. It was for show, nothing more. Even the framed photos on the low shelves were no more than framed copies of the newspaper article photos he'd already seen. Nothing from the life he'd claimed back home in Devon.

A closed door at one end of the room gave onto a large, modern kitchen with dark grey concrete counters and red appliances. Black cupboards made him feel as if he was in Baba Yaga's lair about to brew up a strange concoction. The air even smelled funny. He checked the fridge—almost empty except for a half-empty carton of eggs and a wilted head of lettuce. The cupboards carried almost nothing—an unopened box of rice, a single pot and frying pan. A set of four plates and bowls and a matching amount of cutlery. If Collin Archer planned to entertain, he clearly planned to have the event catered. No junk drawer. No takeout menus. No nothing. The place had the gutted feeling of a fish—as if someone had been here before him. To remove anything of importance? It seemed the old guardian of the building entrance had not only fibbed about someone's attendance, but had also been a bit disingenuous about not allowing anyone into the apartment.

The garbage bin contained the remains of a dinner of noodles and rice and vegetables in a dark spicy sauce—all now covered in a blue frosting of mold. The mess was the source of the odor in the room. Three days the security guard had said. Perhaps it was longer, age doing what it did to an old man's memory. So where had Collin Archer been?

He returned to the living room and spotted an obvious panel designed like a secret hiding place set into the far wall opposite the kitchen. Such things had been all the rage in Fergana about seven years ago when someone had taken the country's unspoken fear of invasion and made it fashionable. The panel opened with slight pressure of his fingertips to reveal a bedroom. The room had the same opulence as the dining room, with white coffered ceiling, ornate navy-blue walls and, against the far wall, a large, white, four-poster bed draped in navy bedding. This room had a slightly different air—a scent as if a person lived here. Pheromones. The scent of unwashed clothing and old skin sluffed off in bedding. A dresser sat under another cold window, but the heating vents were on here and, so far, able to hold off the cold.

Drawers revealed the dead man's clothing. Underwear. Socks. A white t-shirt. A black t-shirt. White shorts and polo shirt suitable for racket sports.

He found the closet and bathroom behind another supposedly secret panel. Large bathroom with tub, shower, and a vanity that contained cold medicine and a bottle of lotion that tingled on Kazakov's fingers when he tried some. Skin bleach? It was a reasonable possibility. But the sheer lack of anything else said this was a very careful man. Or someone had helped him along.

In the closet, the impression was reinforced with freshly laundered clothing all held in individual plastic coating. Nothing in pockets—he checked. No boxes on the shelves. Even the shoes had had their soles cleaned. All of the clothing bore labels Kazakov recognized as coming from Anglo-German designers.

Perhaps that was odd in and of itself. Most people were not careful about only purchasing items manufactured at home, and with trade across the globe, more and more designer clothing could be made anywhere in the world.

Frustrated, he returned to the living room. The man had left no sign of his existence beyond a body, a few newspaper clippings, and a woman's statement.

He was wasting his time here. He was sure of it. And he was fairly certain that Archer's office would be just as carefully devoid of the man. But there was another place Archer had spent his time.

Kazakov returned to the bedroom closet, dug to the back, and pulled out a sterile plastic-wrapped package of white breeches and polo shirt. Embroidered on the breast pocket was the name: AngloTec Polo Club.

He tossed the clothes back into the closet and headed out the door. In the downstairs lobby, he returned the keys to the crafty old security guard.

In all of New Moscow there were only three polo clubs. He knew that much. One had its stable and clubhouse to the south in the foothills. The other two shared facilities and were located westward out of the city toward Kokand. He remembered reading about it in the newspaper, because the second club was patronized by AngloTec.

He checked his watch. Six thirty. All those businessmen had to exercise their string of polo ponies some time.

He started his car and headed west.

Outside the sprawling city, the houses died away and the land flattened out. In summer, it would hold rolling fields of wheat and corn. Fergana's many irrigation canals had been dug to steal water from the Potemkin River. In exchange, the farms offered up vegetables and sweet Dunhuan melons in the long summer days. Now the silent fields were dark, reflecting moonlight that filtered through a spectral layer of clouds. Here and there lay the huddled, low-slung shapes of houses and farm buildings amid the fields.

He reached the stables, only a short drive off the highway, just after seven. White-fenced fields were empty, but a large, covered arena leaked light through large windows placed above metal siding. Stables made sloped rooflines off the sides of the arena like the full skirts of a tribal Kyrgyz woman.

The parking lot was full of expensive Ziln, Bosphorus, and Autowunder vehicles as he pulled the Perseus into a space among them. His trusty vehicle looked like an ill-bred Kyrgyz mount amongst sleek racehorses. Any one of the imported vehicles could have bought and sold his dacha ten times over. He climbed out onto the well-cleared lot and hunched toward the nearest stable. The large sliding barn door had a smaller human-sized door in the middle with a bright amber light overhead. He opened the door and stepped through.

Quiet and warm were his first two impressions. The air lay still and pungent with hay, leather, and horse manure. Along the length of the long breezeway between two rows of stalls, three horses were tied and men were working over them with brushes. The two men working on the horse closest to him glanced in his direction. They were young and fit, clad in breeches, puffy down jackets, and high black boots.

Feeling out of his depth—he had never had occasion to get comfortable with horses except for the small mountain breeds of the tribesmen who had visited the dacha woods—and bulky beyond belief in his long wool coat, he approached the first animal and its handlers.

"Detektiv Alexander Kazakov, New Moscow Police. I am conducting an investigation. Can you point me to whoever is responsible for this place?" He left out the nature of the investigation in the belief that in an environment like this the news would travel like wildfire, thus potentially ruining witness testimony.

"Y-ees," said one of the young men brushing the horse as if he doubted his own ability to provide the information. He carefully brushed out the animal's mane. "What's this about?" His Russian was stilted, but whether Anglo or German, Kazakov couldn't tell. He was young, broad-shouldered, and blond, and by the gleam that remained on his clothing under the horse dust, he came from the money now infiltrating New Moscow's wealthiest families.

"It is a police matter. Now the directions, please?"

The young man waved him toward a door in an alcove and Kazakov left them whispering as they brushed the horse. Beyond the door he stumped up a flight of stairs and found himself in a heated lounge, complete with wet bar and leather-clad tables and chairs. On one wall hung a painting of an English countryside with horses and riders galloping, painted in an almost oriental style. Lounging in one of the swivel chairs nearest to a broad expanse of window overlooking the arena sat a woman also clad in a pair of those ubiquitous boots and breeches and a down vest over a heavy knit multicolored sweater.

She glanced over her shoulder and smoothed a palm over chestnut, shoulder-length hair. By the fairness of her skin, Kazakov expected freckles and as he approached her, he wasn't disappointed.

"So? She asked from her chair, her attention back on the arena where a horse and rider were going around in circles. She didn't even shift the long legs that were stretched out before her. "What do you want? Police, correct?"

Her accent was thickly Anglo—a transplant, then. Possibly brought in to help introduce the Anglo version of polo.

Kazakov introduced himself and she already looked bored. "That is an unusual painting," he said. "I'm not familiar with the style."

She rolled her eyes slightly. "It's Neuvo-Briton—the latest thing a few years back. A blend of Anglo and our Asian friends' styles. Made popular by the painter Henry Chow, if you must know. That's one of his. What of it?"

Kazakov studied the painting. So perhaps Collin Archer *had* been reflecting Anglo-German tastes. He turned back to her. "Just interested. It's an interesting style given its heavy Chinese influence."

She held him steady with her gaze. "I guess that was the point."

Time to change the subject. "I need to talk to you about an AngloTec rider."

She glanced at him, an arched brow awaiting the answer to the obvious question.

"Collin Archer?" he asked.

She sighed and sat up, her heels pulled into a prim position on the floor. "So how is dear Archer? We haven't seen him for a few days. His ponies miss him. So do the bookies."

She turned back to the arena and appeared to study a second man working a horse in a circle on the end of two long lines.

Damn it, he needed her attention. "Well, he won't be here for either horses or bookies again."

She blinked three times as if processing that information.

Then she swung her chair around to face him.

"Tell me about him," he asked, hooking a chair forward to sit down facing her. He pulled out his notebook. "Your name?"

"Charlotte Newcomb. I'm married to Brett Newcomb, the Anglo attaché to the Ambassador."

As opposed to the German attaché who would also be attached to the Ambassador. Though the Anglo-German Empire had a single royal family, the two cultures were distinct enough that care had to be taken to retain the uneasy peace of the Anglo-German alliance even after two hundred years of being one empire.

"And what is your role at this polo club?" he asked.

She shrugged. "Manager, I suppose, though the mysoginist club members barely acknowledge even that. I make sure the feed for the horses is here and arrange the matches—that sort of thing."

Kazakov nodded and noted it down.

"So, you said Collin Archer won't be back. What's happened to him?" She shook her head. "Something bad, I'm thinking—given you're here."

He studied her from the tops of his eyes. "He's dead."

Charlotte Newcomb showed almost no reaction. Then she sighed and nodded. "How did he die?"

There was no way Kazakov was providing the details. "Let's just say that there were unusual circumstances. So, what can you tell me about Collin Archer?" He held his pen poised as she rolled her head on her neck.

"Unusual circumstances. Why doesn't that surprise me," she said with a hint of laughter. Then she turned serious. "Well… regardless of what he told everyone, he was a very poor horseman and a not much better gambler." She shook her head and leaned forward as if warming to the subject. "Collin never did have much affinity for the animals. He's got good ponies—the best money could buy or train, actually— but unlike the other riders, he never did the work himself and seemed to expect horses to just be like a vehicle: you climb behind the wheel and they go where you tell them." She shook her head.

"Anyway, Collin Archer was one of those men I like to call a Golden Eagle—not good for much except swooping in and taking the credit. You know eagles are very much carrion birds, don't you? He'd swan in here and spend time flirting or talking, let others ride his horses, and then swan in again when a game was on. Don't get me wrong. He could ride. But it was more like he went through the motions, not that he was passionate about it."

"You don't sound like you cared for him very much."

Charlotte shrugged. "What difference would it make if I did? I'm just one of the follow-along crowd. I might ride dressage horses, but in this stable it counts for nothing." She lifted her chin at the horse in the ring. "They're doing it all wrong. The way they're working him, the horse is learning to drop his shoulder and fall onto his forehand. Not what you want in any horse, but god forbid I should say anything."

"The people around here don't like your advice?"

She smiled sweetly but there was a touch of acid in her gaze. "They are men in a man's world. Who am I but the wife of somebody, even if I own this barn?"

Surprised, he looked down at his notes. "You said you were the manager…"

She shrugged again. "To them that is all I can ever be, even if I'm also the money behind the operation."

Her bitterness was so harsh that he chose to ignore it. "You mentioned bookies before. What did you mean?"

She leaned back in her chair, appraising him. "So is this where we get to the heart of the matter? Collin Archer. He had a gambling problem. Perhaps that's what caused his—what did you call it?—the unusual circumstances of his death?"

He leaned back, too. "Tell me about this gambling. What do you know?"

She appeared to consider for a moment and then rolled her gaze heavenward. "What don't I? Archer and his buddies were deep into gambling. They even tried to rig a polo match until I caught them. I told them that if they ever bet on a polo match, they were out of the club and the stable, no matter how much they paid in dues. I would not stand for it. I do not like scandal. So as far as I know, Collin took his gambling elsewhere."

"Can you think of anyone who might have wanted to do Collin Archer harm?"

Her steady gaze glittered at him. "Aside from me, Detektiv?"

He cocked a brow in question and she looked away. "Let us just say that he was no gentleman. He might be of good Anglo stock, but there was something about him. He might speak the right words, have the right accent, but there was something very—wrong—about him. Don't get me wrong, it was nothing major—just many little things like how he would fold a coat, or expect me and others to answer to him. I mentioned it to my husband, but he told me I just didn't like the guy. Maybe that was the case, I don't know. I suppose that sort of attitude could come from the nobility, but I never heard that about Collin. I used to tell Brett that I thought he was a psychopath—absolutely no concept of anything other than what he wanted, and what he wanted was money and influence. He was always trying to sidle up beside the right person at the wrong time, but I guess some people are like that. Made for very awkward social situations from time to time."

She shifted uneasily in her chair while Kazakov simply watched her.

"The last rumor I heard was that he had lost big on a football match and his bookies were demanding payment." She shrugged. "Sometimes you reap what you sow, Detektiv."

"Do you know who these bookies might be?" he asked.

She shook her head. "Someone in New Moscow, I suppose. I'd heard he'd already had to trade favors in lieu of interest on what he owed. Something about someone's nephew getting a job beyond his competence level. I think there may be a lot of that thing in Fergana. But then I suspect you would know that, Detektiv." She spoke as if she suspected as much of him.

He noted the information down, but frankly it didn't sit right with him. Why would a spy go out of his way to be noticed—and for all the wrong reasons? It made no sense—and yet—who would ever suspect someone with Collin Archer's personality of being more than a difficult to deal with foreign company hack? If Collin Archer was a spy, he was either the most incompetent or the most brilliant spy he'd ever heard of.

Not that he'd heard of many.

But clearly Charlotte Newcomb did not know who the bookies were, or she took pleasure in not telling. Which meant he had little more to go on. He was going to have to track down the bookies through standard police procedures.

He thought about Collin Archer and how much he didn't know about him.

"There was a charity polo match of the old-fashioned kind. It was held to raise money for a youth musical conference. Were you involved in that?"

She grimaced as if the whole event had been distasteful. "Live goats." She shuddered. "I organized the event at the request of my husband and some politicians. They thought it would provide a marquee event that would provide good press for AngloTec and the government. Embracing culture and all that."

Kazakov again made a note. "What happened during the event?" He left it open for her interpretation of what was important to report on.

She shrugged. "We hosted the event. It was well attended by Fergana's well-heeled. The game was held with a reception afterward with food and music and much schmoozing." Another lift of the shoulder as if it was nothing. Clearly Charlotte Newcomb was well trained in the art of leaving much unsaid.

"There were newspaper articles about the event…" he said and held her gaze until she shifted in her seat and looked away.

"There was one small problem. One of our guests had words with one of the caterers—or at least we thought the young man was one of the catering staff. It turns out he was uninvited and was trying to cause problems. The police were called, but the young man disappeared before they arrived. That was all there was to it."

Kazakov nodded. "Tell me, if this was to benefit student musicians, surely some of the musicians must have been in attendance."

"Definitely. There was a chamber orchestra. They were not that good, but then they had been drawn from a number of schools."

Including Yekaterina Weber, most likely. "And can you tell me which guest this unknown youth troubled?"

Charlotte Newcomb looked puzzled. "What does this have to do with Collin Archer?"

"Please. Just answer the question." He held his breath.

"Why, it was Boris Bure. We had to work very hard to convince the press to leave that little fact out of their articles." She grew thoughtful. "Come to think of it, it was Collin who helped make that possible and he also came to Boris's rescue."

Kazakov was writing as fast as he could. "Why would he do that, do you think?"

"I—I'm not sure."

And for a woman as certain as Charlotte Newcomb, that was something.

"Perhaps Archer was simply currying favors—again. But I seem to recall that Boris and Collin might have been talking when the young man interrupted. They were off to one side, in a small garden that grows next to the polo field and reception area. I suppose Collin was the only one around to help Boris." Another shrug as if it didn't matter.

But it mattered to Kazakov. In those circumstances, he could see young Semetai Manas trying to make contact. He could have followed the two men into the garden in order to talk to Boris Bure when the two men were finished their conversation. Had he heard something he shouldn't have or was it simply that he had tried to speak to Bure about his stepdaughter? Obviously, Charlotte Newcomb would know nothing of that. He decided to change the direction of enquiry, but the familiar tingling in his chest said that he was onto something. He just needed to learn more about that day.

"These places." He encompassed the arena and stables in his wave. "There must be some place that the riders maintain their possessions."

She sat up. "You mean their lockers?"

He nodded. "That might be it. But it may not be, too. Lockers tend to be small." Too small for a spy who would need to have access to equipment. "Did Collin have any other place that was his own within the complex? A place he could store things in private?"

She started to laugh and it was both amused and annoyed. "A space? A small space, he asked for. The least of spaces—where a man could relax together with his friends, he said. It was a card club! A damned card club!" She leapt to her feet and paced around the carpeted room, her booted feet thumping hollowly on the floor.

Then she turned to him. "Come with me."

She grabbed a knee-length shearling jacket that would cost about half a year of Kazakov's pay and ran down the stairs from the viewing room to the stables, then threw open the door to outside and marched into the night, Kazakov at her heels.

Outside, she strode across the snowy parking lot to a large truck and trailer parked to one side. The stable lights reflected in its darkened windows and on the chrome grill work. The truck was commercial grade, made for hauling large loads over long distances—the same type that hauled cargo up and over the mountain passes between China and Fergana, but the trailer was custom made—a large horse-hauling van with a large living space up front.

Charlotte stormed up to the living quarters stairs, fished a key ring from somewhere on her person, and threw open the door.

"There!" she said turning to him. "If he had anything stored privately, it would be here. And if you want his locker, I will be here for another hour." Then she stomped back down the stairs and away across the silent parking lot to the arena.

10

Kazakov's breath steamed around him as he turned back to the open door above the three retractable iron stairs that led up to the trailer entrance. Grabbing hold of the side of the door, he hiked himself up into inky darkness. There were few windows and the open door provided only a narrow alley of light. His eyes adjusted gradually and his fingers fumbled on the wall until he found a small switch. He toggled it on and a low hum filled the room. Then a soft flickering glow began from a single overhead light and a whiff of heat came from somewhere down by his feet. The place had a generator. Very nice. And expensive.

He closed the door behind him as the light increased and steadied.

The room was about ten feet long by seven feet wide. Cupboards filled the upper walls above a half-sized sink, electric oven, and a single cooktop gas burner. Low, cushioned, bench seating around three sides of a small table sat beneath a shuttered window opposite the door. Two small doors gave off toward the rear of the trailer. He checked one and it gave onto the length of the horse area. The other door gave onto a tiny bathroom with toilet and shower. In the main room's heat, the dusty-sweet scent of horse sweat slowly permeated the air.

It was clearly the change and lounge room used by the riders when away at a match. What had Collin Archer turned it into?

He began with the cupboards.

The uppers revealed packs of playing cards and dice and opened and sealed bottles of vodka, imported Anglo whiskey, German beer, and even a bottle of sake. Cartons of Anglo crisps, jars of pickles, and tins of something called herring and sardines filled the rest of the upper cupboards. The fridge contained delicacies of cheese and sausages he had only seen in specialty shops catering to expatriate shoppers. Everything looked reasonably fresh, as if it had been replaced only recently. It certainly *looked* like the lair of an Anglo gentleman who liked his comforts of home. Or else it was a perfect place to make other Anglo gentlemen feel at home, and those who were not Anglo feel like they had stepped into a rarified world of plentiful exotic food. A place of comfort. A place among friends.

He crouched down and went through the lower cupboards. They smelled of astringent and antiseptic. Large bottles of strange brown liquid sloshed when he shifted them. Tins of hoof unguent, sprays to enhance the shine of a horse's coat. A plastic workman's rack filled with brushes and other paraphernalia he couldn't identify. Long strips of bandages. Hair tonic. Boot black.

And exactly nothing that told him anything more than he already knew about Collin Archer.

He sat back on his heels as the humming cut out. The room had reached a temperature that he no longer needed his coat. He stood, removed it, and placed it on a hook by the door.

The bench seating had thick cushion backs and seats. He pulled off each one, unzipping the faded cover—this was clearly a well-used trailer—and felt inside the dense foam. Nothing in the side cushions, but when he unzipped the larger cushion from the back of the bench seat, he found a line of small slits in the foam just big enough to slip two fingers inside.

There was nothing in the three exposed by the zipper.

Simply an imperfection of the foam, or something cut more recently? He pulled the slipcover right off and laid the foam wedge across the table to check each slit. On the second to last one, his fingers hit something. He pulled his fingers out and parted the foam to peer inside.

Buried in the foam was something small, about an inch wide, that looked like tan-colored plastic.

Wishing for a camera to document the evidence, he dug the plastic piece out onto the table.

Not quite an inch wide and about two inches long, the small plastic rectangle was cut by a seam around the waist. He couldn't tease the two pieces of plastic apart with his fingernails and finally picked the rectangle up and pulled the two ends. It came apart in his hands, one piece clearly a protective lid for what he had uncovered.

It was a small metal prong that reminded him of an electric plug, but he couldn't think of anything small enough to plug it into. It wasn't shaped like a normal three-prong plug, either. This had two plugs on one side, so close together as to almost be one and delicate enough looking he could probably bend them off with a finger. The third prong sat at the other side of the end of the plastic and was a simple small metal rod or wire.

Replacing the lid on the rectangle, he pulled out a plastic bag and placed the contraption inside. Then he kept searching. There was nothing further in the cushion. He pulled the cover back on and placed the evidence bag in his pocket just as the door pulled open, letting in a blast of cold air and the young man he'd spoken to when he'd first arrived at the stable. The young man entered as his blue eyes scanned the room.

"I figured it would be messier," he said in an atrocious German accent.

Kazakov arched a brow at him.

"You know. You're searching old Collin's secret hideaway, aren't you? A cop doing his job?"

Kazakov slowly nodded, not quite sure what to make of the man. Friend of Archer's? An ally? Of Archer or Kazakov?

The young men grinned, revealing crooked white teeth in his otherwise handsome face. "When Charlotte came storming back I figured she probably wouldn't have showed ya the tricks of this place." He shook his head. "Charlotte. She's had a hard-on for Collin ever since he turned her down when he first arrived. She likes to have her way with each of us and then toss us aside. I think it makes her feel better. But Collin wasn't having any and she resented him for it. Couldn't stand a man with morals greater than her own, I guess." He lounged companionably against the closed door and looked around the room.

"So just what's happened to Collin and what are you looking for?"

It was unusual for people to be so easily forthcoming. If Collin Archer was truly a spy, would he not try to ingratiate himself and fit in? But then perhaps he had—with the men.

"What can you tell me about Collin?" Kazakov asked.

The young man shrugged. "Damn good polo player when you can get him on the ponies—or maybe it's the expensive horseflesh that makes him look good. Either way he was a good man to have on your team."

"And beyond polo?"

Another shrug. "I didn't really know him. Quiet sort of bloke except when it came to the gambling. He's pretty serious about that. Made for quite a few good parties." He grinned his crooked grin. "A lot of money changed hands a time or two because he wasn't that good at it—the gambling I mean. He's into me for a few pounds. A few of the others, too. But he provided the liquor and the food and that's too good a deal to turn down, isn't it?"

Kazakov patted the cushion back, sat down and pulled out his notebook. "Tell me about these parties."

The young man settled across the table from him. "What's there to tell? We get together and play cards and get soused."

"Who is we?"

"Well, me of course."

"And your name is?"

"Richard Spencer. I'm assistant to the Anglo-German Ambassador." Kazakov scribbled.

"And then there's Henry Scott, he's in the foreign trade department.

And George Kinsey. He's in security—top secret stuff, you know." Another crooked grin. "Rodney Swift. He's in communications. He comes in from time to time. A few others, but we're the main ones."

"And what do you talk about at these parties?"

The young man leaned back in his seat. "I don't know. Women, of course. The damned snow in winter. In summer, the heat and dust. What we miss from back home—you cannot get a decent beefsteak here—or shepherd's pie or clotted cream." He shook his head as if it pained him. "Work, at times. The horses or the last game or football, of course. Who cheats the worst—usually that's Collin!" Another disarming grin.

Kazakov thought for a moment. If he had been Collin Archer, getting a few fools together talking about their work would be a good way to learn the Anglo-German position on matters of trade and foreign policy, but the Anglo-Germans weren't the Chinese enemy. That was the Ottoman Empire. Why would such a carefully prepared spy be wasted on these people and why was he dead?

"Did Collin Archer have any enemies?"

The young man's gaze narrowed and his grin disappeared. A calculation came into his eyes that said he was no fool. "You said 'did'. Why are you asking me all this? Has something happen to Collin?"

Kazakov met his gaze. "Answer the question first."

Richard Spenser shook his head. "Like I said, he keeps more to himself. None of us knows him that well. We didn't exactly run in the same circles back home, but he's a fun enough bloke to be with. Aside from Charlotte, I never saw him have words with anyone."

"Collin Archer's body was found three days ago in Yekaterina Park."

"Jeezus." Richard Spenser looked stunned. "Robbed? He always did like to show that bank roll of his…"

"It did not appear to be a robbery." Kazakov looked at his notes and made a note of bank roll and question mark. "What did Collin Archer usually wear?"

"Out here? Boots and breeches mostly. Like the rest of us. He had a few nice pieces, though. That navy coat of his was Saville Row, and he had a few fine suits. Mostly his things were bought here—when he had the money, and that was usually when he'd won a pot or a bet or something."

"Can you think of anything Collin was involved in that would make him a target?"

"A target? Are you talking premeditated murder?"

Kazakov didn't say anything and Richard Spencer seemed to collapse back into his seat.

He rubbed his face and looked apologetically up at Kazakov. "First time this has ever happened to me. I came out here for a bit of a lark." He waved around the trailer. "But then I came to Fergana for a bit of a lark, too, didn't I? Jeezus."

He leaned forward. "Listen, I didn't know Collin that well, like I said. He wasn't exactly a cuddly bloke. But I will say that the past month or so he's seemed a bit on edge. I thought it was just the heebie-jeebies that come after you've lived in this hole of a country for a few months, but maybe he was expecting something to happen. I guess something did."

Making a show of checking his watch, Richard Spenser slid out of the bench seat.

Kazakov stopped him with a raised hand. "I expect you were at the charity polo match along with the others?"

Richard Spenser looked like a man who had just missed his escape. "Yeesss. I was there. A good match, too, though I'm not too partial to the live goat thing." He shuddered. "What of it?"

Kazakov held his gaze, then glanced at his notes and up again. "There was an altercation at the reception. What can you tell me about it?"

Cautiously, Spenser slid back into his seat. "There was nothing to tell, really. Some guy crashed the event and got into an argument with one of the guests. Collin intervened, I guess. He had scraped-up knuckles and a mark on his cheek."

"Where did this altercation occur?"

Spenser shrugged. "I was told in the garden. Odd, because at that time of year, it gets cold outside in the evening. I guess people wanted a break from the crowd. Some privacy, so to speak."

Which meshed with Kazakov's thinking.

"Do you know who the party crasher was? Could you describe him?"

"It was a kid, actually. I caught a glimpse of him leaving when everyone else was running toward the noise of the altercation. I'd hung back to get another drink when this young guy scurries across the room and out the door. Dark-haired kid. Looked young, too. He looked mighty angry." Spenser brightened. "Could he be the killer?"

Kazakov maintained a noncommittal expression. "One more question: what's your understanding of what the altercation was about?"

Spenser shifted in his seat as if the question made him uncomfortable. He shook his head. "You've got to understand. I wasn't there so I don't know for sure, but I've heard a couple of stories. One is that the kid was dating someone's daughter when it wasn't approved. You know how fathers can be." He shrugged as if that was all he had to say, but Kazakov wasn't going to let him off that easy.

"And the other story?"

Spenser blinked as if he didn't like being caught, but he grinned his bright grin and shrugged. "Rumors, old son. Simply rumors, but I've heard it said that the gardens are a place of private conversations and the kid might have been eavesdropping."

Kazakov held Spenser with his gaze. Was this truth or fabrication? The clarity of Spenser's gaze said it was either the truth or he was the consummate liar. Kazakov wasn't sure which to believe.

Spenser took the opportunity to scramble up. "I'd best be going. I've got an early day tomorrow. Oh. And if you're searching this place, check the walls. Charlotte had it fitted with a number of 'secret' panels for stowing extra gear when we were traveling. Sometimes it's not good to have everything out for customs to see when you're crossing borders."

"Pardon me?" Kazakov wasn't sure what he'd just heard. "Like here, see?" Richard Spencer pressed a panel in the wall by the door.

The panel of wood sprang open to expose an empty bit of shelving. "Sometimes the border crossings confiscate some of the horse medications. They're expensive, so Charlotte had this done."

Kazakov eyed the space and realized that he had a lot more searching to do. "How often do you travel outside of Fergana?" he asked.

Richard Spencer frowned. "Last year it was eight or ten times all over the eastern Ottoman and once down into the Moghul South. The last trip was just a few weeks back. It was a hell of a trip at this time of year. I swear I won't do it again over those roads. But then, I survived, didn't I? This year Charlotte's talking about traveling as far as Bagdad and Damascus and maybe up into Constantinople itself. A hell of trip to tell my grandkids about." Another of those crooked grins and he checked his watch again, nodded, and ducked out the door into the night.

It was a lot of information to take in. Kazakov let it sift into his brain and then took rapid notes. So there was the possibility that Semetai had overheard something. Something important enough it could warrant his death? But if that was the case, why was Semetai allowed to live all these months since the eavesdropping occurred? And a Chinese spy on trips through the Ottoman empire. Was Archer actually spying on the Ottomans? That gave a number of motives for his death. It might also explain his odd actions and attitudes in Fergana. He wasn't spying on Fergana—he was using it as an axis hub while he spied on the Ottomans. But his body was found perilously close to the home of a high-ranking Ottoman, Enver Pasha. He could not see any Ottoman doing that purposely.

Those thoughts in mind, he stood and inspected the cubbyhole that Richard Spencer had shown him. It was a narrow space between the inner and outer walls of the transport. This one held shelves that still carried a few bottles. The labels were for horse medications. He opened the bottles one by one and the pungent astringent odor set him back a pace. The shelf ran ten inches to either side of the opening. That was a lot of storage, but there was still three feet of space between the secret cupboard and the floor.

He pressed the paneling below the opening, but nothing happened, then went around the room pressing any exposed panel. Four more cupboards sprang open, all of them set comfortingly at chest height and all equally as disappointingly empty.

Something about this wasn't right. Charlotte or whoever had installed the hidden cabinets had left the better amount of the wall's potential storage untapped. Why just build the cabinets in the top part of the wall?

He went to the first cabinet by the door and examined the bottom shelf. Solid wood by the look of it. He ran his fingers along the shelf inside the left of the cupboard. There was nothing. On the right his fingernail caught in a small protrusion of wood. He pressed it and there was still nothing, but then he pressed it again and leaned on the shelf.

Click.

The shelf dropped away, exposing a dark, empty space that appeared to run to the floor. He grabbed a flashlight from his pocket and exposed a space perfect for storing contraband. He'd bet good money that Charlotte Newcomb smuggled more than horse drugs in this trailer.

He repeated his discovery in each of the other cabinets. Of course, it was the last one that wasn't empty. Slid into the narrow dark space was something wrapped in a muffling cloth. To hide it or to protect it? He reached in and pulled it out. Heavier than it looked for the size. Not square, the item was about twelve inches long by nine inches across and two inches deep when he set it on the table. The muffling cloth was not a cloth at all, but butter-soft leather that he unwrapped to expose something rectangular and metal.

The metal was burnished on the top and sides and it looked like it was made of two pieces fit one on the top of the other and connected by a hinge. On the side of the lower portion were a series of holes, one pattern like it would accept three prongs. He pulled the baggie with the small rectangle out of his pocket. Could it be?

He retrieved the small, pronged rectangle from the baggie and pulled off the top to try the exposed prongs in the hole pattern. The small prongs slid right in as if made to do so.

So the two items were meant to be together, though for what purpose he wasn't sure. Gingerly he separated the top from the bottom of the larger metal rectangle. It swung upward to expose a tray of lettered keys and, on the upper half, a blank black screen.

"*Derr'mo,*" he swore softly. He knew what it was, though he had never seen anything like it before. The screen and keys were too similar to the new German-made data machine at his office, but this was incredibly small. So small he could not believe that it could actually do something useful.

Beyond the keys, a small round button sat just below the screen. He pressed it and the box began to hum. A machine. It was a machine, like the one that held the police and government database.

A database. The machine itself must be worth a fortune, but what did it carry? Secret information? And the small rectangle that he had found hidden separately. What did it do?

The screen swirled to life with red Chinese characters and too many dots, dashes, and slashes to make any sense at all. It was clear that he wasn't going to make any further discoveries here. He clicked the top down and pulled the small rectangle from its side, reinstalling it in the baggy and then rewrapping the data machine in the leather.

He scanned the transport one more time. Charlotte Newcomb had built an almost perfect vehicle for smuggling. Had she known what she'd done? But if she had, why would she have led him right to this evidence? No, Charlotte smuggled for her own purposes. Collin Archer had just taken advantage and no one had been the wiser because Collin Archer was regarded as a bit of a fool.

In a way, it was a more brilliant disguise than the facial reconstruction.

He left the stable in the dark with the small data machine placed like a bomb on the Perseus's seat beside him, the small slotted rectangle in his pocket, and too many questions. There was no question that along with the information that proved the connection between Semetai Manas and Collin Archer, he'd found something important. And there was no question that if the owners of these items knew what he'd found, they'd want them back. Hell, this was most likely what they'd been looking for in Archer's apartment.

The night-bound highway stretched before him, the traffic limited to the huge transports carrying cargo to and from New Moscow. Their headlights filled the highway with a ghostly blue glow that left him half blind after they passed by. His eyelids were heavy. It had been a long few days with very little sleep. The Perseus's heater churned out comforting warmth, but couldn't erase the chill he felt. Just what did the death of a smuggling spy have to do with the deaths of Yekaterina and Semetai? What had the teenagers gotten involved with that got them killed? What had they known?

He might have thought he had it all wrong, but the fact that Collin Archer had been identified as one of the people in pursuit of Semetai and that a prior connection was known—well, that proved the connection between the cases. This box might tell him why three people had died.

A part of him felt the quiver of excitement that always came with an important clue, but it was tempered with frustration. What did he know about data machines? He'd barely managed to turn the thing on and it appeared that everything was in Mandarin or some other dialect. And if he couldn't access whatever was on the machine, he had exactly nothing at all.

Maybe Rostoff had been right that this was a case he should leave alone.

He shook himself. That had to be fatigue talking. All cases came with difficulties.

Like the dog kept within a walled garden for too long, if he just kept scratching at the walls, eventually they would be gone.

He headed for home to sleep and think, driving the snowy roads to bypass New Moscow up into the hills. His headlights caught on the unmarked lane leading to Agafya Ryabkov's home—he would need to bring her more supplies in the next few days—and then he turned into the ruts left behind from the Perseus's wheels in the driveway up to his home. A welcoming light gleamed from the dacha window when he came out into the clearing.

Carrying the leather-wrapped machine, he went into the dacha, his feet sounding hollow on the newly swept stairs. A whiff of lavender greeted him at the door along with the luscious scent of leftovers from the day before. His mouth watered. A lit lantern sat on the counter beside the woodstove, a covered plate beside it. Maria lay cocooned, asleep in his covers, Koshka curled in close to her breast.

One hand was curled close to her chin like a child. Framed by her mane of dark hair, her face held a radiant peace the likes of which he'd never seen. Annushka had always slept with arms and legs flailing, just as she lived her life.

Sighing at the thought of another night on the floor, he shrugged out of his coat and hung it on the peg. He sat down to pull off his boots and then checked the fire, added a log, and straightened. It was while he was wolfing down the cold remains of the delicious beef and potatoes that he realized Maria's eyes were open. So were Koshka's. Both sets seemed to study him.

"Thanks for the food," he said around another forkful.

Maria pushed up on one elbow. "So? Have you found out anything?"

He shrugged and shifted the extra blankets and pillow, which had spent the day in a folded pile on the couch, onto the floor next to the now-ticking woodstove. By the rumble in the chimney, the fire was building in heat. Soon the dacha would be warm and he might stand a chance at sleep.

"I found this." He patted the machine he'd placed on his desk.

"What is it?" she asked.

"Damned if I know. A data machine of some kind, I believe. Collin Archer had hidden it at the stable where he kept his polo ponies."

She sat up farther. "What does it say?"

He shrugged again. "All the answers to all the questions that have plagued mankind—or nothing at all. I've no idea."

He hung his holster and weapon off the back of a chair and shucked his shirt and trousers before using the water closet. Then he washed his face in the sink and went to climb between the blankets.

"Don't!" In a flash Maria was off the bed and beside him. She caught his wrist and looked up at him. "You've had a very long day. You need your bed."

She stood too close, her sleep-warmed lavender scent flooding him, her skin golden in the lantern light.

"I—I will sleep on the couch," she continued. "It is fine. Definitely long enough for me."

She released his arm and scooped up the blankets before smoothing them into a bed on the couch. She plopped down and slid her legs beneath the coverings. "See? It is long enough." She had to curl her legs up tightly to fit.

"Get up," he said. There was no way he would sleep in the bed and leave her contorted on the couch. That wasn't the way he'd been raised.

She burrowed into the blankets until he caught her wrist and dragged her up. She staggered against him and he caught her shoulders to steady her.

Soft—her skin would be soft. He could tell even through the old t-shirt. The flickering lantern light placed a mist in her eyes as she met his gaze. Then she stood on tiptoe and kissed him.

Sweet and soft and filled with longing. When she pulled away she laid her head on his chest. "When you did not come back for so long, I was worried that something had happened to you."

His hands came around her back almost as if they belonged to a separate person. Her waist was so trim. Her body warm in his arms. He rested his chin on the top of her head and wondered what he was doing. Blood stirred in his limbs. It was a long time since he had felt like this —alive. Potent.

"I need to sleep," he said, but led her to the bed. She climbed in and, after dousing the lantern, he climbed in beside her, pulling her in close. The scent and texture of another living being suddenly important.

She did not try to turn their arrangement into a sexual encounter. She simply curled into him, as if she'd understood something from the night before.

He fell asleep almost immediately and was lost in a lavender-scented forest where a chicken-legged house danced in a circle and a wicked, misshapen crone laughed and laughed.

He woke to the dacha ticking around him. It was still dark outside and by the hush in the air, more snow was falling. He sat up. Something had woken him beyond evil dreams. He slid out of bed to Maria's protesting murmurs and went to the door. Pulled it slightly open and cold air froze his face. Snow sifted in over his bare feet. It was the predawn darkness, the deepest of the night when the whole world seemed to gather itself in preparation for the leap into day. Usually this far out from the city there was absolute quiet, but the throaty rumble of at least two approaching vehicle engines broke the stillness.

He closed the door and turned back to the bed. "Get up. You have two minutes to get up and dressed. Move!"

He pulled on his shirt and trousers, a handmade sweater of thick brown wool Annushka had bought for him years before, and his shoulder holster. Then he pulled on his coat and his old fur hat.

Maria gazed confusedly up at him from the bed. Sleep still half held her.

He grabbed her and hauled her out of the covers. "There are people coming for us just as they came for Collin. Don't ask me how I know. Now get dressed."

He'd been a damned fool bringing the machine here. Someone at the stable had reported that he was there. Someone had reported he had removed something. Charlotte Newcombe? Richard Spencer? But Spencer had all but handed him the data machine. And they were Anglo-German. Why would they come after him? He needed time to think. Time to assess everything he had learned, but events seemed to conspire against him.

Maria was up and had her stout trousers and shirt pulled on. She pulled on her coat while he thrust his feet into his boots and tossed hers to her. Yanking open the door and carrying the data machine, he hauled her out into the night and stopped. The engines were closer. Almost to his lane. Dragging Maria behind him he set off for the lane, following the Perseus's tire prints.

He just had to pray that the enemy would drive up the lane and make it harder to follow their tracks. In the darkness, it was just possible he and Maria might get away.

They were halfway down the lane when vehicle engines slowed. His eyes had adjusted to the snow and the night and he could now see shapes and contours. He floundered through snow off of the lane and into the forest and down the hill. Maria came after him. "Who are they?"

He shook his head.

"Why are they here?"

"For you. For me. For us both. They want to tie up loose ends."

By the sound, the vehicles had turned into the laneway. If he was lucky they'd drive right to the house and make his and Maria's tracks less clear.

Whoever these people were, he'd bet that they wanted to get in, get the job done, and get out. They wouldn't like having to search. If he and Maria could stay disappeared, they might be safe.

A glance over his shoulder showed something shiny moving through the trees, though there were no headlights. He waited a moment but a second vehicle didn't pass up the driveway. They were going for the house but they had stationed one vehicle at his driveway entrance to block escape that way.

He turned back to his trail and waded through the snow, making a path for Maria. If the men searched, they'd find his and Maria's trail. And then they would come for them.

He stopped and pulled Maria in close. "Listen. I have to stop them from finding our trail. Straight through the woods that way," he pointed. "There is another dacha. It is owned by an old woman who lives there. Her name is Agafya Ryabkov and she is a loner and suspicious. I bring her groceries. Go to her house and explain. She will, hopefully, take you in. Stay there until I come for you."

Her eyes caught whatever light there was as she peered up at him. "I'm sorry. I've brought you only trouble since I've known you."

"No." He shook his head. "You've brought me—I don't know what —but I feel—" Like what? A foolish old man? Like he had found an inkling of life again? "I feel like you've shaken me out of a long bleak winter." He caught her shoulders and leaned down to kiss her. Sweet lips again and he realized he was hungry for kisses and so much more. Annushka was the past. Maria might hold the future.

He pulled back and, praying he wasn't placing her in more danger, handed her the data machine. He pointed again. "That way. Go. I will try to stop them."

She looked as if about to protest, but he shoved her in the right direction and then headed uphill, circling back toward the dacha.

11

____

The snow thankfully was only part way up his shins in most places and closer in around the trees there was even less. Snow still sifted softly down and masked all sounds. The air smelled of ice and pine pitch as he slid through the night shadows to come at his dacha from the rear.

They must have arrived by now. Perhaps they'd even discovered that their quarry was gone. If they'd found his and Maria's trail, the two of them were doomed.

Downslope, through the trees, he made out the greater light of the clearing and the dark bulk of his home. Flashes of light against the snow said that someone or someones were searching the area. So they'd been inside and realized they were too late.

From inside the dacha came a crash as if someone else was relieving their frustration. A snarling yowl expressed Koshka's opinion. Hopefully the little black cat would get away.

A door slammed and voices reached him through the trees. The flickering lights of four flashlights fanned out from the house. They'd seen the Perseus. They knew he and Maria were on the run, and on foot.

Four against one. Not great, but they would be blinded by their lights and he—was not. That had to be worth something. That and the fact they had yet to discover his and Maria's trail. He hoped.

Loosing his weapon in his holster, he slid closer to the clearing as the men struggled through the deeper snow in the open. Their breath made huge clouds as they puffed through drifts.

The closest man's flashlight tracked back and forth across the snow. Kazakov stayed immobile in a stand of trees and let the man blunder closer. He was tall and lean and by his stance, experienced with weapons. He gripped a pistol in the hand not holding the flashlight. The tracker entered the trees and came even with Kazakov's hiding place but still didn't see him. Then his flashlight found the deep trench of Kazakov's footprints. He stopped, inspecting the trail, and Kazakov stepped out from the trees. The man had time to look up as Kazakov clocked him on the temple with his pistol. He went down, heavily and hard, and Kazakov relieved him of his weapon.

Three to one. Better odds, but still not good.

He used the man's belt to bind his hands to a tree, checked his face with the flashlight, and stopped. Sergei Alenin from the squad. What the hell?

Kazakov flicked off the light and looked back at the cabin. Was Rostoff there? It was almost a sure thing that Antonov, Alenin's partner, was. He thought of Antonov's suggestion that Kazakov should change and felt sick to his stomach.

The fact it was Kazakov's brother officers meant so many things that he could not fathom. Right now, all he could concern himself with was living through the night. He straightened and set off following another bobbing light.

This one was down lower, on the north side of the dacha. Kazakov wallowed through the snow, trying to stay silent, but he found himself puffing, his breath great gouts of steam. He had to be careful. If it was Antonov, the burly detective was powerful—a man you wanted at your back in a fight. He was also deadly accurate with his weapon, scoring top of the heap in their annual weapons qualifying. Incapacitating Antonov's partner would only make him angry, but surely Antonov and

Kazakov's history together had to mean something. If Antonov was his enemy, would he have tried to warn Kazakov off at the office?

A lesser man might not—but Antonov—he would try to do the right thing first.

Kazakov eased carefully through the trees. Their branches were heavy with snow. If he knocked one, the snow would cascade down, alerting the searcher to his presence.

The man was searching the snow along the tree line, but just as Kazakov came even with him, he straightened.

"Sergei! I don't think they came this way. I'm not finding any sign."

Antonov. Kazakov held his breath. The detective's voice carried, his short, hulking form visible through the trees.

"Sergei?"

Antonov turned uphill, in the direction Kazakov had come.

"Sergei!"

He stopped and listened, then swore under his breath. His hand snaked inside his coat and came out armed with a pistol. Then he turned and cautiously followed the tree edge around the dacha. He'd find his friend's tracks soon enough and now he was on watch. That would make Kazakov's task more difficult.

Kazakov turned back the way he'd come, following his path back through the snow and praying he could beat Antonov back to Alenin's body. But the snow was still heavy and now he was going uphill and his path was longer than Antonov's because it wound back through the trees.

The bobbing flashlight Kazakov had been tracking suddenly dropped to the ground. Although there was no outcry—Antonov was far too cagey to alert an adversary to his whereabouts—Kazakov knew that he had lost the race.

He crept forward. By the glow, Antonov had set the flashlight down in the snow and was on his knees examining his partner. If he was doing that, there was a good chance that he had holstered his weapon. From behind, and with an element of surprise and his greater height, Kazakov could probably take him. Silence was certainly better than using his weapon; the gunshot would bring everyone running.

One step forward. Another. Kazakov edged behind Antonov as he checked Alenin's pulse and released his bonds.

Bent under branches, Kazakov gathered himself to leap. The snow shifted under him, sending him sideways against a branch. The frozen tree limb cracked like a gunshot.

Kazakov threw himself. Antonov leapt up, whirled, fumbling for his weapon.

Kazakov slammed into Antonov's side, grabbing for the pistol. It went off and the sound burned a hole in the silence. Something hot slammed through his side, stealing his breath and his limbs went weak.

The pistol swung toward him again. He slammed his fist into Antonov's face. The pistol wavered and he grabbed its hot metal. Grabbed Antonov's thick gun hand, jerked and twisted, and felt-heard something give. Antonov roared.

Tearing the pistol from Antonov's hand, Kazakov tossed it away. He slammed his fist into Antonov's face again. Again. Again. Antonov slumped under him and went still. Panting, Kazakov stood over him.

Shouts came from downhill. Two flashlights bobbed up the lane. Kazakov stepped free of Antonov's body, turned, and ran.

Into the trees, his breath burning his lungs and something burning his side. The night was very cold and he knew he needed help but there was none to be had. They'd mount a search for him, so he had to keep going. It would work in his favor, actually. It would lure them away from Maria and Agafya Ryabkov's dacha. He headed farther uphill toward the mountains.

It was the pain that finally stopped him—that and the now knee-deep snow. He doubled over beside a tree where a large eagle owl sat in a crook of a branch. The bird took flight silently as he tried to listen to the pursuit over his ragged gasps for breath. Night was lifting its dark wings from the sky, leaving only the feathers of darkness under the trees.

His breath steamed around him. Steam came off his side and a crust of frozen red had formed down the side of his coat. He unbuttoned the coat to inspect the damage and inhaled the reek of iron.

Blood and sweat soaked his sweater and the top of his trousers. When he shifted, more blood seeped out of a deep hole in his side. His shirt and sweater were packed into it. And there wasn't a damn thing he could do about it other than seek help.

Or get caught. He legs felt weak enough that he wasn't sure how much longer he could keep going.

His breath slowed and he focused on listening. The wind rustled in the tree tops and sent snow sliding and thumping down from branches. Above him the eagle owl cried, but otherwise there was only the sound of his heartbeat and of blood pounding in his ears.

In this silence, he would hear any pursuers' voices. Had they actually given up? Not particularly efficient of them.

But then maybe they thought he'd die out of here of his wounds. Or maybe they hadn't come for him...

Maria.

Swearing, he started down the hill, following his blood-spotted trail back the way he'd come. The breeze picked up, sifting snow off the trees down over his head and shoulders, freezing his face and dusting his clothing. He finally reached the spot where the pursuit had apparently stopped. Three men had been here, by the different treads on the boots. Most likely two who he had seen around the dacha and another from the second vehicle. They had either decided he wasn't worth the effort to pursue further or something had drawn them back.

And if there had been four men in the first vehicle, he doubted that there was only one in the second.

He reached the dacha when it was still early morning. The weak winter sun angled across the snow revealing the pattern of many footprints. There were no strange vehicles present and no sign of his attackers. The Perseus was still there, but someone had stabbed both front tires. It wasn't going anywhere soon.

There was no smoke from the dacha's chimney, but that didn't mean no one was waiting. Carefully, he approached from the rear past the Perseus. There were no windows here for anyone to see him. Close by the walls he stopped to listen, but there were none of the soft thumps and bumps that came with footfall in the dacha. Perhaps it was uninhabited, or perhaps whoever waited was perfectly quiet. It was possible, if an unusual skill.

From the rear of the house he skirted down the side to one of the windows that flanked the front door. He eased up on the first step and leaned up to peer through the window corner—pulled back.

From what he could see, no one was there. He pulled out his pistol and peered around the clearing. If someone was here, surely they would have finished him off by now. He crept up the stairs and yanked open the door. Then sidestepped inside to keep his profile small. No one was there.

The place had been tossed, all his evidence torn from the wall. The photocopy of Yekaterina lay on the floor beneath the woodstove. He had to believe the rest of his evidence was burned. From the darkness under the bed came a plaintive mew and Koshka pushed a black nose out to him.

"I know. I know. I am worried for Maria, too." He needed to be away after her, but he had to take care of his wound or he'd be no good for anyone. He just had to pray that she'd made it to safety and that the men had not found her trail.

He didn't want to think about the fact that they'd turned back without finishing him off.

He went to the sink and washed his hands, then roughly pulled off his coat and stripped off off his blood-soaked clothing.

The wound oozed red. A slightly larger wound on his back showed where the bullet had gone right through. It had cut through the extra flesh he had gained from too many years of sausages and good brown bread since Annushka had left off cooking for him, but the bullet seemed to have missed anything vital. He would live but it hurt like hell. A cleansing with alcohol had him swearing and knocking back a long pull of vodka straight from the bottle. Then he found a bandage from his first aid kit and covered the wound. It still hurt, but it was the best he could do and at least he'd stopped the worst of the bleeding. He hoped. What was going on inside his flesh he had no idea.

He straightened and groaned at the tug of torn flesh, but dug in drawers for clean clothing and pulled them on. The others were ruined.

His coat he rinsed in the sink and watched the blood swirl red down the drain. He wrung it out as best he could and pulled the coat back on. Feet back in his boots, he fed Koshka her tinned food and put out the bag of kibble for free choice, gave her a pat, and went out to fix the Perseus. Thankfully, he had enough spares in the lean-to on the back of the dacha. An hour and a half later and sweating profusely in the cold, he had four intact tires. He climbed in and collapsed, shivering, back in his seat. A trickle of warmth down his side said the bleeding had started again, but there was no help for it. He had to make sure Maria was safe. The Perseus's engine roared to life. Time to collect Maria and find somewhere else else to hide. Koshka would fend for herself and if he didn't come back, the little cat could escape out her cat door and feed on mice. She'd been a feral when she came to him. The cat door had been a compromise to keep her with him.

He rumbled cautiously down the lane to the road. The plow had finally passed by, leaving a huge drift blocking his lane. He drove the Perseus right through it and headed down to Agafya Ryabkov's turn-off. Instead of plowing through the drifted-in driveway, he parked the Perseus at the side of the road and hiked in, ignoring the pain at every movement. There were no tracks in the driveway, so that was good. Antonov and company hadn't paid a visit to Agafya's place so Maria should be waiting.

In the clearing, the place looked immensely peaceful, the stone and log walls gone honey-colored in the sun. A spiral of blue smoke rose straight up from the chimney. The wind had died down. Thankfully, there was no sign that anyone else had been here this morning, but then the snowfall last night had most likely helped to fill in Maria's tracks.

He climbed the stairs and knocked, closing his eyes at the thought of seeing Maria again.

"Who is it?" Agafya's querulous voice came through the stout door.

"It's me, Kazakov. I've come for Maria."

There was silence a moment. "There's no Maria here." The old woman had to be hiding her.

"Agafya Ryabkov, this is Alexander Kazakov, your neighbor. Maria is my friend. I sent her here last night for safety. Surely she came."

The door opened an inch and the old woman peered out, eyes glittering. "When I say there's no Maria here, I mean it. What were you thinking, sending a stranger to my house?"

What indeed. By the suspicion on her face, even if Maria had come there was every chance the old woman would have turned her away. His heart started pounding. If Maria wasn't here, where was she?

"Did someone knock on your door last night?" He turned from her to scan the yard and saw the truth. Only his footprints crossed the pristine layer of new snow. What he'd thought of as good news at the lack of faint indentations in the snow was actually a scarier truth: Maria hadn't come here.

He looked back at Agafya. "If a woman comes named Maria, please take her in and keep her safe. I will be back for her."

He plunged down her stairs and back to the road, climbed back into the Perseus, and reversed back to his lane.

Had she gotten misdirected in the dark? Was she still walking, exhausted, through the forest? In this cold that was dangerous.

Fighting the pain stitching his side, he followed the Perseus's track up the lane and found the place where he and Maria had set out through the trees. There were three sets of boot prints over theirs.

He swore. He never should have left her alone.

Dreading what he would find, he pushed on through the woods, the sunlight placing bright bands of light and shadow over his vision. His breath steamed. His vision misted. His side throbbed and his legs wobbled. He needed to rest. He needed to eat, but he kept going until he reached the spot where his path branched off. A pair of tracks overlaid his.

He'd been lucky, because he'd had no idea someone was in pursuit. If they had come upon him while he was hunting Alenin and Antonov, he could have ended up with more than a bullet through his side.

A single large set of prints followed Maria's trail.

He followed, noting how Maria's strides had lengthened, though they were still not as long as her pursuer's strides. She knew she was being followed and she was trying to escape. Then her path split, one of her tracks clearly heading for the road, while the other went forward. The snow around the forward path indicated that she had backtracked and turned aside to the road.

Kazakov stopped. What the hell had she done?

He followed the forward track and then backtracked as she had done. What had she seen that would make her do this?

He stood at the spot where she'd turned aside. The snow was deep here. Had she thought the road would give her more speed? If so, why the few strides ahead and then backtrack? She could have just turned toward the road.

In the panic of last night for her to do this spoke of either great confusion or purpose. Cautiously, he retraced her forward path to the turnback point. There had to be some reason. Something that had turned her back last night.

A gunshot? The sound would have carried but surely concern for him wouldn't have turned her around to face the man chasing her. He stopped in the tiny clearing where she had reversed her direction and turned around, studying her footprints to get a sense of her actions. In the sunlight and shadows there were so many prints it was almost as if she was masking her tracks, laying confusion upon confusion as if she didn't know what to do.

But most of the tracks congregated on one side of the clearing.

To hide intent there?

He scanned the brush but there was no sign of a hidden track continuing. He turned back to the clearing. Or were the heavy tracks to draw attention away from elsewhere. He crossed the clearing and peered into the brush.

No trail showed, but only visible because of the angle of the sun was a rectangular slot in the snow. He reached in a gloved hand and pulled out the data machine. His legs gave and he thumped down in the snow.

"Aah, Maria." He bowed his head. She'd known this was important so she'd wasted time hiding the damn thing, thereby risking herself.

He staggered up, feeling suddenly exhausted, and retraced his steps back to where her path cut to the road. He followed, dreading finding her body in the snow.

Through the trees he followed the signs. Maria's stride was a staggering stumble and half fall against the trees as she tried to outrun the man behind her. A snow angel where she'd fallen. A tree cleared of snow where she'd bumped it.

And then the trees parted and the plowed road appeared, but on the side of the drift were the signs of what had happened. A flurry of flattened snow and deep indentations that caught the sun and shadows. Someone had been pushed into the snow in a caricature of a snow angel, on either side the indentation of knees.

There was blood in the snow where the angel's head had been.

12

With the pain radiating out from his side, the world was a distant concept that he could not quite grasp as he steered the Perseus down the slope from the mountains. Maria had been captured and Antonov and Alenin were part of it, though he could not fathom why. He would make them tell him where she was.

The open steppe, the houses that devoured the open fields, played across his windscreen like the latest movie. It was there, but not really. All a dream. All a dream just like Fergana was a dream. The dream of a people and New Moscow was his nightmare, because Maria had been taken and he'd promised to protect her. And failed. He'd failed in so much in his life. Failed to live up to his father's expectations by being too bookish, even though he had joined the police force. Failed his marriage. Failed to find Yekaterina and Semetai's killer. He could not fail in this.

Beside him in the still freezing vehicle, even though the hot breath of the heater filled his face, lay the damnable data machine still wrapped in its protective leather. What was protecting Maria?

She had given herself for this machine and it was not a good trade.

The streets of New Moscow were filled with sunlight glinting like knife blades on snow. Antonov and Alenin. They would know where

Maria was being held. The concrete streets filled with a film of dark snow. Frost covered the edges of the Perseus's windshield as he pulled into the curb as close to the police station as he dared.

He sat for a moment, inhaling the stale scent of wet wool and old blood and preparing himself for the confrontation. Then he secreted the data machine under the front seat and stuffed his emergency blanket in after it. Opening the door, he climbed out. It took a moment to steady himself on the side of the Perseus. His legs were watery. His feet too many thousand feet below him.

But his pistol was in his pocket and he knew where he was going. He struck out around the vehicle and down the sidewalk. The ten steps up to the station's front door were a cliff face he scaled. Through the doors, he focused on not staggering across to the secure inner door. The officer on guard recognized him and let him in so that he could reach the elevator. When he faced forward before the doors closed, there were too many people looking at him.

The doors slid closed and he slumped against the wall as the elevator lifted him to the third floor. When the door dinged open, he straightened and stepped into the squad room.

Old tea and sweat and a little bit of iron fear scented the air as he scanned those present. Blond Pavel Chelomeyev and Sherepov, his trainer and partner, looked up from their desks by the wall. They stopped their discussion. Then Detektivs Razin and Pogolin stepped out of the coffee room. Both stopped dead when they saw him.

"Jeezus, Kazakov," Chelomeyev said. "What the hell happened? That looks like blood."

"Are you okay?" Razin asked.

Kazakov looked down at himself. The bandage job he had done was clearly insufficient. Fresh blood gleamed wetly through the thickness of his black wool coat. He felt dizzy for a moment and braced a leg against a desk.

"Where're Antonov and Alenin?" His voice was a rough growl.

"Out on a case at Yekaterina Park," Chelomeyev said.

Kazakov felt his heart miss a beat. He turned to leave.

"Kazakov! Wait! Let me call you a doctor!" Chelomeyev called.

Kazakov stabbed the elevator door and it slid open. Chelomeyev came after him, but the door thankfully slid closed.

Down the three floors and he squared his shoulders. He knew he wasn't thinking straight but he had to get to Yekaterina Park. Something about the location filled him with ill-ease. He shook himself. He had to find and confront Antonov and Alenin. Demand that they tell him where Maria was. Do whatever was necessary to get Maria released. He'd trade the damned data machine if it would do the trick.

The walk to the Perseus was miles farther than he'd thought. He climbed in and slumped behind the wheel, wishing he could just go to sleep. But Maria needed him. He started the vehicle and pulled out into traffic so abruptly that brakes squealed and horns blared at him. He steered the Perseus through traffic far faster than he should, turning onto the quiet streets that fronted the park and the Red Veil. Red and blue lights flashed at the end of the treed park. The coroner was there and uniformed police. He accelerated down past the false quiet of the Red Veil and came to a stop on top of the curb behind the coroner's van.

Antonov and Alenin. He staggered out of the Perseus, feeling drunk with rage, betrayal, and pain. Where were they? The wind off the mountains rattled tree branches together like bones. Two uniformed officers stood aside smoking, much as they had when Collin Archer's body had been found. Khalil Khan stood beside the cloth-covered body, making notes on a clipboard.

In his heart he knew it would be Maria.

He lurched over to Khan. "What happened?"

He leaned down to shift the cloth, but Khan knocked his hand away.

Khan looked him up and down. "What happened to you?"

Kazakov waved the question away. "Who is it? Is it the woman?"

By the size of the body, it looked like it.

Khan must have read the fear Kazakov felt. The M.E. hesitated. "Where's Antonov? Alenin?" Kazakov demanded.

"I don't know." Khan shook his head, his gaze apparently held by Kazakov's bloody clothing. "They left when I arrived."

Kazakov looked down at the tarp-covered body and thought he might be sick.

No Antonov or Alenin to be found. None to be confronted. Kazakov felt his strength unraveling. He glanced down at the body. Another to be added to the rolls of Yekaterina Park's dead. The tsarina who had left a trail of bodies across Asia was still doing so here.

"What have you got?" he asked softly, fighting back his fear and urgency. He carefully erased his emotions from his face and nodded at the carefully shrouded figure in the snow.

"Woman. Maybe thirty. Beaten to death."

His knees threatened to give way and he staggered. Khan caught his arm.

"I need to see," Kazakov said, bracing himself.

Khan frowned. "Perhaps not. It is not—pretty."

Swallowing, Kazakov nodded and Khan bent to twitch the tarp off the face.

Maria.

Kazakov groaned and felt the tears well. He dug at his eyes with finger and thumb because he should not feel this ball of tangled emotion clotting his chest. He barely knew her and yet he knew her too well, her sun-kissed olive flesh gone gray in the snow and battered with bruises. The flesh was split on her brow, blood pooled in her gaze. Her refined nose was twisted sideways from a horrible blow. Her sweet lips mashed and pulped.

He started to fall, but Khan caught him. "What the hell's going on, Detektiv?" His hand slid Kazakov's coat open and slipped inside, then pulled out again, full of blood. "Allah save us." He scanned their surroundings. "You need a hospital."

Kazakov shook his head.

Khan's mouth pressed into an unhappy line. "Then at least let me look at your wound. I'll drive you to the hospital."

Kazakov shook his head again. He was not leaving his vehicle here. If he went with Khan, it would only be for a bandage and then he would continue his search for his two fellow officers. He turned toward the Perseus and staggered, only Khan's quick steadying hand stopping him from falling.

"You can't possibly drive yourself."

"I can drive." It was a promise. An oath for Maria. But could he really? He felt like collapsing. His legs felt weak. And a terrible anger surged through him, heating his blood. Antonov and Alenin. They would pay for Maria five-fold.

Khan resignedly guided him back to the Perseus. "I shouldn't let you do this. I should be calling you an ambulance. Now listen: you will follow me to the hospital, do you understand? You will follow me and we will deal with your wound."

"And her. Maria." Kazakov looked back at the body. Leaving her here, so close to the Red Veil had to be a message. But why, when they could have used her as a trading point to get the data machine. Unless —did they not know he had found it? Or did they know and was this a warning of what would happen to him if he did not return it? But return it to who? The Chinese embassy?

"It is the woman I delivered to you," Khan said.

Khan pulled the vehicle's door opened and tsked at the bloody seat. Kazakov slid inside and lay his head back. "Her name is Maria di Maria. She was a witness in the Collin Archer case. I was protecting her until they came for us last night."

"Is that when you were shot?"

Not opening his eyes Kazakov nodded. It was so tempting to sleep. So tempting to just curl up in a ball and admit defeat. "There was evidence taken from this crime scene," said Khan.

"There was evidence of a fight and the perpetrator left something behind this time—unlike Collin Archer."

Kazakov opened his eyes and sat up. "Like what?"

Khan shook his head. "A hat like the one you're wearing, except far newer." He slammed the Perseus's door shut and rapped on the roof. Attendants were already carrying Maria's body to the wagon and Khan climbed into the coroner's van. It pulled out and Kazakov started the Perseus, wincing as the vehicle thunked down off the curb.

Overhead a film of cloud was dampening the sun, and the mountains were fading into a gray distance. All except Yekaterina's mountain.

The Perseus's cab filled with a sound like engines and he scanned the sky, just as he had done so many times in his life, for signs the final battle had begun. There was nothing there, but something was coming. He knew it as surely as he knew Baba Yaga would likely figure in a Russian fairy tale. He accelerated down the snowy street to catch up, and Yekaterina Park, the scene of so much death, fell behind.

If Antonov and Alenin thought that leaving Kazakov's hat at the scene would stop him, they didn't understand who they were dealing with. He would put things right with Antonov and Alenin in his own final battle. But first he needed Khan's help—and not the way the little M.E. thought.

Traffic increased as he careened unsteadily through the roundabouts onto and then off of Suvarov until he found himself at Our Lady Yekaterina Hospital. He sat in the parking lot, resting his forehead against his hands on the wheel. His hands shook. His legs felt weak. But he had no time for such things. He pulled the data machine out from under the seat, shoved the Perseus' door open, and stepped out into the shuddering cold. Khan stood waiting by the stairs down to the morgue. Kazakov limped over and refused Khan's help down and inside.

The receptionist's eyes were black sparks that took in too much of him. By the downturn of her lips, there wasn't much she approved of.

"There are calls for you," she said to Khan, as if to remind him he had duties beyond his troublesome companion.

Khan collected the slips and then led Kazakov down the hall to his office. Inside, Khan slid off his heavy winter coat and pulled on his white physician's coat. He looked neat and tidy, his darker skin counterpoint to the white of the cloth.

"Care to tell me what the hell's going on? Why are people shooting at you?"

Kazakov only slumped in a chair and winced. When he looked up, Khan was studying him.

Finally, the M.E. sighed. "Let me look at your wound."

"Not why I'm here." Kazakov leaned forward and placed the leather-wrapped data machine on Khan's desk. "I need your help with this."

Khan shook his head. "We'll get to that. You're gray as a hospital sheet, and believe me, gray is not your color. By the look of your coat, you're bleeding and you've been bleeding for a while."

Kazakov looked down at his side, and damnation, there *was* more blood seeping through the thick wool. "But I bandaged it."

"Not good enough, it would seem. Now stand up and let me see how bad it is."

"Most doctors would provide a me with a place to lie down," Kazakov mumbled.

"Most doctors don't work with living patients in the morgue." Khan grabbed Kazakov's arm and proved himself surprisingly strong, hauling Kazakov up out of the chair. He groaned and leaned on the desk as Khan helped him remove his coat.

"So, what has that thing on my desk got to do with you being shot?" Khan asked as he studied Kazakov's bloody shirt and trousers. He hauled the shirt up and found the blood-soaked bandage. Tsked. When Kazakov didn't answer, Khan met Kazakov's gaze. "By the look of this, you need an emergency physician, not the coroner. Yet."

"I'm not going anywhere where I might be reported. They would have finished me if they could have found me. They probably thought I bled to death in the mountains—until I kindly informed them otherwise by going into the office." He shook his head at his stupidity.

"So instead you came to my crime scene to die? Am I supposed to be flattered?" Khan shook his head. "As if my situation isn't already tenuous enough. There are parties in the hospital administration who do not trust a Muslim doctor—even for the dead."

Kazakov steadied himself on the desk because the room was spinning. "I didn't come looking for you. I was looking for Antonov and Alenin."

He saw understanding flare in Khan's dark eyes.

"And now she is dead and I *will* find them. I need your help with that." He tilted his head at the desk. "I came for that, not the kindness of your medical help." Yet he held still for Khan's examination.

"And yet without medical help you are not going to be able to do anything about anything else." Khan shook his head. "Stay here."

He left the office and returned after ten minutes with a basin of warm water, a pail, and a stack of bandages. "Sorry I took so long. You'd be surprised how difficult it is to find bandages in the medical examiner's office. Now sit on the desk and take the shirt off."

Kazakov did as bid and out of the pail Khan produced a set of scissors and expertly cut free the sodden bandage. The wound was ugly in the fluorescent light, pulsing with blood with each movement and each breath.

Khan inspected it and the wound in Kazakov's back. "A through and through gunshot."

"Pistol." Kazakov said through clenched teeth. Even the air's touch hurt.

"You washed it?"

"Tried to. Used some vodka to disinfect it."

Khan frowned. "Not too effective."

"It was good vodka."

Khan looked up at him and actually grinned. "Well, this is going to hurt like hell, because we don't normally need local anesthetics in this department. I suggest you prepare yourself."

"You're enjoying this just a little too much."

Khan swabbed away the worst of the blood to inspect the wound, then used a squeeze bottle to spray clear water. Pain shot through Kazakov's side and up to the top of his head. He gripped the corner of the desk and clenched his teeth as Khan applied fiery antiseptic and then poked and prodded. He pulled strands of dark sweater wool from inside the opening.

"Better to do this now than close the wound and let it fester," Khan said as Kazakov groaned.

"It doesn't feel any better knowing that."

"There. Done. Just consider yourself damned lucky that the bullet didn't do anything but notch your love handles." Khan threaded a circular needle and did quick, neat sutures to close the wounds on Kazakov's front and back. Each small stitch sent a sharp blade of pain through Kazakov's head. The wound burned as Khan smacked white bandages on and wrapped them around Kazakov's waist to hold them. "No more gun battles and no revenge for a few days. You need to rest."

He went around his desk and pulled out an ancient prescription pad. Grimaced. "Not too much use for such a thing here, but it comes with the coat."

He wrote something indecipherable and then tore the page off the pad and handed it to Kazakov. "Antibiotics. I suggest you take them." Then he let his gaze drop to the leather-wrapped rectangle on his desk. "Now, what's this?"

Kazakov heaved himself unsteadily off the corner of the desk to pull on his blood-stained shirt and slump in the chair across from Khan.

"I'm not sure what to do with that. I figured you had more experience." He dipped his head at the data machine console in the corner of the room. "You know how to use that far better than I do. I thought maybe you could figure out what this is."

Kazakov reached forward, intending to uncover the machine, but the sutures pulled too tight and stopped him.

Khan waved him away and unfolded the leather. When he was done, the metal carapace of the machine gleamed dully in the middle of his desk.

"What is it?"

"Open it and see. The top is hinged at the back."

Khan found the edge of the top and lifted it open. His brown gaze widened and he glanced at Kazakov, then bent over the machine. "Are you telling me this is a data machine?"

"You tell me. You're the expert. I can barely key in a name in the squad room. There's a button at the top that seems to turn it on."

Khan gingerly pushed the button and a low hum filled the room. "Allah protect us," he swore softly as the screen flickered on and placed a green glow on Khan's skin.

He touched a pair of keys, and the machine beeped. Khan jerked back.

"It's clearly a machine, but I know nothing about its workings. I can do queries on my office machine, but that's because I was taught how. You need someone with far more skill than me. A programmer, I think they are called."

Kazakov slumped in his chair. "Listen, that woman in the park. She gave her life to protect this evidence. I need to find out why it's so important, and hopefully that information will lead me to whoever killed its owner and Maria. If you can't help me, who can?"

Khan steepled his long fingers and thought for a moment. "There are men in the government…"

"No government. They may be involved. And no AngloTec either."

"You suspect them also?" Khan said.

It was so hard to know. Kazakov shook his head. "Them. The Chinese. The Ottomans. Any of them could have had reason to kill Collin Archer—and others."

Khan went still, his gaze assessing. "This is still about the girl, isn't it? That Yekaterina Weber. And the Manas boy?"

Kazakov looked away uneasily, scanning the various government policy bulletins pinned to the bulletin board by the office door.

"No. Yes. Maybe. I don't know. Perhaps."

Again, the barest inkling of a smile crossed Khan's lips. "You and your definitive answers. I think I've missed you, old friend. Even if you bring problems like a plague of locusts."

Kazakov sighed. "Part of my charm. So, can you help me?"

Khan placed his hands palm down on either side of the offending machine as if he was a psychic conducting a reading. "I can make a suggestion, but you may not like it."

He waited for Kazakov's nod before continuing.

"A few months ago, I was at a conference and at lunch I was seated beside a fellow from the United States of America embassy. We got to talking about changes in our work and he was very excited about technology. He had worked for a time with the Anglo-Germans as a data programmer, but had since returned to his home in a place called

Charleston to work with a large research firm. Apparently, the Americans are presenting themselves as a hotbed of technological development. He is here as part of the delegation making overtures to our government about building closer alliances. He may have the expertise to help you."

An American. One of those who approved of slavery.

Kazakov sighed. It had been eight hours since Maria disappeared and probably not much less since she died and yet it felt like years. His failure weighed his shoulders. Was agreeing to deal with such a man simply one more failure and erosion of his morals?

"How long will it take to set up a meeting?" he asked wearily.

Khan picked up his phone and dug in his top desk drawer for a card before dialing the number.

Someone must have answered almost immediately.

"This is Khalil Khan. We spoke not long ago." He nodded. "The pleasure is mutual. It was an enjoyable meal." His gaze met Kazakov's and there was calculation there. "I—I have a friend here who you simply must meet. He's brought me a toy that is, I think, unique. Interested?" He nodded and mmh-hmmed a few times. "We are at my office at the hospital. Where should we meet?"

Kazakov looked up. "The library. The tables at the back of the first floor. It is public there." And yet quiet. The same area that Natania Bure had frequented.

Khan relayed the location "We will see you in a little while."

He hung up and turned to Kazakov. "He will meet us there in twenty minutes."

Kazakov looked at his watch. "There are people out there laughing because they think they have silenced everyone. I need to show them they are wrong."

Khan steepled his fingers under his chin. "Revenge does not look good on you, friend. It is a demon that has plagued my people for a thousand years and yet we have not learned the lesson. Revenge eats you from within and leaves a living carcass behind. Is that what you want?"

"A living carcass—isn't that all that's left of Fergana? We all walk and talk, but really, we live in a purgatory dreaming of a great past and what might have been. We're nothing more than a façade in this country and our enemies know it and take advantage. Hell, from what you say, even those upstart Americans come here to feed on us."

"Or make us greater. You do not know."

It was a bare fifteen minutes before Kazakov found himself and Khan seated at a table in a corner of the library's first floor. They had taken Kazakov's Perseus with Kazakov driving, though Khan had clutched the door handle the entire way. The library was busy enough on the main floor, with patrons coming and going, but at the rear, an area usually preferred by students after school, the time of day had the place largely empty. It was good because anyone paying too much attention to their impromptu meeting could easily be identified.

Promptly five minutes later, Khan stood at the approach of a man unlike anyone Kazakov had seen before. Kazakov considered what it meant that Khan could get such a quick response from this almost stranger. What did that tell him about his old friend?

The stranger was tall like Kazakov, at least six feet two, but with a ramrod straight back that made him seem taller. So did the tall, wide-brimmed hat he wore that held a layer of snow on its gently curled felt brim. A coat much like Kazakov's minus the blood, and a pair of pointy-toed boots that had been tooled in opulent curls and leaf patterns completed the ensemble. Not exactly the sort of thing that would work well in the snow and cold of Fergana, but the man probably didn't plan to be in the country that long.

"Eric. Welcome." Khan held out his hand and the two men shook. "I'd like you to meet my friend, Detektiv Alexander Kazakov of the Fergana police. Kazakov, this is Eric Clinton of the American Embassy." Kazakov lumbered to his feet and swayed. "Eric, Kazakov has brought me a little problem that I thought you might be more adept at solving." He tapped the machine on the table beside him.

Clinton cooly looked Kazakov up and down; his blue gaze clearly registered Kazakov's bloodied wool coat, but the expression smoothed swiftly away again. Here was a man who guarded his reaction like a lesser man might protect his gold.

"You will please pardon my condition. There are people who are less than happy with my investigations," Kazakov said and sat down heavily again.

Eric Clinton had a ruddy, outdoorsman's face shaved smooth—as opposed to the usual five o'clock shadow most Russian men sported. He shook Kazakov's hand with an impressive grip, made more impressive by the rough work calluses on his fingers and palms. Then the newcomer went around the table to Khan's side. He stopped dead when he saw the screen Khan had exposed in the data machine.

"Holy hell. What is that?" He shook his head. "No. I know what it is. I've heard of them, but I've never seen one. Where the hell did you get it?"

His Russian came out with a nasal twang that made much of what he said almost indecipherable.

Khan waved him in Kazakov's direction and Eric Clinton looked at him expectantly.

"It was found hidden amongst a murder victim's belongings." Not quite true, but it gave a flavor of where it had been located.

"Do you mind?" Clinton eased into Khan's chair and pulled the little machine closer, scanning the screen as if the chicken scratch of Chinese figures, hashtags, and numbers meant something. He leaned over the keys tentatively pecking, then picking up speed.

Kazakov heaved himself up and around the table to peer over Clinton's shoulder. Then the dark screen cleared to light blue with a list written in another language.

"What is it?" Kazakov asked as he leaned closer to scan down the unfamiliar writing.

"A menu of records."

"What language?" he asked.

"English," Khan and Clinton said in unison.

Clinton whistled. "There's a hell of a lot here." He glanced up at Kazakov. "Who did you say this murder victim was?"

He clicked on one of the names and the screen shimmered and changed.

It held copies of letters. Clinton leaned in close and then swore.

The letter was in Russian, correspondence between the small Fergana defense department and the department of agriculture regarding the lease of a large tract of prime farm land for an installation. It discussed how to go about shifting the large population of Kyrgyz farmers and referenced negotiations between Fergana's government and the Ottomans.

"What's an installation?" Khan asked.

Clinton sat back in his chair. "I'd say probably weapons. It sounds like someone in your government is finally choosing sides. Shit." He shook his head. "We were hoping Fergana might be interested in forming an alliance of independent nations."

"One department of government does not necessarily speak for all Fergana," Khan said softly.

Clinton looked back at the data machine and closed that file to open another. This one had documentation filled with Chinese characters. Clinton closed the file and looked up at Kazakov with the file menu still on screen.

"It looks like your boy's been very busy. Ottoman information. Chinese, too. Just who was this guy?"

Kazakov stopped scanning the menu, his attention caught by one word closer to the screen bottom.

"Open that one." He pointed.

"Bure?" Clinton tapped on the keys and suddenly the screen changed again.

An image of a newspaper article filled the screen. It was a headline article.

Tragic Accident Kills Leading Family.

Kazakov remembered the event, if not the article. It was part of the Boris Bure mystique. Bure and his family had been traveling back from a holiday in the mountains when their car left the road. When their vehicle was finally discovered, the driver, mother, father, and two sisters were dead. Seventeen-year-old Bure was gone and had apparently wandered off into the mountains.

Clinton scrolled down and a second article came up, this one screaming that Bure had been found after four long weeks in the mountains—further story to follow.

Clinton kept scrolling down through an interview with Bure talking about his miraculous winter survival in only city clothing, to the next article.

It wasn't a headline, but the typical type of article you would find inside the paper and below the fold.

Prestigious School Student Questioned in Rape.

The article was brief and named no names, but said that a senior student at New Moscow's premier education center was being interviewed as a suspect in the rape of an eleven-year-old female student from nearby Education Center #5. The girl was still in hospital due to emotional and physical trauma.

There was nothing else in the record but the date— approximately thirty years ago.

Clinton looked up at him again. "This means something to you."

A statement not a question, but Kazakov nodded. "So, who was your victim?"

Kazakov glanced at Khan, who gave an almost imperceptible nod. He had already trusted this stranger with so much.

It was telling as well that Khan knew this Eric Clinton well enough to judge.

But who else was there? The evidence was too broad and too vague and yet something he had seen niggled in the back of his brain.

Biting back a groan from the pain, he returned to his chair across the table and sank down. The first floor of the library was quiet with just a few voices coming from students who had taken possession of the far corner and the drone of the check-out kiosks out front. "When we first found him, we thought he was simply a homeless man. Investigation indicated that his name was Collin Archer, but he may have been far more than a manager at AngloTec."

Clinton ran his fingers around the rim of the small machine.

"A spy, you mean. This is the data machine of a spy."

Kazakov nodded and checked over his shoulder. "He also had this. Can you tell us what it is?" He hauled out the small plastic stick and placed it on the desk in its baggie. Let it carry the answer to Maria's murder—to all the murders.

Collin eyed it. "What is it?"

"No idea."

Clinton picked up the bag. "You ever seen anything like this?" he said to Khan.

The M.E. shook his head thoughtfully, but then his gaze brightened. "May I see it?"

Clinton gave it to him and Khan turned the device over in his hands. "I'm almost sure of it…" He looked at Kazakov. "If you read my report, you saw the bit about the odd flap of skin I found on the victim."

"It was on Archer's left side—a small flap of skin about two inches long and an inch wide," Kazakov said.

Khan nodded and held up the small rectangle in the bag. "I think it just might fit, don't you?" He shook his head. "If we were still at my office we could check."

Kazakov and Clinton bent closer to look at the device. It was virtually the same size as the small flap of skin.

"But what is this thing?" Clinton took the baggy back to examine the device.

"It fits into the side of the data machine," Kazakov said.

"What?" Clinton and Khan rounded on him. Kazakov nodded and wished for his bed. His knees felt like rubber and his vision was like murky glass.

"When I found it, I realized it had prongs that fit into a socket on the side of the machine."

Khan pulled the small device from the baggie and Clinton plugged the little device in.

The screen shivered. The machine beeped and then the screen went dark again.

Clinton's fingers danced over the keys once more and this time a different list came up. Two items, both with names that meant nothing to Kazakov. He shook his head but Clinton sat back, satisfied, then leaned forward and touched another key.

The screen cleared again, this time bringing up a new list of items.

"Your device carries other information." He tapped the little rectangular device. "With this kind of technology, your man could have been transferring intelligence to his associates almost unnoticed. It wouldn't take much. A drop in a coat pocket. A handshake. A hug. The information could exchange hands. By the look of this list, a lot of it, too."

"Or a man could transport such a device across borders in the flap of skin and then place it in his coat pocket for someone else to retrieve," Kazakov said, realizing that he had the information he needed.

"I'm going to leave this with you to keep safe," he said, heaving himself up and heading for the entrance beyond the bookshelves.

"What are you doing? You're in no condition to be going anywhere." Khan came around the table as if to stop him. "Besides, you're my ride."

Kazakov shook his head. "Clinton will have to get you back to the hospital. I'm going to arrest Archer's killer."

13

———————

The Perseus's seat was sticky with old blood as he pulled into the curb in the late afternoon, but that couldn't be helped.

At least Khan's bandage held—or Kazakov thought it did, but he wasn't going to check. Pain throbbed like a fist grinding into his side and the vehicle's heated cab smelled like iron and old meat.

All too bad. So was the cold that ate into his hands and feet and sent shivers through him even though the Perseus's heater chugged warmth.

Across the street the Red Veil sat peacefully, its white façade glowing in the growing dusk and the swirl of the new dusting of snow. Soon the lights in the lower windows would come on and the Ziln limousines would begin to arrive for the evening. The streetlights flicked on in the gathering gloom and he should do what he had come for while he still had the momentum of arrival. It had come to him as they discussed the small data holder.

According to Maria, Archer had shown no interest in sex, but he had gone through the motions as if it was an expectation. But what he had done at each visit was spend time in the dining room listening to the other patrons talking. Those people might change, but there was a constant in his visits beyond his trysts with Maria, who was perfect for him because she was not prone to gossip like the other girls. What better place to pass off his data than a place where it was automatic that all patrons relinquish their coat?

He climbed out of the Perseus and felt his stitches pull. At least the pain had died down to a throbbing ache like a vice crushing his side. Better than the screaming pain it had been. Thankfully, his legs felt solid enough—for the moment.

Unfortunately, his coat and clothing were still crusty with dried blood, but that wasn't going to stop him from what needed to be done. He just wished he knew how Archer's spying linked back to Semetai and Yekaterina's deaths. Was Bure perhaps an unwitting source of the information Archer was trading? Did something in Bure's past allow him to be blackmailed? If Semetai had overheard an exchange of information…

He started up the Red Veil's daunting flight of stairs using the railing as support. By the time he reached the red door he was puffing and he took a moment, peering out into the growing dark where the swirl of flakes was becoming a white veil across the park. The Red Veil and the White—both masked so much darkness. He used the knocker once on the door and once more it pulled open revealing the delicate oriental flower with the secret smile: Prae.

Her eyes widened as she recognized him and then the smile faded away, but not the secrets. Her gaze still held those. Gone were the offer to take his coat and the gentle subservient bow of the head.

"What do you want?" she said. "Frau Zelinka is indisposed."

He stepped past her into the hall, though she tried to block his way. She was dressed in demure scarlet silk with a collar high around her neck and a bodice and skirt that sheathed her body like a blade. Her black hair was coiled in ropes high on her head. "And if I asked to see Maria, would she be indisposed, too? How about Collin Archer, Prae?"

Her gaze flickered for a moment, but then her chin lifted. "Frau Zelinka doesn't want to talk to you."

He grinned down at her. "Amazingly, this time I want to talk to you, Prae. You see, I know what's been going on here. I know what Collin Archer was."

"He was a patron. That is all."

"Not all, Prae. He was a spy and a courier. He brought the data to you and you took it from his pocket each time he came and probably passed it to someone else each time."

Her impassive expression turned to a glare. "I don't have time for this. Clients are coming."

Kazakov grabbed her arm and dragged her into the parlor just off the foyer. It was an opulent room rich with burgundy and dark blue carpets and brocade furniture. Gossamer burgundy veils concealed the corners and oriental incense conveyed the sense that he had stepped into another time and place. An idealized Silk Road, perhaps. A man could imagine himself as Marco Polo, a man of the cold western world experiencing the pleasures of the east for the first time.

"You will tell me who you work for. Who ordered Archer's death? I know he was a spy. I suspect he double-crossed you."

She jerked away. "You know nothing!"

"So tell me." He crossed his arms, but blocked her escape from the room.

"I'll tell you nothing."

Behind him the front door burst open. Kazakov spun around. The unwelcome figures of Antonov and Alenin zeroed in on Kazakov as he fumbled for his weapon. Loss of blood slowed him down. They beat him to their guns and advanced into the room. He should have known. Should have expected. And there was nothing he could do. Barring using Prae as a human shield, they were two and he was one and they were ready for him. Slowly he raised his hands.

Prae stepped past him to Antonov's side.

"Good. You're here." Her voice changed, becoming stronger, and sharp edged. "I told you to get rid of him, and yet he shows up here. What do I pay you for? Do you know what jeopardy everything is in?"

From a simpering apprentice whore, her expression changed and he realized just how wrong he had been. "You run the Red Veil. Frau Zelinka—she's your front, your puppet!"

She turned a haughty expression on him. "That slut's only good for enticing fools like you and Rostoff. Let him think we are just a whorehouse paying our bribes. I have the business sense. I have the loyalty. Unlike that *hún dàn*, Archer, after all the money spent on him."

"He betrayed you."

"All the years of building a web of connections across Asia and he planned to sell out to them—the Ottomans." Her hands curled into fists. "He became too much like the Anglo-Germans."

"It was you who made him look like them, sound like them."

"Think like them, too, apparently. Duplicitous bastard. I should have known when I saw him with Enver Pasha."

"So you had Archer killed. Maybe by your friends, here." He nodded at his fellow detectives, wondering how they had fallen so far. Was it only the money? He'd never have thought it possible of Antonov, who now stirred uneasily where he stood.

She just looked at him. "I am not a fool, Detektiv. I might play one, but I will not provide an admission to you."

She looked at Antonov and Alenin, nodded, and ducked around Kazakov to disappear down the hallway. Both detectives were stone-faced. Then Antonov nodded. Alenin remained inscrutable.

"Alexander Kazakov," Antonov said, but his voice hitched as if he did not like his predicament. "You are under arrest for the murder of a prostitute named Maria di Maria."

"You expect me to simply surrender to you due to some trumped up evidence?" Kazakov asked. He doubted whether he'd ever see the station. It was far more likely that these two would drive him to some quiet spot and take care of a problem.

"Strong evidence." Anontov said, with something akin to regret in his voice. "A fur hat with your name in it left at the scene."

"Of course. Get rid of me officially and you don't need to kill me. Anything I say will be discredited and you can bury me in Fergana's darkest prison. Tell me, just how long have you been working for the Chinese?"

Antonov wouldn't meet his gaze.

"At least we're doing something to help our country. I don't do everything they want. Just the things that will help Fergana resist the bastard Ottomans," Alenin said. "But then you wouldn't understand something as great as taking a stand. Of doing what's necessary to help the greater good. Some people just have to die, sometimes. But you're too bloody impressed with your own reputation as the detective who solves everything. You just couldn't leave well enough alone—even after Antonov warned you."

A swirl of evidence coalesced in Kazakov's brain and he swayed for a moment at what it meant. "You were there. You were the two men with Archer who chased down Semetai Manas. You helped kill him."

Antonov shrugged. "Archer wasn't sure if the kid overheard anything, but then months later he started making threats to important people. Seems he was determined to marry the girl. We couldn't afford to have information leaking out. And then there was the fact that he killed the girl."

Kazakov staggered. It couldn't be true. Semetai had loved Yekaterina. There was no reason to kill her.

Unless there was.

All the figures of the investigation swirled around him and his legs felt weak trying to wade through them.

Antonov caught his shoulder and shoved him into the veil-draped wall. "Sorry, old friend."

Alenin patted him down and confiscated his pistol.

Then Antonov grabbed his hands and twisted them behind his back. From the hallway beyond the parlor came the sound of voices swirling down from the upstairs. Prae must be holding them there until the situation was dealt with and Kazakov was gone. Metal cuffs imprisoned his wrists and he was shoved out of the room and out of the door.

"You should have listened," Antonov murmured.

Kazakov almost fell down the long flight of stairs, but his captors must have taken pity on him. Somehow his wobbly legs got him to the street.

They shoved him in the back of a police vehicle and climbed in. The engine roared to life as he pondered Semetai Manas and what could make him take the life of Yekaterina. The lad had loved her enough to abandon his family's traditional ways. It didn't make sense. But then nothing made sense in this case. Nothing was as it seemed.

A woozy sense of disorientation flowed over him as the car cruised through the streets. It was like a circus parade and he was the prize lion caged for all to see. Surprisingly, instead of taking him to a quiet spot for execution, they pulled into the *politseyshiy* garage, parked, and hauled him out of the vehicle and up the elevator, half dragging him into the squad room. It was surprisingly busy, with two witnesses giving statements at desks and detectives pecking at their typewriters. Young Pavel Chelomeyev froze as he exited the coffee room, two cups of coffee in his hands.

All discussion stopped and all eyes followed him as he was guided through the desks and shoved into an interview room. The door slammed shut behind him and he was alone. He collapsed into a hard wooden chair at the table bolted to the floor in the center of the room. The air tasted of old sweat and stale fear and he knew that a camera was on him. He closed his eyes, visualizing the evidence he had hung on his wall at the dacha, trying to put the pieces together into a new pattern. How did it go?

Yekaterina and Semetai's photos were at the top, their families off to the side. Semetai's parents, his father looking fierce in a traditional fur hat, his mother faded, eyes downcast. On the other side, Boris and Natania Bure. Beneath the photos of the young people had been Collin Archer's death photo. He had been, if not responsible, then closely involved with Semetai's death. Kazakov had considered that he might have been involved in Yekaterina's death too. Somehow that would have been fitting—a spy for the Ottomans and Chinese destroying the latest in a long string of Yekaterinas.

But it didn't fit now. Not if Alenin's off-hand comment had been true.

His memory scanned down the rest of the wall. The Red Veil and Frau Zelinka and Prae. He knew who had killed Collin Archer, or at least who had had him killed. Also at the Red Veil were Maria—killed for what they thought she knew about Archer's death—and the other girls including pale Katya—almost the image of Yekaterina…

It was like he was swimming in Yekaterinas. A tsarina who had destroyed a nation through her greed. A girl's notebook that survived a time of great strife and rose above the ashes. A schoolgirl dead in a park bearing her name and a whore whose face was almost the same.

Too many, and yet. And yet. There was something almost there. Almost aware in his brain. He almost had the connection.

The interview door burst open and Antonov and Alenin came in bearing a large paper evidence bag and a file that they dumped on the table. Antonov slumped into the chair opposite Kazakov while Alenin released Kazakov's hands and then retreated, scowling, to slouch his lanky frame against the wall. Classic interview. Good cop, bad cop.

Kazakov filed away the tingling sensation of almost awareness and returned Antonov's fierce regard. It was classic step one: intimidate the suspect. The only problem was that Kazakov had almost as many years on the other side of the table. The fact he sat here today didn't matter at all. He crossed his arms, waiting.

Like a staring contest where the winner was the one who didn't blink, the power here was in silence. Let the Double A team break the silence first.

Finally, Antonov stirred and flipped open the file, appearing to scan its meager contents. "You know why you are here."

"Enlighten me," Kazakov said.

Antonov didn't look up from the file. "A woman's body was found in the snow in Yekaterina Park. Evidence suggests that you knew her. More evidence suggests that you killed her. Tell us what happened."

"Aren't you supposed to ask me if I would like an advocate present for the interview? Is that right not enshrined in Fergana's constitution?" He asked it mildly, as a training officer would ask a recruit. These two knew better and just chose to forget, though their version of the interview would doubtlessly state that such an advocate had been offered and declined.

"Why would Semetai Manas kill Yekaterina Weber," Kazakov asked. "Everybody says that he loved her. He was risking everything by going against his faith to be with her."

"This isn't about the death of some teenaged slut. This is about the woman in the park," Alenin said.

And the woman in the park was a whore. But why consider the girl a slut? She was in love, yes. In love with a Muslim boy and that would not be popular.

And she was pregnant.

Kazakov straightened as Alenin roused himself from his slouch and crossed to the desk. "Don't play silly bugger with us, Kazakov. We've got the evidence we need. We have your hat at the scene where her body was found and I'll bet forensics will find her fingerprints all over your house."

Kazakov only half-heard the evidence. Surely his theory couldn't be right, but there were the newspaper articles. There was the fact that Boris Bure was even now being groomed to assume leadership of the Reformation Party. How it was all linked to the Red Veil he wasn't sure, but something was there.

"Dammit, Kazakov, we asked you a question!" Antonov pounded his fist on the table and Kazakov started. The clue connections faded, but hung around like wispy chimney smoke vapors amongst the blue trees of winter.

He blinked at his interrogators. "Repeat the question, please."

"Tell us how you came to kill Maria di Maria," Antonov repeated.

Kazakov shook his head. "I wish an advocate to be present."

"Then tell us what you know of this?" Alenin upended the paper evidence bag and out tumbled a furred winter hat Kazakov recognized. The ermine and lynx fur he had chosen himself, matched so the red tipped hairs caught the light. He knew inside would be his name, carefully embroidered by the wife of the tribal man who had crafted the hat.

He glanced up at Antonov and sensed Alenin's leer. They thought they had him. He sat back with his arms crossed and winced as his side burned. "There is more evidence than this and it will not convict me."

"Evidence can disappear, friend. Now tell us what you know," Alenin said, his mouth a grim line.

"I want an advocate."

Antonov leaned over the desk but his expression made Kazakov wonder whether the man's heart was in it. "Tell us how it happened. Was the whore your lover? Was there a lover's spat?"

Kazakov's fingers curled to fists. "I want an advocate."

Antonov glanced up at his partner. "I told you he would not play this game." He leaned over the desk. "Be careful or you will leave us few choices, friend."

Alenin rounded the desk to loom over Kazakov. "All right. We'll call an advocate. In the meantime, we can move you down to cells. There's a lot that can happen in transit."

His breath smelled of a meal of sausage and garlic and Kazakov's empty stomach curdled. There was likely a beating in store for him and there was nothing he could do about it. But as long as he was alive, there was a chance he could come through this. There was a chance he could bring the right people to justice. Alenin hauled him to his feet and Kazakov realized he needed the help. The damned wound had hurt him more than he thought, but he kept his head up as he was pushed out into the squad room. Again, all eyes were on him. Most were neutral. Some resentful of a comrade who would allegedly kill a woman. Pavel Chelomeyev, actually met his gaze and nodded as if he knew the truth of Kazakov's situation. For the youngster's sake, Kazakov hoped he didn't try to intervene.

Beyond the squad room, they took him to the back stairwell that led down to the cells. Prisoners had fallen down these stairs. Some had even broken their necks. Tales of those misadventures that he'd chosen not to believe in the past now took on an additional menace. How many other suspects had been innocent men who had fallen prey to the swirling currents of foreign interference? How many of his comrades were bought and paid for by the Chinese or Ottomans?

He couldn't think of one he would trust—at least not fully. He started down the stairs gripping the stair railing.

"You move like an old man, Kazakov. Don't tell me a little flesh wound has you off your game," Antonov said.

Kazakov tried to move a little faster. Two steps down to the landing. Then two hands found his shoulders and shoved. He stumbled down to the landing, flailing for balance as the hands once more found his back. Another stairway welled ahead.

His fingertips grazed the railing, but missed. He flailed again, slamming down on his shoulder halfway down the staircase. Something cracked as he bumped down the stairs. As momentum sent his hips up over his head, he covered his skull, his neck. Over. Over. Slamming to a stop on his back at the next landing.

Sharp pain in his shoulder. His wound screamed. He groaned and rolled to get up, but a boot found his wounded side and the world came apart.

"That's enough," Antonov growled.

He opened his eyes against the pain as strong hands heaved him up. He tried to get his feet under him, but they didn't want to work.

"Looks like the *'khu i* has just about had it." They dragged him down the last flight of stairs and down the short hall to the basement booking room.

The world swung around him, colored by pain and the knowledge that something was horribly wrong. Yekaterina, Semetai, Collin Archer, Maria. Something about the names. Something about how they fit together. Too many lies and too many truths.

He slumped against the counter as they emptied his pockets. Once upon a time there was something he'd had in his pockets. Something important, but he couldn't recall what. They took it all and half-shoved, half-dragged him down a gray concrete corridor to a cell. The solid door clanged opened with a squeal and they shoved him forward. He staggered in, going to his knees beside a metal cot. The cell door clanged shut.

14

———————

Kazakov lay his battered forehead against the cool metal cot. The cell's chill air smelled of urine and old blood—perhaps his. There was no blanket and the gritty floor radiated cold. For a toilet there was a bucket in the corner—thankfully emptied. Four bare walls. No window. One metal door—locked. Not a particularly helpful situation except it confirmed everything he'd suspected about Antonov and Alenin. They were in this far too deep to ever get out again and they were going to make sure he wasn't around to cause any problems. Fatal accidents in cells were not unheard of and an enquiry after such a death might be easier to rig than an outright murder investigation. They were cleaning up loose ends— just with more subtlety than he would have expected of them.

The beating he'd endured was but an overture. He would never make it to trial. Antonov and Alenin and a woman named Prae would undoubtedly see to it. For a moment he mourned the Antonov he'd known. They might not have been good friends, but there had always been respect between them.

Groaning, he crawled up onto the metal cot and rolled onto his back. The bolt heads from the supporting bars dug into his shoulders. He tried moving the shoulder that had been injured in his fall down the stairs. It hurt like hell, but probably wasn't broken. Torn tissue, then. That was something to be thankful for, at least. His nose, unfortunately, was full of blood.

A cell like this was supposed to have a mattress, but he doubted that he would ever see one. The single light bulb in its mesh cage glared down at him, the light catching on ceiling cobwebs and the flyblown concrete. Lower down, previous occupants had scrawled their epithets and burdens. He wondered what bodily fluid had been used to create the ink.

He closed his eyes against his surroundings and thought of princes trapped in Baba Yaga's basement dungeons. Not that he was a prince. Not that this was a fairy tale. No one was coming out of this and living happily ever after.

He'd been close, so close. The exciting tingle of pursuit was still sparking in the back of his mind. He just needed to put all the facts together and some place to take them. He doubted Rostoff or the brass would be interested.

On the other hand, the tingle in his brain could just be the result of a blow to his head. With his good hand, he gingerly felt the huge goose egg growing on the back of his skull.

The case of Collin Archer was surely solved, his death due to his duplicity toward his Chinese masters. The only question possibly outstanding was just who had held the knife. He'd bet good money the knife wielder was Antonov or Alenin. Was it Rostoff or Prae who gave the orders? The difficulty was proving it. The same went for solving Maria's murder. He had only circumstantial evidence—the fact that the two men had come after him, the fact that Maria had been alive when he last saw her and far away from Yekaterina Park. Of course, it was exactly the same kind of circumstantial evidence that Antonov and Alenin were using to rid themselves of the Kazakov "problem."

His word against theirs.

But it was the case of Yekaterina and Semetai that still made no sense. Regardless of Antonov's comments, there was no way the boy would have killed the girl he loved.

Her body had been so pale and still on the dead October grass. So ripe for the future that she had been robbed of. From the walls of his memory, her dead face peered out at him, the evidence pinned around her. The autopsy report. The lines linking her to her strangely unconcerned mother, her cold, self-important, politically connected stepfather. They'd acted like it was Yekaterina's fault that she was dead. A foolish girl at the dinner table and then she was murdered. Whatever had led to the fight at her last meal wasn't going to be revealed, beyond the fact that it had something to do with Semetai. And then there was Natania Bure's plea, *don't look any further—not if you truly care for Yekaterina.*

There had been pain in those words and fear in Natania's gaze.

But why? Sighing, he closed his eyes.

Layers of Yekaterinas. Tsarina, diarist, victim. Even the girl Katya at the Red Veil. Katya was only a shortcut for the seemingly omnipresent name. Katya who had been bought for the Red Veil at a patron's request and who had been Boris Bure's favorite.

Kazakov sat up, and winced. He swung his legs over the side of the cot. Katya with the gossamer blonde hair and the looks of a sixteen-year-old.

"Holy mother of God. *Eto piz`dets.*" What he was thinking was so fucked up.

He had to be wrong; and even if he was right, there was no way to prove it. Everyone involved had been too careful and very, very smart. As if Bure himself was protected by a patron who would, if it was true that the boy killed the girl, take care of the boy who could tell what he knew. The same patron then killed the spy to destroy any link between the two.

He scrubbed at his temple and winced. He had to be making this up. It was too farfetched. He could not believe Semetai would kill Yekaterina.

His shoulder throbbed and that arm felt weak. Blood soaked his shirt and bandages. He was bleeding again and who knew how long it would be before he received any medical attention. His wound hadn't even been mentioned at admission. He pressed his hand over the blood and applied pressure.

Hours passed. At least it felt like it. It was hard to tell with no daylight or watch to portion out the time. Voices rose from other cells. Prisoners swore. Prisoners yelled. Footfalls and jingled keys passed by his door, but no one stopped. No one even paused. Hell, no one but his enemies even knew he was here. Somewhere a metal door much like his clanged open and there was a shout, the muffled sounds of a fight, and then the sounds of heavy feet and something being dragged.

He staggered up and limped to the door. That would likely be him in an hour, a day, a week. Whenever they thought his resolve might be weakest.

He slammed the door with his fists and grabbed the handle.

Locked, of course. He slammed the door with his palm one more time and retreated to his cot. Beating his fists against the walls would solve nothing and waste his precious energy. He sat down to wait.

Long past the clang of the meal cart that seemed to have forgotten him. Long past the footsteps and the jiggle of the locks as the guard did his rounds, Kazakov sat and waited. Beyond the door the cells had quieted, leaving him in silence with the graffiti curses.

He lay back with his forearm over his eyes and must have dozed off—to wake to the sound of footfall in the hall. A single tread, so not Antonov and Alenin—they never went too far from each other. He sat up, listening as the footfall came to a stop. Then keys jingled softly and he was on his feet, ready.

The lock clicked and the door swung outward in the hand of Pavel Chelomeyev. The blond youngster looked pale with high points of color in his cheeks. His his shoulder holster bulged with a pistol. Their eyes met and Chelomeyev's gaze widened.

"Mother of God, what did they do?" he asked, scanning Kazakov's bloodied face and torso, and then checked over his shoulder.

Kazakov shoved past him into the hall. To hell with what he looked like.

"What you'd expect. Why are you here?" A trick? A ruse? A setup to get him out where he could be dealt with as an escaped prisoner? He could see Antonov and Alenin doing something like that. The question was whether Chelomeyev was knowingly part of it.

Chelomeyev shook his head. "I—I saw what they did. Your hat. I saw them take it from your drawer a few days ago. A joke, I thought. Until suddenly it is evidence against you." He swallowed. "I see you work. I see you solve cases far more than anyone else. I—I would like to learn from you."

His young face was so earnest, Kazakov had to look away. Was it really possible for someone in this place, in this job, to have hope and faith? Kazakov had lost his long ago.

"Not a good idea if you want to live—or succeed. Besides, you have a partner." But he took advantage and started down the hall between the line of locked doors to the open door to the guard room. He stopped, Chelomeyev crowding up behind him.

In the guardroom, the guard lay collapsed over his desk, eyes closed, blood on his temple. Papers from the desk were scattered over the floor.

"What the hell have you done?" Kazakov demanded as he crossed to the guard and checked his pulse. Steady. Slow.

"I hit him with my gun. I hope it wasn't too hard."

Kazakov glanced back at the youngster. "You shouldn't have hit him at all. You shouldn't be here. Don't you understand that this is a career-destroying move? I'm a prisoner. You're aiding and abetting my escape. You'll end up dead like me, or leastwise your career will." He rifled the guard's pockets for keys and went to the effects lockers, checked the list and unlocked his locker to pull out his bloody belongings. He pulled on his shoulder holster, his coat, and boots. His gun and mobile phone were gone.

He glanced back at Chelomeyev. "Let me see your gun."

The young detective freed his weapon, opened it, and handed it to Kazakov.

"I'm going to do you a favor. I'm going to trust that you were smart enough that our friend here didn't see it was you who hit him."

Chelomeyev nodded.

"Good." Kazakov checked the gun, flipped it closed, and stepped toward Chelomeyev. "Remember that when you wake up and you still have a job."

He clocked the gun across Chelomeyev's temple. The young detective crumpled, but Kazakov caught him and eased him to the floor with an apology. It was for the kid's own good. If this wasn't a setup, he could claim he came down for a visit and met the same fate as the guard after someone unknown freed Kazakov. He was, after all, now a criminal. If this was a setup, then the kid got what was coming to him.

Stuffing Chelomeyev's weapon in his own holster, he pulled on his coat and headed for the door, but the sight of the guard's desk phone stopped him.

Risk a call to Khan from here? If they knew about Kazakov's investigation and had seen the evidence that he'd collected, they'd know that Khan had evidence, too.

He picked up the phone and dialed through to Khan's cell; the phone purred lightly in his hand, but Khan didn't answer. After fifteen rings he thumped the phone down, wondering what to do as he hauled his crusted coat on, stuffed his pockets with his car keys, and prayed that the Perseus was still on the street by the Red Veil. He headed to the rear door that led into the police garage.

Large and poorly lit, the broad, concrete space worked to his advantage. So did the fact that at this hour of the night many of the uniformed officers had their vehicles parked in the city's quiet corners so they could catch a few hours of sleep.

He walked briskly through the marked vehicles to the sedans used by the detective squad. In his effects were the keys to the sedan he'd abandoned for the Perseus. It seemed like a lifetime ago. The vehicle fit him like an old tired glove, but the engine started and the vehicle slid out of its parking stall and cruised out of the garage without a hitch.

Snow was falling softly as if this was a holy night. October was behind them. November was almost gone, and early Christmas lights twinkled in the windows of a few of the downtown shops. Their glow and the hush of the snow gave the night a feel as if this time, this space, existed somewhere outside of the Fergana he knew. This was as Fergana might be, pristine and clean and sacred. The holy mother Russia people dreamed of.

A fairy tale, and it was all a lie.

The streets were quiet as he reached Yekaterina Park and cautiously cruised past the Red Veil. Even the brothel's lights were out except one that glowed near what must be the lower floor rear door, as if all of Fergana was sated except one ravenous soul. He knew whose light it was, but Prae would keep until he had Khan and his American friend safe. Besides, a light like that was a perfect lure for a man seeking revenge. A perfect lure for a trap.

He cruised by and slowed past the Perseus, inspecting the snow. By the lack of imprints around his vehicle, no one had been near it since he left it there. He pulled the sedan to the curb. Though the police sedan might have about equal chance of being spotted by the police once they realized he had escaped, the Perseus was far superior in the snow. If he needed to escape New Moscow, the Perseus would be the better vehicle. He climbed into the trusty Perseus and the engine caught with a grinding start. Even in the cold, the vehicle reeked of old blood. Thankfully the blood on the seat had either frozen or dried, but he doubted if he would ever get the Perseus back to its once pristine condition.

The Perseus chugged through the snow like a workhorse and he wound through New Moscow past the gaudy lit domes of Saint Basil's and the faux frontage of Yekaterina's old palace, lit up by spotlights through twisted walnut trees so the shadows and the walls were contorted.

Somewhere, his country had gone wrong. Perhaps it was being surrounded by superpowers, but the inferiority complex of his country was clear in every one of its attempts at grandeur. Gradually the number of streetlights lessened until they finally relinquished the streets to the night and he entered the honest darkness of the gray mud-daub buildings of the old city.

He didn't know where Khalil Khan lived, though it was certainly on record somewhere. Khan had kept his roots and his home life private even after all the years they'd known each other. Though Khan was a friend, the man hadn't trusted him with a home phone number. But then, Kazakov hadn't invited Khan to the dacha, either.

For a moment he wondered why, but the answer was obvious. There was a divide of faith in Fergana and though Kazakov wasn't a religious man, somehow he'd come to obey those edicts. He sighed at the realization.

He stopped and parked when the streets narrowed, and climbed out into the silent night. This far into the old city, the lights and traffic noise of the new city didn't penetrate. The snow was a silent veil of white, the occasional house light a glowing beacon and the shadows a welcoming shield. He set off trudging through the snow until he reached the glass front of the narrow print shop and knocked on the door.

The rap sounded like thunder in the quiet street, but it couldn't be helped. He felt exposed and kept checking over his shoulder. Finally, a dim light appeared inside the shop as if someone had shifted the curtain from the back storeroom to expose light from the living area. Movement stirred the shadows inside the shop and then a face appeared briefly beyond the glass.

A lock clicked and the shopkeeper's narrow face peered out at him. "What do you want?"

He was clad in a knee-length sleeping shirt as he checked the street behind Kazakov.

"I need your help to reach a friend. They're after us for what we know. I have to warn him."

The shopkeeper checked the street again and finally nodded. "Come. Come."

He stepped back and Kazakov ducked inside. The warm scents of paper and ink were welcome after the cold. The sounds of life reached him from deeper inside the house and for a moment he regretted his lack of family.

Maria.

He sagged and the shopkeeper caught his arm. "You're injured more than bruises and blood on your face."

Kazakov shook his head. The shop's darkness hid his bloody side. "It doesn't matter. I need to warn Khalil Khan that they may be coming for him. I need you to contact him."

The shopkeeper went still.

"I know you don't fully trust me, but you trusted me enough to help me gather evidence from those who saw what happened to Semetai. Now two of his killers are after me and probably Khan. Phone Khan and tell him I'm here with a warning. Let him decide whether to talk to me."

Finally, the shopkeeper hustled to the phone on the wall behind the shop's counter. He didn't have to look Khan's number up as he dialed. The phone must have rung for a long time on the other end, but finally the shopkeeper spoke softly to someone—in Arabic, the holy language of the Koran.

Then he held out the phone. "He will speak with you."

Kazakov took the phone. "Khan?"

"What is it? Have you looked at the hour?"

"They came after me, Khan. They arrested me at the Red Veil. They took me in, but I escaped. It might be a setup so they can kill me on sight—an escaped prisoner. I think you're on their hit list, too. They know your evidence on Maria's death wouldn't convict me. They know you have evidence on the Archer death and Semetai and Yekaterina's, too. If they get rid of us, they'll have gotten rid of anyone who could cause trouble."

Khan paused at the end of the line.

"Listen, old friend. They won't stop at you. Your whole family is likely to disappear, too."

Kazakov heard soft voices in the background at Khan's end.

Khan came back on the line. "My wife says there's someone knocking on the door."

"Shit." Kazakov thought a moment. "Your friend, Eric Clinton. Call him. I'm on my way."

Kazakov hung up and swung to the shopkeeper. "I need you to take me to Khan's house."

The man shook his head. "I would need his permission to do that."

"We don't have time. There are people there now and there's a very good chance they are there to kill him."

The man read Kazakov's face. Then his refusal faded. "Let me get my coat."

He ran through the curtain to the storage area and the rest of the house. Kazakov heard shouts. A woman's answer. Then the man came back with a coat buttoned over his sleeping wear, his feet deep in knee-high boots, one of the ancient tribal rifles in his arms. He handed Kazakov a damp cloth for his face.

"Follow me," he ordered as he yanked open the door and plunged out into the night.

Kazakov followed, yanking the door shut behind him as he wiped his face clear of the worst blood. Then he hurried to catch up as the other man loped down the street. The snow was deeper here, for the wind had difficulty blowing the snow into drifts. Its depth was uneven from the passage of many feet, and the new snow masked the treachery. His feet slipped. He almost fell and twisted his side so the pain punched through him. The shopkeeper kept on going. He didn't look back. Then another armed man joined him. And another.

A third man, unarmed, arrived and slid to Kazakov's side. He was young and tall and Kazakov recognized him as Semetai's friend who had provided evidence at the group interview.

"You are hurt?" he asked.

"The bastards shot me last night. They killed a woman who could have given evidence against them."

The young man's expression hardened. "They will pay, these men. There are many coming."

Many coming. Somehow the shopkeeper had called for reinforcements. But if all they had were the antique weapons of their forefathers, this could be a bloodbath against the firepower of Antonov and Alenin's modern pistols.

"We have to catch up to the others and make a plan. There'll be too many killed otherwise."

The young man's brow rose. "Too many of them? They have things to pay for."

Kazakov looked forward and realized that the shopkeeper and the others had disappeared and there were no more footprints to follow. He stopped dead realizing that he had missed the place where the others had turned.

"What the hell is this? This is my fight and my investigation! Now where the hell are the others? Where's Khan's home?"

The boom of a rifle report negated any need for an answer. The sound echoed off the maze of flat-sided buildings making it difficult to get his bearings.

More shots, these the sharp bark of modern pistols. A man's scream of mortal pain.

"Idiots! They told you to keep me away, didn't they?" He grabbed the young man by the scruff of the neck.

"Ye-es," the youngster said.

"Well, you better damn well get me there or they'll all be dead. Or are you going to make me waste time backtracking for their trail?"

The young man hesitated, then nodded. "This way."

He set off at a run down a side street that wouldn't even pass as an ally in the new parts of the city. Cracked, gray-brown walls showed marks where weather had washed away the stucco. More shots came from ahead and Kazakov stayed on the young man's heels. The effort cost him. By the time they slowed at a corner, Kazakov was panting. He'd allowed his fitness to wane before this and with the wound, this was almost beyond him. Chasing down alleys was a young man's game.

More shots and something thudded into a wall across from them. Kazakov stopped the young man from stepping beyond the corner.

"Where from here? Where's Khan's house? Is that where the others were going?"

"Khan's house is down that street. He has the whole house. The front is his medical clinic. You can't miss it because of the sign."

Kazakov studied his face. He was smooth-cheeked, dark-eyed, and handsome like Semetai had been. "What's your name, son."

"Adilet. Adilet Sultanbek, sir."

"Well, Adilet Sultanbek, you will stay here. This is no place for an unarmed youth. Do you understand? There are men beyond that corner who will kill you. They use real bullets that kill a man, even one named for justice, do you understand?"

Adilet looked away, perhaps surprised that someone not Kyrgyz understood the meaning behind his name. Kazakov grabbed him by the collar. "You listen to me. I've had to look into the dead faces of too many young people who thought death couldn't catch them. I've got news for you. Death comes to us all. For some sooner than later. Semetai greeted him. So can you."

That seemed to shake the young man's bravado a little. Kazakov released him and went to the corner. There was a pause in the shooting.

He knelt and poked his head around the corner. A shot pinged off the wall next to his head and he threw himself backward, but not before he'd seen two bodies in the street. Both appeared to be Kyrgyz men. The fools had run right into the firefight.

"Adilet, is there another way in to Khan's house?"

He looked over his shoulder. The damn kid was gone. "*Derr`mo!*" He scrambled up, his side radiating piercing blades of pain. The damn kid hadn't listened to a word he'd said.

Adilet's footprints were clear in the snow, though the falling flakes would erase them. The prints led back the way they'd come and then turned at the next corner. That had to be the way closer.

The gunfire started again.

Kazakov set off at a limping run, the snow tangling his feet as he reached the end of the next block. He skidded to a stop and knelt to peer around the corner.

Two men stood at the end of the block facing out into a small square. Adilet hugged the wall behind them. From somewhere a light illuminated the front of a building with a single doorway, above which hung a small sign with Arabic writing and the image of a stethoscope underneath. There were no windows. Outside of his long hours as an M.E., Khan was also a doctor for his people. The little M.E. was far more than he seemed. He had bucked tradition and turned the single door that led to the usually immensely private living space into a public entrance for a community medical clinic.

But the door to the doctor's office hung loose on its hinges and something—a desk perhaps—had been thrown up as a barricade. The men from the old town had the attackers pinned down for the moment, but that didn't mean that the attackers hadn't killed Khan and his family.

Kazakov pulled Chelomeyev's pistol out of his holster. The thing looked impressive with its blue-black steel, but was too heavy in the barrel to be a truly good weapon. He checked the chambers—thankfully loaded, but he had only six shots to do whatever it was he was going to do. Not get into a shooting match, that was certain. Not when his wound would impact his aim and not with a sharpshooter like Antonov.

He edged along the wall until he could see into the square.

More bodies that he hadn't seen from the other angle. The man across from him glanced back. It was the copy shop owner and his face was angry.

"How many have you lost?" Kazakov asked.

"Five, at least. Two were able to crawl back to cover in that doorway." He nodded at a doorway that gave onto the oddly- shaped common area. At one side, an ice-bound fountain still trickled water for the local women. In this weather, it would soon be frozen solid.

Kazakov nodded. They needed to get help to those men and the other fallen, if they lived. They needed this ended.

He held up his hand to the Kyrgyz men.

"Antonov! Alenin! I know it's you. Come out with your hands up and you just might live through this." He just had to pray that they had already used a large portion of their ammunition.

"Kazakov! I should have known." Antonov's grating voice carried across the square, but there was no sign of movement beyond the shop barrier. "We've got your little friend. His family, too. Give yourself up and we might let his family go free—at least the little boy."

"I don't believe you. Khan had the chance to barricade the door. He and his family are safe and you're trapped."

There was a disturbance in the medical office and then a scream, a shriek, and suddenly a small boy was swung over the barricade by his feet.

"That look safe to you? Now get your ass in here and let's have this out."

Sight of the child brought shouts from the armed men outside. The printshop owner turned and grabbed Kazakov's arm. He hauled Kazakov forward. "You go. You save the boy."

Kazakov yanked loose and fell back a step. "Hold on. Hold on a moment."

There had to be something he could do. The fact the child was still alive was a wonder. If they already had Khan, they would have killed him and the rest of his family. No, something had gone wrong. Somehow Khan's family had been caught, but probably not Khan. He said as much to the men he was with and scanned his surroundings seeking an answer.

The building walls had barely a crack between what had been ancient homes of these people. The building walls were blank slates except where the antique stucco had fallen away revealing old mud, straw and animal hair. The streets were narrow and cobbled, and looking up it was as if the structures leaned together so that they loomed over him. "Make a difference," the ancient walls seemed to say."If you can."

So much destruction they had seen. From Ghengis Khan and Timur through to the Russians.

The night sky was gauzy with snow and cloud.

"How can I get into these houses?" He asked, patting the wall beside him.

"Why?" demanded the shopkeeper, no longer so friendly. He'd seen too many of his friends fall.

"If I can get to the roof, there's a chance I can reach Khan's house. If I can reach Khan's house, then I'm betting Khan will let us in through the roof. But I don't think we have much time. The threat to his children is too imminent. He'll give himself up to save them."

The shopkeeper met his gaze and Kazakov nodded.

"He's my friend. I know him. His family is everything, but he would try to hang on. He knows we're coming." But did he? Khan had as much as told him to get out of his life—that he could not take the risk of having Kazakov as an associate, let alone a friend. And yet the man had been there for him, had even brought in the American.

The shopkeeper jerked his head back down the street. "Adilet, take him. We'll provide cover when you are ready."

Sighing, Adilet led Kazakov back the way they'd come, but turned aside to knock at a stout wooden door. Adelit shouted something in his own language and soon the door swung open. Adilet slid inside, speaking quickly to the man who had answered. When Kazakov entered the dark passage beyond the door, their greeter gave him the once-over and shook his head.

"You don't look fit for anything, let alone what you propose." He was a slim man, as all of these tribal men seemed slim and just newly parted from small rugged horses who would gallop them across the mountain steppes. He had a rugged face that had seen wind and rain and snow glare, and his mouth was filled with absences of teeth that he exposed in a grin.

"I guess we'll see," said Kazakov, "But if you want Khalil Khan as a neighbor, you'd best let me try."

The man nodded and hurried down the arched-roof passage and out into a courtyard of snow-covered paving stone. Broad balconies shielded doorways and windows from the snow on the first and second floor. On one side, near a single glowing window, a stairwell led up to the second floor coming out even with the top of a leafless pomegranate tree. Kazakov crossed the courtyard snow, his boot prints defiling the pristine nighttime white. He climbed the stairs and spotted a rickety wooden ladder that led to the roof. Not waiting for Adilet, he made the climb, feeling the frozen wood sway and creak under his weight. A trapdoor blocked his way at the top, but he shoved it open and climbed out.

A gust of wind surprised him and sent him stumbling sideways. He caught himself against a wooden lean-to that would provide shade in the summer. Between the low walls that edged the rooftop, lines were strung and hung with wash. The women would beat them free of the frozen wash water in the morning.

Ducking under the clothes lines, he reached the side of the house that overlooked the street and fountain. Keeping low to minimize being seen, he took a chance and peered down.

The bodies still lay in the street. The print shopkeeper and his man still stood sentry on the side street. From this height, he spotted three more groups of men guarding other paths of escape. There was no way Antonov and Alenin were getting out of this alive.

Unless they had a hostage.

That was why they hadn't killed Khan's family. They were caught, but they still had a card to play. Let them continue to think that.

The other side of the roof gave onto the street that separated this building from Khan's house and clinic. It was a long way down to the snow-covered street where another body lay. A span of seven feet separated the two buildings. From the ground, the distance between the rooftops had been deceptive.

Well, there was no help for it.

"What do you think?" Adelit asked from behind him. "It is far, is it not?"

"Not so far." When Kazakov was younger he would have made the jump in a heartbeat, without thinking. Now, as a man in his forties, it was no longer so simple. He took off his coat, for the weight would make the leap more difficult. "Hold onto this for me and stay here."

He tucked Chelomeyev's weapon in the waistband of his trousers and walked back as far as the clotheslines would allow. It was barely fifteen feet. Barely far enough for him to break into a run and then there was the low wall to clear.

Ignoring Adelit, he paced it out, then did a few painful jumping jacks to get the blood running. It was already running down his side.

It was time.

One. Two. Three.

He had that many strides before he drove himself up off the rooftop, up over the wall, up into open air, arms reaching, body straining.

He soared up over the street, but already knew it wasn't enough. The blood loss had sapped him of his strength. Already he started to fall.

His reaching hands caught the edge of Khan's rooftop, scrabbled there, and managed to cling as his body slammed into the stucco side. Oomph and the air went out of him. All the muscles in his hurt shoulder screamed.

His feet scrabbled for purchase where none existed. If he could just grab the other side of the roof wall, he could pull himself up. He scrabbled with his feet again and found the barest crack in the stucco with one booted foot. He kicked it and kicked again and heard stucco falling, then hiked himself up, daring to release one fingerhold to grab the other side of the wall.

His foot slipped. He slammed into the building again. This wasn't going to work. It wasn't going to work because his shoulder was too injured and he'd lost too much blood. He was going lose his hold and fall and die just as surely as if Antonov and Alenin had killed him. Already his hands were freezing and the wind stripped all warmth from him.

He shook himself. That was the kind of thinking that ended empires, it was not the kind of thinking that the original Yekaterina had when she tried for greatness beyond anything ever seen in a woman. It might have resulted in a country dreaming of past splendor, but Russian blood ran in his veins. That was worth something. For Yekaterina, he was a fighter.

Ignoring the tearing pain in his shoulder, his feet scrabbled again and caught something firmer. He threw himself up just as his foothold broke free, and caught his torso across the roof edge. The roof edge wall cut into his wound.

The pain pulsed through him and he couldn't breathe. He kicked and rolled onto the roof to stare up at the heaving clouds. When he could breathe again, he hauled himself to his feet and waved back at the moon that was Adelit's face and checked for his weapon. Still there.

He hurried to the trap door on the roof and tugged on the worn wood handle. The door didn't budge.

"*Derr`mo!*"

He knelt beside the door and tried it again. No movement.

He knocked softly, then harder, pausing to press his ear to the edge of the opening. Maybe there was a sound but it was hard to tell in the wind and with his teeth chattering in the cold.

He knocked again, softly. "Khan. It's Khazakov. Let me in."

Then he stepped back, weapon drawn in case he'd been wrong.

15

The night was cold, the wind off the mountains stiff so that Kazakov's bloody shirt and trousers blew around him like flags and he was freezing as the stinging snow swirled around him on the flat roof. The distant lights of New Moscow were a glow through the haze of flakes like an imagined world. There were clotheslines here, too, but most were empty. What remained of the wash looked like medical bandages that ran a long, ragged beard through the wind. A small shack leaned on one corner of the roof and the floor seemed to slope underfoot as if the roof had sunk in past rains.

The slick sound of a well-oiled bolt came through the trap door and Kazakov tensed with the pistol ready. The trap door lifted a few inches exposing only inky blackness beyond. Kazakov lunged forward and caught the edge of the door, yanking it back so it fell into the snow. From within the blackness, he faced the well-oiled steel of another antique rifle.

"Kazakov?" Khan's voice was a hoarse whisper.

"Khan." He came around the edge of the trapdoor and peered down at his friend. Khan's normally solemn face was grave and pale as the night was dark around him. Even the darkness couldn't hide the huge circles bruising Khan's eyes.

"They've got Anfisa and the children. I won't give myself up until they release them."

"I know, old friend. I know." Kazakov stuck the gun back in his waistband and climbed down through the trap door into a warm room that smelled of—old wool and spice. In the almost total dark at the base of the ladder he caught Khan's shoulders and felt the little M.E. shiver. "So now we free them, yes?"

Khan nodded. He wore a glowing white night shirt shoved into a pair of hastily pulled on trousers. Kazakov's vision adjusted enough to make out Khan's usually neat hair standing up wildly around his head. Fear and gratitude warred on his face. Finally, he composed himself and looked Kazakov up and down. "And you? Your wound? How did you get here?"

Kazakov shrugged. "I ran. I jumped."

Khan frowned and pulled Kazakov's shirt open, then glanced up at him. "You abuse my work."

"And you're in my way if you want to free your family." Kazakov tugged his shirt closed. "Show me where they are."

He buttoned his shirt as he followed Khan out onto a balcony that ran around the house's interior courtyard. Khan tugged him back against the wall. "They can see movement unless we are in the deepest shadows. I think one keeps watch here and one guards the front of the house. He nearly caught me once, but I shot back and may have caught him."

"Then you've made my job easier for me." Kazakov looked down at Khan's ancient weapon and gained a new respect for the M.E. But then, there was a reason the old weapons were treasured by the tribal families. He'd just never thought of Khan as connected that way.

"Describe the layout," Kazakov asked.

"The stairs are there," Khan pointed beyond the bare branches of an apricot tree that grew up from the courtyard. By the low humps in the snow, the courtyard was likely a garden of potted plants in the summer. A low, boxy structure stood in one corner of the courtyard just outside of the balcony cover. "The bedrooms are all up here. The parlor is there." Khan pointed to one side. "Kitchen is at the rear of the house, of course. The clinic used to be a prayer room." He pointed at a doorway masked in balcony shadows that would have a clear view of the stairs down from where he stood.

Kazakov nodded. "Is there any other way down?"

Khan hesitated. "There is an old stairway that leads to the kitchen, but that brings you out below us, directly into their line of sight."

Not a good option, but then neither was going down those courtyard stairs. If he was younger he might chance a leap off the balcony, but he wasn't younger and he'd already reopened his wound.

"All right. I want you to give me ten minutes to get down the kitchen stairs and into position below. In the meantime, I want you to go up to the roof and tell Adelit to signal the men out front to start shooting. Then get back here as fast as you can and cover me. We'll split their attention and just maybe have a chance to take them."

Agreeing, Khan told him where to find the stairs to the kitchen and then faded back into the shadows toward the roof ladder. Kazakov followed the balcony and found the door to a small storeroom. He slipped inside into darkness and the smell of cedar and had to feel his way past shelves to a low, servant's door at the rear. He pushed it open, its hinges creaking, and found himself looking into a pit of more darkness.

No windows. No lights that he dared flick on. Only velvet darkness ready to swallow him down. He slid one foot forward, feeling like he was stepping into an abyss, until his foot found the stair. He stepped down and kept his hand on the wall, feeling each step and counting. Twenty steps in the dark with the only sound his breathing. He came out into a space that smelled of cooked beef and noodles and, faintly, of turmeric and saffron. It was lighter here, from an open-air cooking area at the rear that in the summer would hold a cooking fire. Gradually his eyes adjusted enough to make out the bulk of a modern stove and fridge. So perhaps the cooking fire was not needed. Neat shelves lined the walls.

Carefully, he edged between the stove and butcher-block counters to the hallway that led to the courtyard. His feet whispered on tile. His fingers traced the wall—smoother than anything in the dacha—and with his other hand he drew out Chelomeyev's gun.

Still in the shadows, he peered across the courtyard. The clinic door was open, the window beside the door closed and curtained so no one could see inside. There was no light in the clinic and he could only assume that, like him, either Antonov or Alenin were in the shadows keeping watch. His money was on Alenin given Antonov's sharpshooter skills would be put to test fighting off Khan's friends outside and if, as Khan had suggested, Alenin had been shot, he would be very, very angry and on guard.

Kazakov edged forward until he was almost to the courtyard. The good thing was that as far as Antonov and Alenin knew, Khan was here alone with an inferior weapon. Kazakov tested the weight of Chelomeyev's gun once more. For all intents and purposes, they might be right.

He waited, contenting himself with breathing, with keeping watch for movement inside the clinic doorway. There was no way Antonov or Alenin would let their hostages near any escape route. These men were killers, but with police training. That meant they would be careful— and thorough. Maria's poor battered body proved that at least one of them could also be cruel. Even traitorous Collin Archer had been killed more cleanly. But then Maria had betrayed her mistress by abandoning everything in that life. Archer had simply had pretensions of grandeur —had thought he was good enough to play one power against the other as if he was a game master. A gambler to the end.

From the balcony above him came the soft fall of footsteps. Khan was back. Kazakov took a deep breath. It was beginning.

From the street, beyond the stout house walls, came the sound of shooting. The city men were firing at the front door. Answering, muffled shots came from inside the clinic and Kazakov tensed, praying that he wasn't hearing the deaths of the hostages. More shots came from overhead, blasting plaster off the wall by the clinic's courtyard door and window.

Something moved in the inky clinic shadows. A gun barrel appeared, aimed at Khan's position. Kazakov used the wall to brace himself and aimed at the darkness beyond the shadows. If Alenin was shooting in proper police style, his body would *there* as he steadied his pistol.

Kazakov fired. Chelomeyev's pistol bucked sideways in his hand. A shout came from the clinic and the pistol disappeared. Kazakov leapt out of the shadows, zigzagging across the courtyard, leaping the heaps of snow that he was pretty sure were summer flower pots as Khan's gunfire hopefully kept Alenin pinned down. He made it up the one step to the roofed porch that encircled the courtyard and shaded the ground floor rooms and the clinic door from the summer sun.

A gun barrel flash sent him leaping sideways, but the bullet slammed him into the snow five feet sideways from the door. Pain seared through his chest and beat consciousness away in white-hot waves. He fought for breath and clung to awareness.

Maria. Khan. The cold. The gun.

Somehow, he still held it. He opened his eyes and looked into the door's shadows—right into the barrel of Alenin's gun. The crew-cut blond towered above him, his finger already tightening on the trigger.

"You have a bad habit of living," Alenin said, but time distorted his voice as if a tape had been slowed.

It was over. He was done.

Kazakov blinked up at him trying to understand. Had Alenin taken out Khan? Had Antonov killed off the attacking men?

Taking aim, Alenin stepped out of the doorway's shelter, but he was still hidden from Khan's view from the balcony above. He used his boot on Kazakov's bloody side. White heat exploded in his brain and then turned to blackness. Kazakov fell through the pain, fighting for consciousness, the gun lost from his hand.

"Hey!" The shout echoed in the courtyard.

Alenin's head snapped up as someone tackled him. Kazakov rolled away, fighting nausea, and stumbled up as Alenin whirled and took a shot. A double report echoed forever in the courtyard.

Alenin sagged. He looked at Kazakov in surprise, a Hindu third eye blooming in his forehead before his knees gave. He crashed to the snow.

Kazakov staggered to Alenin's gun and dug Chelomeyev's from the snow. His chest was on fire. His gasps came with a red mist that froze in the air. Someone called his name.

In the snow beside Alenin lay the Kygyz youth, Adelit, his blood blooming in the snow from the hole in his throat. His hands flopped as he tried to stop the bleeding. His lower body didn't move. Then Khan was there, kneeling in the snow, fighting to staunch the wound.

Kazakov went to help him, but the sounds of gunfire from the clinic turned him around.

He stepped through the clinic door.

The dark space echoed with the violence of the battle taking place at the front of the clinic and the stink of cordite. Antonov apparently hadn't noticed the silence from the rear of the place.

Kazakov picked his way through a storeroom and office, past doors marked as exam rooms. Through one of the doors came the sound of sobbing. Life. But not in front of him. From the front of the clinic came the raining sound of death. Bullets slamming into the walls. The report of Antonov's weapon. How many rounds had he and his partner brought? They had apparently come prepared, if not expecting their own deaths.

"Alenin! What's happening! Did you get him?" Antonov called in a pause in the barrage.

Kazakov came to the end of the hallway. Beyond was a single room with a desk—now thrown on its side to barricade the lower portion of the doorway—and a tangle of chairs meant for waiting clients. On the walls, tattered bits of paper fluttered in the cold wind—all that remained of health message posters. Silhouetted at the edge of the now open door crouched the squat form of Antonov.

"Afraid not," Kazakov said, leaning against the wall because his legs were shaking. "Put the gun down, Antonov. Give yourself up."

Antonov didn't move. His hand flexed over his gun. "Or what, Kazakov? You shoot me? An honorable man like you? I don't think so."

He turned slowly, his gun still gripped in his hand and he smiled when he caught sight of Kazakov. "You don't look so good, old friend. If this is a stand-off, I think I can out-stand you."

Kazakov nodded. "Probably. One last chance, Antonov. Put the gun down. You were a good cop once. I don't want to kill you."

Antonov's hand swept up. Kazakov pulled the trigger.

The bullet found Antonov dead center. He slammed back against the desk in the doorway, looking down at the hot bloom on his chest. A blast of bullets caught him from the street. He danced back into the clinic on already dead feet and collapsed to the floor in front of Kazakov.

Alenin's gun slipped from Kazakov's hand. The white-hot pain of his chest was spreading again. This time the bullet hadn't gone right through. This time it had hit something and the damn wall shifted away from him, leaving him without support.

Leaving him falling.

16

The wind was cold and dry out of the eastern mountain ranges. It swirled flakes around Kazakov's shoulders. This late in December there was always more snow blowing in, smothering the earth, the city, and Fergana's hopes and dreams, but this year the snows had come earlier. At least that was how it seemed, standing in the graveyard above the cleared plot that marked the spot where Maria di Maria was buried.

It was on a hillside that faced west, toward Yekaterina's Mountain, not that the sullen clouds allowed any sense of direction. There was only swirling snow, but his hope was that in the spring the distances to the west might be revealed and Maria's spirit might see her way across the far-flung Ottoman deserts, past the crumbling might of Constantinople, and on to the remains of her small village in the Anglo-German province of Italia. It was the least he could do for her. She had been good-hearted and trusting and kind and he had allowed her to die. Another lost soul just like the Russian remains who dwelt in Fergana these days. He realized that now. They were all ghosts, figments of a past that was gone and that clung too closely to a fairy tale.

Kazakov shook his head, the nap of his latest lynx fur hat caressing his cheek in the wind. "We're all trapped, Maria. But you have gotten free. Perhaps I envy you that."

"Talking to the dead? I thought that was my job." The slight figure of Khalil Khan appeared out of the snow behind him. The small M.E. was swathed in a heavy wool coat that reached below his knees to tall black boots and a hat much like Kazakov's except black with golden tips. Mink, perhaps, or ermine. He came up beside Kazakov.

Kazakov sighed. "I suppose I was. Since I got out of the hospital, coming here has become a habit. Perhaps it's one I'll continue."

Khan shook his head. "I didn't save your life to let you spend it with the dead. You need to laugh. You need to find joy again."

Kazakov remembered a fleeting touch of soft skin, the warmth of Maria's mouth and body. Perhaps he'd almost found it.

And lost it again.

"I suppose I can't find that sort of thing standing in a graveyard, can I? It's just—I feel that I owe her. Not only did she trust me enough to come to me with evidence, she died to keep the evidence from falling into Chinese hands. And the Ottomans."

"And our American friends thank you—and her—for it. The evidence on that data machine has changed the dynamics of Central Asian politics I think. At least Eric thinks so. The deals the Ottomans were brokering with Fergana seem to have fallen aside and we're officially back to neutrality. Again."

Kazakov gave Khan a sideways glance. "You know a lot more of politics than I ever heard you speak before. It's an interest you've hidden."

Khan looked at his hands and shrugged. Perhaps he hadn't meant to let that fact slip, or perhaps he was putting Kazakov on notice. Khan had secrets just like all of them.

The M.E. looked out into the snow toward Yekaterina Mountain. "Did you know that we call it Suleiman's Throne?" He lifted his chin at the five peaks almost masked in the snowfall. "It is said that Mohammed prayed there. Babur, too. It is not well known, but of vast importance as a symbol of my people."

Kazakov hadn't known all of it. "And we renamed it for you."

Khan shook his head. "For yourselves, perhaps. For us it is still the same."

That was the thing. Fergana was built on memories and stories layered over top of reality. Perhaps that was where his people had gone wrong.

At the base of the hill, the snow appeared to lessen and the abstract puzzle of New Moscow's towers and the domes of Saint Basil were momentarily visible, like a dream.

"I did that DNA testing you suggested. I got the results today. I thought you'd want to know," Khan said.

Kazakov nodded as he watched the forms of New Moscow blow away in the wind and snow. More flakes caught in the lettering on Maria's new headstone. *Maria di Maria. Daughter of Italia. Gone but not forgotten.* He didn't know her birthdate and could only guess at her age, but in the end that didn't matter.

"So? Did it tell us anything?"

Khan was silent a moment. "The father of her child was not Semetai Manas."

"Bure," Kazakov said.

Khan nodded again. "How did you figure it?"

Kazakov sighed, thinking of girls in pink sweaters and undying love between a traditional Muslim boy and a Christian girl.

"It was a lot of things that came together. The story about the young girl who was assaulted by a school boy in Bure's file. The fact that a young, blonde prostitute was bought by the Red Veil because he liked her. The way the mother and Bure reacted when Yekaterina died and the horror the mother felt about me investigating further." He shook his head. Natania Bure had been her daughter's Baba Yaga— sometimes good, sometimes bad, living in a small house that might as well have danced on chicken legs for all the safety it provided her daughter. But then, perhaps unknowingly, each person was a Baba Yaga to somebody. He thought of Maria.

"I should have seen it sooner," he said. "Maybe I would have, if I'd been able to continue the investigation in the open. Antonov and Alenin didn't lie when they said Semetai killed her. He loved her, but then she told him she was pregnant with her stepfather's child. How could a boy raised in a traditional Muslim home deal with that? He'd risked everything to love her and then he's told that. He killed her, probably in abhorrence at the child she carried and then they killed him for fear of what he knew. Perhaps he actually threatened Bure somehow. So Collin Archer killed him to protect Boris Bure but then somehow Archer's people found out about his duplicity. Or maybe they couldn't take a chance on him being arrested for Semetai's death. Two cases, except they weren't. Did the Americans get the police to take action? Did Prae get arrested?"

Khan shook his head as another gust of wind found them and Kazakov raised his collar against the cold. He was still recovering from the gunshot wounds after losing a kidney. He'd been offered a pension and Rostoff encouraged retirement, but Kazakov wasn't sure that was what he wanted. What did he know about retiring?

"From what I heard, they went to the Red Veil but the woman was already gone—back to China probably. Frau Zelinka has been arrested, but I don't know what they'll charge her with. From what I hear, she's cooperating as much as a madam might be expected."

Kazakov eased his side and leaned on his cane—temporarily, he hoped. Overhead the clouds were thickening and dusk was gathering around the flakes. Another day ending, with holy Russia like a fairy tale heroine, lost in the deepening Siberian snows.

"And Bure?" he asked wondering again why Prae needed to protect him. Because he was a favored patron, or was it something more?

Khan shrugged. "What can I say? We could cause him some trouble with the news of his stepdaughter's pregnancy, but there are too many people paid to smooth that bit of trouble away."

As they already had.

"There's something about him. Something that doesn't fly right. Why would the Chinese care if Bure rises or falls?"

"Old friend, that is an investigation that could blow up in your face," Khan said softly into the wind.

Kazakov swirled the tip of his cane in the snow. He was tired of the implement; would be glad when it was gone, but for now it was the one solid leg he had. "You have your family to protect. I have nothing to lose."

He set off down the hill, feeling his way through the white forest of snow. When he looked back, Khan was no longer there.

Kazakov went on alone.

JOIN K.L. ABRAHAMSON/ KAREN L. ABRAHAMSON'S MYSTERY READERS!

If you'd like more of K.L. Abrahamson's mysteries, join other mystery enthusiasts and receive a free novel, a novella, and an award-nominated short story. To get your free books, go to www. karenlabrahamson.com.

DON'T GO YET. PLEASE LEAVE A REVIEW!

If you enjoyed this book (and even if you didn't), it would be immensely helpful if you would leave a review at your favorite website, such as Amazon or Goodreads. Reviews help gain me visibility and they can bring my books to the attention of other readers who may enjoy them.

Thank you!

ABOUT THE AUTHOR

Backpack traveller, police and corrections officer, speech writer, and consultant are among the many previous lives of Karen L. Abrahamson. All of them color her writing. Karen is the author of literary, mystery, romantic and fantasy fiction including the highly regarded Cartographer fantasy series. Her writing reflects her passion for other cultures and countries around the world, but British Columbia, Canada is her favorite place to come back to. She lives on the western edge of North America with two Bengal cats that aren't quite as well traveled as she is, and killer whales, bears and bald eagles for neighbors.

When she isn't writing she can be found with a camera and backpack in fabulous locations around the world.

To find out more about her and her writing, visit
www.karenlabrahamson.com

THE DETEKTIV KAZAKOV MYSTERY SERIES

Set in an alternate history Russia, the series introduces Detektiv Alexander Kazakov, a loner detective committed to finding the truth for the dead and murdered. The series takes place in a world where Catherine the Great's conquest of the Crimea woke the slumbering Ottoman Empire and brought the armies of the great Khans down upon Moscow. Two hundred years later the remains of the Russian population dream of Russia's past glories, while their new country of Fergana lays like the gristle in a joint between the rumblings of the Ottoman and Chinese Empires. The death of a young Russian girl sets Kazakov on a series of investigations that have implications for the entire world.

Books in the Series:
After Yekaterina
Mareson's Arrow
The Tsarina's Mask
Ivan's Wolf

PREVIEW: MARESON'S ARROW

"Deep in a forest filled with snow an old couple lived. The snow was so deep that the old man could not hunt on his weak legs and so he and his wife would starve. As a result, the old couple decided to slaughter their mare to have food for the winter.

"A raven at the window overheard their plan and flew to the stable to warn the mare. "You'd best break down your stall and jump the fence before the deed is done," the raven said.

"And so the mare did, escaping deep into the forest. She wandered for maybe a long time or maybe it was short, for who can say how far was far in those distant times. She came to a cloak thrown across the snow and found upon it a dead man of the east. She took a bite out of his right knee and then of his left, and found herself pregnant.

"When the mare gave birth, she named her son Ivan Mareson. He grew into a handsome lad and when he was old enough to be on his own she told him to make himself a bow and arrow and every night stick the arrow into the earth. That way she would know that he was alive. If he did not stick the arrow into the earth she would come looking for his bones."

Old Mrs. Ryabkov words seemed to hum in the warm dacha air as she stopped her recitation of the old Russian folktale. She peered at

New Moscow Police Detektiv Alexander Kazakov from the tops of her eyes across the worn wooden table her long-dead husband had made. Her bird eyes glittered in the light from the single candle between them and so did the half-empty bottle of vodka and the cracked edges of the old china bowls that had held their supper. Her old cabin's stone walls were lost in shadows. So were the cobwebs amongst the rafters of the low-ceilinged structure and the neatly made up narrow cot against the rear wall.

Agafya Ryabkov's dacha was small, built like a part of the earth, so that Agafya, her house and her story seemed to have grown out of the dust and rock of this country. But instead of the usual dusty scent of the herbs drying amongst the rafters, the single, low-ceilinged room smelled of the warm scent of the *kutia* in their bowls. Kazakov had made the traditional Russian Christmas Eve honeyed porridge this afternoon, but the rich poppy seeds, berries and nuts that he'd included seemed inappropriate to enjoy alone, so he'd brought it through the snow to her house. Oddly, he hadn't wanted to spend this evening alone even though he normally preferred to be on his own.

"Continue, please," he said to her, awaiting her spin on the miraculous tale of the mare's son who had wonderful adventures and who died and was raised from the dead many times. It was a story of resurrection that was near and dear to the hearts of the exiled Russian people in their adopted homeland of Fergana. It was as if they expected Holy Mother Russia to rise the same way. It was *not* something he had expected his ancient Kyrgyz neighbor to choose. But then he had learned to always let the storyteller choose the story and the way of telling. An artist always chose a first story they could tell with confidence. Later, with coaxing, the storyteller would tell the tale that touched her soul. You could always tell by the emotion in their voice. It was the same with witnesses.

Or suspects, for that matter.

Agafya set her spoon down and sat back in her chair. It was one of two that her Russian husband had carved. The chairs, the table, the stone house and his bird-eyed wife, all that he left behind him when he died.

She gave a single, stubborn, shake of her head. "It was my husband's tale. Or that of his people—not mine. I thought I could tell it, but…" Agafya's Kyrgyz heritage shone through in more than her diminutive size and her attitude. She still wore the felted embroidered skirts and leggings of her girlhood. What remained of her fine grey hair was wound around her head and her black gaze glittered with old suspicions. "What is it to you? What do you want here?"

Kazakov eased his stiff side and shoulder—the penance he paid for being shot twice and thrown down a set of stairs—and straightened. He nodded at the table. "It's January 7th—Christmas Eve, remember. I brought the kutia to celebrate."

Lips tightening over her teeth she shook her head. "Pah on your Christmas.." She shoved the bowl away. "This is not what I cook."

Kazakov tried a smile. The January 7th date was the Christmas of the Russian Orthodox Christian faith that had not spurned the Julian calendar as had most of the world. Of course, Agafya was not Christian of any stripe, but Muslim.

"But the Kutia's good, yes? My mother made it this way. I've spent years trying to recreate her recipe."

Agafya shook her head and took a long drink of the cup of vodka he'd poured her. "I am not your mother." She looked away. "I want to be alone."

Kazakov sighed. Agafya Ryabkov was a fierce woman, perhaps the strongest he'd ever met, save for the one he'd lost most recently. Agafya had always been the perfect neighbor, asking for nothing and barely tolerating when Kazakov came checking that she was safe and well. He knew when her limited tolerance for visitors was surpassed.

He pushed himself up from the table. "All right. I thought it would be good to share Christmas Eve with a friend, but I will leave you to your peace."

As he pulled on his muffling, wool great coat and heavy boots, she stood and shuffled to the old woodstove where he'd put the pot of kutia to keep it warm. He held up his hand. "Keep it and enjoy the kutia. I'll pick up the pot in a few days." For regardless of what she'd said, she'd polished off her bowl in record time. The old woman was made of twigs and skin and he had no idea how she survived. He'd been bringing her groceries for years.

Thankfully, she didn't argue, but continued fussing around the cabin. He pulled on his lynx fur hat and tugged up his collar. "Thank you for the hospitality, Agayfa. It was good to hear the old tales again."

She only harrumphed, so he grabbed his cane and let himself out, closing the door behind him.

Black night greeted him and cold. January in Fergana was usually chill, but it was in the mountain foothills like this that winter truly came and this year more than most years. The air was still, except for a few flakes that tumbled down. Even the smoke from Agayfa's chimney rose straight up for a hundred feet before swirling into calligraphy against the stars. The new moon was only a sliver and the air carried the scent of wood smoke and pine from the surrounding forest. To the east a passing cloud picked up the amber glow of New Moscow's streetlights.

This far away he could almost imagine the city slumbering and at peace, but he knew better. Under the white covering of recent snow was the scurrying of rats—both in animal and human form. Rats with guns who had left him minus one kidney and, at forty-five, needing to help himself with a cane like an old man. He hoped it was only temporary.

He limped down Agafya's stairs to the trail his arrival had laboriously cut in the snow. The tip of his cane fought him as he lumbered across the clearing that during the summer would hold Agafya's small garden, and down the treed driveway towards the road. Halfway down the driveway, where the snow was heavier, waited his trusty Perseus vehicle. He'd parked here for he hadn't been certain whether even the Perseus could navigate through the heavy snow around Agafya's home.

He sank into the driver's seat and realized that he was sweating. Since when had a two-hundred-meter walk stolen all his strength? The answer was simple: since the shooting in late November and the surgery that had left him convalescing. He had done nothing to keep in shape, instead diving deep into reading— folk tales that glossed over the horror of too much killing and that left him trying to determine the stories' purpose; mysteries that left him ready to toss the book across the room; histories that were determined to present the victors in the best light possible and to vilify those on the losing side.

Fictions all of them.

In response, he'd turned back to the news and non-fiction, but even those he'd come to suspect were not the truth.

He turned the Perseus' ignition and the engine roared. Through the frosted windscreen a white world was revealed in the headlight beams. Truth, it seemed, was in short supply these days. Even the shooting deaths of two police officers who had been responsible for Kazakov's injuries hadn't been reported accurately. But then, who in the New Moscow police force was going to damn two of their own?

Apparently, no one.

Perseus in gear, he carefully backed out of Agafya's driveway, following the tire tracks in his rear taillight's glare. At the road the vehicle bumped over the snowplow's most recent drift and onto the narrow road, before starting uphill.

The drive to his dacha was not quite half a mile along from Agafya's. His next nearest neighbor was over a mile farther on and he liked it that way. He guided the Perseus into his drive and under the sheltering dark pines and pale naked poplars, but something about the driveway wasn't right.

The snow clearly showed the tracks of his departure and the half-filled ruts of his comings and goings prior to the most recent snow. But now another set of tire tracks, wider than the Perseus's, followed the upward slope of the driveways and obscured his tracks in places.

He slowed the vehicle and felt his heart beat a little faster. The last time strangers had come to his dacha uninvited had been the first time he'd been shot. The last time a friend had come to the dacha was well back in November just after he'd been released from the hospital. No one had visited in December and that was just fine.

Back up and leave whoever was waiting for him or see who it was? He wasn't in the same situation as he'd been in November, working a case that technically wasn't his and another that he'd clearly been ordered to leave alone. Now he wasn't involved in anything.

Technically.

So. He might as well see who had disturbed his isolation. He eased his foot off the brake and the Perseus chugged up the slope into the clearing around his dacha. A blocky, black sedan sat waiting, its windows fogged with frost as if whoever waited had chosen to wait in the car.

Interesting. Such a vehicle was the choice of the New Moscow police department.

Jaw clenched, Kazakov drove the Perseus past the unknown sedan. He parked in the shelter behind the dacha and then climbed out. The cold stung his cheeks. The heavy timbers of the dacha's walls were pitch black in the night, but overhead a thin trail of smoke rose from the chimney, so the fire he'd left banked was still burning.

He pulled himself up to his full six feet two and almost set the cane away, but there was too good a chance that without it, he'd fall. His strength might be better than it was, but he wasn't a young man anymore. He picked his way around the house and the sedan's driver-side door clicked open.

Out stepped a tall, thin, baby-faced blonde man who looked as if he should still be living with his mother, but who was, in fact, the youngest member of the New Moscow detective squad. Pavel Chelomeyev was the son of a senior member of the New Moscow police, which was most likely why he had been promoted to detective when most recruits were still taking notes for their training officers. He'd been partnered with one of the hard-case detectives on the squad, though he had worked with Kazakov a time or two in the past. One could argue that Chelomeyev was also responsible for Kazakov being alive today.

"Kazakov!" Chelomeyev's strong baritone was always a surprise, more so when it echoed back from the thick line of trees. He stood swathed in a thick wool coat down over his knees and black fur hat that seemed ungodly large for his scarf-wrapped neck. Kazakov only nodded and hooked his head at the dacha, then thumped up the four snow-covered stairs to his front door.

He stepped inside and Chelomeyev crowded in behind him while he lit a kerosene lamp. Koshka, Kazakov's rebellious female black cat, twined around his legs. The single-room log cabin was comfortably warm and quite adequate for Kazakov on his own or perhaps with another, smaller, person.

The place had no electricity and had been built by his father when Kazakov was a boy. After his mother died they had spent many summers here. After his father died and Kazakov's disastrous marriage ended, the dacha was the only thing Kazakov had held onto. He'd moved in then, and had no plans to move out again, though he was considering installing a complete bathroom to replace the water closet attached to the kitchen.

At the moment, however, the place did not feel big enough for both Kazakov and Chelomeyev as they removed their coats and hats in the small area between the woodstove that stood against one wall and the table that filled the center of the room. Another, narrow table stood against the wall beyond the woodstove and served as Kazakov's desk. A small kitchen filled one corner and a narrow bed sat opposite the desk. A small couch filled the final rear wall. It didn't leave a lot of room for someone whose arms were as long as Chelomeyev's. As usual, Koshka mewed plaintively for food though she had been given her dinner only a few hours before.

"Go on with you." Kazakov used the side of his boot to gently send Koshka on her way as he hung his coat and hat on a peg by the door. In disgust, Koshka leapt up to the shelf above his bed to curl up and hold him in a disapproving glare.

Kazakov turned back to the young detective in his neat grey suit and expensive tie who was trying to figure out what to do with his coat. Kazakov wasn't going to help him. He might have invited the young detective in, but that didn't mean that he'd told the youngster to make himself at home. Chelomeyev settled for folding the garment over the back of one of the two spindle chairs at the table.

"Why are you here?" Kazakov asked, dispensing with any of the niceties. This was home. If he wanted guests, he'd invite them, but Chelomeyev wasn't on the very short list of people Kazakov would consider inviting. No one from the police department was, but at least Chelomeyev was polite enough to wait in the car rather than invade the cabin to wait for him.

Chelomeyev looked back at his coat, perhaps rethinking the garment's removal. "I—I thought I would check up on you. It has been almost two months. Surely you will be coming back to work soon."

Arching a brow at the younger man, Kazakov went to his kitchen and retrieved a bottle of vodka and a single glass, then thought better of it and grabbed a second glass. "You expect me to believe that?"

He thumped the bottle and glasses on the table and studied the younger man. Chelomeyev sidled uneasily where he stood— nervousness—not a good thing in a detective.

"You want something, then." He lifted his chin at the chair. "Sit. Have a Christmas drink with me."

Obedient as a school boy, Chelomeyev sat. Kazakov swallowed a smile. The youngster still had some growing up to do. A shame his father hadn't allowed him to do it the way every other officer matured into the job.

"How long were you waiting?" Kazakov asked as he poured two tumblers and set the bottle down. The sweet glow from his meal with Agafya had worn off, but then Chelomeyev was an unwelcome intrusion of the real world.

"About an hour."

Odd how he felt so resentful when he should be appreciating the youngster's patience in waiting—and waiting in the cold, at that. But Kazakov had been waiting for someone from the police force to come to try to change his mind ever since he'd refused the offer of early retirement from Detektiv Chief Inspector Rostoff. He drained his vodka back and poured himself another as Chelomeyev sipped. The slow sweet warmth crept from his belly to his heart and then his arms.

"So?" Kazakov asked leaning back in his chair. "How are you? I won't ask about the department because I know it will be fucked up as usual." He eyed his tumbler, but limited himself to matching

Chelomeyev sip for sip waiting as the youngster found his courage. Clearly it had not been an easy choice to come here. His father would not approve and neither would Rostoff nor the other detectives.

"Where is Sherepov?" Sherepov being Chelomeyev's surly partner.

The young detective set down his glass and drew in a deep breath. He shoved back from his chair and stood to pace around in the cramped room. Kazakov watched him and took another gulp of vodka, certain he wasn't going to like anything that caused Chelomeyev such consternation.

Chelomeyev's movement stirred the kerosene lamp shadows so the room seemed to expand and contort as if they were inside the old witch Baba Yaga's chicken-legged house with miraculous adventures awaiting beyond its confines. He knew better—unlike Ivan Mareson from Agafya Ryabkov's recent telling, there was no one to put him fully back together again when the bullets came flying. He still ached where his one kidney was missing.

"I've been involved in these investigations," Chelomeyev began. From where he stood in the shadows he looked eternally young, like a tragic figure lost beyond the mythic River Styx who wished to come home.

He shook his head, his bright blonde head of hair shifting on his forehead. "I don't know what to do. Sherepov is off on sick leave and one of these is my first murder investigation on my own—like you." He gave Kazakov a proud, but hopeful glance. Kazakov was the only detective in the department who worked alone, whether because he distrusted his co-workers or they distrusted him, he no longer cared. Clearly, Chelomeyev had come to him as a last resort. Asking for help would be a sign of weakness. Asking Kazakov for help would damn the young detective in the eyes of the squad.

And just like that, the illusion of safety in the comfortable light and shadow of his dacha disappeared and became only shadows, the outside world intruding.

He shivered. A piercing knife blade cut through his side and he hissed out through his teeth. Did he want any part of this after all that had happened? He took another gulp of vodka, emptying the glass, and poured again.

But this was Chelomeyev and Kazakov owed him. "What is the problem?"

Chelomeyev returned to his chair and leaned across the table. "Rostoff has told me to close the files. There is not enough evidence, he says. But my gut tells me that there is something there." He shook his head, his expression both pained and hopeful. "No one believes me, just like they never believed you."

Kazakov closed his eyes against that look. He had seen something similar in Maria's gaze before she died. He did not like the guilt. "Your superior officer has told you to close the file. To do anything else is a poor career move. Think about it. Your father would not be happy."

"You say that now, but listen to the cases—the facts as I know them."

A rustle of fabric and Kazakov opened his eyes. From somewhere Chelomeyev had produced two manila envelopes from inside his woolen greatcoat. From outside the dacha came the sound of the wind stirring in the eaves as if something else was trying to come in—or draw him out. Chelomeyev slid the top envelope across the table to him.

For a moment he almost pushed it away. The lantern light gleamed beckoningly on his tumbler of vodka. Then he tipped the envelope contents onto the table. Police investigation evidence that should be in a police file in the department, not here in his dacha. On top was a photo of a body splayed over strewn documents. Male. In his fifties, though he looked trim and fit. The body wore an expensive-looking blue suit and white shirt, both covered in blood, but what likely killed him was the gaping second mouth in his neck. Blood blackened the edge of a Bokhara carpet, and the hardwood floor under him, but through it you could see the expensive haircut, the manicured hands.

The man was clearly somebody. "Messy," Kazakov said.

"His name is Grigori Ivanov. He runs—or ran—an import-export business in New Moscow specializing in tobacco products and in particular expensive American brands. He was found in his home office like this last Monday morning by the housekeeper who comes in three times a week. He was alone in the house," Chelomeyev said.

Kazakov slid the photo aside to look at the M.E.'s report underneath. Numerous bruises on the body, but the M.E. confirmed his assessment of the mortal wound. According to the report the neck wound would have required considerable strength, but the bruising indicated a beating that could have slowed the victim down. The document was signed neatly with the familiar signature of Khalil Khan, the lone Kyrgyz M.E. in the country and possibly its only Kyrgyz doctor.

Kazakov glanced back at the photo. Physical strength, and also a strong stomach.

He closed his eyes again feeling the old awareness of his country creep back into his soul—something he had been trying to avoid for the past month. Fergana was his people's second chance after the Ottomans drove Yekaterina the Great out of Moscow. After escaping eastward into Siberia, followed by a long diaspora, they had found the tribal Kyrgyz people welcoming and had settled here—only to do to the Kyrgyz what had been done to the Russians by breeding more quickly, taking the land and then simply by excluding the Kyrgyz from the opportunities of modern Ferganese society. The Kyrgyz might still have the ancestral connection to their traditional lands, but they no longer owned it. It made Agafya's bitterness understandable.

He glanced back at the photo. "What about the wife?" he asked. "A bloody death usually speaks of a crime of passion. It would not be so difficult to slit a throat once the victim is down."

"Not this woman. And she was out of town visiting friends." Chelomeyev frowned. "How did you know there was a wife?

Kazakov tapped the photo. "Rings. Not all men wear them, but this man does. It suggests the marriage was important to him—and the wife. You've checked her alibi of course." He glanced up at Chelomeyev who nodded and leaned across the table.

His long pale fingers sorted through the documents to a statement. "Hers."

Kazakov's hand itched for his vodka glass. If he was to get

involved in a case, it would be a case of his choosing—one that still haunted him.

The statement of Svetlana Ivanova was brief. She was out of town for the weekend with a friend and then her return was delayed for twenty-four hours due to road conditions in the mountains. She last spoke to her husband the day before she left. She had phoned him at work to tell him that she had decided to accompany her friend, Olga Gruenwald, on a ski trip to the mountains. Her husband had complained a little about her going without him, but he was busy dealing with some crisis or another at work and—as usual—had chosen work over her.

He glanced up at Chelomeyev. "Her words?"

The young detective nodded. "As close to verbatim as I could capture."

Kazakov turned thoughtfully back to the papers. The phrasing suggested the wife was less than happy in her marriage. But if the case was that obvious, why was Chelomeyev here? Had someone sent him? Someone intent on ensnaring Kazakov in a case again? But surely Chelomeyev wouldn't do such a thing given how much the young detective had risked to help Kazakov on his last case. On the other hand, perhaps this was his penance to save his career...

Kazakov kept reading. The wife and her friend had left on Thursday afternoon and traveled by automobile for the four-hour trip to her friends' dacha in the small mountain village of Biysk, named after another town long lost to the Ottomans. They went to ski and enjoy the clear air and the natural mineral baths. She returned on Tuesday, the day after the body was discovered and was shaken and worried that someone might come after her, too. She could think of no one who would want to harm her husband. He was a well-regarded member of the community. He and she were involved in charity work together. It made no sense.

"And does it make no sense?" Kazakov asked.

Chelomeyev shrugged as if it didn't matter—never a good gesture on a detective, and yet he was here.

"Her alibi is strong. Her friend and her friend's employer both confirm her presence at the dacha. It would be impossible for her to get back down the mountain over the weekend, because they truly were snowed in."

Nodding, Kazakov pawed through the papers. "A mistress?"

"If there was, they were unusually discrete. His office knew of no one."

There had to be something. There was always something. And the death wounds spoke of ferociousness and high emotion that led to the killing. Or the killer was a psychopath.

He read through the wife's friend, Olga Gruenwald's, statement that confirmed the Svetlana Ivanova's alibi and stopped dead half way through, the sudden surge of memories almost overwhelming.

Quickly, he fanned out the other papers across the table and found what he had hoped to find: a photo that likely confirmed Svetlana Ivanova's presence in the mountains. In the photo two women stood arm-in-arm swathed in thick fur coats, their heads encased in matching fur hats that tipped toward each other as fast friends were likely to do. Clearly the wind was blowing for their cheeks were rosy, their furs were blown flat on one side of their bodies, their long hair catching on their faces.

One woman was dark haired and lean featured, but even swathed in the furs, he could tell she had curves in all the right places, though her body was thin. The other woman was blonde with high Slavic cheekbones and bright, intelligent blue eyes. He knew they were intelligent because he knew her—or at least had met her while investigating his previous case. The case that had killed Maria. The case that had resulted in him being shot.

He reached for his glass and drank, holding himself to a sip when he wanted to drain the glass.

"Her." He tapped his finger on the photo. "Let me guess. That is the friend, Olga Gruenwald, yes?"

When Chelomeyev nodded, Kazakov leaned back in his chair and closed his eyes fighting back the nausea and the vodka burn twisting his gut. He had spent the past month telling himself that he had done all that he could about Maria's death, including identifying the murderers, and yet there was something more. Something that connected her death to a rising star politico named Boris Bure. During the investigation a name had come up, but he had never had the chance to investigate further. The name involved was Olga Gruenwald's employer.

There was something here. He knew there was. Olga Gruenwald's employer was a man named Enver Pasha, an Ottoman businessman, a representative of one of the two most powerful empires in the world and one of the empires that sandwiched in the small Russian country of Fergana. The only reason Fergana hadn't already been swallowed up by the Ottoman Empire was because the Chinese Empire of the Sun was pressed right up against Fergana's eastern border and would take aggression against Fergana as aggression against their empire. Fergana was the gristle grinding between the two massive entities and both China and the Ottomans were apt to meddle in Ferganese affairs.

Enver Pasha had been a person of interest in his previous case, both as a possible instigator of a murder, and as a possible target.

Solving the case had killed the woman Kazakov might have loved and left him minus a kidney. He eased his side and looked back at the papers on the table. And now here was Enver Pasha again, like an ill wind.

Chelomeyev's pale face hung like a moon in the shadows of the dacha. Outside the wind had sent a loose shingle tap-tap-tapping like a mad woman trying to get in.

If he was going back to work, this was a good case to sink his teeth into. If he was returning to active duty, then he could partner with Chelomeyev until Sherepov returned, or until he preferred to work on his own.

If he was going back to work.

The trouble was, he wanted the freedom to conduct an investigation that the police department's senior management would never countenance, not investigate a simple murder even if it might give him grounds to access people he otherwise might not have a right to.

He inhaled and the muscles in his side sent a sharp stab right through his heart. No. He wasn't ready yet to make a decision. His injuries were still healing.

When he could breathe again he shuffled Chelomeyev's papers back into a pile and stood, leaning heavily on his cane to limp over to his bedside.

"I can't help you. I don't want to be dragged into a case like this." He sank down onto his bed and would not meet Chelomeyev's gaze. "I'm sorry. I'm not ready to return to work."

Chelomeyev shuffled the papers back into the envelope and shoved back from the table. Without a word, he hauled on his coat and hat and, with the envelopes, went to the door. "I just wanted your opinion of where to start. All my leads have led to dead ends so far."

Kazakov chanced a look in Chelomeyev's direction and caught the disappointed gleam in the young man's gaze. Another hero shot to hell. The lad lived in Fergana, he should get used to it.

"It was good to see you, Pavel," Kazakov said and suddenly he didn't want to send the young man empty-handed out into the cold. But it was too late. Chelomeyev opened the door and stepped out onto the porch.

Kazakov lumbered to his feet and across the room to catch the door before it was fully closed. He hurriedly hauled on boots and stepped outside into the wind and swirl of new flakes as Chelomeyev headed down the stairs.

"Pavel."

The young man swung back to him, the light of the kerosene lantern through the dacha window catching on his brow and cheekbone.

"All I can suggest is to look into Enver Pasha. It was the one thing I neglected to do in the Weber-Manas case. There might be something."

Chelomeyev frowned and then nodded, before turning back to his vehicle. He opened the door and slid inside.

"And—and for God's sake be very careful," Kazakov called, but the door thunked shut so Kazakov wasn't sure that Chelomeyev had even heard.

He stood in the swirl of snow and the wind and watched as the red taillights disappeared down his driveway. Then came the silence of his life—except for the wind off the eastern mountains.

He went inside and poured himself another tumbler of vodka.

To read more of Mareson's Arrow, go to http://www.karenlabrahamson.com/books/maresons-arrow/

ROMANCE, MYSTERY AND FANTASY
FROM K.L. ABRAHAMSON

If you enjoyed this book, you might enjoy other titles available from Karen L. Abrahamson in your local bookstore or wherever e-books are sold.

www.karenlabrahamson.com

KAREN L. ABRAHAMSON
WRITING AS KAREN L. MCKEE
In a land steeped in light and dark, the truth hides in shadow.
SHADOWPLAY
ROMANTIC SUSPENSE

THROUGH
DARK
WATER
A Phoebe Clay Mystery
"... much more than a mystery. [A] spine-tingling tale involving whales, eagles... and murder."
-Joanne Pence, USA Today bestselling author The Angie Amalfi Mysteries
K. L. ABRAHAMSON

SHE HAS THE POWER
TO REWRITE THE
LANDSCAPE -
OR ERASE IT.
AFTERBURN
The American Geological Survey Series Book 1
KAREN L. ABRAHAMSON

HANK HUDSON AND THE ANUBIS

BY

CLARK CHAMBERLAIN

Raven International Publishing
Idaho Falls, ID

Hank Hudson and the Anubis © Copyright 2016
by Clark Chamberlain
All Rights Reserved

Hank Hudson and the Anubis
ISBN- 978-1-944107-04-8
First Edition

Raven International Publishing
PO Box 52112
Idaho Falls, Idaho, 83405

Book design and Illustrations by Clark Chamberlain

www.RavenInternationalPublishing.com
www.Clark-Chamberlain.com

To Riley and Jed.
Thank you for showing me
the magic of these stories

TABLE OF CONTENTS

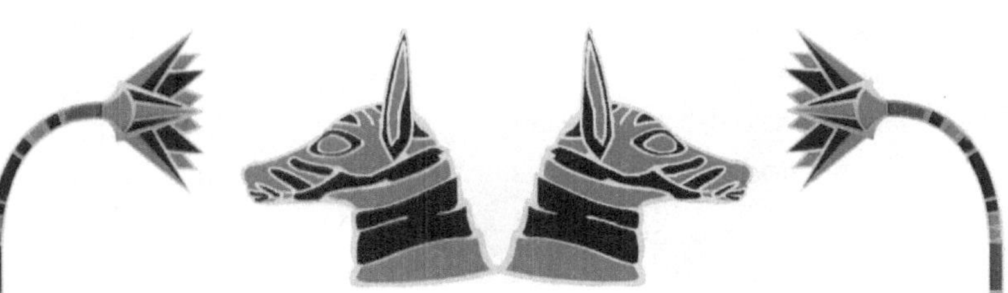

1
TRAINING

October 27, 1933, 10 miles north of Fruitland, North Carolina

If two months ago someone had told Hank Hudson he held the power to turn invisible and store energy from something called ley lines, he'd have said they were crazy. But that was then. Now, Hank understood a few things about this new world: the ley lines, a terrifying force called the Darkness, the power to turn invisible, and the ability to talk with dogs. Hank might only be twelve, but he knew deep in his gut he'd only seen the tip of the iceberg.

He glanced across the grassy fields that spread out from the shore of the reservoir. Tents and gypsy style caravans dotted the landscape. Word had spread like wildfire about what happened in Fruitland, and people poured in to offer their help to Hank and his friends.

"Hank!" Stin shouted.

Hank spun his attention to Stin. As always, the man wore his heavy overcoat from the Great War. Stin had been Hank's first introduction to this amazing world. They'd met when Hank had spotted him stealing food. At that time, Stin found it odd that Hank had even noticed him, since only people who were like Stin could see him when he turned invisible. Hank and Stin were alike in that regard. They both

had the ability to turn invisible at will. They were not alike when it came to training to use the ley line energy.

"Can we continue?" Stin asked.

Hank nodded. The grass, still soft and green under Hank's feet, seemed to be holding out against the inevitable change of season. Hank flexed his hand around the crusty feel of a geode about the size of a baseball. He eyed Stin, who was standing about twenty-five yards away.

Stin stared back.

Hank took in a deep breath of the crisp morning air. Stin seemed like a statue carved from marble. *What's he waiting for?* The only sound came from the rhythmic lapping of the waves on the shore. He relaxed his shoulders as he exhaled.

CRACK!

A blast of energy shot from the geode Stin held, rocketing towards Hank. His own geode wasn't heavy, but lifting it again felt like trying to move his arm through tar. He shouldn't have relaxed.

He was just a half second too late to form a defense. The energy hit him full in the chest, powered by Stin's emotions and channeled with stored ley line energy from the geode.

Hank laughed as the blast knocked him down. He slid across the grass and came to a stop. Still laughing, he stood, but not because he thought being thrown on the ground was particularly funny. It hurt quite a bit, especially his fractured ribs he'd received in his fight with the Darkness. The laughter came from the emotion with which Stin had hit him. When the energy hit Hank, he'd caught a glimpse of Stin's memory: a man's face, a silly joke, a release from the intense feeling of dread, and Stin laughing.

But Stin wasn't laughing now. "You're not trying."

Hank brushed back his blonde hair. "We've been doing this too long. I need to take a break. My ribs," Hank said as he did his best to cradle his side, looking away from Stin. They really didn't hurt that much. Although the ley line energy from the crossing by the reservoir didn't heal him, it powered two significant abilities. First, it allowed for incredible physical endurance, and second, it could channel emotions into energy. The second ability allowed Hank to drive the Darkness away in Fruitland four weeks ago.

Just thinking about the Darkness sent a chill up Hank's spine. It was a mass of dark energy that took basic shapes and forms. It could choose when it wanted to be seen. But even invisible, Hank could still feel it. The Darkness projected a great weight that crushed Hank's chest. The Darkness had untold power, but, more importantly, it had taken Hank's parents, making Hank's main focus finding the Darkness and rescuing them.

Understanding the ley line energy, how it connected with emotions, and what a person could do with it had been Stin's main focus. The only weapon they had against the Darkness came from the ley line energy, and Stin stood determined they learn to use it correctly.

But for Hank, the training seemed pointless. They needed to be searching for his parents or any sign of the Darkness. Instead, they were doing drills with the geodes.

The geodes Hank and Stin held were small, but they could hold a charge from the ley lines that allowed them to get a few blasts of energy or even create a shield. Stin, and the others who'd been training with them, had to use the geodes, but for Hank, it was different. The Darkness had called him a vessel. He still had no idea what it meant to be a vessel. In his daily training, Hank had learned one thing: His body could charge in the ley line energy crossings just like the geodes.

He'd go to the hill overlooking the reservoir and stay in the ley line crossing all day and through the night. Twenty-four hours in the ley line would give Hank enough energy for a week's worth of training. The energy he held inside let him ignore his injuries and also gave him physical endurance. Hank didn't need to take breaks.

"Another break? It seems you've been taking a lot of those lately," Stin said.

Hank shifted his weight and looked back at him. "We've been training every day for the past four weeks, and what's the point? We're no closer to finding my parents or going after the Darkness!" The words tumbled out before Hank could stop them.

"That's exactly why we need to train. We both need to know how to use this energy, so when we find out where your parents are, we have a shot at rescuing them." Stin hesitated like he was waiting for Hank to respond.

Hank didn't.

"It's time to get serious about this," Stin said.

"I am taking this seriously! It's my parents that thing took! It's me that it wants! I'm doing the best I can. Sorry if I can't just shut my feelings off like you do," Hank shouted. He dropped the geode and sat next to it.

Stin came closer. "You think I'm turning my emotions off?" His voice was calm.

Hank shot a look at him. He'd wanted those words to hurt. He'd have to try harder. "Well, you still haven't even opened the letter from Adam, and all you do is train! All day. You don't join us at night. It's like you don't know how to be normal."

Stin's hand went to his inside coat pocket, like a natural reflex to protect an open wound. Hank guessed the pocket contained the letter from Stin's dearest friend, Adam. He'd taught Stin a little about the ley lines and helped him use his invisibility to save soldiers during the Great War, the same war that took Adam's life.

Hank stared at him.

Stin said nothing and moved his hand back down.

He'd hoped hurting Stin would feel good. It didn't. He looked down and pulled at blades of grass.

"Get back up, Hank. Let's go again."

Hank didn't move. "We need to be out looking for my

parents, not training," he muttered.

"I said, get up!"

Hank got to his knees, not ready to take another hit from Stin. He put his hand around the geode, the same one he'd used when he'd fought the Darkness in Fruitland. Each time he picked it up, it reminded him of his missing parents.

"Thank you. Now, let's get back to training. I want you to concentrate on using the energy as a barrier."

"Why? When we get there it's just going to be the Darkness. Putting up a barrier won't stop it."

"You don't know that. We both need to learn how to use the ley line energy if we have a chance at getting your parents back."

A flash of anger shot through Hank. He was sick of it—sick of training, sick of sitting around instead of going after them. No one had made any progress, so why should he?

"You want to keep going? Try this," Hank said as he lifted the geode and focused on his anger. The blast shot out and cracked through the air, blowing grass and fallen leaves in its wake. The moment the energy left the geode, Hank regretted it.

Stin moved to defend himself. He pushed up an energy shield, but it wasn't strong enough to stop the anger Hank had used. It only slowed it down.

Stin screamed in pain as the force of the anger emotion tied to the ley line energy hit him. Stin flew backwards twenty-five feet. He arced across the sky and landed in the lake with a giant splash.

"Stin!" Hank shouted as he ran after him, his heart beating faster. *If I knocked him out, he'll drown.*

Before Hank could get to him, Stin stood, water pouring from his coat pockets. He faltered for a moment, seemed to get his footing, and limped the five feet to shore.

Hank stood by, eyes wide. "Are you okay? Did I hurt you?" Hank's voice trembled with fear. "I'm sorry. I didn't mean..." Hank fell silent as Stin lifted a hand. He limped past him, placing the same hand on Hank's shoulder.

"Maybe we should call it a day," Stin said, his voice empty of emotion.

Hank stood speechless as he watched Stin limp towards the encampment. He wanted to run after him to tell him how sorry he was, but instead, he stood still, looking into the distance as Stin got smaller. Hank balled his fists and kicked a rock into the lake.

He collapsed, closed his eyes, and listened to the water hitting the shore. He rolled to one side, his ribs tender. He glanced across the field. No one was around, but just to be safe, he cleared his mind and went invisible before pulling off his shirt. Even though he couldn't feel much pain, he could see the deep bruises over his ribs. They weren't healing well.

He slipped out of his pants, went to the cold reservoir water, and eased himself into the liquid to soak his sore ribs. He hoped it helped. He'd gotten into the habit of taking cold soaks after training, either in the lake or in the creek that now flowed behind the former physician, Mr. Swenson's, property. The ley line energy might allow him to ignore the pain, but he had to try to heal his injuries. He thought the cold helped.

Mr. Swenson. If the former surgeon ever caught sight of Hank's ribs, he'd throw a fit. Mr. Swenson had tended to Hank's wounds after the fight with the Darkness. With the ley line energy, Hank had made it seem like his injuries were all healed so Mr. Swenson would let him out of the house.

The water rolled across Hank's ribs as he watched a hawk circling above. The Darkness had flown through the air too. Hank wondered if there was a ley line energy that would let him fly. It looked so peaceful. But even peaceful things could be dangerous. The hawk dove after a small fish swimming at the edge of the surface. The bird hit the water, claws out, snatching the trout in one smooth motion.

Hank stayed in the same position for an hour before climbing out of the cool water. He dressed and sat on a soft patch of grass, watching the sun reflect off the water. Thoughts of his parents filled his mind. Not taking action for so many weeks made him sick. They were out there somewhere, being held by the Darkness. What good was training if they never went looking for his parents?

The sun dipped into the horizon, just as Dog padded up to the lake.

Dog didn't bark a word as he plopped down and rested his head on Hank's lap. Hank rubbed the back of Dog's neck as they watched the sun sink.

Dog gave a soft bark.

"Just a tough day. I hurt Stin. Twice."

Dog gave a whine.

"I'm glad he's okay. I feel so stupid. I just want them back." If there was anyone in the encampment who Hank could talk with, it was Dog. He couldn't remember a time without him. He'd always thought he was talking with Dog, and when he met Stin, he'd confirmed it. Going invisible, shooting energy from stones, and talking to dogs. It felt bizarre, and yet, at the same time, made so much sense. The carefree days of being a boy were long gone as he faced the unsure future in this new world.

Dog nuzzled his nose deeper under Hank's hand. Directing his anger at Stin hadn't done Hank any good. What if it had been Dog? Would he have been so anxious to lash out? Stin was the best human friend Hank had.

Hank stood, leaving the geode on the ground. "Come on.

I need to go talk with Stin."

They walked the winding road to the encampment. Fires cracked and popped, sending sparks into the night air. Each glowing ember seemed to sit in the heavens and then morph into a twinkling star. Mr. Swenson had been teaching him the constellations and how to navigate using their positions. Were his parents looking at the same twinkling lights?

Hank felt at home here, and not just because of the people and the familiarity of the area. He was learning to make his own way with more confidence. That was part of what home meant now. Hank hoped Stin would forgive him. He hated to think what would happen if he lost his friendship.

Just outside the encampment a rustling in the nearby trees brought Hank out of his thoughts. He froze, his heart beating faster. He hadn't been paying attention, and now he might pay the price. A shadow grew larger from behind a tree. Dog looked right at the spot.

Instinctively, Hank's hand grasped for the baseball-sized geode. He didn't have it, but he still had enough energy stored in his body from the ley lines to put up a strong defense.

2

THE BOND OF FRIENDSHIP

Hank shifted the weight on his feet. He was as ready as he could be. "Stop sneaking around and come out!" He tried making his voice sound deeper. It didn't work.

The shadow shrunk as a body entered his view. "I'm not sneaking," Lina said as she stepped from the trees. "Hey, where have you been all day?"

Hank's heart slowed as he saw her concerned face.

She looked at his hand cocked behind his body. "Were you getting ready to attack me?"

Hank felt a little silly now. He smirked. "Can't be too safe out here."

"Especially if you run into Fast-Draw-Hudson at night."

Hank giggled. "Sorry."

Lina brushed her black hair behind her ear. She was a year older than Hank, and the two had become fast friends over the past weeks. Hank didn't have the butterfly feeling every time she came around like he did when they first met at the dance, which was good. He'd found it difficult to train with butterflies making such a mess of his insides.

Dog barked.

"Well, why didn't you tell me it was her?"

Dog raised his ears and gave a whine.

"I think it's so cool you can talk to Dog," Lina said as she crouched and scratched the center of his head. Dog closed his eyes and panted like he was in heaven.

"I think it's pretty cool too. I'm sure you could learn how. Stin, Kiska, Misha, and Mr. Swenson all know how to speak it."

"I don't know," she said as she stood up. "They could do it before they were my age. It might just be something you're born with. You forgot to add Mr. and Mrs. Dubois. I know they can talk with Dog."

He hadn't forgotten. Just hearing their names tied his stomach into a knot. Hank had met them when his parents moved across the country and had accidentally left him behind. At first, Hank thought Steve and Julie Dubois were the greatest people in the world. They fed him, gave him a job, and made him feel like he was something special. They'd also told him they were sending letters to his parents, so they could come back and get him. Hank had believed them. They were adults after all. But they hadn't sent any of his letters.

After Hank ran away, they finally got in contact with his parents. They were even there during his fight with the Darkness. But the truth of what they'd done to him felt raw. Steve and Julie Dubois might have everyone else fooled, but Hank kept a sharp eye on them.

Lina looked at him. "Seriously, though, where have you been? I was going out to practice with you but ran into Stin. He said practice was done for the day." She reached into her satchel and pulled out some fragments of a geode. "I need to get another one. I was playing around with it and dropped it."

Hank welcomed the change of subject. "You don't need a new one. Those pieces will still hold a charge," he said. "Just not as much as before."

"All of them?"

"Yep. It's the crystals in the geodes that hold the power. At least that's what it says in Adam's journal." Adam had left three geodes for Stin. When Stin understood what the geodes could do, he'd gathered as many as he could find.

Lina put the pieces back and smiled as she dug around in the satchel. When she pulled her hand out, she was holding something between her finger and thumb. "What about this piece? Will it hold a charge?"

Hank looked at it closely. "I think I see some crystal fragment, so yeah it should." He laughed. "Looks like you've got the world's smallest geode."

She held it triumphantly. "Just let the Darkness come!'

They both laughed at the thought.

Dog barked his approval.

Lina put the tiny fragment back, looked at Hank, and said in an eager tone, "So, did you go somewhere today? Did you learn more about the ley lines? Did Stin send you on a secret mission?"

Stin. Hank shook his head and stared at the dirt.

"What happened?"

"I did something really stupid," Hank said, still not making eye contact. He spent the next few minutes telling her about the training that morning and how he hurt Stin. Lina listened to every word.

"So, now I'm hoping he can forgive me and that he's okay," Hank finished.

"I'm sure he'll forgive you. Stin knows how crazy it must be for you right now," she said.

Hank nodded but wasn't convinced he'd be forgiven.

She must have been able to see his doubts. "If someone really cares about you, they find it in their heart to forgive. My mom was so upset when I started training with you and Stin. She said, 'Let the women be women and the girls be girls.' But she forgave me and tries to understand why I need to do it."

Hank laughed.

"What? It's not funny."

"I'm not laughing at her being upset with you. She says the same thing to me all the time, but with men and boys." Since fighting off the Darkness and losing his parents, he didn't feel much like a boy anymore, but he was to Lina's mom, Mrs. Nieves.

She'd taken Hank under her wing, and although he knew she didn't want him out training, he'd never seen her angry, and therefore couldn't imagine it. He tilted his head. "I didn't know she was upset with you. So why risk her getting mad? You certainly don't have to train with us."

"I want to be there. With you." The last two words brought the butterflies back and seemed to leave his mouth inoperable for speech.

Silence bloomed between them, but Lina quickly withered the blossom by adding, "Helping you against the Darkness ... or anything else."

The Darkness. That thought wrangled the butterflies and returned his speech to full operation. "You can't."

"What do you mean, I can't? I'm just as good as you and a heck of a lot better than most of the people Stin is teaching," she snapped.

"No, that's not what I mean. You're incredible working with the geodes. No one can bring up an energy shield like you."

Her pale features softened.

"I just meant that I don't want you to get hurt. What I did to Stin today—what if that were you? What if the Darkness takes you too? I couldn't..." He trailed off and looked away.

She took his arm. "Come on, that won't happen. Not with you and Stin there."

He gazed at her. Her eyes looked golden instead of their usual brown. She seemed so sure of the fact. He straightened, nodded, and with a little chuckle said, "If I can get Stin to forgive me."

"He will. He's at Misha's fire," she said and turned.

"Don't you want to come with me? Team support?"

She looked over her shoulder. "Sorry, I've got to get home. My mom may forgive me for training with you, but she won't forgive me for getting home late." She smiled and walked into the trees.

Hank and Dog continued down the path. The sound of guitars, accordions, and tambourines floated on the night air. Normally, it was a treat to be at the encampment at night. He stepped through the trees and stopped. Misha's campfire burned just ahead.

The aroma of smoked meats tantalized Hank's taste buds. He spied Misha removing kabobs from the fire. The large man was built with muscles on top of muscles. Misha had been a world famous strongman in a circus.

Hank liked him the first time they met. The man had such a large heart and a zest for life, and he'd do anything for the ones he loved, especially his wife Kiska, the bearded lady whom Misha had met while working with the circus. He protected her like a precious flower. He handed a kabob to his Kiska and then to Stin.

Stin almost never came out at night to the campfires. Since finding the journal, Stin withdrew from the group to focus on continuing Adam's work. Misha joined him every day on the hill to examine the equipment Sheriff Anderson had brought to build a derrick. There was a lot of speculation in the encampment. The only thing they knew for sure was that the sheriff had a plan to use the derrick with the ley lines and the Darkness.

Somehow, the sheriff had held a connection to the Darkness that allowed him to control it. No one had any idea how the sheriff did it or what the derrick would do when constructed over the ley line crossing. After the sheriff was arrested, he'd been moved to the state penitentiary and wasn't allowed visitors. Not that it mattered. Even when he'd been locked up in Fruitland, the sheriff refused to answer any questions.

Now, as Hank looked at Stin, he could see that spark Stin had shown when they ran into Misha in Atlanta. Stin had been alive that night. He had been a man among old friends.

Hank hesitated to walk in. "Maybe I should talk to him in the morning. He looks like he's having a good time," he said in a whisper to Dog.

Dog gave a short bark and pushed him with his head.

"Okay," Hank said and marched forward.

"Hank! Come join us for a song!" a man shouted from another campfire.

Hank waved at the man and tried to give a real smile, but his nerves were holding him back. He still wasn't used to everyone knowing who he was. He stopped just before Misha's campfire. Stin stood nearby, popping meat and vegetables from the kabob into his mouth. Hank's nerves tightened.

Misha and Kiska smiled at him. Hank could do this. He moved next to Stin. "Can I talk to you?"

Hank looked at Stin but could feel Misha's and Kiska's eyes on him. He rubbed his hands and wished he could go invisible in front of them, but they were like Stin and Hank who could see the unseen. "Alone," Hank added.

"Of course," Stin said.

They strolled away from the fire until they were out of earshot.

"I'm so sorry. I shouldn't have done that to you today," Hank said as his eyes studied the ground.

Stin put a hand on his arm and Hank looked up. "It's okay. I shouldn't be pushing you so hard. I've let my feelings cloud my judgment."

"No, you've been doing a good job training me."

Stin smiled and rubbed his leg where Hank had hit him. "Maybe I'm training you a little too well. I had no idea you could pack that much punch into one shot."

Hank gave a short laugh. "Are you okay?"

"Just a bit bruised. Nothing broken. But you're right. I've been turning away from everyone. I've been traveling by myself for so long, and when we found Adam's journal, it brought back a lot of feelings, feelings I've tried to bury since the war." He stopped a moment and cleared his throat. "I've been having a hard time getting back into the swing of society. Even with my friends," Stin said and then motioned with his hand. "Come on. Let's join the others."

Hank smiled, the weight of his angry outburst lifting from his chest. He ambled past Stin who placed a comforting hand on his shoulder. Hank sat opposite Misha who gave him a wide smile.

"Little Fish, I think you will be excited to hear this," Misha said, clapping his hands together and leaning forward as if he were about to offer the secrets of the universe. "I have just received word that my brother, Volk, was seen in Idaho."

Hank had heard of Volk and his arrogant wolf, but didn't see how this was exciting to hear. *Where's Idaho? The mid-west? Maybe. Or was that Ohio?*

Misha kept looking at Hank. Was Misha waiting for him to act excited?

"That's great news about your brother," Hank said.

Kiska smiled, her beard catching the light of the campfire. "He barely knows a thing about your brother," she said to Misha.

"Let me do the honors," Stin said and sat. "Volk spent the last few years experimenting with ley line energy."

"He's had run-ins with the Darkness too," Kiska said, her tone sour.

Hank recalled Misha telling him about the Darkness that attacked his wife.

"And he could be our best bet for finding your parents," Stin said.

Hank's heart seemed to skip a beat. He stood, excited.

"When will he get here?"

Misha's face went from excited to thoughtful. "Well, we only know he was in Idaho. There is a chance he's already gone."

"So, when do we leave to find him?" Hank asked, looking at both men.

"That's not what they were saying!" Kiska exclaimed.

"Exactly," Stin said. "You should stay. Misha and I can travel there and see if we can find him. We'll be gone about a week. I've already talked with Julie Dubois and she'll keep up your training."

Hank gritted his teeth. "You can't leave me behind, especially with her." As the words came out, he realized they were too harsh. He made a quick turn to lighten the mood. "I mean, what happens if you get into trouble? Who's going to bail you out?" He gave a sideways grin.

Misha and Stin looked at each other.

"You said he was the one that fought off the Darkness in Fruitland," Misha said.

Kiska slapped Misha's arm. "Don't encourage him!"

"Nyet, I'm only saying the little fish has done something none of us have."

"That he did. And I guess with what he showed me by the lake today, he might be able to do even more this time," Stin said, his hands crossed over his chest. He seemed to be saying, "Yes, but I don't like it."

Hank grinned. "I'll get ready to go!" He turned to leave before Stin changed his mind.

"Wait," Stin said.

Hank's heart sank an inch as he turned to face him.

"Let me walk you back."

Dog fell in beside them as they made their way to Mr. Swenson's home where Hank and his siblings had lived since their parents were taken.

They'd walked a hundred yards, and Stin still hadn't said anything. Maybe he was waiting until they were farther away from the encampment so Misha wouldn't hear him telling Hank he couldn't go. Hank kept his mouth shut. He wouldn't give an easy opening for Stin to tell him no.

They strolled another fifty yards before Stin said, "I opened it."

The statement was so plain that Hank didn't connect the words with the meaning. He asked, "Opened what?"

"It, it."

Hank stopped, his eyes widened. "You opened the letter? What did it say?"

Stin reached into his coat and handed the letter to Hank.

My dear friend Stin,

As if the war around us wasn't bad enough, I have started to frequently dream about my death. The dreams don't feel like fears manifesting in my sleep. They feel like the future waiting to happen. I can see the place and know the time. I know my end is coming. In fact, if you're reading this letter, it means I have gone from this world.

I'm not filled with sadness. I certainly will miss you and those we left at home, but there is a joy in my heart because you found my letter. Now, I know you've taken a big step into understanding who you really are.

You were always skeptical about the power of the ley lines. It always made me laugh inside that you so easily accepted your ability to turn invisible but not that there could be other power out there in the world. There is. You feel it now. The ley line power is how I came here to leave this for you. There is so much it can do. But I only had enough ley line energy to make one round trip. I could have saved myself, but you know me; that's just not who I am. There are others in this world that deserve my life more than I do.

I left you my journal as a guide. I know there will still be much to learn, but it will build a strong foundation for your life.

Thank you for being here with me. This bloody war has been filled with hate, desperation, and greed, but you have been my center through it all. I will never regret making the decision to come here. Through all the pain of being beaten and trapped like animals, I'm still glad we are here. If it wasn't for us, our comrades would be lost to the ravages that have besieged us.

For you, the war is over, and now you must live your life. Know that inside you is tremendous power. We are different from others in this world, and yet, through that difference, we are drawn to others like us. I do not believe it was an accident that you and I found Misha, Kiska, Volk, and your Elizabeth.

Learn from those who understand more and help those along that were once like us, ignorant and alone.

Farewell my dear friend. I hope your life is filled with love and laughter.

Yours friend always,

Adam

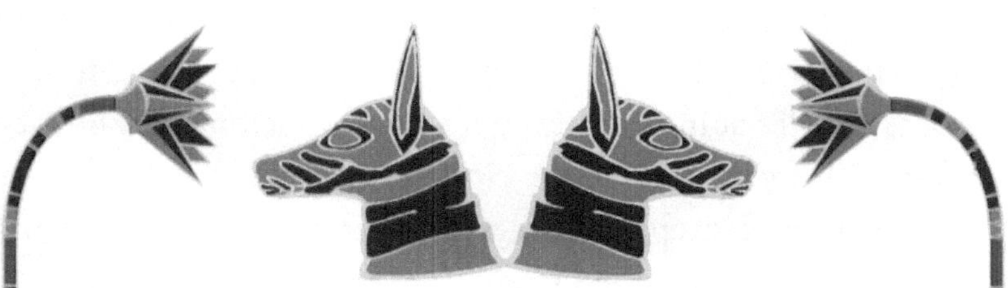

3

CONTRAPTIONS

Morning at the Swensons' had become a mad house since Mr. Swenson opened his doors to the Hudson children. The girls shared a single room, the only spare room in the house, while the boys tucked themselves away wherever they could. One morning, Hank walked into the kitchen and found his younger brother Thomas sleeping on the counter. To say the house wasn't big enough for everyone was an understatement, but Mr. and Mrs. Swenson enjoyed the full house, especially Mrs. Swenson. She woke early every morning to make breakfast. She usually cooked so much they'd take the heaping plates of leftovers to the encampment.

This morning was no different. Hank woke to the smell of frying eggs and bacon. He hadn't had much sleep. His mind kept him up as it raced over the contents of Adam's letter. *Traveling by ley line.* The thought stuck fresh in his mind. Stin had said it would take them a week to make the trip to Idaho and return. What if they had the traveling power of the ley line? Could they cut the trip in half? Would the power fly them there or increase how fast they could drive?

But they didn't have the power, and Adam's letter didn't tell them where they could find it. Adam had drawn a rough map with a few ley line crossings, but none of them were labeled with what power they created. With or without

the traveling ley line power, Hank was still excited to leave for Idaho. He sprung from the couch. Today, they were moving forward, actually doing something to find his parents. He hurried to dress with a grin on his face. Nothing could ruin today.

He passed Joseph, his oldest brother, sleeping in the corner of the hall, his feet extended straight up so he could lay sideways. Hank smiled. Joseph had been a big help when they were escaping from the sheriff in Fruitland. Now, he helped Mr. Swenson with the work around the property and joined them every few days to train. Joseph hadn't gotten the hang of using his emotions with the geodes just yet.

Hank entered the kitchen. "Morning ma'am."

Mrs. Swenson looked up from her skillet and smiled. "Good morning, dear. Pull up to the table, and I'll get you a plate."

"Yes, we want to make sure you're ready for the journey," Mrs. Nieves added.

"Oh, hi, Mrs. Nieves. I didn't know you were here."

"Of course, I'm here. Someone has to try and talk some sense into you. You should let the men do this alone. No one knows what dangers you could face. Stay here and be a boy, Baxt."

He should have expected she'd try to get him to stay. He didn't know what to say.

"Nicoleta, you know you can't stop him," Mrs. Swenson said. "He's a larger part of this than any of the others. Who you should be trying to stop is my Albert. He's too old to be jaunting across the country."

Mrs. Nieves scrunched up her nose. "Well, get them both to stay." She glanced at Hank. "Please, Baxt. Stay."

She'd called him Baxt from the moment he'd met her. He asked Lina what it meant one time. "It's something like luck, or good luck charm," she'd said. Hank had often felt he'd brought people bad luck and trouble. It was nice to think someone thought of him as a good luck charm.

"I've got to get my parents back," he said. "And I feel like I

24

can help on this trip."

Mrs. Nieves placed her hands on her hips and stared him down. Hank swallowed hard. What else could he say to convince her?

"They all have to grow up sometime," Mrs. Swenson said.

"But not at twelve!"

"All my children grew up faster than I wanted. It'll be the same for your Lina too."

Mrs. Nieves raised her hand, her pointer finger extended at Mrs. Swenson.

Hank spoke without thinking. "Is Lina here?"

Mrs. Nieves and Mrs. Swenson shot Hank a surprised glance, like they'd forgotten he was standing there.

Mrs. Nieves shook her head. "She was, but left get something from the camp." She turned her attention back to Mrs. Swenson. "I might not be able to stop Baxt from going, but you won't be seeing my Lina—"

There was a knock on the back door, cutting off Mrs. Nieves. *Saved.* Hank turned his head and stopped short. He hadn't expected to see *her.*

Julie Dubois stood smiling on the other side of the door. She was younger than his own mom by at least ten years. Her face seemed all apologies, but Hank didn't want any of them.

He narrowed his eyes. As if the conversation Mrs. Nieves and Mrs. Swenson were having wasn't already bringing down his mood, seeing Julie brought it to a crashing halt.

Mrs. Swenson opened the door and welcomed Julie.

"Hi Hank," Julie said, as she placed a strand of her umber hair behind her ear.

Hank didn't respond. Instead, he looked at Mrs. Swenson and Mrs. Nieves. "I'm actually not hungry." He stomped past Julie and out the back door.

"Hank, wait," Julie called after him.

Julie and Steve had been making big efforts to win back

Hank's trust, but with each instance, Hank remained strong on his stance.

He picked up the pace.

"Please, Hank. Just let me talk to you," Julie said.

He stopped. His mom and dad had done a good job of teaching him respect. He took a quick breath and turned, but couldn't hold her gaze. Her iron blue eyes were filled with tears.

"I'm sorry, Julie. I just can't talk."

She nodded. "I'm the one who's sorry, Hank. Both Steve and I are sorry. We should've never lied to you. We just wanted you to be safe, and we thought we were protecting you. We didn't want something to happen to you like it did to me."

She'd never mentioned anything happening to her. *Be strong.*

"I—" he started, but stopped before he finished saying anything rude. "I just can't talk right now. I have to get ready to go."

"That's just it. Stay. Stay here. You don't know what can happen out there. Stay and train with me and the others."

He shook his head. "You may have them duped, but I won't be your rube again." Maybe his mom and dad hadn't been complete in teaching him respect.

"Everything okay?" Mr. Swenson asked as he walked over from one of his sheds.

"Yes, I was just leaving," Julie said.

"I thought you were staying for breakfast?"

Julie shook her head. "I just remembered something I needed to get. I'll be back this afternoon."

"It's good to see you, Mrs. Dubois," Mr. Swenson said with a wave of his hat.

She nodded to him and looked at Hank. "I'm sorry."

Hank kept his lips tight. She walked away, her head down and shoulders slumped.

Mr. Swenson was beside him now. "She's not a bad

person."

"She's not a good person either." The words came out a little hotter than Hank had meant. "I'm sorry, Mr. Swenson."

"It's not me you need to be apologizing to. I know you're hurt, but holding on to pain just leads to more pain." He pulled two pieces of salt water taffy from his shirt pocket and handed one to Hank. "Now, give me a hand with this contraption."

Hank unwrapped the taffy and popped it in his mouth. *Blueberry.* Mr. Swenson led him to a barn that sat on the far side of his property. The barn was at least twice the size of the house. Hank had never been one to rummage through people's things, so this was the first time he'd been out here. The twins loved to rummage and said the barn was packed with cars and trucks. The twins had a habit of exaggerating everything. Hank had a hard time imagining him loading his barn with cars he didn't use.

"Grab that handle and pull," Mr. Swenson said, pointing to one of the large bay doors. Hank took hold of the handle and slid the door back while Mr. Swenson pushed the other door. The smell of oil and grease hit Hank. He stepped inside and looked around. The twins weren't exaggerating. The entire barn seemed to be crammed with cars, trucks, engines, and tools.

"Contraptions have been my habit since the Great War. I thought they'd be easier to work on than people. Not so sure about it now."

Hank stepped into the barn, gazing at Mr. Swenson's contraptions.

"I've never even seen you drive, sir."

"I don't like driving. Just like to work on them," Mr. Swenson said.

Where animal stalls might have been were tools, cars, engines, and trucks. Mr. Swenson led the way through the maze of vehicles.

Halfway through the barn, Hank stopped and stared. Just ahead sat the largest truck Hank had ever laid eyes on. Massive seemed the only word appropriate. It looked like the cab had been stretched to add a second set of doors.

Mr. Swenson looked back and smiled. "Yep, that's the contraption we're after. She's a 1922 Mack truck," Mr. Swenson said. "I had to fabricate the cab to add the extra bench seat."

Hank wandered closer, gazing at the cab that loomed over him. "How tall is it?"

"With the new rubber wheels I put on her, she stands ten feet and eleven inches. I've been working on her for the last two years. I rebuilt the engine and increased the sprocket size on the chain drive."

Mr. Swenson might as well have spoken in French. Hank had never learned anything about automobiles, except they were nicer to ride and easier to get into than a moving train.

"Go ahead. Take a look for yourself," Mr. Swenson said with a huge smile and pointed at the underbelly of the truck.

Hank looked under the truck and saw the large metal chain that ran from the engine to the rear axle. He wished he could say something truck smart. Instead, he asked, "How fast will it go?"

"I'm getting one hundred and fifty horse power out of the new engine."

A term Hank had heard but didn't understand. Mr. Swenson must have seen the look of confusion on his face.

"On a flat road, fifty-five miles per hour."

Hank grinned. That was a number he did understand. "So, how far is Idaho? How long will it take us to get there in this?"

"About twenty-five hundred miles from here. So, with stops to rest and fuel up, we should be there in three or four days."

Hank stood and looked at the bed of the truck. Instead of a flat, open bed with some guard rails, the truck bed held what looked like a small house, bigger than the bunkhouse he was locked in at the Dubois's property.

"Do we need to unload the house?" Hank asked, pointing at the windowless wooden-looking house.

"That's where we can sleep. It's like a caravan. I've put shingles on the top for rain, and it even has a cook stove inside."

"How do you get in?"

"There's a door on the back."

Hank ran to look. Sure enough, there were two steps leading up to a door. He climbed them and opened the door. It was like a small bunk house. There were fold-down beds, a chair, a little table, and a cook stove. A stove pipe extended out the top.

"She'll sleep eight people comfortably." He hesitated and then added, "Well, with Misha coming, it might not be that comfortable."

"This is amazing," Hank said as he exited.

"I'll get her fired up and moved out. Then, as soon as Stin and Misha get here, we can go," Mr. Swenson climbed into the open cab. He poked his head out the door and shouted, "Stay clear. Sometimes she likes to backfire."

Hank stepped away. The engine roared to life on the second try. Mr. Swenson revved it a few times. The engine rumbled deep with power. Although loud, Hank found it soothing. Another rev came from the engine.

BANG!

Anything soothing about the sound vanished as the engine backfired. Hank jumped and tripped on something behind him. He tumbled and landed on the hard wooden floor. Mr. Swenson trotted up. "You okay?"

Hank sat up and rubbed the back of his head. "I think so." He looked up to see what tripped him. The front wheel of a motorcycle gleamed at him. There wasn't a speck of dust on it, and the tear-shaped tank, seat, and fenders shone brilliantly in the sunlight.

Mr. Swenson offered him a hand and pulled him up. Hank had only seen a couple of motorcycles in his life, and those had been speeding through town. He'd never met anyone who actually owned one. Hank touched the handle bar.

"She's a real beast. Sorry she bit you," Mr. Swenson said.

"Really, I'm okay. I wasn't paying attention. What's that?" Hank asked pointing to a seat on the other side of the motorcycle.

"A sidecar. It lets you have a passenger or at least bring more than what you can carry on your back."

"It looks fast."

"She is. Some modifications of my own, of course. She's a 1928 Harley Davidson JDH two cam motorcycle. Even stock, she could run almost ninety miles per hour down a flat stretch. After adding the sidecar, normally it would bring the speed down, but not with my modifications. I've bored out the cams, increased torque, and added a few other little secrets. She'll hit a hundred miles per hour and not break a sweat."

A hundred miles per hour. Hank didn't know that was possible outside of flying. "Now that's fast. Maybe we should just take the motorcycle."

Mr. Swenson gave a laugh. "Can you imagine Misha riding on that?"

Hank pictured Misha crammed into the sidecar and laughed too.

Kiska and Mrs. Nieves seemed to have settled on the fact that they weren't stopping Hank from going because they both brought boxes filled with baked goods, smoked meats, and cheese.

After saying their goodbyes, the five travelers loaded the truck with Stin and Mr. Swenson in the front seat, and Hank, Dog, and Misha in the back. Most of Hank's brothers and sisters had come to say goodbye. Joseph had gone to work that morning, and the twins weren't there, but that wasn't surprising. Most days, they could be found exploring some area or another. Sarah, his oldest sister, waved excitedly at them as they pulled away. Each wave seemed to move her thin body back and forth like wheat in a windstorm.

It was great to have everyone say goodbye, but Hank's

heart sunk a step as he realized Lina still hadn't returned.

Stin shifted into the next gear.

"Hank! Wait!"

Hank's heart pulled itself free as Lina's voice drifted into the cab. He looked out his window but didn't see her. "Excuse me," he said to Misha as he climbed over him to peer out the opposite side.

Lina came running down the drive a package in her hand. Hank rolled the window down and leaned out to wave at her.

"See you in a week!"

She jogged beside the truck. "Hank, be safe," she called over the roar of the engine.

"I will," he said and wished he'd been able to come up with something smarter to say.

"Here, catch!" she said and tossed him a wrapped bundle. He reached out his hands as her gift sailed through the air. He clenched his teeth. He might not catch it. He had a three fingers on it, but the soft fabric slipped through them. Another hand shot under his own.

"That was a close one," Misha said as he handed the bundle to Hank.

"Thank you!" Hank shouted to Lina.

Stin drove, as Mr. Swenson wanted nothing to do with being behind the wheel for such an extended period of time. The Swenson's home shrunk from view. Hank looked at the wrapped bundle from Lina.

Dog barked.

"Da, open it," Misha said in agreement with Dog.

"Maybe later," Hank said as he placed it on the floor. He didn't really want to open it with everyone watching.

"Ah," Misha said as if he'd just discovered something. "Maybe it has sweets. Sweets from a sweetheart." He smiled and nudged Hank in the ribs.

Hank could feel his skin flush. He probably looked as red

as a tomato. He needed to change the subject. "So, where in Idaho are we going?"

Misha, Stin, and Mr. Swenson chuckled at once.

"It's a small town called Minidoka," Stin said, saving him from any more embarrassment.

"We won't be stopping much. We've got a lot of miles to cover, and I want to be there in three days," Stin said.

Three days. In three days, he could finally have some answers on how to find his parents.

4

STOWAWAYS

An hour into the journey, Hank's throat hurt from trying to talk over the roar of the engine. It must have done the same to Stin, Misha, Mr. Swenson, and Dog because after the second hour passed, everyone fell silent.

By nightfall, they had driven for over fifteen hours and had only stopped for bathroom breaks and fuel. Stin was determined to drive the entire time, even though Misha offered to switch with him. Hank offered too. They'd been teaching him to drive, and he'd gotten pretty good, but Stin stayed behind the wheel.

The truck bounced twice as it slowed to a stop. The sudden end to the jostling movement and constant roar of the engine woke Hank. He wiped his eyes and looked into the black of night.

"Where are we?" Hank asked, his voice tired.

"About thirty miles outside of Kansas City," Stin replied. "We'll camp here tonight and get going as soon as the sun's up."

They piled out of the truck. Hank's legs were stiff from sitting so long. He lurched his way to the back of the truck, opened the door, and climbed the steps. Mr. Swenson

followed.

"Here," Mr. Swenson said and handed him a box of matches. "In the lower cupboard there should be a lantern. Get it lit so I don't trip and hurt myself."

There were no windows in the caravan, not that they'd help. The moon hid behind the clouds. Hank inched to the cupboards, opening the doors when he reached them. He couldn't see a thing. "Which side of the cupboard should the lantern be on?" Hank called back to Mr. Swenson.

"Left, I think," he replied.

Hank reached his hand left and felt the glass bulb of the lantern just outside the cupboard. He took hold of it and stood up, but stopped. *It was floating outside the cupboard?* He bent down again and thrust his hand into the cupboard, hitting something soft. No, not something. Someone.

"Ouch!" a small voice cried out.

"Get out! Both of you get out of there," Hank shouted at the cupboard.

"What's going on up there?" Stin asked as he entered the caravan.

"We have stowaways," Hank said. He struck a match, and he could see the twins' eyes looking back at him.

"We'll lose two days worth of time if we take them back," Stin said.

Everyone sat in the caravan now. The twins in one corner, a shared sad look on their faces. Misha sat against the wall opposite them. His massive frame seemed to make the room feel even tinier than it was. Mr. Swenson had taken up residence in the only chair, a stern look on his face. Stin paced back and forth. Hank had dropped down one of the beds on the wall and sat on it with Dog by his side.

Mr. Swenson took a deep breath. "And we can't take them with us. I was adamantly opposed to Hank coming."

Hank's shoulders dropped.

"But at least he has the ability to take care of himself," Mr.

Swenson said.

Hank felt a little better, even if it was just his abilities that were being recognized.

"These two will find ways to get in trouble no matter where they are. At least if they're with us we have the ability to protect them," Misha said.

"Mr. Swenson, we'll stay out of your way," Kathy said.

"And we'll do whatever you tell us," Kyle said.

"Just don't take us back," they said together.

Hank had seen that angelic face before. It looked sincere, but it always seemed to lead to more mischief.

"Oh, brother," Mr. Swenson said. "Now I really think we should take them back. And to be honest, my wife probably has a search party out looking for them."

"You're probably right, Mr. Swenson," Hank said as he looked at his brother and sister. "But I agree with Stin. Two days could mean catching up with Volk or missing him."

"Fine," Mr. Swenson said in a huff. "But it's on your heads when these two end up blowing up a house or shooting a cow across a river."

The twins grinned.

"Don't give them any more ideas," Stin said.

"It's nothing they haven't thought of before. You should see all the trouble they've caused at my place."

"Well, we need to find a telephone or a wire to let Mrs. Swenson know we have them with us."

The next morning Hank was surprised at just how well behaved the twins were. They helped with breakfast, didn't play tricks, and when they made stops during the trip, they even came as soon as Mr. Swenson called.

The troop stopped for the night by a small moving stream of water called Muddy Creek, about fifty miles east of Cheyenne, Wyoming.

"Doesn't look that muddy," Kathy said.

"Maybe it's named after someone with the name Creek,"

Kyle said.

"Who would be named Creek?" Kathy retorted.

"I don't know. Who would name their kid Muddy?" Kyle said.

Stin came up behind the twins. "Why don't you use some of that deductive reasoning and find us something out in that grassland to build a fire with."

The twins bounded off and Dog followed. "I'll help them too," Hank said as he sprinted to catch up.

Wyoming looked as flat as Nebraska, with grassland and scrub brush as far as the eye could see. Tonight, with the moon shining brightly, they could see far into the distance. The twins were pulling at a short scraggly looking bush without much luck.

Hank looked around. There was a small group of trees about two hundred yards away. "I'm going to check up there," he said to the twins and Dog as he pointed toward the trees.

The twins grunted an acknowledgment as they pulled harder on the branches of the bush. It held tight to the ground.

Dog barked.

"No, you should stay with them. I don't want them getting lost out here," Hank said.

The stars were bright in the dark night sky. Hank noted the direction of the North Star. He didn't want to get lost out here either. He plodded toward the trees, his mind thinking about the twins. They were only seven, and if they were hurt while on this trip, he might never forgive himself. Maybe if he'd stayed behind the twins wouldn't have thought about stowing away.

He could imagine how furious his dad would be right now if he were here. The twins were always up to no good. It seemed like they lived for a thrill. Hank wasn't searching for a thrill. He wanted to get to Idaho, find Volk, and get his parents back. Wherever they were.

He could only hope they were still in good health and alive, because if he lost that hope...well, he didn't want to think of that. There was one thing he couldn't get out of his mind. This— the Darkness, ley lines, and everything involved—seemed to be centered around him. If he hadn't tried catching up with them, his parents would have never been in Fruitland. They never would have been taken by the Darkness.

Hank looked at the ground. There was nothing hindering his movement, but his legs seemed to be heavier than normal.

His fingers tingled from the chilled night air. He cupped them to his mouth and blew hot breath on them, rubbed them together, and then stuck them in his pockets where he felt something soft. The fabric bundle from Lina. He'd forgotten it. He'd planned on opening it the night before, but with the discovery of the twins, it completely skipped his mind. He pulled it out and examined the bundle in the moonlight. It was the size of his hand and didn't weigh much more than a sandwich. He untied the fabric, a handkerchief with embroidered flowers on the end.

Inside the bundle was a little tin box. He held it to the light and inspected the top. It read:

Whitman's Prestige Chocolates.

His mouth watered. He couldn't remember the last time he'd had a chocolate. He opened the box. It held no chocolates. Instead, a piece of paper lay in the tin. He pulled it out and turned it to the moonlight.

The world's smallest geode to keep you safe on your adventure. -Lina

Hank grinned. Moonlight reflected off the tiny crystal shard. He put the note back in the box, closed it, and placed it in his pocket. He pulled his shoulders back and took in a refreshing breath.

With a newfound spring in his step, he picked up the pace and ran the distance to the trees, jumping over scrub brush and skipping past gopher holes. And then he stopped. The trees were only twenty-five yards away. He wasn't tired. He reached his hand forward. The warm sensation of a ley line trickled across his fingers. *Stin.* Stin would need to come out here and feel this.

Hank turned to head back to the camp and froze. He spied someone about one hundred and fifty yards to his left. Someone in a long trench coat.

"Stin?" Hank called out.

"Hank! Come over here. I found a ley line marked in Adam's journal!" Stin exclaimed.

"I found it too, right here," Hank said as he stepped into the energy stream. It traveled east and west, but Stin was moving more north, indicating that his ley line traveled perpendicular to Hank's. Hank jumped up and down with excitement. "We didn't find the same one! It's going to cross!" Hank jogged forward along the ley line.

Stin dashed towards the crossing.

"You're too slow!" Hank shouted.

"You want to see fast?" Stin said, picking up speed. It was a race to see who'd make it to the crossing of the ley lines first.

Hank focused on his line's path. It would be close. Stin's would cross about twenty yards ahead. Hank moved his legs as fast as he could.

Fifteen yards.

Stin was almost there.

Ten yards.

There was a rushing noise coming from behind Hank.

Five yards.

They were both almost there.

A flash of fur and four legs barreled past Hank and cut in front of Stin.

"Dog! That's cheating!" Hank cried in mock outrage.

Dog barked and rolled around in the ley line crossing.

"I could run that fast if I had four legs," Stin said.

Dog barked again and sat up. His tongue lolled to one side as he panted with pride.

"Yeah, I think he'd look silly too," Hank said as he patted Dog on the head. "Good run."

The lines didn't feel the same as the seven crossing at the reservoir. It felt warm but without the intense feeling of power. Hank put his hands out, one into each ley line. He could feel it flowing through him.

"What do you think it does?" Stin asked.

"Not sure."

"Do you feel any different? Maybe you can fly," Stin said with a chuckle.

Hank thought of the power that Adam had mentioned in the letter. The power to travel with the ley lines. He smiled. Maybe this was it. Hank gave a jump. He didn't get any higher than his normal jump.

"Come on, Hank, you've got to try harder than that."

Hank jumped again and again. He even tried flapping his arms, but nothing. It was a little disappointing, but how could he expect just to stumble into such a power? He shook his head. "Nope. Do you have a geode?"

Stin reached into his coat pocket and handed one to Hank. The small geodes only took a few seconds to charge. He held it in the crossing, counted to five, and returned it to Stin who surveyed the geode like he was waiting for it to say something. "I don't know." I'm not getting much of a feeling," he said.

"See how it works when you put up an energy shield," Hank said.

Stin lifted the geode and pointed it away from them.

"Just a shield," Hank said.

"I'm trying, but it's not doing anything."

"Try shooting a blast."

Stin lifted the geode again. "Nothing."

Hank looked down. He'd hoped this stream would give him a new ability. Maybe not flight, but night vision or fire breathing would have been nice, if those powers even existed. The truth was none of them knew what the possible extent of the powers were. Maybe the ley line crossing at the reservoir was the only crossing that gave powers.

"Well, I can tell there is a charge. I can feel the energy in the geode. It's different than the charge it had when I gave it to you. I just can't tell what it does," Stin said.

"I guess that also means the geodes can't keep the previous charge."

Stin nodded and then added, "I don't think we should

charge any more of our geodes until we can work out what this does."

They took a few minutes to pick up some of the dead wood from the nearby trees, and then they plodded back to the camp.

They were silent for several strides. The letter Adam left for Stin kept popping into Hank's mind. He had to ask. "Stin, in the letter Adam wrote about Misha, Kiska, Volk and a woman named Elizabeth. Who is she?"

The silence continued for a few more strides and then Stin stopped and stared at the horizon. "She was very special to me Hank. But—"

Silence.

Hank wrestled with wanting to know and not bringing up things that made Stin uncomfortable. "You don't have to tell me. I was just curious." Hank took a few steps.

"Wait," Stin said. "We'd talked about getting married. That was before the war. I think we might have still gotten married when I returned, but I'd changed. Everything felt so pointless here. I'd gone from these huge life threatening situations to talking about wedding plans. Nothing made sense."

Dog and Hank looked at Stin but he didn't look back.

"After a month of my coldness she left."

"Where'd she go?"

"Back to her family I guess."

"Have you ever talked with her since then?"

Stin shook his head. "We better get this firewood back," Stin said and tromped off.

Dog whined.

"I know," Hank said and followed after Stin.

"Thank goodness," Mr. Swenson said as they returned to camp. "Some real wood. Twiddle Dee and Twiddle Dum were about to reenact the burning bush."

Hank looked over to see the twins standing around a ring of rocks with an uprooted bush in the center.

"It'll burn," they said.

"Good effort, but let's use this first," Stin said and replaced the bush with the wood he'd brought.

Hank put his down too. "I'll get the matches and the axe." He climbed the steps to the caravan, put his hand on the door knob, and yanked. The door ripped from the hinges. Shocked and still holding the door in his hand, Hank looked at the others.

Mr. Swenson gave a blood curdling scream, like he'd just witnessed a murder. He jumped up and threw his hands in the air. "What did you do?" His voice teetering on full blown anger.

"I don't know. It just came off," Hank said, his voice jittery. Mr. Swenson was sometimes a little grumpy, and he always spoke his mind, but Hank had never seen him angry, and he didn't want to start tonight.

5

STRENGTH OF ARMS

October 29, 1933, Muddy Creek, Wyoming
Everyone gathered around the broken door.

"Why'd you break it?" Kathy asked.

"I didn't mean to break it." Hank said. "It's like it just popped off."

"Why didn't you help us pull out that bush? You could've got it in one yank," Kyle said, with a tone of awe mixed with disappointment.

Stin stepped over to a scrub brush. Its roots spread deep into the earth. He held the geode with his right hand and grabbed the scrub brush by its base in his left hand and heaved. It was like he pulled up a carrot.

"No resistance at all," Stin said. "I can feel the bush, but it's like holding a feather."

The twins rushed over to Stin. "Let me try! Let me try!"

Stin seemed to be deaf to their pleas. He pushed the bush into Kyle's hand and walked over to the truck. "Come here, Hank."

Mr. Swenson sprung forward at Stin. "What are you planning?"

Hank had never seen the old man move with such speed.

"I just want to test Hank's strength."

Mr. Swenson wedged himself between Stin and the truck, throwing his arms out as if to protect it. "Not with my truck, you're not. He's already torn off the back end. I'm not about to let you have him tear up the middle."

Stin exhaled. "He didn't tear off the back end. Just the door."

"And I'm going to have to fix it before we leave tomorrow. I don't have any intention of getting stuck out here in the flatlands," Mr. Swenson added.

Stin stepped back, his hands in the air in a surrender. He looked around the camp. "We won't touch your truck. Hank, don't open anything else," Stin said as Hank nodded in agreement.

Hank could imagine himself tearing off the truck doors as he tried getting in. He didn't want to see just how mad Mr. Swenson would be if he destroyed one of his contraptions.

Stin continued, "But let's try a couple things. When we were at the ley line crossing, you jumped in the air, but if the crossing had given you super human strength, it seems like it would have made you jump higher too. Try it again."

"Okay," Hank said as he squatted down.

Mr. Swenson, the twins, and Dog backed up a few steps and covered their faces as if Hank were about to explode. He jumped as high as he could, but it wasn't any different than before.

"Now try to pull up a bush," Stin said.

Hank reached down and tugged. The bush came up without any effort. Stin picked up the door and handed it to Hank. It felt no heavier to him than the bush. He shifted his grip from the center of the door to one of the ends, lifting it straight out.

"It's weightless," Hank said with a grin.

"Keep holding it," Stin said as he scooped up Kathy and set her on the door.

"Same. I can feel the door, but there's no change in the weight."

Stin clapped his hands and rubbed them together as he looked across the camp. "Misha!"

Misha lumbered over as Kathy hopped down from the door.

No change.

"Get on the opposite end," Stin told him.

Misha gave a big smile to Hank from the other side of the door.

"Push down on it Misha," Stin said.

Misha lifted his right hand and waved it at Hank. It was like looking at a canned ham with five big sausages attached.

"Ready, Little Fish?"

Hank gritted his teeth as Misha placed one finger on the door and pushed down. It didn't move. It was already quite a sight to see Hank holding a door in his hands parallel to the ground. Misha's eyes widened as he looked at Hank, then the door and back at Hank. Misha pushed harder.

No change.

Hank laughed with delight.

"Push, Misha! Push!" the twins chanted. They clapped their hands in rhythm and cheered Misha on.

Misha put his whole hand on the door. It didn't wiggle. He pressed both hands down. Still not a tremor of movement.

"Are you just fooling with me?" Hank asked Misha.

Misha snorted, rolled up his sleeves and pushed down. The veins in his bald head popped out like the lines of a road on a map.

"I think you've proved your point," Mr. Swenson said.

Misha must not have heard him, or at least he ignored him because the next moment he grunted and threw his fist down on the door.

"I think it moved a little. Maybe," Hank said.

Misha snorted, backed up four steps, and lowered his shoulders. He dug the ball of his foot into the ground. "I'm Misha, the strongest man the circus has ever seen! I'll get it to move!" Misha declared with great gusto.

Mr. Swenson stepped closer. "Seriously boys—" he tried to say but was cut off.

"Watch this," Misha said, took three quick steps, and jumped, his massive form strangely aerodynamic as he sailed through the air.

"Hank!" Mr. Swenson shouted. "Stop it!"

The shout made Hank jump, he looked away from Misha and saw the concern on Mr. Swenson's face. Without even thinking, he let go of the door just as Misha's belly touched it.

The twins, who were standing on either side, dove for cover as the door collapsed to the ground, Misha falling squarely on top of it.

CRACK!

Hank spun his gaze to the conquering hero. Misha got to one knee. "I told you I could move it."

"No!" Mr. Swenson cried.

Misha stood and Hank could see the door was now in two jagged halves. Mr. Swenson dropped to his knees beside it.

"I can help," Hank offered.

Mr. Swenson stared at the broken door, not saying a word.

"I'm really sorry about the door," Hank said.

Mr. Swenson let out a sigh and collected the pieces. "I know you're sorry, Hank, and thank you for the offer, but I really think I'd rather take care of this myself."

As Mr. Swenson stood, Hank could see a tear in the old man's eye. He hauled the broken door to the truck.

Stin motioned for Hank, the twins, and Misha.

"I think we should give him a little space tonight," Stin said in a hushed tone.

Everyone nodded in agreement.

"I've never seen him so upset before," Hank said.

"It's my fault. I got too excited about testing the new power," Stin said. "Let's just give him some space for an hour, and I'll talk with him and make sure he's okay."

Everyone stood still for a few moments. Mr. Swenson was pulling tool chests from the back of the truck.

"I think I'm going to head over to the crossing. I want to sleep in it tonight and charge up," Hank said. It sounded more like a question than a statement.

"I don't know. This one seems a little unpredictable," Stin said.

"I can pay attention to what I'm doing. Now that I know what it can do, I'll just move a little slower. Besides, it's nice to the strongest one for a change," Hank said as he patted Misha on the back.

"For now, Little Fish. Just for now," Misha said with a laugh.

Mr. Swenson stopped moving tool boxes around. Hank looked over and caught his eye for a moment. *He's so sad.* "Come on. Let's get out of his way," Hank said to the twins and Dog

Stin and Misha stayed behind to work things out with Mr. Swenson. Hank lay in the center of the ley line crossing. The twins and Dog were lying in it too, all their heads close together in a circle.

"I don't feel anything," Kathy said.

"Me either," Kyle said.

Hank opened an eye and turned his head. "Really? You don't feel it?" The power of the lines washed over Hank like a rapid river. He couldn't imagine how someone could be in it and not feel the energy flowing along. It would be like sitting in a tub of water and not knowing you were wet. "What about at the reservoir?"

They shook their heads.

"But I've seen you use the geodes. Can you feel it then?"

"Holding the geode makes my fingers tingle, like they're asleep," Kyle said.

"Same with me," Kathy said.

Hank closed his eyes. He felt the ley lines. It was the most fantastic thing. He couldn't imagine not being a part of these lines.

"Now you're strong and can shoot things," Kyle said.

Hank realized for the first time that, like the geode Stin had him charge, he must have changed too. Was it a good trade? The strength was cool, but could it really help him against the

Darkness? *Probably not.* He let out a little sigh.

"Actually, when you charge a geode, it replaces the old energy with the new." Saying the words sent a little sting to his belly. He needed to remember in the future not to switch the charge in his body before learning what the new power did.

"But you're not a geode, so maybe it doesn't work like that," Kathy said in a sleepy voice.

"What did you say?" Hank asked.

"She said you're not a geode. And of course he's not a geode. He's our brother," Kyle said.

Hank lurched up. "I'm not a geode."

"Yeah, we know," Kyle said.

"No, I mean you're right. Maybe it doesn't work the same with me. No one else here can charge up. Maybe I work differently. I'm the vessel, " Hank said the last three words in almost a whisper.

"You want to wrestle?" Kyle asked.

"Not wrestle. I said vessel. Never mind." He'd tried to push the Darkness' words far from his mind. Tried to forget the term vessel. He was Hank. He never asked to be a vessel.

He stood and thought of something happy. *The world's smallest geode.* Closing his eyes, he pushed the feeling out and took hold of the ley line power inside him. He could feel the emotion move up his body and down his arm. He opened his eyes. An energy shield about the size of an umbrella extended from his hand.

"Wow!" Kyle said.

Hank turned to see the twins and Dog staring. Kathy reached out her hand and touched it.

"Ouch," she said with a smile as she jerked her hand back. "That stings."

"Sorry," Hank said, the energy shield fading away. He hadn't noticed it before, but now he could tell there was a difference in the energy he carried.

Kathy glanced at her finger, then with wider eyes and a mischievous smile looked at her older brother. "You were thinking of Lina," her voice in a teasing sing-song.

"I was not," Hank lied.

"I saw a flash of her. You used a memory of her to power the shield, didn't you?"

"Quiet," Hank said and lay back down. He'd have to be more careful what memories he thought of when using the ley line energy.

"She is really pretty," his sister said, dropping her voice.

"I said, quiet."

"She is. And really nice too," Kyle said.

"Let's forget about it and get some sleep," Hank said. He could feel his face going a deeper shade of red with each new comment.

Dog barked.

"Seriously, you too? Some man's best friend you are."

6

TRAIL OF THE WOLF

When the sun crested over the horizon, Hank woke with a wonderful feeling, like he'd had the best sleep of his life, fully rested and recharged. Hank wasn't the only one in better spirits. Mr. Swenson smiled as he showed the repaired door.

The door looked pretty good, considering the rough treatment it'd received. Mr. Swenson's skills as a builder were only rivaled by his skill as a mechanic and surgeon. It was a good feeling, knowing they had him.

They drove across Wyoming, up through Utah, and over to Minidoka. It was close to one in the morning when they stopped for the night. The next morning they'd set out to locate Volk, if he was still there.

Minidoka was more of a railroad stop for the farmers than a town. The welcome sign listed a population of 236. There were only two stores: a small variety shop with an attached post office and a blacksmith shop directly across the street with a new, hand-painted sign sporting hasty thick black letters. It read:

Any Engine Repaired!

All seven of them piled out of the truck in front of the store.

"So, what's the plan, Misha? Where's your brother?" Mr. Swenson asked.

Misha stretched his massive arms high in the air. "The telegram said he'd been here five days ago. He's a person that people remember."

"Maybe he picked up supplies," Hank suggested.

"Good idea. Let's check with the store owner," Stin said and turned to enter the shop.

Everyone followed. Stin held the door. A small bell rang and the shopkeeper looked up. Her grey hair bobbed up and down as she moved. Hank guessed she might be the same age as Mrs. Swenson.

The store wasn't much bigger than Mr. Swenson's caravan, and as they all filed in, it felt smaller and smaller. Misha ducked his head under the door frame. The shopkeeper's face puckered as if she'd taken a big bite of lemon.

"Maybe we don't all need to come in," Stin said.

There were nods of agreement as everyone but Stin and Hank filed back out.

"Good morning, ma'am," Stin said, approaching the counter.

"I suppose so. I suspect you're more of those government workers. Come to clean me out of my supplies again."

Hank and Stin gave each other a quizzical look. "No ma'am," Hank said.

"We're hoping to catch up with our friend. Maybe he came in here. He's tall, about six foot two. And skinny as a post," Stin said.

She gave a humph. "There have been so many of you government workers coming in and out of here. How am I supposed to remember what any of you look like?"

"But we're not-" Hank started.

She cut him off. "Every day it's the same thing. You come in here for enough food to feed an army, asking all kinds of questions about the area. Another thing: we think what you're doing is wrong. That land out there shouldn't be blocked off just to give people jobs. And the worst part you're not even hiring locals, bringing in people by the truckload. Sure, we get to sell more, but what I really want to know is when will you open the area back up? I understand people need to work, but now I can't even ride my horse to my favorite fishing hole."

Stin nodded. "Of course, ma'am. I can see your frustration, and I'm sorry you've lost access. I don't have the answers you want. We won't take any more of your time."

She nodded, and they walked out.

Hank closed the door and looked at Stin. "What was that all about?"

"I couldn't say what it's all about, but the federal government created a lot of public work jobs. I guess this is one of the areas where they're putting people to work."

Hank looked up and down the small street. The little town seemed to be doing better than a lot Hank had seen. No signs for soup kitchens, no one asking for work, and everything seemed clean.

"So, what now?" Hank asked.

"We just keep talking to people until we meet someone who saw him. Let's find Mr. Swenson and the others."

A truck drove past. There were three men in the front and eight in the truck bed. Painted on the door of the truck were the words Tennessee Valley Authority.

"Tennessee? They're a long way from home," Hank said, as the truck rolled down the road.

Stin stood quietly, watching the truck drive into the distance.

"What is it?"

"I don't know," Stin said, still looking at the truck.

"It's something."

"They are a long way from home. And it's like the woman said, why not just hire locals? It has to cost more to bring men all the way from Tennessee." Stin took a step and looked back at Hank. "Come on."

Just as they entered the street, the door of the blacksmith

shop opened. A short man no taller than Hank walked out. His face and clothes were covered top to bottom in grime and oil. Trailing behind the man were Mr. Swenson, Dog, Misha, and the twins. They were making a beeline for Mr. Swenson's truck.

The man stopped in the center of the road and raised his arms. "This is fantastic! How in the world did you ever come up with this idea?"

Mr. Swenson smiled widely. "I had just seen one of those old horse-drawn caravans and thought, why not build it on a contraption?"

The grimy man looked back at Mr. Swenson. "I like that. Four doors on a truck?"

"I call it a double cab," Mr. Swenson said.

The blacksmith dropped to his hands and knees. "Do you mind if I take a peak under the frame and hood?"

"Not at all," Mr. Swenson said, now taking the lead.

Hank and Stin fell in beside Misha.

"Any luck?" Hank asked.

"Nyet. Mr. Swenson and the blacksmith haven't stopped talking about machines."

The blacksmith rolled out from under the truck and looked to Mr. Swenson. "This is just ingenious. Double chain drive...and is this a complete custom built engine?"

"It is. Had to if I wanted to get it over sixty miles per hour with the double cab."

The blacksmith popped up. "Sixty? In a truck this big?"

"Of course, we usually keep it right around fifty. Don't want to wear it out."

The blacksmith took a few steps back, as if he were trying to take in a wider view of the truck. "It sure is impressive."

"If you're interested, when I get back home, I could mail you a set of my engine plans," Mr. Swenson said.

"Would you do that for me? I'd certainly be in your debt."

"It'd be my pleasure."

The blacksmith smiled. "So, where are you folks headed anyway? Not much out here, especially now that the TVA has everything shut down."

"Actually, we're looking for my friend's brother. He was here earlier this week," Mr. Swenson said.

"We've got a lot of people coming in and out of town since the TVA showed up here."

"He's my twin brother," Misha said.

The blacksmith looked at Misha and shook his head. "I'd certainly remember a man like you coming through town."

"Actually, he's a skinny pole of a man, but the facial features are the same," Stin said.

The blacksmith looked at Misha's face more closely.

"And he travels with a wolf," Stin said.

The blacksmith snapped his head and looked at Stin. "Wolf? Why didn't you just say so? I can see the resemblance now. Yeah, he came into my shop, had me build him a couple of rods for holding rocks."

"How long ago?" Hank asked, excited to get some good news.

"Oh, about three days ago."

"Is he staying in town?" Hank asked.

"I don't think so. He said he was taking geological samples out by the lake. But honestly, he didn't seem like any of those other government types out there searching."

Mr. Swenson shook the blacksmith's hand. "We appreciate it. What's the fastest way to the lake?"

Searching? The word lodged in Hank's thoughts.

The blacksmith pointed down the road, the way the TVA truck had driven. "That way about twenty miles, but you won't be able to get there. The TVA has all the access roads shut off."

"Excuse me, sir. You mentioned the TVA is searching for something."

"Well, that's our best guess. My friend and I went up one afternoon to go to a fishing hole using the same roads I just told you about. Anyway, we got out there alright. Two hours went by, and we heard a truck. It was clear out in the distance, but we saw men walking a line. Not sure what they're doing. I hear it was some kind of geological survey."

Hank gave Stin a quick glance.

"There's an old sheepherder trail we used. It could get you there. Let me go get my map," the blacksmith said.

Stin reached his hand in his coat pocket and fished around. "I've got one." He opened it and spread it out on the hood of the truck.

The drive to the sheepherder trail took them across single track roads, between farm fields, and through desert sagebrush. Over an hour passed before they arrived at the location the blacksmith marked on their map. They'd been driving on the refuge for almost two hours, and still no sign of Volk.

The bumps and jostles kept Hank from falling asleep. His mind focused on what the blacksmith said he'd built for Volk: "Rods to hold rocks." Those had to be designed for holding geodes, but why would Volk want to handle the geode without touching it to his skin? How could he use it? Stin and Hank figured out early on in order to use the geode, it required skin contact. If the geode was in Stin's pocket, he wouldn't be able to use the power. But if he tied a string to it and wore it around his neck, the geode made skin contact with his chest and he could call up the power. Hank couldn't figure out why Volk didn't want to touch the geode.

He stared out the passenger window. The landscape looked so foreign. Back home in North Carolina everything seemed green, like the land was painted from the same pot of paint. The only place he'd ever been that looked anything like this Idaho desert was Fruitland, but Fruitland had been barren. At least here, sagebrush and odd shaped bushes grew.

Hank spied a particularly large stand of sagebrush. It waved at him. He squinted, taking a closer look. Just then, ten antelope bounded from the bushes. Their nimble frames darted toward the side of the truck.

Hank shouted, "Look out!"

Stin looked left and right, and then slammed his foot on the brakes.

SNAP!

The noise echoed in the double cab and the truck lurched, throwing everyone forward.

Misha asked, "Where in the world did they come from?"

Stin shook his head and looked around the cab of the truck. "Is everyone alright?"

Kyle and Kathy nodded.

"Da."

I think so," Hank said.

Mr. Swenson didn't say a word. Hank looked at him to make sure he hadn't been knocked out. He was awake with his jaw clenched tight.

"What spooked them?" Kathy asked, looking out the window at the antelope in the distance.

"Don't know. Maybe the truck," Stin said.

Hank still watched Mr. Swenson. His jaw still clenched tight, but his body trembled. Hank reached out to put a hand on the man's shoulder, but before he could reach him, Mr. Swenson threw the door open and clambered from the front seat. He moved much faster than Hank imagined he could.

Stin looked back at Hank. "Is he okay?"

"I don't know."

A moment later Mr. Swenson shouted, "No, no, no, no!"

Hank and the others poured out of the truck. Mr. Swenson was on all fours looking under the truck.

"What's wrong?" Hank asked as he got on his hands and knees to join him. Pieces of metal were resting in the dirt road.

"It's the train drive. It snapped," Mr. Swenson said, his tone defeated.

"Can you fix it?" Kyle asked.

Mr. Swenson shook his head. "If I had my shop, sure, but not out here." He stood up and dusted his pants off. "If we walk back into town, we could be there tonight. We can get a tractor out here to tow the truck to town, and I can get it working again. Only grab food and water," Mr. Swenson said as he walked to the back of the truck.

The others followed him, but Hank didn't move. "Kathy, I think I found what spooked them." His voice was just above a whisper.

"What?" Kathy called back.

He stared out at a hulking white wolf, which was less than thirty-five yards away. The wolf had stalked out of the sagebrush and now sat staring at Hank. "Wolf," Hank said.

Misha dropped down next to Hank.

"Is it Volk's wolf?" Hank asked.

Misha peered at the wolf, scrunching his eyes. "Right size, but too far away to tell for sure."

"What's his name? We can call to him."

"Nobo. Not that he'd come. He's—what is the word? Arrogant."

Dog scooted in beside Hank.

They both watched the wolf. The twins knelt next to Hank, and Stin took up the spot to the right of Misha. The wolf sat, staring in their direction.

"You think it sees us?" Kathy asked.

"Yes. I think it's waiting for us," Hank said.

Dog whined.

"It's not going to eat us," Hank said.

"It might eat Kyle," Stin said.

"What? I don't want to get eaten," Kyle said, his voice jittery.

"Don't worry, Kyle. You just need to run faster than Mr. Swenson," Misha said with a chuckle.

"I heard that," Mr. Swenson said. "Now are you six going to sit under there all day, or can we get on the way to town?"

Hank stood. "We can't go back yet. That could be Volk's wolf. I think it wants us to follow him."

Mr. Swenson shook his head. "Nonsense. It's just a wolf looking for an easy meal."

"I don't want to get eaten," Kyle cried from under the truck.

"Nothing is going to eat you!" Hank exclaimed.

Mr. Swenson ignored the interruption. "Besides, if it was

Volk's wolf, then where's Volk?" He put his head under the truck. "Misha, is it Volk's wolf?"

Misha shrugged his shoulders. "Maybe."

"We can't waste time on a maybe," Mr. Swenson said.

"Maybes are all we've got," Hank said, pointing a finger toward the hulking frame of white fur and sharp teeth. "We came here to find a wolf, and there's a wolf."

Mr. Swenson scratched the back of his head, looked out at the wolf, and then back at Hank. A moment passed, and then he nodded.

Hank smiled. "Come on." He took a step toward the wolf, who turned and leaped into the sagebrush.

"See? It's not his wolf. It's just a regular, old, scared wolf," Mr. Swenson said.

Hank stopped and turned to say, "Then I guess I'll be right back." He knew this had to be Volk's wolf. He jogged over to the edge of the sagebrush. "Nobo?"

"Don't get eaten!" Kyle yelled at him, his voice mixed with some encouragement and some relief.

If it wasn't Nobo, he could be walking right into dinner. He took his steps with precision. He pushed through the sagebrush. It smelled like campfire and mint. The branches pushed against him as he squeezed deeper into the stand. He stopped and listened. No huffing, no puffing, no growls—just the sound of his own breathing.

He pushed through to the other side. No Nobo. No Volk. He looked around. There were clusters of sagebrush all across the desert. Fifty yards ahead, the earth made a gentle rise. Two more stands of sagebrush were silhouetted. The hulking white wolf popped his head out between the two bunches and stared at Hank.

Hank called back to his friends. "It's him. I'm sure it's him! Come on!"

They hiked after the wolf for over an hour. Each time they'd get too far behind, the wolf would stop and wait for them to catch up, but wouldn't let them get too close. The wolf always stayed one hundred yards ahead, much too far for Misha to identify the wolf as Nobo. Mr. Swenson reminded Hank every five minutes that they were walking farther away from town and from getting the truck fixed. Hank nodded and made a mental note. Mr. Swenson was up to twenty-three reminders.

"Do you feel that?" Stin asked Hank.

"Feel what?"

"It's faint but I think—"

"A ley line!"

Hank and Stin took a moment to circle the spot, trying to find the ley line.

"Are you two coming?" Mr. Swenson shouted back.

"In a minute," Stin said.

Hank shook his head. "I can feel it here," he said, pointing at the ground where he stood. "I know it should be here, but I can't feel it flowing through me."

"Maybe it's ahead," Stin suggested.

Hank closed his eyes and concentrated on the feeling. He took a step forward, and then another. He took several steps in the opposite direction and then looked at Stin. "I think you're right. It's like I can tell the direction it's moving, like the current in a river."

Stin stepped next to him. He took a few steps forward, a few steps back, and then shook his head. "I feel it faintly, but I can't feel it moving." He looked ahead at the others. "Come on. We better catch up."

Hank and Stin trotted to catch up.

"So nice of you to come back on this wild wolf hunt. You know, we're now a day and a half away from getting my truck fixed," Mr. Swenson said.

Hank added another tally to Mr. Swenson's total. *Reminder number twenty-four.*

"Just a bit more. And if Volk isn't there, we'll turn back," Hank suggested.

Mr. Swenson exhaled his exasperation and walked on.

The wolf had disappeared from sight, crossing another ridge. The travelers tromped another fifty yards and then crested the same small ridge as the wolf.

All of them stopped, silent.

The other side of the ridge dipped into a natural bowl about thirty yards in diameter. All around were stands of sagebrush, tall grass, and other desert plant life. In the bottom of the bowl, nothing grew, but it wasn't empty. Unnaturally white sand filled the floor. Seated in the white sand were large, rectangular-shaped stones that started on the outside of the bowl and circled to the center where there sat a highly polished black stone large enough for four people to stand on.

Kyle broke the silence with a whisper. "What is that?"

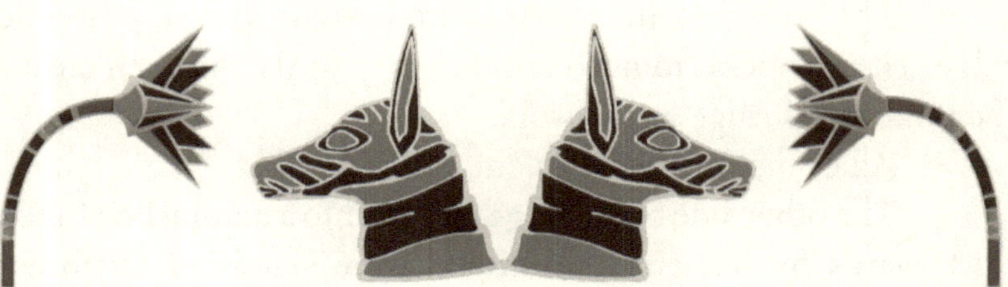

7

A CIRCLE OF ROCKS

October 31, 1933, Minidoka, Idaho

The ley line energy surged just ahead. "I found it," Hank said.

"Found what?" Misha asked as he stared at the stones.

"The lines Stin and I were feeling."

Stin smiled. "It's been under us."

"And it's pouring through this place," Hank said, pointing into the bowl. He caught sight of the wolf sitting on the opposite side. It looked at them and howled.

"That's rude," Hank said.

"That's Nobo," Misha said as he stepped into the bowl.

"Stop!" a voice boomed from the opposite side.

Hank saw a thin man. His facial features had a resemblance to Misha, but that was as far as the similarities went. *So this is Volk.* His beard dangled to his chest. Like asphalt, the beard reflected no light.

"Don't enter the Apep's lair. Unless, of course, you enjoy being attacked," Volk said in his thick Russian accent. He removed his trapper style hat and ran a hand through his inky hair before returning it to his head.

Apep? Lair? Hank thought.

Volk put the trapper hat back on. "What are you doing here?" Volk added in a tone of contempt.

"Brother!" Misha cried out. He bounded across the rim of the bowl and hoisted Volk into a bear hug.

Hank and the others took delicate steps as they followed in Misha's wake.

"Come here," Misha said. "I want you to meet some new friends." He placed Volk on his feet again.

Volk pulled back and brushed his flannel shirt. "I'm not that interested. Your 'friends' could cause a lot of trouble for me," Volk said.

Misha's joy seemed to dry up. Hank gave him a quizzical look, but Misha just shrugged. Hank didn't like the feel of this.

"What is that?" Kyle asked, pointing at the stone in the center of the bowl.

"Something you should stay away from. You should all stay away from this place. It's taken me almost a month to find it, and I'm not ready to lose it because of you!" Volk said, jabbing his finger at Misha.

Hank glimpsed the anger in Volk's umber eyes.

Misha's head and shoulders slumped as he turned from Volk.

"Fine. You're here. Come on. My camp isn't far. You can tell me what you want and be on your way," Volk said and set off in the opposite direction from where they had come.

The others followed Volk. Hank held back a minute, looking at the stone. The ley line energy called to him, and the energy radiated around him. The force held him there for a moment. It felt enormous. It would only take a moment for him to run down the slope and charge, just a little.

Dog barked.

Hank shook his head as if he had awoken from a dream. "What?"

Dog barked twice.

"Coming," Hank said and jogged down the dirt path to catch up with the others.

A rock outcropping gave Volk the perfect place to build his shelter. He'd done an excellent job of camouflaging it into the surroundings. If Volk hadn't lead them to it, Hank would have never seen the little camp.

Hank looked in. There wasn't much room inside the shelter, but every inch of space was being used. A blanket, a supply of food and water, a couple of books, some metal rods, a small pile of geodes, and a few other things an explorer might own filled the small space. Hank guessed Volk liked to travel light. In all, there wasn't more than someone could carry on their back.

Nobo pushed past everyone and entered the shelter. He circled three times on the blanket and dropped, his massive white coat rippling as he came to rest. The spot must have looked comfortable to Dog too because he followed a moment later. Nobo growled and Dog retreated.

"Why's he so mean?" Hank asked Stin.

Volk shot a scowl at Hank. "He's not mean," he said. "He just doesn't feel it necessary to share his space with riffraff." He turned to his brother. "And speaking of riffraff, why is this gaggle of beggars at my door? Especially that one," Volk said sternly, pointing a finger at Stin.

Hank's stomach turned.

Stin stepped between the Russian brothers and said, "Oh, I'm sorry. Have we disturbed the czar in his splendid palace? What's wrong with you?"

Volk took a step forward and pushed a finger into Stin's chest. A large burn mark ran the length of Volk's hand.

"What's wrong with me? You left him to die! Then you come back and break her heart! And if that wasn't enough, you leave us too! And now, you have the audacity to ask what's wrong with me? You have no place here with me," Volk said. He punctuated his words by spitting on Stin's shoe.

"Brother!" Misha said as he pushed Stin back and stood eye to eye with Volk.

Stin dropped his head. "I didn't leave him to die." He

turned and walked away.

A sickening silence spilled over the group. No one said a word, except for Nobo who snickered.

When Stin had gone from sight, Misha confronted Volk. "Why do you always have to be so boorish? You think he needs reminded about Adam or Elizabeth?"

"I think he needs to know he doesn't get to choose when to come and go. You don't leave family like that. First him, then Elizabeth, and finally you and Kiska. You've all left me. That was your choice. You chose to leave. I get to choose how to treat you now," Volk said. He turned before Misha could respond and entered the little shelter.

"Please give me a little time with my brother," Misha said to Hank and the others.

"Why don't we check out what's here," Mr. Swenson suggested to the twins.

Hank, Dog, and the twins followed Mr. Swenson the opposite way that Stin had gone. There wouldn't be much to see out here. The area looked the same—sagebrush, wild grass, dirt, and thistles.

When they were out of hearing, Kyle spoke first. "Is Misha going to be safe? I don't want Volk to feed him to the wolf."

"That wolf isn't going to eat anyone," Kathy said.

Hank put an arm on Kyle's shoulder. "He's going to be fine. Misha will make it okay. You'll see." Hank stopped. "Hey, I think I should catch up with Stin and make sure he's okay."

Hank went to turn, but Mr. Swenson caught his arm. "Give him some time alone."

"But—"

"No buts. Let's just take a nice walk in the desert and then go back and check on the brothers."

Hank nodded, but shoved his hands in his pocket. Dog gave him a sympathetic whine and they continued walking.

No one spoke. The only sound came from nature. Grasshoppers chirped, and birds sang out as they wandered through the desert. It must have been thirty minutes before Mr. Swenson finally stopped. He squinted at something on the horizon. Hank followed his gaze and caught a reflection.

"What is it?" Kathy asked.

"I don't know. Maybe a truck," Mr. Swenson said.

"Yeah, it's a truck. It has those letters TVA on the door," Kyle said.

"You can't read the letters from this distance," Hank said, skeptical.

"Look for yourself," Kyle said and handed Hank a pair of small binoculars.

Hank look dumbfounded at them, and then at Kyle. "Where did you get these?"

"I saw them in Volk's shelter."

"The wolf man's shelter? The same wolf you're concerned about eating you? That's whose binoculars you stole?" Hank asked.

Kyle kicked at the dirt. "I didn't steal them. Just borrowed them for a minute." He added in a timid tone, "Do you think he'll be mad?"

Kathy shook her head in disbelief.

"Yes. Yes, I think the angry Russian with the giant angry wolf will be mad if you steal his stuff," Hank said as he turned back from his brother and looked through the binoculars. "Some of them have guns, and—"

"And what?" Mr. Swenson asked.

"You're not going to like it," Hank said and handed the binoculars to Mr. Swenson.

"My truck! They're stealing my truck!" Mr. Swenson took four quick steps, like he was marching to get his truck back.

"Mr. Swenson, what are you doing?" Kyle asked.

Mr. Swenson stopped, looking back and forth between the kids and his truck. He sighed and returned to Hank and the twins.

"Are the men with guns coming this way?" Kyle asked with an inflection that sounded like he might want them to come.

Mr. Swenson looked through the binoculars again. "No, they're headed parallel to us. Come on, we need to get the others.

I'm not letting them take my truck!"

As they neared the shelter, they heard voices floating through the air.

"Are they fighting?" Kathy asked.

"Is he mad about the binoculars?" Kyle added.

Dog barked twice.

"I think you're right," Hank said with a smile. "I think they're singing."

"Just needed some time," Mr. Swenson said.

The song was in Russian, and Hank wasn't sure if they were singing it well or not, but they were singing it with great gusto. Misha and Volk rested on the ground, arm over arm. They swayed back and forth as they sang. Nobo, still in the shelter, clamped both front paws over his head. *Maybe they weren't singing it well.*

Misha turned his attention to the returned group. "Now, a proper introduction." Both he and Volk stood. "This is Mr. Swenson, Dog, Kathy, Kyle, and the little fish I was telling you about—"

"Mr. Hudson," Volk said, stepping forward and shaking Hank's hand. "You fought an Apep and drove it back. I am impressed you are still standing. Forgive my rudeness. I didn't know we were fighting on the same side. Sit down. We have much to discuss."

Hank looked at Misha. Misha gave him a bold smile and nodded. Hank sat in the dirt.

"Get up, Hank! All of you get up! They're taking my truck!" Red splotches spread across Mr. Swenson's cheeks, which added to his already flushed expression.

Volk stood, canteen in hand. "I think you should sit and have some water."

Mr. Swenson pushed the canteen away and shook his head. "There's no time for water! Aren't any of you listening? They're stealing my contraption! We have to go—"

Mr. Swenson's eyes rolled back, and he collapsed into

Volk's arms.

"Mr. Swenson!" Hank jumped to his feet.

"Calm down, Mr. Hudson. He's fine," Volk said. He laid Mr. Swenson on the dirt floor.

"I think he had a stroke! We need to get him to town!"

Volk chuckled as he poured water over a cloth. "He's fine. I just gave him a little something to help him calm down." He placed the cloth on Mr. Swenson's forehead and turned back to the group. He held something in his hand.

"A geode? You knocked him out with that?" Hank asked.

"Yes. If I hadn't, he might have injured himself."

"But what about his truck?"

Volk shrugged and sat in the dirt. "I thought you came here looking for answers, not for trucks."

Hank looked at Mr. Swenson sleeping in the dirt, his face returning to its normal color. *He's okay.* There were a million questions flying through Hank's mind. He sat back and asked first, "What's an Apep?"

The others sat around the two, and Dog plopped down next to Hank. Volk eyed Hank with a serious expression.

"An Apep is what you have called the Darkness. He's also been called the Snake of Chaos and Apophis. There's an ancient legend from Egypt about a great, dark serpent that opposed the God Ra. But the legend skewed the truth. First, it isn't just one. There are seven."

"Seven?" Hank asked and swallowed hard. One was almost unstoppable. How could he get his parents back if there were seven guarding them?

"Yes, seven. They were once men. Great scholars and leaders of Egypt who had discovered and harnessed the power of the ley lines. Have you seen the great pyramids in Egypt?"

"Just in pictures," Hank said.

"The pictures pale in comparison to seeing them with your own eyes. When you look at it in person, you realize what a truly incredible feat it would be for humans of that era to build such a magnificent structure. But with the ley lines—"

Hank's mind flashed to Misha and the door, and he said with realization, "A man could lift the stones."

"Yes. Increased strength, not growing weary, precision cutting of stone, even the transportation—all done with the power they gained in the ley lines. They built a kingdom like the world has never seen again, and then these men who had everything craved more," Volk said.

A shiver ran up Hank's back. "What else could they want?"

"To become immortal and rule their kingdom for all time," Volk said.

"The ley lines could do that?" Hank asked.

"Yes, the seven men became immortal. They built a great apparatus that transformed them. But it didn't work the way they had intended. They became energy, much like the ley lines."

"It wants a vessel," Hank said flatly as he remembered the Apep's slick voice in his mind. It told Hank he could be his vessel. Until this moment, Hank didn't understand exactly what that meant.

"Yes, a vessel. A container to hold their energy. If they could find a person who could maintain their energy, they would have a body to use. Thankfully, they've never been able to get one."

"Yeah, that's a good thing," Hank said, shifting is weight on the hard ground.

"It is also how they were captured," Volk said.

"With a person?" Hank asked.

"No, a geode. A huge geode. All seven had been imprisoned for centuries, but during the Great War, the geodes that held them were damaged or destroyed, and now, they are loose again in the world."

A silence drifted over the group. Hank thought about how seven of these Apep were roaming the world, searching for a vessel. Searching for him. Then, he thought about his parents. "I don't care what they want. I just want to get my parents back."

Volk tilted his head. The man's look brought silence to the group.

Nobo broke the silence with a howl.

Mr. Swenson sprung to his feet as if he'd just been launched by a catapult. He looked around, his face covered with confusion. "What's going on?"

No one answered.

Volk looked at Nobo. "How close are they?" Volk asked as he stood.

Nobo stepped out of the shelter and sniffed the air. Dog raised his head and did the same, giving a quick yap. Nobo glared at him and gave a short growl.

"Dog says they're about three hundred yards," Hank said.

"I understood him," Volk said with a snap.

"Who's coming?" Misha asked.

"Probably those TVA workers towing my truck," Mr. Swenson said.

"Where did you see the TVA?" Volk demanded. "And why didn't you tell me you saw them?"

"Because you—" Hank started to say, but Volk raised his finger and glared at him.

"We'd walked about thirty minutes north of here. They were at least a half mile farther, and I told you they had my truck. What's going on?" Mr. Swenson asked.

"I don't care about your truck. They're looking for the lines," Volk said.

Hank caught a glimpse of Kyle. He slipped the binoculars out of his pocket and rested them on the dirt floor of the shelter.

Volk continued, "The government wants to contain all the ley line crossings."

"Why?" Hank asked.

"Didn't you listen to me tell you about the Apep? They want the power of the ley lines." Volk sprung over the twins and shoved his belongings into a bag. "We need to get going." He lifted the binoculars and stopped. "I don't remember leaving these here," Volk said to no one in particular.

Kyle's eyes widened and his body froze, but Volk didn't say another word about them. He shoved the binoculars into the bag and continued loading his other belongings.

Hank poked his head into the shelter and said, "Why are they looking for the ley lines? Why wouldn't the Apep just tell them where they are? Aren't they working together?"

Volk didn't stop his packing. "The Apep doesn't like to share. How do you think they were captured before? It's a game of balance. The government wants to control the Apep and the power while the Apep wants to use men to gain back its total control." Volk shoved the last of his things in the bag and turned.

"But I don't—" Hank started.

"We don't have time for any more history. With all of you, I don't think we can get out of here without an incident."

There was movement from the far side. Volk pulled another geode from his pocket and pointed.

Stin walked into camp and looked at Volk. "Hank and I can slow them down."

Volk's eyes narrowed. "How?"

Hank smiled. "They won't even see us."

Volk stared a moment longer, then nodded. "Fine. You two take care of them and meet us back here. I have to get something before we can go."

8
DANGEROUS GEODES

Hank and Stin crouched behind a large stand of sagebrush. On the horizon, Hank spied the silhouettes of men. They walked in a row with an equal distance between them. Their steady pace and formation reminded Hank of a time, in his home town, when a little girl disappeared in the woods. The town gathered together and formed long lines to walk through the forest. They searched for two days using the rows of steady moving people until they found her. Now, here in Idaho, these men used the same technique, but these men weren't searching for a lost child.

"They're looking for the ley line crossing," Stin said.

"Why can't they feel it? Volk made it sound like they were working with the Apep. Some of them must be like us," Hank said.

"Probably not, and even if they were like us, these lines don't want to be found. They must have hundreds of men walking this desert in hopes of finding the crossing."

"Do you think the government wants the power?"

"I don't doubt it."

Hank waited for Stin to continue. He didn't. Instead, he stared at the line of men in the distance. Hank couldn't put his finger on it, but Stin seemed to be gone.

"Are you okay?"

Stin opened his mouth and then closed it again. He didn't look at Hank.

The line of men made a steady advance. If they continued on their path, they'd reach the ley line crossing at the center of the bowl in less than fifteen minutes.

"Stin?"

Stin squeezed his eyes shut and looked at Hank. "Sorry. Just had a moment where I felt I was back in Europe. Are you ready for this?"

Hank sucked down a quick breath. "Ready as I'll ever be."

"Let's go slow them down."

Hank cleared his mind of his family and friends. *Don't be seen,* he thought and stepped out of the sagebrush.

They needed to buy themselves at least an hour's head start to get out of the desert. The silhouetted men towed Mr. Swenson's contraption behind their TVA-marked vehicle. Stin and Hank could get to it, but they had no way to fix it. The truck towing Mr. Swenson's contraption looked half the size. Transportation would be a problem. Volk said he'd handle it, but Hank couldn't imagine the rough-looking woodsman owning a truck as large as Mr. Swenson's. Hank could imagine Volk owning a covered wagon pulled by a team of woolly wolves.

Right now, he needed to concentrate on slowing this group of government men. Hank continued to follow Stin. They crept straight toward one of the men on the end. The man was less than fifty yards away and looking straight at them. His eyes held no hint of recognition. He didn't see them.

Hank smiled to himself but immediately thought, *Don't be seen,* just to be safe. Stin motioned for him to stop as he pulled a geode from his pocket. Hank nodded, and prepared to back him up.

Stin closed the distance and stuck his leg in the man's path. The man's eyes widened and he shouted as he tripped over Stin's leg. He fell, but caught himself before crashing to the ground.

"Are you okay?" another man yelled to the first.

"I'm—"

The man on the ground was cut off as Stin shocked him with the geode. The other men might not have seen Stin and Hank, but they'd have a hard time not seeing the flash of energy from the geode. The other men shouted and raced toward the unconscious man on the ground.

Hank tensed up, ready to fight. Then, Stin motioned for him to follow. Hank stepped over the unconscious man and jogged to the truck, passed the driver who had just exited to run towards the commotion.

Stin stopped at the back of the truck. "Think you have a little strong man left in you?"

Hank concentrated on his body. Over the past few days, he'd noticed a difference in the ley line energy he held, like he could tell how much remained of each type. He knew he stored some energy but didn't know if he contained the strength of arms, the emotional amplifier, or a mixture of both.

Hank put both hands under the truck's bumper. "Only one way to find out," he said. Like he was preparing to lift a heavy box, he gritted his teeth and flexed his muscles. He needn't have bothered. The truck's back end lifted like he'd picked up nothing more than a chair. Hank smiled and then looked at the other end of the truck. The tires still rested on the desert floor. "Watch this," Hank said, his smile widening.

He lifted the entire truck in the air, turned it over, and set it down, wheels up. "That should take them a while to turn over."

"So considerate. I'd have smashed it," Stin said.

"Well, I don't want them to get stuck out here all day."

"What the devil!" The driver of the truck called out.

The other men stared at the truck.

"I think that's our cue to exit," Stin said.

"Right behind you."

They made it back to find Volk's camp empty except for Dog, who barked at their arrival.

"Thanks for waiting for us. Where'd they go?

Dog led them back to the bowl. Misha, Nobo, and the

twins were in the center. Volk and Mr. Swenson watched from the top.

"Back so soon? I thought it would have taken longer to kill so many men," Volk said to Stin.

Hank's stomach turned. "We didn't kill anyone! Why would Stin and I do that?"

"Stin said you were going to take care of them." He turned to Stin. "This is a war. I thought that's what soldiers did," Volk said, then spit on the ground.

"Yes, soldiers do that. But those aren't soldiers, Volk. They're not wearing uniforms. They're just regular men trying to work. There's no war going on here."

Volk stepped toward Stin, the two eye to eye. Hank clenched his fist. He'd stop Volk if he had to.

Volk wagged a finger in Stin's face. "That's what you think, but soon you'll know that this is war."

"Volk—" Stin started, but Mr. Swenson cut him off.

"Boys, you need to calm down."

Stin and Volk stared at each other. Neither seemed willing to break eye contact first. Hank still clenched his fist. He'd just picked up a truck. Volk wouldn't be a problem.

"We just put them in like this?" Kyle called up from the bowl.

Everyone looked down. Kyle held a geode by a metal rod over the center rock. Misha and Kathy stood beside him, also holding metal rods with geodes on the end.

"Just like that, but remember, don't touch the geode with your skin," Volk said.

"Why can't they touch it?" Hank asked as he watched.

Volk held his hand out to Hank. The slight scar he'd seen earlier spread across Volk's palm. It looked like the pockmarks Hank had seen on some of the geodes.

"It did that to you? And you've got my brother and sister down there?"

"My brother is there too," Volk said.

Hank rushed into the bowl.

"What are you doing? You shouldn't go in the ley lines! It knows you just like it knows me!" Volk called after him.

Hank didn't listen. He wasn't going to let Kyle and Kathy be hurt. "Kyle! Kathy! Don't touch those!"

They looked back at him with questioning eyes.

"Those geodes are dangerous!"

"We know," Kathy said. "Volk warned us."

Hank gritted his teeth. He took a short breath. "I don't care that he warned you. What would happen if you got hurt? You shouldn't even be here with us. Now, put those down, and let's get out of here."

Misha set down his metal rod and took Kathy's. "I'm sorry, Hank. I shouldn't have let them help."

"Hank! Come back up here," Volk shouted at him.

Hank slowed down as he neared the center. He'd entered a stream. The ley line energy moved through him. It felt warm and tingly. He walked along the line toward the center.

"It's okay, Misha. I just don't want anything bad to happen to you guys. With Mom and Dad—" he stopped cold. Hank's eyes widened as a freezing chill moved through his body.

"What's wrong?" Kyle said.

"Run!"

"What?" Misha asked.

"I said, run! It's coming! The Darkness is coming!"

"I warned you! That's why I sent them in to retrieve the power!" Volk cried out.

Misha sprung forward and scooped up both Kathy and Kyle in his massive arms. Hank was right behind them, running up the side of the bowl. The crushing weight of the Apep closed around him.

As they exited the bowl, Volk waved for them to follow. "Hurry. We need to go this way, to the lake!"

Dog and Nobo led the way through the desert scrub. The weight of the Apep grew as it pushed down on Hank.

"It's almost here," Hank said to Stin. "We have to fight it, give Misha some time to get the kids away."

Stin nodded as Misha looked back.

"Don't slow down, Little Fish," Misha said.

"You keep going. We'll be right behind you," Stin said.

Misha looked at Kathy and Kyle, gave a solemn nod to Stin, and kept running.

Volk and Stin stood beside Hank as he turned to survey the empty desert. The weight of the Apep crushed down, but it still hadn't materialized. Stin reached into his coat pocket and pulled out two geodes. He handed one to Volk.

"What does it do?" Volk asked.

"Just think about how much you hate me and focus it on that monster. Hank, do you have enough energy?" Stin asked.

Hank concentrated on his body. The warmth of the ley line energy wavered inside him. "I think so." *I hope so.*

The weight of the Apep increased, but still, Hank couldn't see it. The empty blue sky gave no sign of the storm rolling through them. Hank's heart beat faster. He could hear it *thump, thump, thumping* against his chest. Would this Apep be the same one that took his parents? Could he beat it again, or had it been dumb luck in Fruitland?

The sounds of nature vanished, replaced with the beating of Hank's heart and the deep breaths from Stin and Volk. "It's close." As soon as the words exited Hank's mouth, the sky darkened

9

FLIGHT OF THE LOON

Hank pushed back his foot to brace himself against the Apep. It hadn't materialized, but it blackened the sky, and its weight tripled against him, making each movement a labor, like slogging through mud.

"Where is it?" Volk asked.

Volk and Stin both swiveled their heads back and forth, searching for the Apep.

"It's here. It's playing with us," Stin said.

A gust of wind shot against Hank's back. He spun around, his blood racing.

No Apep.

"Show yourself!" Hank shouted at the dark, empty sky.

No answer. Last time Hank fought an Apep, it talked to him. It had felt like an invasion because the Apep's words poured into Hank's mind, not his ears. Hank never wanted to have that slick voice drip through his mind again, but now, he'd prefer it to this cat and mouse game.

"Arhhh!" Volk screamed as he flew through the air and smashed hard into the desert ground.

"Volk!" Stin shouted, backing against Hank.

Hank clenched his teeth, waiting to be hit. Volk rolled over and rose to his knees. The sky above them darkened

more, like the sun had gone down. Hank looked up as the Apep materialized. It coiled slowly in the air, like a long snake made of smoke. Hank's breath caught in his chest.

Stin didn't hesitate. He stepped in front of Hank, pointed his geode at the Apep, and let out a strong blast of energy. White light lit up the sky. The Apep recoiled for a moment and then snapped forward, striking at Stin, who pushed Hank out of the way as the Apep struck him dead center. The force knocked Stin off his feet.

Another energy blast, this one brighter than Stin's, smashed into the Apep. Volk smiled as the Apep recoiled again. It shot high into the air, making a large circle above them. Volk rushed to Stin's side and helped him up.

Hank looked at the two and then at the Apep. "Let's all shoot at the same time!"

Stin and Volk pointed their geodes at the Apep. Hank pointed his hand and shouted, "Now!"

Three blasts of ley line energy flew at the Apep. The sky lit up. A smile crossed Hank's lips, but fled, as the sky darkened again, and the Apep sprung at Stin and Volk. Hank didn't hesitate. He lunged forward in a sprint, aiming at the Apep.

"Hank, don't!" Stin yelled.

It was too late to stop. The Apep smashed into Stin and Volk at the same moment Hank smashed into it. Piercing pain ripped through Hank's body. He clenched his teeth hard, trying not to cry out. Stin's and Volk's screams echoed in Hank's ears as they flew through the air and tumbled across the ground.

The slick, inky voice entered Hank's mind. "So, you do exist," the Apep said.

It sounded almost the same as the one he'd fought in Fruitland.

"I did not believe the rumors that a vessel had been found. But then, I felt an odd sensation as someone entered my ley line. I had to see if it was you."

Hank looked at the ground. The Apep moved him higher in the air. From this height, if the Apep dropped him, he'd splat like a bug hitting a truck window.

"I'm no one's vessel!"

"But maybe you would be. For the right price," the Apep said.

Hank squeezed his eyes tight as another flash of pain tore across his body. He bit through the words. "There's nothing you have that I want!"

"Really?" the Apep said, its voice taking on a sympathetic tone.

Hank opened his eyes, but he didn't see the Idaho desert. Now, he floated in a warehouse. He looked around the room and saw them. His parents.

"Mom! Dad!"

Even though they were awake, they didn't respond to his voice. They huddled against each other, a look of fear on their faces.

"Mom, Dad! I'm right here!"

"They can't hear you, Hank Hudson." As the Apep's words hit Hank's mind, his vision shifted again, back to flying high above the desert.

"Let them go!"

"Be my vessel," the Apep hissed. "I'll make sure they are released."

He could do it. His parents had done so much for him. It would be an easy trade. His life for the lives of his parents.

"You're brave, Hank Hudson. You have no fear of your own sacrifice. You will give me the body I need to rule this world!"

Hank blinked. The Idaho desert had changed from one of sagebrush to one of sand. Hank looked down to find himself standing on the top of a pyramid.

"My kingdom. You will give it back to me. Say yes."

Hank looked over the complex of pyramids. There were thousands of people looking up at him as they were forced on their knees. *Slaves.* Could he really trade his parents' freedom for the enslavement of the world?

Before he could say yes or no, the sky lit up from an energy blast. The Apep shrieked in pain. It bucked and spun, and Hank lost his grip. The air rushed past his body as he dropped toward the ground. His heart beat faster as he braced for the inevitable splat. Stin he cursed at Volk for shooting. But that did nothing to slow Hank's decent.

Hank closed his eyes. He saw his family, Dog, Stin, Lina, and Misha. *I'm sorry.* He'd thought he had the power to save them and protect the ones he loved, but now, he had reached the end of his short life.

The impact hit him hard, but it wasn't nearly as bad as he thought. Why did it feel like he was still moving through the air? He opened his eyes. The Apep had caught him.

"I won't lose you so easily, Vessel."

Hearing the words caused a snap. Hank's muscles tightened as his anger flared. "I'm never going to be your vessel! I'd never let you use me to hurt the ones I love!" The power of the ley lines rushed from his body as he let loose the entire store he held.

The energy flashed across the sky, switching the darkness for a blinding white light.

"Nooooo!" the Apep screamed.

Hank's body again plummeted toward the ground, but this time only ten feet. He hit hard. Stars danced in front of his eyes, but the darkness in the sky was gone. The Apep's crushing weight vanished.

"Hank!" Stin yelled as he ran forward. Both he and Volk reached Hank at the same time. "Are you okay?"

Hank sat up. His head pounded and his cracked ribs hurt more, but he was alive. "I think so."

"Good. We need to go, quick!" Volk said.

With their help, Hank got to his feet. The sound of the desert returned, and in the distance, a motor roared.

"It must have told them," Volk said.

"Told who?" Stin asked.

"The Apep. It must have told the government goons where we were before it attacked us."

"But I thought they weren't friends?" Hank asked.

"There's no time to talk the politics of Apeps and men. We have to get to the lake!"

Hank didn't question him. They ran, and with each step, Hank's side hurt more.

The lake rose on the horizon, but the sound of the engines closed on them. They wouldn't outrun the vehicles. Hank's lungs burned, and his ribs screamed at him with each step. He'd used up the last of the Fruitland ley line energy and his endurance with it. He couldn't take the pain of his broken ribs. "I don't think I can make it," he said to Stin.

"Nonsense. We're almost there," Volk said.

"Almost where?" Stin asked.

"To the Loon," Volk replied.

"What good is a bird going to do us?" Stin asked.

"That bird is going to save us."

Hank looked over his shoulder. Three cars approached at top speed, a few hundred yards behind them. Men hung onto the cars and rode on the running boards. A flash of light and a crack of sound refocused Hank's efforts. It wasn't from a geode.

"They're shooting at us!" Hank yelled.

"I told you. It's war!" Volk spat.

"This isn't time for 'I told you so!'" Stin shouted back.

They crested the last ridge before the lake.

"There she is," Volk said.

At first, Hank didn't see it. He spied Kathy and Kyle jumping up and down, waving their arms. Next to them in the water, a large sea plane rocked back and forth.

"The Loon," Volk said and rushed forward.

Hank ran down the hill after him. He tripped on a rock and tumbled forward. Arms grabbed hold of him and set him upright.

Stin pulled him along. "Come on. You can make it!"

The cars were on the ridge. Bullets zipped past Hank, throwing up dirt and rocks as he ran. The others jumped into the plane.

Hank clenched his teeth tight and pushed himself to give

everything he had.

Only fifty more yards and he'd make it to the plane. The engines fired up, and the twin propellers spun to life.

Misha popped his head out of the plane door. "Hurry!"

The Loon inched forward on the water. A bullet struck inches from Hank's foot. *I wish they couldn't see me.* As soon as he thought it, he yelled at himself for being so foolish. He cleared his mind and went invisible.

Stin made it to the door of the plane first. He turned back, pointing his geode at the men shooting down. Energy arched across the sky.

Hank didn't look back to see if Stin hit his mark. He rushed into the Loon as Stin fired another blast.

"That's it. Hit it!" Stin shouted to Volk.

The engines roared louder as the Loon jerked forward. Hank doubled over in pain. Every inch of his body hurt.

The Loon picked up more speed, and in a moment, Hank felt that all too familiar feeling of being airborne. He closed his eyes and collapsed on the floor.

10
TRAVELING HOME

Mr. Swenson knelt beside Hank and wrapped a wide cloth bandage around his lower ribs. Hank winced.

"Sorry, but you should have told me sooner that you were still hurt this bad," Mr. Swenson said.

Hank clenched his teeth as the former surgeon tied off the bandage. Each breath Hank took brought with it a tight constraint to his lungs. He laid down on the metal floor of the Loon. "Honestly, when I'm filled with the ley line energy, I don't notice the pain."

Mr. Swenson shook his head. "Not feeling your injury and being healed are two different things. When we get back, I'm ordering you on bed rest for at least a month."

"No!" Hank shot upright. His whole body contracted in pain from the sudden movement.

"Yes, and lay back down." Mr. Swenson stood. "Also, just to keep your body aware of its injury, I don't want you in the ley lines."

Hank groaned.

"I think you just killed him, Doc," Stin said.

"I guarantee he'll end up getting himself killed if he keeps doing things like this. It's too dangerous."

Stin nodded, and Mr. Swenson walked to the back of the plane to sit by Misha. Stin scooted closer to Hank and

gave a sideways glance toward Mr. Swenson. "Here, this will take the edge off." Stin slipped a geode from his pocket and put it in Hank's hand.

There wasn't much of a charge left in the geode, but Hank could feel the pain in his body melt away as the energy flowed into him.

"Thank you."

"Of course."

Hank closed his eyes. The Loon vibrated in every inch of its metal frame. Each bump and jolt would easily keep Hank's ribs in constant pain, but now, with a little of the ley line energy from Fruitland, he might have a better chance at sleep.

"You know he's right. This is too dangerous," Stin said.

Hank opened his eyes and looked at Stin, his face filled with concern.

"Dangerous or not, that thing, the Apep, has my parents. I saw them. They're scared. I got them into this, and I'm going to make sure they get out of it," Hank said and closed his eyes.

Stin touched his arm. "I know. That's what worries me most."

A few bumpy moments passed and Hank's thoughts kept jumping from his family to Stin to Volk to Elizabeth. Hank opened his eyes.

"Volk mentioned Elizabeth, after you left."

Stin looked at the wall.

Hank didn't say a word.

The time stretched between them until Stin opened his mouth. "Maybe if I'd been more like you, more concerned about keeping my family safe and intact things would be different. But I made the wrong choice." Stin leaned back and pulled his hat over his eyes.

Hank shouldn't have mentioned her. He stared up at the ceiling of The Loon. If Hank ever wanted to know more about Elizabeth and what happened he might to ask someone else.

The flight back to Fruitland went much faster than the drive to Idaho. Hank tried sleeping, but the rattle of the plane and the thoughts of his parents kept slumber far away. A few hours later, they landed on the reservoir. The Loon skipped across the water, causing the twins to shout in excitement. Everyone bounced off their seats and then hit down hard with a groan. Hank winced against the pain. He'd used all of the ley line energy to mask it, and now his supply was depleted.

With Hank in so much pain, Mr. Swenson had Mrs. Nieves bring a truck to drive Hank to the house. Hank protested, but he couldn't argue with Mr. Swenson backed up by Mrs. Nieves. Once he'd changed and settled into bed, Hank couldn't complain too much about the decision. It felt good to rest.

"I'll make you some chicken noodle soup," Mrs. Nieves said.

"Thank you," Hank said.

Mr. Swenson picked up the clothes Hank wore on the trip. He sniffed them and made a sour face. "When was the last time these things were washed?"

"I don't know. A little while."

"A little while in a boy's life is much too long a time to go without cleaning your clothes. I'll get my wife to wash them."

"No, Mr. Swenson." Mrs. Nieves said. "She has too much to do already. Let me take care of it," She took the clothes and felt in the pockets. She pulled out the Whitman's chocolate tin and shook it. "Empty." She made to toss it in a waste basket.

"No!" Hank said sitting up. He clenched his jaw against the pain.

"What's wrong?" Mr. Swenson asked.

Hank took in a breath. "Could you please just set that on the mantle? It's from—" he hesitated as he looked at Lina's mom. "It's my good luck charm."

"Baxt, you don't need a good luck charm. You are one," she

said with a smile and put the tin on the mantle.

"Okay, let's give him some quiet," Mr. Swenson said as he ushered Mrs. Nieves from the room.

Hank lowered himself in bed again and closed his eyes.

Mr. Swenson kept everyone out of the room, even Dog. A blanket of silence fell over the house, the only silence the house had known since the Hudson children arrived. And in that quiet, Hank found his first easy sleep.

The dream didn't arrive for a few hours. He stood in a familiar room, the one the Apep had shown him.

"Mom? Dad?" Hank called out.

The only answer came from echoes of his voice. *Where are they?* He crept deeper into the room. Each step took all his strength, like he wore large weights instead of boots. The darkness in the room seemed thick enough to swim through. *Darkness?* Icy fingers crawled across his back and up his neck.

He looked up. His eyes widened, and he bit back a scream. He couldn't see the ceiling through the coiling mass of Apeps. He also couldn't see where one ended and another began. The weight of the Apeps pressed down. He wanted to run, wanted to find a place to hide, but the weight held him in place.

Sobs reached his ears.

He shot a quick glance to the end of the room. His mom and dad were there, huddled together. Tears streaked their dirty faces, and there was terror in their eyes.

He looked at the Apeps. They hadn't seen him yet. Hank cleared his mind to make certain he wouldn't become visible. Through gritted teeth, he dragged one foot forward. He had to get to his parents, no matter what.

He gulped down a breath. He didn't want any sound to alert the corkscrewed cluster of Apeps. His heart beat against his ribs, and his stomach clenched tight, but he could do this. His parents were a few short steps away.

The weight from the Apeps shifted. Their force pushed him from side to side. He looked up. They circled faster and faster.

The faces of his mom and dad were covered in fear as they watched the Apeps.

"We see you, Vessel."

They saw him. How could they have seen him? Hank made a run for his parents.

One of the Apeps bolted from the ceiling, it's smoky body barring Hank's path.

"So glad you've chosen us," the Apep hissed into Hank's mind.

"I didn't choose you! I'm getting my parents out of here!"

He tried to fire a blast of ley line energy. Nothing happened. *I'm drained.* He had nothing with which to attack the Apep or defend himself.

"Hank, look out!" his parents screamed.

He turned his head just in time to see a second Apep. It flew at him with incredible speed. He tensed his muscles, preparing to be thrown across the room. He didn't move.

He looked down and saw the Apep enter his body. "No!"

The other Apeps followed. Each one entered Hank.

"Get out! I won't be your vessel!"

His pleas did nothing to stop them. He looked at his parents. They reached their hands through the bars. He reached for them, but was a foot too far away.

He screamed in pain.

"Hank! Hank!"

His body bounced and shook.

"Hank! Wake up!" Mr. Swenson said, shaking him.

Hank opened his eyes. The nightmare ended. He could feel his body drenched in a cold sweat. "I'm awake. I'm awake."

Mr. Swenson removed his hands and eyed Hank. Concern and fear filled Mr. Swenson's gaze.

"Bad dream," Hank said.

"I'd say so. I thought you were having a fit."

"I'm okay." Hank sat up. He gritted his teeth against the pain in his ribs.

"You're not okay. You're hurt and need to rest."

"There's no time to rest. The Apep isn't resting. My parents aren't resting. They're out there, scared to death, and I need to get to them. I can't do that here in bed. I know you're just looking out for me, but I have to do this."

"You don't have to do anything. In fact, if you do this, we could lose you and your parents."

"I just—" Hank looked away. "They want me. They want me because of what I can do."

"Who wants you?"

"The Apeps. I'm a vessel. I think that means I could give them a body. My body. I can't let them have me, and as long as they have my parents—"

"Then, they have something to hold over you," Mr. Swenson finished. "That's a hard feeling to deal with, but there are others who can do this. Stin, Volk, Misha—even me."

Hank nodded. "I know you can all help, but I can do something no one else can. You have to believe me, Mr. Swenson. If I had any other choice, I'd take it." Hank stood, expecting Mr. Swenson's protests, but he didn't try to stop him.

"Hank," Mr. Swenson said.

Hank turned. "Yes sir?"

Mr. Swenson looked at him, and then shook his head. "Nothing. I'm sorry it has to be like this for you."

Hank nodded and left the house. He didn't want anyone else to carry his burden. He went to the ley line crossing first and charged for an hour. The energy filled him and washed away his physical pain.

He made his way into the encampment. A single fire at Misha's tent burned. Misha, Kiska, Volk, Nobo, Stin, and Dog sat staring at the fire while Volk spoke.

"These monsters control people. People don't control these monsters."

Hank stepped into the light of the fire.

"Hank!" Stin said with a cheerful expression.

Dog sprung forward, throwing his paws on Hank's chest and licking his cheek.

"I thought the Doc ordered you on bed rest," Stin said.

"He did, but there's no time, not with my parents still out there." Hank sat with Dog by his side. "What were you saying about control?"

"Volk doesn't think Sheriff Anderson could have been controlling the Apep, even though we all saw it," Stin said.

"I don't care what you think you saw. He couldn't have been," Volk said.

Volk and Stin stared at each other. Hank had seen the sheriff control the Apep. He'd heard the Apep call the sheriff "Master."

"If they can be captured, couldn't they be controlled? Maybe with a ley line?" Hank asked.

Everyone looked at Hank as if he'd just explained the process of building a train to the moon.

The group sat silent for a moment. Stin was the first to speak. "Yes," he said.

"Maybe," Volk said as he stood and paced back and forth. "If he had a power that caused the Apep to be controlled, that would explain what you saw." He stopped and looked into the night sky. "You know what this means?"

"We need to talk with the sheriff," Stin said.

"But he's in prison," Misha said.

"Break in?" Volk asked.

"We're not breaking in to a prison," Stin said.

Volk glared.

"What about the judge? He said he'd help us if he could," Hank said.

Mr. Swenson lent a car to Volk, Stin, and Hank to make the trip to the state penitentiary. Kiska and Mrs. Nieves again protested that Hank had no business going, but this time, Mr. Swenson put a stop to it, adding that "Hank is a bigger part of this then any of us. He'll go where he feels he needs to."

Hank slept most of the way as Volk kept his icy disposition toward Stin, and when Hank tried talking with Stin, Volk would add snide comments.

The judge had been surprised by Stin's call. Placed in solitary confinement, it would take a lot of work to get them in to see the sheriff. The judge arranged a thirty-minute visitation. Volk said it would be more than enough time and smiled. Hank didn't know what the smile had meant or what Volk had planned, but the judge had been clear that they were not to harm the prisoner.

When Hank heard the judge, he gave Stin a quizzical look. He didn't understand why anyone would harm a prisoner until he looked at Volk. He didn't know him well at all, but Hank somehow knew that Volk wouldn't have any qualms about harming someone without a second thought. On the other hand, Stin was different and Hank felt confident that he'd keep the judge's instructions.

Sheriff Anderson had been sentenced to Central Prison in Raleigh, North Carolina. Hank knew the prison well enough. Its large, castle-like walls and turrets could be seen on his walks to and from school. He'd never been inside the prison and had never really wanted to be.

As they drove toward the prison entrance, a funny feeling washed over Hank. He was coming home, returning for the first time to Raleigh since setting out to catch up with his parents. Part of him wanted to return to the house and take a look at the tire swing. He longed to return to the simple life he'd once complained about.

"Are you okay?" Stin asked

Hank knew he couldn't go back. It would never be the

same again. "Yeah, I guess."

"Prisons scare me too," Volk said.

That wasn't what was bothering Hank, but he didn't feel like correcting him. Instead, he said, "Yeah, I just want to get out of here." He looked in the direction of his old house.

Stin looked at him, but didn't say a word.

Volk parked the car, and they made their way into the waiting area for prison visitors. A barrel-chested prison guard sat behind a tall desk guarded by a wire fence. A solid, iron door seemed to be the only way into the prison. A chill ran up Hank's back as the guard eyed him.

"Visiting hours aren't until Saturday," the guard said.

Hank stepped forward. "Sir, we have an appointment to see a prisoner. Anderson."

The guard looked at him for a long moment. "First off, the judge didn't mention nothing about no kid. I can't have a kid in the room with a solitary confinement prisoner. And second, the judge said there were three of you coming."

Hank looked at Stin, who mouthed sorry and went back to the door. Stin must have been invisible to the guard.

"Sorry, had to put something in the car," Stin said as he returned.

The guard looked at Stin, now visible. "Well, I still can't have you take the kid in."

"Why don't you wait for us in the car?" Stin suggested to Hank.

Hank opened his mouth to protest, but Stin winked at him. Hank walked out, cleared his mind of the desire to be seen, and returned. The guard opened the iron door for Stin and Volk. Hank slipped in behind them.

The guard led them to a small room with a wooden table and six chairs. "You have thirty minutes. I'll be out here waiting. And no funny business," the guard said as he stepped out and closed the solid wood door.

Hank took in a sharp breath of air as he looked at Sheriff Anderson. The sheriff looked like a shell of the man Hank had crossed paths with in Fruitland. Hank could see the outline of bones, like the sheriff had shriveled up. And if Hank had to pick a color, he'd call the sheriff's skin gray, but not as gray as the man's hair. In Fruitland, it had been dark and full. Now, it fell in long strings to his shoulders. He gave a crooked smile, showing gaps where teeth had been. The remaining teeth appeared yellow and brown with rot.

"Well, well, got a couple of visitors. What can I do for you fellas?" the sheriff asked.

The sheriff kept his right hand tucked under his left arm, like he was hiding something from them.

Volk slid a chair out and sat opposite Sheriff Anderson. "We have some questions about how you controlled the Apep in Fruitland."

"Apep...Apep..." the sheriff said as he looked around the room. "Now, what's an Apep? Is that some new fizzy drink?" He cackled.

Volk smashed his hand into the table. Hank and Stin both jumped, but Sheriff Anderson stayed still and smiled.

"You're smiling now, but you won't be smiling soon," Volk said as he stood.

"No. Remember what the judge told us?" Hank said.

"Hank? Is that you? Still hiding out?" Sheriff Anderson asked as he looked around the room and under the table. "When we first met, I'd never have guessed you were one of them. Come on. Show yourself to me."

One of who? "No, I don't think so. We want to know how you controlled the Apep and where it took my parents."

"Poor Hank. Reunited with his parents only to have them taken away. Get used to it, Hank, my boy. I don't think you're ever going to see them again," Sheriff Anderson said with a wicked, toothless smile.

This time, Stin jumped up. He stalked to the other side of the table and grabbed Sheriff Anderson by the collar. "You listen here. I will do anything to help that boy get back the life he deserves, even if that means not following the judge's instructions."

The sheriff tried to push Stin back with two hands, one normal and the other black and withered.

"I'm never going to tell you anything!"

"That's what you think," Volk said in calm voice. "I have something that I believe will make you tell us everything." He pulled out a bluish-gray stone rectangle, no larger than a box of matches. He placed it in front of Sheriff Anderson.

"Should you open it or should I?" Volk asked, not taking his eyes off the sheriff.

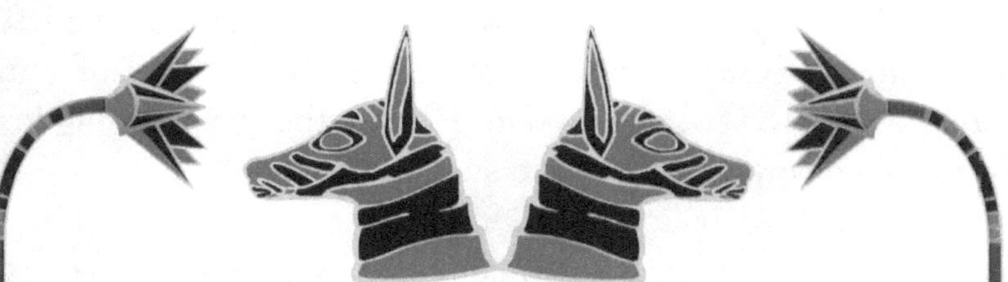

11
BACK TO PRISON

November 3, 1933, Raleigh, North Carolina

Sheriff Anderson stared opened mouth at the box. Hank couldn't understand what had struck him speechless. Stin released the sheriff's collar and took a step back.

"What happened to your hand?" Hank asked.

The sheriff again covered it under his arm, not answering Hank's question.

Volk pulled a chair beside the sheriff and sat. Both men stared at the box.

"I'd hoped it wouldn't come to this. I thought you might be a more intelligent man and be willing to help us. I wanted to save this power for another day. Do you know what's in that lead box?" Volk asked.

The sheriff continued to stare.

"I take it by your silence you've seen something like this before. I've been learning everything I can about ley lines. People can harness the power through the right kind of crystals. Geodes often work best. For the most part, they require a person to touch them in order to activate the power, but a few work without human touch.

"The lead box keeps the power of this particular ley line contained, so it's only used when opened," Volk said. He placed his hand on the lead box. "I'd found this particular

brand of energy in the northern reaches of the continent. I'd heard stories from the indigenous people about a pool of truth, and I just had to see it for myself." He gave the sheriff a long look as if making sure the words had sunk in. "Last chance."

Sheriff Anderson shook his head.

"Okay," Volk said. He lifted the lid. A multi-colored crystal rested on a deep purple cushion of velvet. "How did you control the Apep?"

"I didn't," Stin and Volk said at the same time.

"I didn't either," Hank said, the words running from his mouth without his control.

"With the ring she gave me," Sheriff Anderson said.

Volk smiled. "I've never used this with a group. I'll be more direct."

"Sheriff, who gave you the ring, and how did it allow you to control the Apep?" Volk asked.

The sheriff tensed his muscles and clenched his jaw. He must have been trying everything to keep from speaking the truth. He wasn't strong enough.

"Cabot. Evelyn Cabot. She said the ring would bind the Apep to me, and I could command it. She'll kill me for talking to you! She probably has members of the brotherhood working here. Watching me." Sheriff Anderson's eyes widened. He folded his arms across his chest and rocked. "She'll kill me. She's got people everywhere. I told her I'd protect her. That I'd never talk."

Hank's stomach turned as the fear in Sheriff Anderson's voice spilled out. In Fruitland, the sheriff attacked Hank and his family, but it didn't mean he wanted to see him killed either.

"Not doing so well with that," Volk said. He obviously didn't care if this man lived or died. "So, Sheriff, you just put the ring on and told the Apep what to do?"

Sheriff Anderson squeezed his eyes shut and put his hands over his mouth. "I had to connect with it," Sheriff Anderson said, his words muffled. "She took me to the reservoir and told me go to the hill where the lines cross. It only took a few minutes before the Apep could sense me there. It sensed the ring."

"Just like in Idaho. Sheriff, why can it find people in the lines?" Hank asked.

"It's looking for vessels and searching for all the artifacts. The ring is one of them," Sheriff Anderson said, uncovering his mouth.

"Vessel? Is that what you mean by connect with it?" Stin asked.

The sheriff shook his head. "No, I can't be a vessel. I'm not even an Anubis. Instead, it connected with me. Like a parasite. It gave me power. The Apep boosted my life's energy, but the ring continued draining it. The longer I controlled the Apep, the stronger the ring drained my life. Now that it's gone, the life is running out of me faster." He lifted his withered hand. The fingers were fused together.

"Can you get it back for me? Can you bring me back to the Apep?"

"No," Hank, Stin, and Volk said in unison.

"What do you mean, Anubis? How is it different than a vessel, and how can the Apep feel artifacts and vessels?" Hank's questions spilled out haphazardly.

"In the ancient legends of Egypt, the Anubis was a dog-headed man. They tell about him being a God, but he wasn't a God, and he wasn't one man. Some people are born special. They called them Anubis. They can talk with dogs and—"

Volk cut the sheriff off. "Enough of the storytelling. We don't have much power left, so answer my questions. It was draining you, but the ring allowed you to control it, right?"

Hank balled his fists and glared at Volk.

"How can you control a tidal wave? It gave me power, but it was a constant fight to stay in control of it. I don't know how much longer I could have kept dominance over it with the ring. The ring pulled at my life to fill the crystal. It's not powered like her other artifacts." A smile again crossed the sheriff's lips. He relaxed and said, "I think we're done now."

Hank reached out to feel for the power of truth, like he often did with his stored power. He couldn't feel even a trace of it. Volk closed the lead box and slipped it into his pocket. Stin knocked on the door to signal the guard they were finished.

"You have no idea who you're dealing with. She will come for all of us. She can't be stopped," the sheriff said as they made to leave the room.

Volk stopped and looked back at the shell of the sheriff. "But I think she'll come to visit you before she finds us. Enjoy what time you have left," Volk said, his words sharp as knives.

As the door shut, Hank saw the sheriff's expression. It looked like fear.

Hank's thoughts ran wild as he walked invisible through the door behind Stin and Volk. Who was Ms. Evelyn Cabot? Why would the sheriff ask for the Apep to be returned but to keep her away? How could a geode or crystal pull the life from a person? And more importantly, what did it mean for Hank to be an Anubis?

The thoughts continued to swirl around in his mind as they left the prison and drove into town. They stopped at a small diner and ordered lunch.

"Hank, are you listening?" Stin asked.

Hank snapped his attention to Stin. He could feel his cheeks warm. "Sorry. What did you say?" He looked at his untouched plate of food.

"The judge says he can't order the prison to release Sheriff Anderson's personal effects to us. Something about prisoners' property having to stay where they're jailed."

Hank gave a sigh of relief. He didn't want anything to do with that ring.

"We need that ring," Volk said.

"Why?" Hank asked, louder than he'd meant.

People looked over and then away. Hank leaned in closer and with a much lower tone said, "Why? It looks like it nearly killed him."

"It's the damage he did with it. We need to have it so it doesn't end up with someone worse," Stin said.

"Yes, like this Cabot woman," Volk added.

It was true. Hearing about the woman and running into the government agents in Idaho had given Hank more reason to pause. They were up against great odds, but would having the ring bring them any closer to finding his parents?

As if Stin could read what Hank was thinking, he said, "I know it doesn't seem like we're getting any closer to finding your folks, but I don't see how we can leave knowing such a device is out there."

"Artifact," Volk said.

Stin nodded.

"He said the Apep could feel the artifacts. So, there must be more. How many?" Hank asked.

"I don't know. It's like we got more questions than answers," Stin said.

"More questions, other artifacts, Apeps, Anubis—none of it matters. The only thing we can do today is get that ring."

Hank nodded slowly. "What will we need to do?"

"We'll need to know when the guards are switching so we can slip in behind them," Stin said.

"And you'll need a layout of the prison," Volk added.

Hank cocked his head at Volk. "You're not coming with us?"

"They'd see me," Volk said.

"But you're like us, right? I mean you talk with Dog and Nobo, and you can see Stin and me all the time, right?"

Volk nodded. "And you can store the ley line energy inside you. We are similar, but not the same. If we really are these Anubis, I don't know which I am or what I can do, but I do know I'm always seen. Eventually."

The three split up from the diner. Volk would go to the town hall and see if the prison had plans on record. Stin would watch the prison. Hank asked what his part would be. "For now, waiting," Stin said.

So Hank wandered off. Walking the streets of his hometown again reminded him of the way dreams sometimes felt:

real and fake at the same time. He kept thinking about the sheriff. The judge had once told Hank that he couldn't imagine Sheriff Anderson hurting anyone. How had this Ms. Cabot changed him so quickly?

Power. The power the ley line energy gave Hank made it easy for him to understand that others would want it too. But harnessing the power of the Apep? Just feeling the Apep on a few occasions, he couldn't imagine trying to control it. It'd be like taking a tiger for a walk with a shoe string for a leash.

His thoughts of the sheriff, the Apep, Ms. Cabot and the idea of breaking into prison kept him so occupied he hadn't realized he'd walked to his old house, more specifically to the tire swing that hung in the backyard. He stood there looking at it, wanting Dog to bound out of the nearby woods to join him.

He took a deep breath. It smelled like home, but it wasn't. No one seemed to be in the house, so he took a few timid steps and sat in the swing. The old tire had that familiar feel. He pushed himself back and forth with one foot. The rock of the tire swing had a soothing effect. Soon, the thoughts of the Apep, the sheriff, Ms. Cabot, and the prison dissolved away with each swing of the tire.

Hank's eyes weighed down on him, and he thought it would be good to close them for a few minutes. In moments, he was asleep.

A hand shook Hank's shoulder. He opened his eyes. Stars shone brightly against the darkened sky.

"Come on, Hank. We're going to be late."

"What?" Hank asked.

"I've been looking all over for you," Stin said. "You missed the rendezvous time. We've only got about thirty minutes before the guards change shifts."

Hank jumped out of the swing and followed Stin to Volk and the waiting car. On the way to the prison, Stin reviewed the plan with Hank. They'd slip in behind the guard, make their way to the inmate lockers, track down the ring, and slip out while no one was looking.

Volk dropped them off a quarter mile from the prison. Stin and Hank could get in unseen but not Volk or the car. They ran through a field to the prison parking lot, trying to make up for lost time.

They came to a silent walk as they reached the main entrance of the prison.

"What now?" Hank asked in a whisper.

"We wait."

Hank watched for cars, waiting for one to bring the new shift of guards. Hank's thoughts of Ms. Cabot, the sheriff, and Apeps quickly focused into one feeling. His hands were shaking. He couldn't bear the thought of being caught by the guards and going behind bars again. He looked at Stin, leaning against the stone building, one foot against the wall like he had nowhere in the world to be and no worries on his mind.

Headlights coasted up the prison road. The car stopped right in front of them, the lights hitting them square in the eyes like a searchlight from the prison tower. *He sees us.* Hank held his breath. The headlights switched off, and Hank could see the guard. The middle-aged man behind the wheel looked in Hank's direction. *We're going to jail!* Hank bit his lip, but the man looked away, got out of his car, and walked to the prison entrance.

Hank let out a sigh of relief. Stin followed the man inside with Hank on his heels.

"Evening, Joe," the guard behind the cage said to the man they followed.

"How's it been today?" The man asked.

"Quiet. Should be an easy night," the guard behind the gate said. He walked around and unlocked the door for the man.

Hank and Stin followed him down the main corridor until they came to a sign that read:

Inmate In-Processing

An arrow pointed right, down another hallway. Hank guessed the white stripe painted on the floor must be for directing new inmates.

Stin motioned for Hank to follow. The main lights in this part of the prison were already off, except for every thirty feet where a small bulb emitted a weak yellow light, which cast an eerie glow down the hall.

A sign hung from the ceiling that read:

Inmates Empty All Personal Belongings into Tray for Storage

Hank smiled. At least they wouldn't have to spend too much time here.

Stin stopped next to a door, a few feet ahead of Hank. Lock pick in hand, Stin worked the tumblers with the small pieces of metal. Hank stepped beside him. A moment later, Stin turned the knob and pushed the door open with a flourish, inviting Hank to enter first. He stepped through the door. With the lights out, Hank shouldn't have been able to see to the back of the room, but he could. He'd noticed his night vision getting stronger. He wasn't sure if it had to do with the ley line energy or something else.

The ceiling rose at least ten feet. Lining the room from floor to ceiling were metal shelves, and on each shelf were boxes on top of boxes.

Maybe they would be spending the night here.

"This is going to take forever," Hank said.

"Keep your voice down." Stin handed Hank a flashlight. "Use this to look for names. It could be alphabetical or maybe by date of incarceration."

Hank took the left side of the room and Stin the right. The metal cylinder weighed heavily in Hank's hand, and the light it poured out on the room wasn't much better than the yellow lights in the hall. Hank looked at the boxes at eye level. Each had a six digit number. No names. No dates. Just the number.

His heart dropped a little. He pulled the first box out and lifted the lid. A leather wallet and some spare change rested on top of a wool coat. He looked through four more before Stin returned.

"We'll never find it like this," Hank said.

"Don't worry. I found a filing cabinet," Stin said. He held up a manila folder. "Anderson's number is 002098."

Hank shone his light on the box in front of him. 001502. The one to the left of it read 001510. "It looks like they get bigger this way," Hank said.

He walked down the long row of boxes, reading each number.

001600.

001700.

001900.

002090.

He stopped mid step and his heart beat a little faster. He pointed his flashlight at the lower boxes, and Stin pointed his at the ones above Hank's head. It wasn't on the bottom selves.

"There it is," Stin said, pointing upward. "Here, let me boost you up." Stin interlocked his fingers so Hank could step in them.

When Stin lifted him, Hank came face to face with box number 002098. He grabbed it at the same time that the lights in the room turned on.

Both Stin and Hank froze.

Stin lowered Hank to the ground and pointed at him and then at the box. Hank nodded as Stin crept along the shelves toward the front of the room. Hank's fingers trembled as he reached down and lifted the lid.

A pocket watch and a wallet were perched on top of some folded clothes, but no ring. Hank pulled the clothes from the box. The pocket watch and wallet clattered on the floor, breaking the silence.

"I know you're in here!" an unknown voice shouted.

Hank felt his pulse quicken. How could anyone know they were here? He pushed himself along, searching each of the pockets.

There was nothing in the jacket.

Footsteps echoed closer and closer.

Hank ran his hands through the pants pocket. *Nothing.* He looked into the bottom of the box. *Empty.*

The footsteps were almost to them. Hank looked at Stin

crouched by the end of the row. Hank reached for the jacket again but stopped as his eyes fell on the pocket watch. He snatched it up and opened it. The ring fell from the watch, clattered across the floor, and came to rest under the shelf.

"There you are!" the guard said as he turned the corner nearest Stin.

Stin grunted and Hank heard the guard fall back, knocking boxes onto the floor.

Hank didn't have time to look up. He reached under the shelf. He could feel the ring just on the tip of his finger. He almost had it.

Another crash from Stin and the guard.

"Harder to fight someone when they can see you!" the guard shouted.

Hank stopped reaching for the ring and looked over to see Stin and the guard fist fighting. *How can he see Stin?*

"Get the ring!" Stin shouted.

Hank reached his hand back under the shelf again. He had the ring. Well, almost had it. He pushed his arm farther, the metal of the shelf digging into his shoulder. He closed his fingers on the ring and jumped to his feet.

"I've got it!"

"Just in time," Stin said. He kicked the guard back.

The guard's eyes opened wide as he smashed against the wall. The man glared at Stin. There was no doubt in Hank's mind: the guard could see them.

Stin grabbed Hank and pushed him forward out of the room, shutting the door behind them.

"How can he see us?"

"I don't know, but we've got to get out of here, fast," Stin said.

The door opened, and the guard ran after them. They were almost to the turn in the hallway that would take them back to the main entrance. They'd be out of here quick enough. Just as Stin was about to make the turn, another guard stepped in his way. Stin and Hank skidded to a stop. The man looked up, but instead of looking at them, he seemed to be looking through them at the guard chasing them.

"What in the world are you doing running down the hall in the middle of the night?" the new guard asked. His voice sounded like a parent scolding a child.

Stin and Hank slipped around the new guard, unseen, and continued down the hall

"Nothing. Go back to work!" They heard the running guard say.

"You see these stripes, Greenhorn? This means I ask the questions and tell you what to do!" the new guard shouted.

Stin and Hank didn't wait to see how the guards' conversation turned out. They continued moving for the front door, but it blocked their escape. Stin looked over the mechanism on the door. It took him a moment, but he moved the necessary levers to release it.

Hank looked back to see the new guard being shoved aside as the one who could see them turned the corner and sprinted down the hall.

Stin turned the main release mechanism.

KER-CHUNK!

The noise of the bolts unlocking echoed down the hall.

"What the devil?" a voice said from inside the room nearest the iron door. The man stood and poked his head out, looking at the door and then toward the guard running down the hall.

"What's going on?"

"Nothing. Go back to sleep!"

Why isn't this guard asking for help?

Stin pushed the metal door open, and Hank followed him into the entry room and then into the night air. They didn't stop running.

The guard chasing them crashed through the front door.

"Split up. Get back to Volk. I'll try to lead this guy away!" Stin said.

Hank didn't have time to protest as Stin turned and charged the guard.

12
THE FOREIGNER

Hank sprinted across the grounds toward town. Behind him there were grunts and shouting. The desire to turn and help Stin pulled at him, but he could feel the metal of the ring in his pocket. He knew Stin wouldn't risk losing the ring, so he kept running.

The fields by the prison gave way to city streets, shops, and homes. Hank brought his legs from a run to a stroll, but his heart slammed into his chest. Five more blocks still stood between him and the rendezvous point.

He slipped down an alley and let himself become visible. With a man out there able to see through his ability anyway, he'd need another way to go unseen.

No lights shone from the buildings. Maybe the shadows would conceal him. He tried to breathe easy, but his heart kept up the brisk beat.

Is Stin okay? The thought repeated in his head. He stepped to the corner of the alley and checked the street. No one was roaming the streets, and like the alley, all the lights were out. *At least something is going right.* He pulled his shoulders back and stepped out of the alley.

"Mr. Hudson?" a strange voice said from behind Hank.

He spun to face the man. A scarf covered the man's

face.

Hank took two steps back. "I don't have any money!"

The man didn't move. "I'm not here to rob you, Mr. Hudson." Even though the man didn't raise his voice, his accent caused each word to sound sharp and dangerous.

Hank looked at the man again. It wasn't just his scarf that seemed out of place. His entire outfit looked odd. The man looked like he'd just stepped outside in his nightshirt.

"Who are you? How do you know my name?" Hank asked, moving behind a bench. It placed something between them, a barrier that offered no real protection, but comforted Hank just the same.

The man eyed him, not responding.

Hank balled up his fist and pulled the energy from the ley line. He was ready to blast this guy into the street if he made a move.

"My name is difficult to pronounce. You may call me Mr. Grey. I know your name because you have caused quite a stir in our ranks. It's being said you are a vessel."

With the last word from the man's lips Hank's heart seemed to stop.

"And I have been given the task to collect you for Ms. Cabot—"

Hank threw his hand out. The fear in his body, mixing with the ley line energy, blasted from his hand straight towards Mr. Grey. The energy lit up the dark street as it flew.

The man contorted to the side, arching his entire body to miss the blast of energy, which smashed with a shower of sparks into a parked car.

"You are a vessel," Mr. Grey said with excitement. "Please do not make this more difficult, Mr. Hudson." He stepped forward.

Hank shot another blast at him. The light from the energy caused odd shadows to dance across the buildings.

Mr. Grey dodged it with almost no effort.

"Please, you can help us, and we can help you," Mr. Grey said.

"Is that what your little group is doing? Helping?" He stepped back again, ready to fire another blast when Mr. Grey sprung forward. The man moved with incredible speed, catching Hank by the wrist and bending his arm behind his back. Hank gritted his teeth as Mr. Grey tightened his hold.

"Mr. Hudson, I have no desire to see you come to harm, but I am under direct instructions. You are either to come with me, or I am to dispose of you."

Hank's blood ran cold. He knew what "dispose" meant, but other questions shot to mind. "How did you find me?"

"I've been watching you since your return from the western state. I've been waiting until I had a moment alone with you. I do not wish your friends or family to come to harm."

"Right. And I bet you don't know what happened to my parents either. You've probably got them tied up with one of your Apeps!"

Mr. Grey didn't speak for a long moment. "Young man, you do not understand. If you would come with me, I could show you what is possible. Perhaps even help you reunite with your parents."

"Liar!"

"I'm not a liar. I'm going to let you go, but please do not shoot at me again. Even if it is a wonderful display of power." A hint of awe tinged his tone.

Mr. Grey released his grip. Hank swung around and moved back, staring at him. His eyes were the only thing Hank could see. The man's eyes appeared tranquil, like the man found this encounter dull.

"I'm not going with you!" Hank said as he pulled more energy from his core.

"I understand, but let me be clear. I am here to offer you a place with us. Because of your youthful arrogance, I am willing to extend this offer two more times. If you reject me thrice, I will follow my commands, and you will be dead, and all those who try to save you will be dead."

Hank swallowed hard as memories of his friends and family flashed across his mind.

"Think, young man. Don't be so proud that you sacrifice the ones you love and yourself," Mr. Grey said with a tone of finality.

A car squealed from down the street. Hank glanced over his shoulder. *Stin!*

"Only two more chances," Mr. Grey said.

He'd only taken his eyes off Mr. Grey for a second or two, but when he turned back, Mr. Grey had vanished. Hank spun in place. He looked up and down the street, but there was no sign of Mr. Grey.

The car raced down the street with Stin hanging out the window. "Hank! Get in," Stin said.

Hank sprinted for the car. It screeched to a halt, and Hank threw open the back door and climbed in. He did a double take. The guard who'd chased them sat tied up in the back seat. The gag in his mouth kept him silent.

Stin leaned over the seat. "Who was that?" Stin asked.

"Who was that? Who's tied up?" Hank asked.

"Just ignore him," Volk said.

Hank looked at the guard, then Volk and Stin.

"We need to ask him some questions. But first, who was that? What just happened to you?" Stin asked.

Hank's stomach contracted as he looked at the guard. He shook his head and met Stin's eyes. "A man. I just fought with a man called Mr. Grey. He followed us here to get me. For Ms. Cabot."

"Cabot! She knows about you? How?" Volk asked.

Hank shook his head. "What does it matter? We have to get out of here! He knows about the encampment."

Volk looked back from driving. "Calm down. Don't say anything more in front of the prisoner. Besides, this Mr. Grey didn't try to take you there," Volk said. "He's a vulture looking for easy pickings. As long as you're with us, you're fine."

Hank shook his head, "No, this man is something else. He's—I don't know. Calm."

"Calm, nervous, weak, strong—it doesn't matter. We'll protect you," Volk said.

"I'm glad you're okay," Stin said. "And I think you're right. We should get out of here."

"With pleasure," Volk said. He revved the engine, and they tore out of town.

Volk pulled onto a dirt road about ten miles outside of Raleigh. No one spoke. Hank looked at the guard. He could see the fear in the man's face. Volk had a glint of glee in his eye, which made Hank's stomach tie tighter.

The car came to an idle, and Volk turned the engine off but left the headlights on. He opened his door, and in a moment, he had the back door open and was pulling out the guard.

The man tried to say something but only muffled tones came out, tones that sounded like pleas for help.

"Volk!" Hank shouted.

"Don't hurt the guy," Stin said, hopping out of the car.

Volk slammed the back door shut and walked the man to the front of the car. Hank opened his door and jumped out. Volk forced the man to his knees, pulled off the gag, and walked back to the car.

The guard looked down at the rope tied around his body. "What are you doing! Let me go!"

"This doesn't feel right," Hank said to Stin.

"Volk! Get back here."

Volk marched back, the guard's gun in his hand. "If he doesn't tell us what we want, we need to kill him. We should go back and kill the sheriff too."

"What? We're not killing anyone!" Hank said, pushing the gun down.

"You don't get it. This man and the sheriff will tell that woman everything. We need to protect ourselves," Volk said as he aimed the gun at the guard again.

"Please don't," the guard begged. "I won't tell anybody anything."

"Then tell us what we want to know!" Volk shouted. "Who are you working for?"

"Cabot. Cabot got me the job there because, well, I can see you. But that's it. I was just supposed to keep you from taking anything from the prison," the guard said, his words splashing over his lips like a bubbling brook.

"Do you know what was in there?" Volk asked.

The guard shook his head. "She didn't tell me anything. I don't know anything."

"Then what use are you to me?" Volk asked and pointed the gun at the guard.

"No, Volk. You can't kill him," Stin said.

"I can. You're the weak man who can't," Volk said.

"Stop it!" Hank stepped between the gun and the guard. "I'm not letting you shoot him, Volk."

Volk's eyes narrowed as he stared at Hank. Hank gritted his teeth and pulled up the ley line energy. There wasn't a lot left, maybe one or two big blasts. It would be more than enough, but could he fire his energy before Volk fired a bullet?

The guard sniveled as he begged them not to shoot.

Hank set his jaw and continued to stare at Volk.

"Fine. But this is on your head!" Volk said as he tucked the gun into his pants and walked back to the car.

Hank breathed a sigh of relief. Stin put a hand on Hank's shoulder. "Let's go," Stin said in almost a whisper.

"Thank you. Oh, thank you!"

"What about him?" Hank asked.

The engine came to life. "Hurry," Volk said.

"We'll call the prison at the next stop and let them know where he is," Stin said.

They piled in the car. Hank looked out the back window as the guard struggled against his ropes.

13

THE BROTHERHOOD OF DARKNESS

The drive back to the encampment was filled with an awkward silence. Volk didn't say a word, but sent an occasional glare at Hank or Stin. Once they parked the car at Mr. Swenson's, Volk stomped off. Hank planned to make a beeline for the house, but Stin pulled him aside.

"I'm worried," Stin said.

Hank looked up at him and could see that worry written across Stin's face.

"About Volk?"

Stin nodded.

"Me too," Hank said. "For a moment, I thought for sure he'd shoot me."

"He's not the same man I used to know. When we were in the circus, Volk was all smiles. He told jokes all the time. He made sure his friends were safe. Now, he's just—"

"Cruel," Hank said, cutting him off.

"Exactly. Cruel and unpredictable. I just don't know," Stin said and looked off in the distance.

"Know what?"

"If we can trust him. Can he help us get your parents back or is he going to take us down a dangerous path?" Stin said.

"Trust." Hank said the word with contempt. "We've

111

got so many people here now. Who knows if one of them could be working for Cabot, like that guard? I don't know who to trust."

Stin looked back at Hank and gave a halfhearted smile. "I'm by your side. I'm not going to let anything happen to you."

Hank smiled back. He knew Stin meant the words, but Stin couldn't be everywhere at once. He'd need to keep his own guard up too.

"Hank!" Lina called from the road. "You're back!"

Hank looked over his shoulder and smiled at her. She waved and walked over with a skip in her step.

Stin ruffled Hank's hair. "Enough talk of deceit. I'll leave you to more enjoyable company," Stin said with a grin. He took a couple steps toward the house and turned. "Hank, let's just keep this between us for now. Okay?"

Hank nodded and Stin walked inside.

Lina took Hank's hand. "I'm so glad you're okay."

Hank just smiled.

"How are you? What happened?"

The desire to spill his guts fought against his desire to just have a moment where none of the last day mattered. "Come on. I'll tell you later."

Lina relayed the misadventures of the twins as they strolled along the path to Mrs. Nieves caravan.

"Baxt! You've returned!" Mrs. Nieves exclaimed as she clapped her hands together. "And you're just in time. I've been baking cookies in hopes you'd come by today. They should be ready."

Hank smiled as Mrs. Nieves went to the wood stove and opened it. The strong smell of sweet cookies filled Hank's nostrils. "I'm starving," Hank said.

"You two sit down, sit down," Mrs. Nieves said.

Describing the caravan as tiny would be a compliment. A person could walk from one end by the wood-fired-stove to the other end by the bunk beds in five steps. Lina and Hank sat in the middle on a bench behind the little table.

Mrs. Nieves put a plate of cookies down. Hank took one

of the warm cookies and broke it in half. The gooey chocolate stretched apart. He gave it a quick blow and popped it in his mouth.

"Mmmm. These are delicious, Mrs. Nieves. Thank you so much."

"Thank you, Baxt. It's so nice to have such a fine and well-mannered boy in the home," Mrs. Nieves said with a wink.

Hank realized the wink wasn't for him as he looked at Lina. Her pale skin flushed a light pink.

"I think there's some cold milk at one of the other tents. Let me—"

"Actually mom, we're heading up to the reservoir," Lina said.

Hank looked at her. *We are?* It was news to him, but he stood with Lina.

"Well, you two kids have fun. And take some cookies, Baxt."

Hank didn't have to be told twice. He grabbed one in each hand and followed Lina, who strode from the caravan. He walked twice as fast to keep up.

When they were out of earshot of the caravan, Lina said, "I'm sorry. My mom can sometimes be—"

"Amazing," Hank suggested.

Lina giggled. "Yeah, she can be amazing. It's amazing how often she embarrasses me. There are days that I just wish she'd give me more space."

Hank stopped. The smile on his face fell.

Lina looked back. "I'm sorry. I didn't mean—"

"I know," Hank said. "I just miss them." Hank absentmindedly took a bite of cookie.

"Hey, so tell me all about going to Raleigh."

They continued to walk up to the reservoir, and Hank filled her in on almost everything, from how the sheriff looked, to the guard who could see through their invisibility, to Mr. Grey and his lightning reflexes, and the ring powered by human life. He held back the part about Volk and the gun.

They strolled along the grassy path to the lake.

"Have you ever heard of a woman named Elizabeth?" Hank asked.

Lina furrowed her brow in thought. "I don't think so. Who is she?"

Hank hesitated, maybe he shouldn't talk about Stin's past life. He bit his lip and then looked at her. "Stin was engaged to her before the war."

"He was going to get married?" Lina asked.

Hank looked around like some might have heard her. "Not so loud."

"I'm surprised."

"Me too."

"What happened to her?"

Hank rubbed the back of his neck. "That's the thing. I don't know and when I've brought it up with Stin he just shuts down." Hank hesitated a moment. "But something happened. I think it's one of the reasons Volk doesn't get along with Stin."

"Well, maybe I can ask Kiska."

Hank chewed the idea around in his mind. "I don't know. I don't want to bring up painful memories."

Lina nodded.

They reached the reservoir edge and stopped walking. Hank bent and picked up a smooth stone. He cocked his arm back and tossed the stone out. It skipped at least fourteen times before sinking through the water's surface.

"How did you do that?" Lina asked.

"It's easy. Here," Hank said and handed her a smooth stone. "You want them to be flat, like this. Actually, as long as they're flat on one side, you can get a good skip. Now, bring your arm back and toss the rock with a little flip of your wrist."

"Like this?" Lina asked. She brought her arm back and tossed the rock at the water. It plopped in with a splash. "I'm terrible at this."

"No, you just have to flip your wrist." He gave her another stone, but this time, he took hold of her hand. "Bring your arm back just like you did before, but this time, when you throw it forward, your wrist needs to flip like this." He moved her wrist a couple of times to demonstrate what he meant by giving it a flip. "Try again."

Lina brought her arm back and looked at him. "Like this?"

"Yep."

She bit her lip and looked at the water. "Here goes nothing," she said and tossed the rock forward.

It sailed out and skipped on the water three times.

"I did it!" she exclaimed, clapping her hands together. "Thank you." She smiled at Hank, picked up another stone, and skipped it.

"Six. That's pretty good," he said, picking up a smooth stone.

Before he could throw it, something else caught his attention. He turned to his right and squinted, trying to get a better view in the bright sunlight.

"What is it?" Lina said.

"Not sure. It looks like Nobo is chasing Dog." The thought of Volk, the guard, and the gun came to mind. Would his wolf be any different? Hank didn't want to take the time to find out. "Come on. I don't want that wolf picking on Dog."

They rushed across the grass towards where Hank had seen Dog and Nobo run into the trees. They slowed as they neared the tree line. *He better be okay.*

A deep growl echoed out of the trees.

"Dog!" Hank yelled as he moved into the trees at a sprint.

"Wait, Hank. Nobo is twice your size!"

Size didn't matter. Hank wasn't about to let Nobo hurt Dog. As far as Hank was concerned, he'd make sure both Nobo and Volk were gone by tonight.

He dodged tree roots and jumped over fallen logs. The growling grew gruffer. *I'm almost there, Dog.* Nobo's growls were joined by Dog's. *Fight back!*

"Hank, come back!" Lina shouted again.

She was close behind him.

Just ahead, Hank could see Nobo, legs bent, fur bristling, like he was ready to spring forward.

"Nobo, leave Dog—" Hank stopped mid-sentence as he entered the clearing. There was Nobo, still growling, but Dog wasn't growling back at the wolf, instead he directed his growls at someone else. Nobo and Dog had a man cornered on the ground.

"Call 'em off! Call 'em off!" the voice pleaded.

"What's going on?" Lina said as she stopped behind Hank.

"I know that man," Hank said as he moved in closer. "You're that guard from the prison."

The guard scooted back onto his elbows. Dog and Nobo stepped forward, teeth bared. The guard continued to scoot back until he hit a tree. His eyes were moving wildly, like he was trying to find some way out.

"Don't let these animals hurt me. Please!"

Hank helped him before, but what good had it done? Here the guard was again. Ms. Cabot and Mr. Grey could be out here too, lurking in the trees, ready to snatch Hank up.

Hank looked around, but in the thick trees, he couldn't see more than thirty yards.

"Dog, you smell anyone else out here?" Hank asked.

Dog stopped his growling and sniffed the air. He gave a sharp exhale and then a clipped bark.

"I'm not with anyone. Come on, kid. Be a pal and let me go."

"Like before? A lot of good that did. Here you are. Maybe this time I shouldn't protect you. Maybe I'll just walk out of here and forget I ever saw you," Hank said.

The guard's mouth fell open.

"Hank, we can't," Lina said.

Hank looked at the guard for a long moment. Volk might be cruel, but maybe he was right. Maybe this was a war. *All is fair love and war.* He stared at the guard's eyes.

Hank's stomach tightened. "You're right Lina, we can't. We're not like him. Get up. We're walking you in, but if you get any funny ideas, Nobo and Dog are here to set you right."

All the way back to camp, the guard didn't say a word or step off the path.

A crowd started to form as the prisoner and his captors walked into the encampment. All eyes were on the guard. Hank stopped the march and the crowd encircled him. Shouts and questions of what was going on and who the man was came from the crowd.

"Make way. I said make way!" Volk's gruff voice echoed over the assembled mass of people. They divided to either side and opened a path wide enough for three men to pass, more than enough room for Volk's skinny frame. Stin and Misha followed right behind him, but stopped when they reached Lina.

Volk did not stop.

"I told you what we should have done with him!" Volk shouted as he marched up to the guard and hit him square on the jaw.

"Stop it!" Hank yelled, his fists balled, ready for a fight.

The man fell to the ground. Volk made to hit him again.

"Stop it!" Hank shouted.

Volk looked at him with contempt. "You stay out of this, boy!"

Hank pulled at the ley line energy inside him.

"I think you need to stay out of this," Stin said. He stepped between Hank and Volk.

"I've had enough of you too!" Volk spit on the ground and swung a wild punch at Stin.

Stin didn't move to defend himself.

Volk landed his punch into flesh, but it wasn't Stin's face. Misha's massive hand caught Volk's fist.

"It's time to go, brother," Misha said.

"Get out of my way!"

Nobo bared his teeth.

This was getting out of hand. Hank still held the ley line energy, but using it might hit all the wrong people.

"Come with me," Misha said.

Volk didn't reply.

"Fine, we do it this way," Misha said. He threw Volk over his shoulder like a sack of potatoes.

Hank gritted his teeth as he watched Misha carry Volk into the encampment. Nobo trotted after them, tail high in the air.

"Show's over, everyone. Go back to the encampment," Stin shouted. He waited for the crowd to disperse before he spoke again. "Why are you here?" Stin asked the guard. He knelt over him and grabbed his collar. "I asked you a question. Do I need to have Volk come back?"

The guard shook his head.

"Then, tell me why you're here," Stin said.

Hank stared at the two men. He wasn't sure he wanted to know why the man was here.

The man looked at Stin and then at Hank. "I'm here to get him and the ring."

"Why?" Hank asked. His insides shivered at the thought.

"I wasn't supposed to let you leave with the ring. I need to prove to them I'm still worth having."

"Worth having to who?" Lina asked, kneeling beside the man. Her voice wasn't demanding.

The guard looked at her and then away, burying his gaze in the ground.

"She asked who? We know about Cabot and Grey. Is it them?" Hank asked.

Stin shot him a quick look, like he shouldn't have said so much.

The guard continued to look at the ground. He didn't say a word.

Lina put a hand on the guard's shoulder. "Come on. Tell us who," she coaxed.

After a long moment, the man looked at her. "They're part of it, but it's not just them that I've failed." The man clenched his jaw. "If you knew what they're capable of, you'd leave right now and never look back."

"They're just two people," Hank said.

The man scoffed at Hank. "The brotherhood isn't just two

people. They've got hundreds. They have the government on their side, and they're growing every day."

The words turned Hank's stomach.

"So, what if you've got a little fraternity? That doesn't mean anything to us," Stin said and then stood. "The only thing I see is that you're here for Hank, and that I can't abide." He turned and walked toward the camp. "I'll be back with Volk. We can't have him hurting you, Hank," Stin shouted over his shoulder.

The guard went white as a sheet. "Wait, wait! Don't kill me! What if I can give you information? I could trade you what I know for my life."

Hank looked at the guard and then back at Stin who'd stopped. He couldn't believe that Stin would really let Volk kill this man.

"You've got nothing we don't know. And besides, how can we trust you?" Stin asked, turning to face the man on the ground.

"If I go back empty-handed, they'll kill me. If I stay here, you'll kill me. The only chance is getting gone for good. I know lots of stuff, like about the brotherhood. I can tell you about it."

"I don't care about them," Hank said.

"You should. They could help you understand who you are."

"I think I understand myself just fine, thanks."

The man looked back and forth. "Okay, maybe I have something you do want. What if I could tell you where the boy's parents are? Would that be worth my life?" the guard asked, his words spilling out fast like water into a sinking ship.

Hank looked at him, the fire in his belly kindling brighter. He tightened his fist. If this man knew where his parents were, he'd find out. One way or another.

"Maybe. If it's the truth," Stin said, stepping closer. "What's your name?"

"Elmer. Elmer Grossman. And it is true. The brotherhood have them. I know where they are, but I need to know I'll be let go before I tell you."

Hank pushed his way in front of Elmer, the ley line energy

still at his finger-tips, waiting to be released. He could give Elmer a little shock, just to make sure he knew he was serious.

Hank shook the thought from his head. "You tell us where they are, and I promise you'll leave here unharmed."

Elmer looked at Hank for a long moment, as if trying to read his mind. He sniffed and then spoke. "They're holding them in Charleston, at a ley line crossing." His beady eyes darted back and forth between Stin and Hank.

"How many people are there?" Stin asked.

"Are they okay?" Hank demanded.

Elmer looked at Hank first. "Yes, they're weak from the Apep, but they're okay. And I don't know, maybe ten. That's how many were there before they sent me to work at the prison."

Hank remembered his dream. All the Apeps circling his parents. One Apep and ten men. It wouldn't be easy, but he had to try.

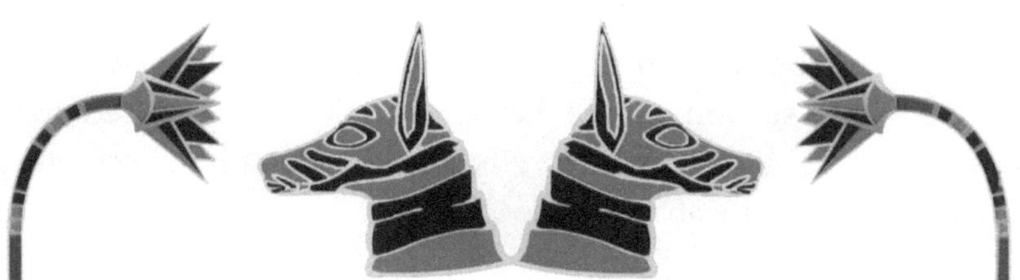

14

MIDNIGHT IN CHARLESTON

November 6, 1933, Charleston, South Carolina

It hadn't taken long for the group to put a plan into motion. They planned to hit the place hard and fast. They'd take every able-bodied person and overwhelm the brotherhood's guards while those who could use the geodes would concentrate on the Apep.

Before they left, Hank picked up the Whitman's chocolate tin and put it in his pocket. It had brought him luck in Idaho, and he hoped it would do so again.

The trucks and cars left the encampment in thirty minute intervals. They didn't want to announce their arrival with a convoy full of carnies and ruin the element of surprise. Hank and Stin might be able to go unseen, but the others would have to use stealth.

Elmer had told them that Hank's parents were being held in an old textile factory by the harbor. If the information the captured man had given them was correct, they'd be able to slip into the factory under the cover of night and rescue Hank's parents.

The part about the factory seemed to be true. Hank looked at the factory as he stood by Mr. Swenson's parked car. They were over a quarter mile from his parent's prison, but he could still see the factory looming high above the harbor.

"It's enormous," Hank said.

"And looks like it should be condemned," Stin said.

This section of the harbor hadn't been updated with lamps or street lights, as if the city knew it was a hopeless cause and had left it to be abandoned.

"Looks quiet," Stin said.

"Well, it's about to get much louder," Volk said, gesturing to the thirty men and women standing behind them.

Hank looked over the faces of these people that were willing to do so much for him. His throat tightened, and he smiled at them.

"Let's go over this one more time. Mr. Swenson and Steve will take their groups to the opposite side of the factory. Volk's and Misha's groups have the front. Julie will cover this side for our retreat, and my group will set up at the rear entrance."

All eyes continued to watch Stin. His tone and manner reminded Hank of a general preparing his troops for battle.

"When I set off the flare, the groups led by Mr. Swenson, Steve, Volk, and Misha will rush into the main and upper floor of the factory to take care of any guards. My group will enter the cellar and deal with the Apep. Once you've taken care of the brotherhood, Volk and Misha will bring their groups down for added punch against the Apep. We get in fast and we get out with Hank's parents. Everyone understands what they need to do, right?"

The group nodded in agreement.

"Good. Let's split into groups. Misha, Volk, Mr. Swenson, Julie, Steve—get your people into position." Stin looked at his watch. "You've got ten minutes to get there. When I shoot the flare, that's the signal to go. Again, move in quickly, subdue any of these brotherhood guys, and let us deal with the Apep. Any questions?"

No one said a word.

"I've got one thing," Hank said.

Everyone looked at him.

"Thank you." A lump formed in Hank's throat. He squeezed

back the tears that were trying to form and cleared his throat. "Thanks for helping me get my parents back."

"Don't thank us until you have them in your arms," Misha said.

As the groups separated, each person walked past Hank and clasped his shoulder. When the last person passed him, he wiped the tears from his eyes.

"You ready?" Stin asked, a look of concern on his face.

Hank cleared his throat again and wiped the last tear. "Ready as I can be."

Dog barked twice and nuzzled his face against Hank's hand.

"Thanks. Let's go get them back," Hank replied.

Stin led the way with Hank, Dog, and three others from the encampment that were handy with a geode. As they crept across the grounds, each step brought a stronger awareness of pressure. *It's here.* That familiar weight that could only be from an Apep pressed against Hank. It was like walking into an ocean wave, and Hank knew it carried all the destructive power of one too.

He'd already cleared his mind and become invisible. The Apep wouldn't be able to sense him. If it did, the element of surprise would be lost and, with it, his parents.

A seagull squawked overhead as the group drew closer to the building. The old factory looked as bad as the buildings in Fruitland. The windows were crudely boarded up, and the wall closest to them had a hole that Hank could easily fit through. Elmer told them that a cellar door would be their entrance and that it should lead right to where Hank's parents were being kept. It would also lead right to the Apep.

Stin stopped and crouched behind an overturned row boat. Hank, Dog, and the other three men took up a position next to him.

"Three more minutes," Stin whispered. He pulled a flare gun from his coat pocket and loaded it.

The weight of the Apep pushed harder on Hank. Each

second that passed left him feeling more anxious. He just wanted to get in there and get them back. He took in a slow breath and tried to exhale his worry.

Another minute ticked by. Hank could see Mr. Swenson's and Steve's groups on the opposite side. He looked at the old factory. The area might have been covered in the darkness of night, but Hank could see them with little effort. He didn't understand it, but his night vision continued to improve. He studied the factory. Still no movement. Hopefully, most of the brotherhood would be asleep at this hour.

The man beside Hank, Gregory Day, cracked his knuckles and rubbed his hands together. He'd come a few weeks after the others arrived in Fruitland. He'd been a carpenter by trade, but hadn't worked in over a year. At least he hadn't worked for money. He'd been good in training with the geodes. He seemed to have a natural ability to increase the damage they could do.

No matter how good he might be in training, though, out here he looked as anxious as Hank felt.

"One minute," Stin said.

Hank clenched his jaw. *Only another minute, Mom and Dad.* They'd all be sprinting toward the old factory as soon as Stin fired the flare. It should take less than fifteen seconds. They'd be through the door, and Hank would be on the Apep before it knew what was going on.

"Thirty seconds," Stin said as he cocked the hammer on the flare gun.

Gregory cracked each of his knuckles again.

Stin raised the flare gun above his head and began to count down from ten.

Hank pushed back his right foot to make sure he'd have a clean start. Dog moved into position as well.

"Three, two, one," Stin said and pulled the trigger.

POP!

The flare shot into the air, casting a red light on the old factory and the people charging it. Flashlights turned on in each group, making it look like an invasion of light. Hank imagined this was what it must have looked like to see men pouring across the trench lines in the Great War.

Gregory was the first to the cellar door. "Ready?"

Hank and Stin nodded.

"Do it," Stin said.

Gregory grabbed the door handle and lifted, the hinges squeaking as he pushed it open. Hank, Dog, Stin, and Gregory ran down the short flight of stairs, leaving the other two men to stand guard.

The light from their flashlights poured across the cellar. It stretched the entire distance of the factory, at least sixty yards. It was a lot of ground to cover with an Apep close by.

"What's happening? It's like I'm walking in quicksand," Gregory said.

"That's the Apep," Hank said in a whisper.

Mold and mildew attacked Hank's nose. He ignored the smell and concentrated on the weight of the Apep. At the far end of the cellar, Hank could see metal bars and two people huddled together. *Mom! Dad!* They were so close. He bit his bottom lip and searched above for the Apep.

"Where is it?" Gregory asked.

"Here, but I thought for sure it'd attack as soon as we came in," Hank said.

The liberators stalked across the cellar, but each step on the stone floor echoed around the room.

Hank could see his parents. He furrowed his brow and continued to look for the Apep before returning his gaze to his parents.

"If it's not going to show, let's get them and get out," Gregory said.

"Agreed," Stin said, extending his stride.

Their footfalls thundered through the cellar. Halfway to the cage, light poured in from outside.

"There's boats out here!" one of the men called from the top of the stairs.

"With big floodlights!" the other man added.

The light cast wide shadows from their bodies, like monsters dancing on the wall. Hank could tell his parent's eyes were close. He sprinted the cage door and pulled out his lock pick kit. Stin had been teaching him, and he'd become pretty good.

"Hurry, guys. There's a bunch of people on the way!" one of the men shouted down, his words jumping out of his mouth like people jumping from sinking ship.

"They wanted us here! It's a trap!" Stin said, his voice filled with anger.

Hank opened the door and touched his parents. "Wake up!"

They didn't move, but something else did. The Apep. Hank looked up. He could feel the Apep swirling nearby, but still couldn't see it.

Outside, shouts and fighting filled the air and echoed into the cellar.

"Hank! Look out!"

Hank looked over his shoulder. There it was. The Apep slithered through the air on a path for him. Hank spun on the spot and pulled up the ley line energy from inside him. He wasn't about to let this Apep take his parents again. The energy pooled from his hands, creating a shield that grew large until it covered his parents. The Apep smashed into the energy and recoiled.

"Get everyone out of here, Stin. I'll be right behind you!" Hank shouted.

Stin pulled a geode from his pocket and charged at the Apep. "I'm not leaving you!" He blasted the Apep with a flash of energy. It brightened the room more, and three men came down the stairs, men he knew weren't with him. Gregory turned and shot a blinding blast of energy.

They needed to go now. Hank dropped the energy shield and knelt by his parents, shaking them. His dad's eyes fluttered for a moment and then closed.

A crash and moan came from behind him. Gregory was knocked to the floor by one of the three men.

The Apep rushed at Stin. Stin fired another blast, but it

didn't slow the beast. Stin hit the wall and crumpled as the Apep vanished. The three men moved in on Stin.

"Dog! Don't let them near him!"

Dog barked and sprung towards the men, teeth bared.

"Wake up!" Hank shouted as he shook his parents.

He could feel the Apep speeding towards him but didn't turn fast enough.

He screamed as the Apep coiled around him and squeezed.

"Welcome back, Hank Hudson. Your power is growing," the Apep hissed in his mind.

"Bad choice," Hank said, bringing up a powerful memory of his family and combining it with a blast of energy.

The Apep shrieked in his mind and released its grip.

"You can't ever have me!" Hank shouted at the Apep.

Hank had thought it would flee, but it only recoiled, like a snake preparing to strike again. He formed another shield and stared at the Apep. It looked like it was trying to find the right moment to strike.

"I'm coming!" Misha's voice carried across the cellar.

Hank looked away for a moment to see Misha clatter down the stairs and tackle two of the three men attacking Stin. He hopped off the flattened men and went to work with Dog to subdue the other.

The Apep moved in lazy motions back and forth as if still considering Hank.

"There's more coming!" Volk shouted from outside.

Misha scooped up Stin and then looked at Hank.

"Misha! Get Stin and the others out of here!" Hank shouted to him.

A conflicted look spread over Misha's face as he looked at Stin in his arms, Hank in the cell, and the Apep coiled above. For a moment, he seemed locked in place.

"Go now!" Hank said.

"I'll be right back for you, Little Fish!" Misha called to him as he ran up the stairs.

The Apep struck out, smashing into the energy shield.

Hank's feet slid back a few inches, but he held tight. The Apep recoiled again.

"Mom, Dad, you have to wake up. I can't hold this thing off much longer."

Hank had put too much energy into his first attack and could feel his pool of power waning.

"Looks like it's just you and me," Hank said, trying to sound as menacing as possible.

The Apep struck at him in a flash. Hank was a second too late with his shield as the Apep sent a tendril smashing into Hank's side. The impact threw Hank against the iron bars on the far side of the cage.

More shouts were echoing from outside.

Hank shot a blast of energy at the Apep. Then another. And another, trying to drive the Apep from the cage. Then another flash of energy spilled across the room, but it wasn't Hank this time.

"Very impressive," a woman's voice said.

Hank shot a glance toward the voice that seemed to have appeared from nowhere. A woman stood in the center of the cellar. She wore long boots with flared pants and a black jacket. Hank had never seen her before. He'd have remembered the short, cropped, sooty hair and piecing blue eyes. She gave him a playful grin as armed men came down the stairs and flanked her on either side.

Hank swallowed hard as his stomach tied into a knot. There was something frightening about her, and it wasn't the men with the guns.

The Apep wound its way toward her.

Ms. Cabot?

Hank had to get out of here. His parents were starting to move. If he could turn invisible and get the others, they could make another attack. It was his only chance.

He cleared his mind and went invisible. *I'll be right back.* He hated the thought of leaving them here for another moment, but what choice did he have?

"Also a very impressive talent. I might not be able to see you, Hank, but I have a dear friend who can," the woman said as a boy a few years older than Hank walked out from behind her.

Hank walked through the cell door and stared at the boy. The boy stared back at him.

"He's just leaving the cage," the boy said in a calm, even tone.

15

SHOOTING STARS

Hank held enough energy to blast his way out, but he'd frozen mid-step when the other boy had pointed at him. It took him a moment to collect himself. He pulled up the energy, ready to strike at the woman and boy.

"You could get away, but your parents will be dead," the boy said. "This isn't a threat, just a full disclosure of the facts at hand." The boy spoke with authority. He was only about five feet, but seemed taller in the way he held himself.

"He's right, Hank. If you leave now, I have no more use of your parents," the woman said, striding toward them.

The boy pushed his thick, russet hair out of his eyes as he followed her.

Hank looked at the woman and then back at his parents. He thought for a long moment and then turned visible.

"That's a smart boy," she said.

"How do I know you'll let them go?"

"It's you I want, Hank. Not them." She placed her hand on her chest. "I'm Evelyn Cabot, and I want to work together."

A shiver rippled across Hank's body. He glanced at the faces surrounding him again. His parents now had their eyes open. The boy looked almost bored, and Ms. Cabot

smiled at Hank. It wasn't an easy choice for him to make.

Hank looked at his parents. "The rest of the kids are safe, and you'll be safe too."

Tears pooled up in his mom's eyes. He turned to face Ms. Cabot with his hands in the air.

"Good." She looked back at the Apep and then at Hank. "I think we should go somewhere more private. I'd like to have a conversation about your future without creatures lurking nearby," Ms. Cabot said. From a pouch on her belt, she retrieved a geode. It was the size of Hank's fist with apple red crystals protruding from the opening.

Hank backed up as she and the boy walked into the cell. "Be a good boy and take my hand," she said as she extended it to Hank.

Hank looked at her hand like it was a bear trap ready to snap.

"We don't have all day, Hank," she said.

The boy had placed his hand over the geode she held. Hank gave a quick exhale and took the hand.

"Hold tight," she said as the geode glowed brightly.

The light seemed to blind him. Everything looked white. He glanced at the geode. It wasn't blinding him with light; it transformed him into light. His entire body glowed as he turned translucent. His body tingled with anticipation.

"Hank!" his mom called to him. "What's happening to you?" She stretched her hand out to him. Hank thought she'd fall through his body, but instead her body also transformed. He could see his dad transform as well. They were now all made of light: Ms. Cabot, the boy, Hank, and his mom and dad.

His entire body seemed to be stretching. He looked up and could see the ceiling get closer while his feet were firmly on the ground. He felt like a rubber band.

CRACK!

In a flash of light, they shot upward, breaking through the ceiling and then the roof of the factory. They screamed through the air and across the night sky. Hank looked down. The ground flew far below him in a blur. He looked forward and then back. They were a flash of long light shooting across the night sky. *We're a shooting star.*

The entire trip took less than two seconds. The light dissipated as his body returned to flesh. Hank blinked several times, trying to see. The bright circles in his eyes dimmed, and he could just see the outlines of the others. He realized he was still holding Ms. Cabot's hand and yanked it back.

"Manners," she said. "What is this, Hank? You brought your parents?" Her voice went up an octave. "They were going to be let go along with the rest of your little band of thieves! Now, I don't know what to do with them." She paced away from Hank.

Waves crashed somewhere in the distance. He took in a deep breath of salty air and realized that the weight of the Apep was gone. It hadn't followed them here. At least, not yet.

A car door opened and a light turned on. Headlights. Hank could make out more of his surroundings. They were in a large cavern by the sea. The sand under his feet didn't give as he turned and knelt by his parents.

"Hank, is it really you?" his mom said, pulling him into a hug.

"Yeah, it's me."

His father's arms came around him next. Feeling the embrace of his parents brought a tightness to his chest and throat.

"What's going on, son? Why do I feel so weak?" his dad asked.

"You've been held captive by that woman over there. She wants me. I'm some sort of vessel to be used for an Apep. That's the monster that weakened you."

His dad gave him a confused look, like Hank was speaking another language. Hank sighed. It was a lot to try to explain to someone who hadn't witnessed everything he had.

"I'm sorry. I don't know how to explain it," Hank said.

"I've been worried every day since you've been gone," his mom said. "I kick myself for not taking the time to double check that you were with us. This is all our fault."

"It's not your fault. I shouldn't have gotten you mixed up in all this."

"Nonsense," his mom said. "Don't blame yourself. I'm just so glad you're okay."

"We love you, son. Love you so much," his dad said, pulling him tighter.

Footsteps approached on the hard, packed sand.

"Oh my. It brings joy to my heart to see such a touching reunion," Ms. Cabot said. "But I'm afraid we have to cut this short. Your son and I have some business we need to discuss." She stepped closer.

"No!" his dad shouted.

"Leave our son alone," his mother said as she pulled Hank close.

Ms. Cabot grinned. "So much love," she said, her tone full of condescension. She closed the distance between them and pulled Hank up by his suspenders.

His parents tried to hold him, but their weak grasp fell away. Hank wasn't going to let Ms. Cabot have them. He pulled up the ley line energy and moved to strike Ms. Cabot.

"I don't think so," she said as she put a hand on his chest.

Her touch felt hot. Burning hot. He clenched his teeth as the fiery sensation spread through his body. His muscles contracted. He couldn't even let out a scream.

"So much power," she cooed.

The burning reached his toes, and as fast as it started, he could feel it pulling back, out of his body, and into Ms. Cabot's hand. She pulled it away, and Hank collapsed on the ground, like he'd just been punched in the stomach with a truck.

"What—did—you—do?" Hank said in gasps of air.

She held up her hand. A large ring rested on her index finger. It glowed ember orange.

"This stone lets me dissipate power."

Hank shook the fog from his head and tried to pull up the ley line energy. It was gone. He sat there, completely empty. Defenseless.

"You like the power, don't you, Hank?" She didn't wait for a response. "I can understand. I've been fascinated by it since my father first introduced it to me as a little girl. But I can only use it through the stones. Not like you."

Hank's parents dragged themselves closer to him. She considered the small family, and then knelt by Hank to whisper in his ear. "You can have more power than you can ever imagine. A never ending supply. You will be a king. No, a God among men."

Hank spit on the ground. "I won't be some monster's puppet!"

She stood. "You misjudge me, Hank. Yes, you are a vessel. The Apeps have used vessels once to take a mortal form in the past, but I'm looking beyond that. They were men, regular men trying to grab the power for themselves. They couldn't hold the ley energy inside them. It consumed their bodies, turned them into—what was the word you used? Monsters." She crossed her arms. "But you could hold the power, complete the process they so desperately wanted. You will be much more powerful than they could have ever dreamed. Most importantly, I believe with that power you could destroy them."

Hank heard the words, but they didn't make sense. "I thought you and the Apeps were partners."

She laughed. "We aren't partners. They want us to be their slaves. I spend every day convincing them that we are, while trying to work behind their smoky backs to bring about their downfall. We've tried to control them, but you saw the dear sheriff. Controlling them consumes life. So, for now, the brotherhood serves them. The Apeps want you, and if they have you, they'll rule the world. But if you have the power..."

She walked back to Hank and extended a hand. "Do the right thing, Hank. Join us."

He looked at her. She smiled, but he could see the hunger behind her eyes. "So, I'd be a God?"

"Yes, Hank," she said with a tone of excitement. "Like the Gods of Egypt."

"I'd be your God to control, right?"

"You'd serve the brotherhood. And we serve the greater needs of mankind."

He looked at her hand and then back at her hungry eyes.

"You've threatened my family, held my parents hostage, and sent a man to kill me if I don't join you. If that's how you help mankind, then my answer is no."

The smile vanished from Ms. Cabot's face. She stood upright and turned. "I'm disappointed to hear that, Hank." She looked at the boy. "Max, kill him."

The boy, Max, stepped forward with a crystal attached to an ornate metal rod, similar to the geode carriers Volk owned but with a higher touch of craftsmanship.

Hank rose to his knees and glared at Max.

"We'll be back for you in an hour. That should be enough time for you to dispose of all three bodies," Ms. Cabot said as she got into her black Rolls Royce.

"You said my parents would live!" Hank shouted.

"I changed my mind," she said as she shut the door.

The Rolls Royce fired to life and rolled out of the cavern onto the beach.

Hank tried to stand, but fell back. He felt so weak from having the energy ripped from him. Max moved closer, keeping the rod in front of him.

"You have to be careful with this one. One touch, and you'll age a year. Another might age you ten. Touch it long enough you'll wither up like an old man," Max said, in that same calm tone.

"Hank!" his mom cried.

"I'm okay, Mom."

"You really aren't okay," Max said standing above Hank. "You should have helped us. Oh well. This will only hurt for a moment." He lowered the crystal towards Hank's body.

"No!" his dad shouted. Hank looked back just as both of his parents lurched forward, hands extended to stop Max.

As they grabbed the crystal, both screamed in pain. Hank reached forward, grabbed Max by the ankles, and pulled. The older boy tumbled. Hank used all of his strength to crawl on top of him.

Max lifted the rod. With a quick twist, Hank grabbed Max's hand and brought the blunt end of the rod into his face. The boy went still.

Hank threw the rod across the cavern. "Mom! Dad! Are you okay?" He rolled over and sat up. They were alive, but they didn't look much like his parents. Both were wrinkled and frail. His mom's hair had gone a silver grey while his dad's had thinned and fallen out. Only small tufts of white hair sat on the side of his face.

"Who's there?" his mom asked, her voice sounding thin.

"It's me, Hank."

"Who?" his dad asked.

"It's Hank. Your son."

"I don't have a son. I've just barely gotten married. Where's my wife?"

"Dad, she's right there."

His dad looked at his mom. He stared for a long moment. "No, where's my wife?"

A family in Hank's old neighborhood had a senile grandfather who oftentimes could only remember his youth. Hank's heart sank. How could he get them out when he could barely move himself? He dropped his hands to his lap, his right hitting something hard in his pocket. *The tin. The world's smallest geode.* He pulled the chocolate tin from his pocket and opened it with the care of a surgeon.

"What do you have there, young fella?" his dad asked, peering at the box. "Chocolates! I love chocolates."

"This is something better than chocolate," Hank said as he placed a finger on the crystal fragment. He could feel the power there. Not much, but it was what he needed. *Strength of arms.* He stood and scooped up his parents, one under each arm.

"Hey, now! Unhand me, young man! This is not how you treat a woman."

"Sorry, Mom, but we have to go."

"Where's the chocolate?" his dad demanded.

Hank ignored their talk and moved out of the cavern to

the beach. Lights from a nearby town glittered in the distance. The energy from this insignificant sliver of crystal wouldn't get him far. Right now, all that mattered was getting distance between him and Max.

16

ON HOLIDAY WITH THE GRANDPARENTS

The strength from the sliver of crystal lasted two hours. Hank had carried his parents parallel to the coastline but stayed away from the main roads or areas where they'd be easily spotted. Just as Hank felt the power wane, he reached the outskirts of a town, found a barn well off the road, and brought them in for the night.

"You're a fine young man. What did you say your name was again?" his dad asked as Hank helped him sit on a bed of straw.

"It's Hank. Hank Hudson."

"Hudson? That's my last name too. Wonder if we're related somehow. I'll tell my wife all about you when I see her." He took a breath and continued. "When will I see her?"

"Soon. I'm taking you to her in the morning."

Hank looked across at the other stall. His mom lay on her side, already fast asleep.

"Ouch! What is this?" his dad asked as he reached behind him and pulled out a pocket knife and a wallet from his trousers.

"Aren't they yours?" Hank asked.

"Never seen them before," his dad replied.

Hank took them from him and looked in the wallet. It was his dad's. *They didn't even take anything from him.* Hank

shook his head. Just how powerful were the brotherhood that they'd leave a prisoner armed? Had it all been set up for him to come after his parents?

He'd rescued them, but they weren't themselves anymore. He slumped against a wooden post, his hands wiping his eyes. He cleared his throat. "These are your—"

A snore from his dad cut him off.

Someone should get some sleep. He opened the wallet again, thumbed past the money, and pulled out the photos. He smiled. They showed smiling faces of his brothers and sisters and his parents, each photo a moment in time. *Better times.* He'd been absent in all the photos until he reached the last one. The picture was of him and Dog. Neither were facing the camera. He sat in the tire swing, and Dog lay by his side. *When did Dad take this?* He wiped a tear from his eye and returned the photos.

The sky grew brighter, but the sun hadn't broken over the horizon line. Hank stayed up all night to watch over his parents, the thoughts of the past few months playing through his mind. How could he have prevented this?

"Is it morning already?" his dad asked.

"Yeah, Dad. Let's get Mom up and find out where we are."

"I'm not your dad, and that woman looks too old to be your mom."

"Sorry."

Hank helped them all the way to the train station. The sign over the main office read:

Saint John

Hank had never heard of a St. John, South Carolina. They'd only traveled like a shooting star for a couple seconds. How far could they be from Charleston? St. John wasn't ringing any bells. Maybe there was a St. John, North Carolina. Even at the height they'd climbed, he couldn't imagine they were farther than a few hundred miles from the old factory.

"Why don't you sit here, and I'll see about getting us tickets?"

Hank double checked he was visible and walked up to the man behind the counter, who smiled as Hank approached.

"On a holiday with your grandparents, my friend?" the man asked, his accent not sounding like any Hank had heard in North Carolina.

Hank raised his eyebrows and glanced around. His eyes landed on his wrinkled and gray parents.

"Oh, yeah. It's been great spending time with them," he said, and then added, "We need to get to Fruitland."

Now, the man gave Hank the confused look. "Where?"

"Fruitland, North Carolina."

"Oh, Americans. Heading back home?"

Americans? Hank hesitated a moment before saying, "We are, sir. Actually we were traveling all night and didn't notice the name of the town. Where are we?"

The man smiled broadly. "Saint John, New Brunswick. The prettiest little town in Canada." The man flipped through some books and wrote some figures.

A train whistle blew in the yard.

"I can't get you all the way to Fruitland. Only freight runs that line. But I can get you to Columbus, North Carolina."

"That will be fine, sir."

The man looked at his book again. "Well, I suppose you'll be wanting to get on that train right now."

"Yes, sir. We're anxious to get home."

"Coach or a sleeping car?"

The whistle blew again.

"Whichever is less."

The man scribbled on his notepad. "That'll be sixty-two dollars, and it will have you there by about seven tomorrow evening."

Hank paid the man, who wished him well as he helped his parents to the waiting train.

The seats in coach faced each other. Only two other people were riding in the car. Hank and his parents sat at the same time that the train lurched forward.

The train rocked like a cradle. Hank's eyelids dropped shut. He forced them wide open and took a quick glance to see that his parents were there. *Still safe.* The cradle rocked back and forth. When had his eyelids put on so much weight? He blinked again, trying to fight against the sleep. He lost.

The cavern entered his dream. His parents were there too. They screamed in pain as the crystal pressed against their flesh. They aged faster and faster, their bodies withering away. He moved to stop the boy from the cavern, but Max wasn't there.

Hank's dad looked up with pleading eyes. That's when Hank realized he was the one holding the aging rod. He was the one turning his parents old. He tossed the rod away, but they didn't stop aging.

"No!" Hank cried. "I didn't mean to!" he pleaded as they withered into a pile of ash.

Hank dropped to his knees as the sand rocked underneath him. It shook him violently.

"Young man. Wake up," a deep male voice said in his ear. "Please, you need to wake up."

Hank opened his eyes and looked towards the voice, expecting his dad. A train conductor stared at him.

"It's your grandfather—"

Hank sprung out of his chair and scanned the seats next to him. His mom slept in one of the chairs, but his dad was gone. "What's happened? Is he okay?"

"He's okay, but I need you to come get him. He's locked himself in the bathroom and keeps shouting."

"Shouting?"

The conductor shook his head. "He's upset. Keeps demanding to know what we did to him." The conductor must have seen the confusion on Hank's face because he added, "He keeps wanting to know who turned him old."

A shiver went through Hank. "Show me where, sir."

The conductor led him to a locked door. "He's in there."

"Da—I mean, Mr. Hudson, can you open the door? It's Hank."

"Go away. I can't let anyone see me like this. What if my wife sees me looking old like this? She'll leave me for sure," his dad said between sobs.

A knot twisted in Hank's stomach. He'd never heard his dad cry. He thought for a moment. "I'm going to help you with that, Mr. Hudson," Hank said. He tried to believe he could help his parents. Through the night he'd been thinking that if there was a way to age someone, there must be a way to reverse it. But how?

The crying quieted. "Can you really help me to be young again?" his dad asked with a snort.

"I can, but you need to open the door and come back with me. This train is going to take us to friends who can help."

Silence. Hank held his breath, waiting for his dad to respond. A long moment passed, but it felt like an hour. The lock clicked. Both Hank and the conductor let out a sigh.

The door opened, and Hank looked at his dad. The wrinkles around his eyes were puffy and red, and streaks of tears lined his cheeks.

"We're right out here," Hank said, pointing down the corridor toward their car. Hank and his dad shuffled side-by-side, down the narrow halls of the train.

They were back in their own car. The other two strangers stared as they walked past. Hank didn't make eye contact with them as he guided his dad back to their seats. His mom, now awake, had a worried look on her face. Their eyes met, but instead of the oblivious look she'd given him all morning, recognition reflected back at him.

"Hank? Is that you?" She stood, but swayed as her legs seemed to disagree with her plan.

Hank reached out and caught her arm, lowering her back down. "Don't move so fast, Mom. I don't want you getting hurt."

She took hold of his hands and squeezed them tightly. "I've been looking everywhere for you, and then your dad and I ended up in a cage, and now, we're here. I feel like I'm going crazy. What's happening?"

Hank smiled at her, but his insides crumbled. "We're okay.

Do you remember last night?"

Her face contorted as she looked down. "I'm trying to remember. There was a flash of light. You were carrying me, and there was pain." She looked at her hands and let go of Hank's to examine the wrinkles and the age spots. "What happened to me?" She looked up at Hank and then at her husband. Fear crossed her face.

"James?" she asked.

His dad met her gaze and looked at her for a long moment. "Margaret, it happened to you too?" He sank into the chair next to her and pulled her into a tight embrace.

Hank could hear their gentle sobs. The belt around his stomach tightened another notch. He gazed out the window. How could he explain this? He grasped at words, but trying to put them in order seemed like a puzzle he couldn't solve.

They were passing a farm field. The white fence posts zipped by. Hank counted over a hundred before his parents stopped crying and wiped their eyes. He looked at them with a forced smile and then opened his mouth to say something that would relieve them, somehow make this all better. But what came out was, "It's going to be okay."

"What's going to be okay, young man?" his mom asked, her eyes blank like she was talking to a stranger.

"This young man's going to help us, dear. His last name is Hudson, like ours."

She looked at her husband and then back at Hank with a sparkling smile. "I like that. Hank Hudson. What a good ring. When we have kids, we'll have to think about naming one of them Hank."

Hank returned the smile and moved his gaze back to the window, his heart dropping to his feet. More fence posts flew by. *Maybe Volk knows something about this.* He'd ask him as soon as they were back, and he'd read through Adam's journal again. There had to be a way to help his parents.

"When you carried us out of that place last night, I saw that crystal attached to that stick. Was that what did this to us?"

his dad asked. He spoke so calmly he might have been talking about the weather.

Hank swung around to face him. "Yeah. You remember last night?"

"I remember you taking us out of there. That crystal. It's funny. I can remember a man and woman talking about crystals, but it has to be a dream because I remember being locked in a jail cell, and I've never been to jail. Couldn't imagine it!"

Hank leaned forward, his breath catching as he spoke. "That sounds like an interesting dream, Mr. Hudson. What were they saying about the crystals?"

His dad pondered for a few moments before speaking. "Well, I don't rightly recall much of it. The woman said they'd found it. Something about a cache they'd been searching for. I thought it was odd because they said it was in Woodbury, Tennessee. I worked just a few miles north of there last summer before I met this lovely woman." His dad squeezed his mom's hand and then shook his head with a laugh. "Funny things, dreams."

"Yeah, funny things." Hank looked out the window. *Woodbury.* The woman could have been Ms. Cabot, but then again, his dad wasn't of the soundest mind at the moment. He spun it over and over in his mind. Maybe they could go to Woodbury and get some answers.

The rest of the train ride went by without any problems. They made good time and got off in Columbus just before six. Hank led them to the Dubois home. He didn't think anyone was there, which was fine by him. He'd pick the lock to the house, and they'd have a real place to sleep. In the morning, they could call someone in Fruitland for a ride.

The streets were quiet. Hank liked taking walks at night. The crisp night air made it easier to think. They turned the corner and walked down the street where the Dubois home sat.

The chatter of people invaded Hank's peaceful evening stroll. Lights spilled into the street, and Hank could see a large gathering in the yard. They were camped out in every spare inch of the property.

"Come on." He urged his parents to pick up the pace.

They didn't.

Hank glanced back and forth between the group ahead and his parents. What had happened since Charleston? Every step seemed an eternity as they neared the home. As they got closer, he recognized some of the people. They were from the encampment.

Misha's voice echoed down the street. "This is only temporary. We will find a new home soon."

A new home? What about the reservoir?

17
A SACRIFICE FOR NOTHING

November 9, 1933, Columbus, North Carolina

"Hank! You're alive!" Hank's older sister Sarah spotted him and ran his way, throwing her arms around him and pressing the air out of his lungs. "We've all been so worried," she said.

"I'm okay, but if you keep squeezing me this tight, I might not be," Hank said with a chuckle as she released him.

Sarah smiled at him as others circled them.

"Are you going to introduce us to your friend?" Hank's dad asked.

Sarah looked at their parents. Her mouth fell open, and her eyes widened. "Mom? Dad?"

"You've got us confused with someone else," her mom said. "We've just gotten married. And then something happened..." she trailed off.

The semi-circle around them fell dead quiet.

Hank's dad looked intently at Sarah. "Margaret, she looks so much like you. What's your name, young lady?"

Sarah stared at them for a long moment, sadness in her eyes. "Sarah. Sarah Hudson."

"Sarah. That's my mother's name. And Hudson—" Hank's mom stopped short and just looked at Sarah. After a long moment, she moved her gaze to Hank. "Please, is there

somewhere we can rest? I don't feel well."

Hank glanced at Sarah. She caught his gaze. The excitement in her face vanished, replaced with flared nostrils and a furrowed brow. She crossed her arms. Hank's shoulders slumped, and he looked at the ground.

Can it get worse?

"Bring her inside," Julie Dubois said from the back of the crowd.

Yep. Her voice grated on Hank's ears. He hesitated, but what choice did he have? They needed to rest. As they walked inside, Misha patted Hank on the back and gave him a smile. Hank returned it weakly. The last two days had been like a tornado tearing through town. What could there be to smile about?

Julie gave his parents her bedroom. Hank made sure his parents were settled, shut the door, and entered the kitchen. Sarah and Stin were seated at the small table. Neither of them were talking. Hank stopped in the doorway, and Julie slipped past him.

"Can I get you anything to eat?" Julie asked.

Hank shook his head. He couldn't eat. "Thank you though," he said as an afterthought, trying to remember his manners. Even if he didn't trust the Julie and Steve he could still be cordial.

He faced Sarah and Stin. No one said a word. Each second that ticked by filled the room with uncomfortable silence. Stin looked tired, but Sarah seemed wide awake. She folded her arms across her chest and drummed her fingers against her arms. She opened her mouth and then clenched it shut. Instead of speaking, she glared at Hank. Her right eye was bruised. What had happened to her, and how had he not seen it sooner? Her hair hung down to her shoulders, unlike the way she normally wore it. A cut across her forehead peeked out under the locks.

Hank looked at Stin, but he stared at the table. His gaze seemed distant enough to be in another world. Hank's stomach tightened. Neither Stin nor Sarah seemed ready to talk about the past two days. He certainly didn't know how to start, so he picked another topic altogether.

"Where's Dog?"

Sarah exploded, slamming her hands on the table. "Where's Dog? That's the first thing you ask? Where's your stupid dog? How about telling me what happened to Mom and Dad? How about asking us why we're all here? How about asking what happened to me? How about—"

"That's enough," Stin said flatly, cutting her off.

She set her jaw and continued to glare at Hank.

Hank looked at the floor. Why was she so cross at him? He'd already failed to protect their parents. Did she have to rub it in?

"We've all been through a lot. Hank, let's start with what happened to you. When I woke up, they told me that one minute you were in the cellar and the next you were gone, and that your parents were gone too."

Hank cleared the lump from his throat. "Ms. Cabot took us. She had some kind of ley line energy that shot us into the sky. We landed in a cavern in Canada. When I wouldn't give her what she wanted, she left us with this boy named Max. He was going to kill all of us, but Mom and Dad saved me—" Hank trailed off.

Sarah stood. "This is all your fault! Our life has been ruined because of you!" She stomped to the door and pulled it open. Just before she stepped out, she looked back at Hank. "You know? You should have given them what they wanted. How could you be so selfish?" She slammed the door like a final punctuation.

Hank's chest tightened. He thought of the dream. He had done this. Even if Max physically pressed the crystal against them, it was still Hank's fault that they were there. Tears welled up in his eyes.

"Hey, don't listen to her. It's not your fault, Hank," Stin said.

He wiped the tears and looked at Stin. "What happened after I left? Why is everyone here?"

"Charleston was a trap. The brotherhood had armed men ready to scoop us up. Only about half of us got away."

"What about Dog?"

"He's okay. We had to lock him up because he kept trying

to run off to find you."

"What happened to the other half?" Hank asked, almost not wanting to know the answer.

"Arrested."

Hank breathed a little easier. "Arrested for what?"

"Trespassing on government property. And while we were in Charleston, Cabot coordinated a raid at the reservoir."

"A raid?"

"That's what happened to Sarah. Armed thugs started rounding people up. Anyone who resisted was beaten. They went through the encampment and the Swensons' home, and they got the ring."

Hank's heart dropped into his stomach. All that work at the prison for nothing. "Where's Lina?" He hadn't seen her in the crowd.

Stin paused.

Hank's heart raced, and his stomach churned. "Is she okay?"

"She's hurt, but not bad. But her mother—" Stin trailed off.

"What, Stin? What happened to Mrs. Nieves?"

Stin looked down and scratched the back of his neck. "Sarah told me that when the brotherhood attacked Lina, her mom went berserk. She attacked three of them and pulled Lina to safety. She was moving everyone away from the encampment when Elmer Grossman showed up. He killed her." The words stuck in Stin's throat. "Shot her in the back."

Hank stared. Why would the brotherhood kill her? "Where's Lina?"

Stin cleared his throat. "Lina stayed with some of the others to bury her mother. After they killed her, the fighting stopped. Elmer told everyone they had until tomorrow night to clear out. He said after that, the TVA would be there to take over the management of the government's newly acquired property. They've taken all of it. From the reservoir all the way to Fruitland. Even took Mr. Swenson's property."

"How can they do that?"

"It's called eminent domain. It allows the government to take land for public use and work projects."

"But it's not the government that wants it. It's Ms. Cabot!"

"I know, Hank, but right now, she is the government. Mr. and Mrs. Swenson are clearing out as much as they can take, but there's no way to fight it."

"What about the judge? Isn't there something he can do?"

Stin clenched his teeth and exhaled. "No one can get in touch with him. His former secretary says he took an early retirement."

"Former?" Hank asked.

"Yep. They've already replaced him with someone more 'favorable.' The new judge was the one who approved the eminent domain. I guess the hearing lasted all of twelve minutes this afternoon."

Hank's legs went weak, and he slid along the door frame. "Sarah's right. I should have let them have me. If I'd gone back when we were fighting the sheriff, none of this would have happened. Lina's mom would be alive, no one would be arrested, the Swensons wouldn't have been kicked out of their home, Sarah wouldn't have been hurt, we wouldn't have lost the ring, and my parents wouldn't be old and senile. Maybe if I go up there now, maybe Ms. Cabot will make it all right."

"No, Hank!"

Hank jumped.

Stin continued. "This isn't your fault. If you gave yourself over to Cabot, your parents' sacrifice would be for nothing." Stin sat by Hank. "Hank, we all choose to make sacrifices. We choose to sacrifice for the ones we love. Your parents, Lina's mother—they would make those same choices to protect you. We'd all make the same choice, Hank. We need you."

Tears poured from Hank's eyes. Wasn't sacrifice meant to gain something? Was he really worth the suffering of others?

Stin put an arm around Hank's shoulder and pulled him close. "We need to honor their sacrifices. You need to move forward with this."

Stin was right. He did need to go forward, but he couldn't risk anyone else's life. He wouldn't let this happen again. *No one should sacrifice for me.* He needed to make this right, especially for his parents.

"Stin, do you have Adam's journal?"

"Of course," Stin said and rifled through his coat. "What do you need it for?"

"I want to see if he wrote anything about aging."

Stin pulled it from a pocket and handed it over.

"Thanks," Hank said. "I think I'm going to check on Dog."

Stin nodded, and Hank walked out of the house.

They'd closed Dog up in the same little building where Hank had been locked in each night while staying with the butchers. Hank neared the little building. Dog ran back and forth, scratching the door. Hank picked up the pace. "Just a minute. I'm going to get you out."

Dog barked.

"I'm okay. Are you alright?"

Dog barked again.

"I'm glad they didn't let you take off after me. You'd be halfway to Canada by now," Hank said as he unlocked the door.

Dog burst out and jumped on Hank, licking every inch of his face.

"I'm glad to see you too!" Hank said, hugging Dog. Hank scratched the fur around Dog's ears. "Listen, I'm going to be gone for awhile."

Dog whined.

"I don't know how long. I guess until I can get this mess taken care of."

Dog gave two sharp barks as he sat and looked at Hank with equally sharp eyes.

"I can't let anyone else get hurt. That includes you."

Dog barked again.

"I know you want to, but look at this. This is all my fault. I'm the one who has to do this."

Dog just looked at Hank. His eyes narrowed, and his ears leaned forward. Hank shuffled his feet. He should have known he wouldn't be able to keep Dog from going. "Listen, I don't know what kind of danger we'll be facing. You have a choice here. I don't."

Dog gave another bark and jumped on Hank again, giving him a quick lick. He dropped down and walked a few feet before barking again.

"Tennessee, but we won't be able to walk there."

Dog gave a short whine.

"Don't worry. I have a plan."

18

HAVE SIDECAR, WILL TRAVEL

Hank and Dog walked through the night. It reminded Hank of the first time they'd traveled this road when he'd run away from the Dubois home. It'd taken him until daybreak to reach Fruitland the first time. But tonight, Hank and Dog had an early start, and they'd be taking a shortcut.

The knapsack on Hank's back dug into his shoulders. He'd grabbed as many geodes as he could find and a few canteens of water. The weight made his already sore muscles cry out. He did his best to ignore the pain. What he carried on his back might be the difference of life or death.

When Hank and Dog reached the cold ley line, they followed it. The two spent three hours traveling through brush and trees until they finally broke through at the clearing by the reservoir.

Hank looked across the field. Even in the dark, he could see the remains of the camp. An eerie feeling walked up Hank's spine. "It's like a ghost town," he whispered to Dog, who nuzzled his head into Hank's hand.

The eerie feeling increased when he saw the caravan. The one where Mrs. Nieves had given him cookies so many times. The one where he'd laughed and shared stories from the road. The one where he'd felt at home each time he'd entered.

"She didn't deserve this," Hank said as he walked out of the brush and trees. There wasn't any movement in the encampment. Stin had said Lina had stayed to bury her mom. What if he ran into her? How could he face her after what he'd done? He swallowed hard.

"Come on," he said to Dog.

They climbed the hill to the ley line crossing, and Hank walked into it. The rush of warmth and power poured into him. In the past month, this place had become his second home, and tomorrow he'd never be able to come back. He closed his eyes and sat.

Dog barked.

Hank opened his eyes and looked at his friend. "I've got nothing left. Give me at least two hours, and then we can go." Two hours would cut it close, but they'd still get out under the cover of the early morning sky.

Dog padded to Hank's side and dropped down next to him. Hank lay back and watched the night sky. Stars twinkled above them. After his trip from Charleston to Saint John, he'd never look at the stars the same way.

"I wish we had the shooting star ley line energy."

Dog barked.

"Ms. Cabot had an energy that turned us into light and shot us through the sky. I think it must have been the same one Adam wrote about in his letter. I don't know where you get that one, but it'd make the trip a lot faster."

Dog whined.

"It didn't hurt at all."

They sat in silence for several long moments. Hank's mind played through the events of the past couple days. Clearly Elmer Grossman, the man they captured, had set the trap, but how had Ms. Cabot known when Hank and the others were going to get there? After they were done questioning Elmer, Mrs. Swenson had taken him back to Fruitland, so the killer couldn't have told Ms. Cabot. He wouldn't have known. It had to be someone who knew the plan.

"Dog, did you notice anything weird about Julie or Steve?"

Dog barked.

"Not like that. She excused herself after the meeting. I'm just wondering if she could have called Ms. Cabot."

Dog whined.

A knot twisted in Hank's stomach. "I don't have it in for them, but I don't believe they're completely honest. They certainly take advantage of situations. If Ms. Cabot offered them a pile of money for me, maybe they'd take it."

Dog barked twice.

"I don't have any proof, but—"

Dog barked, cutting off Hank's words.

"Fine. I'll leave it, but there is someone from the encampment that's talking. Another reason we need to be on our own." Hank put a hand on Dog and stroked his fur.

They spent the rest of their time in the ley line crossing in silence.

"Come on. Hopefully this will be enough," Hank said. If he rationed his energy use, it should get him to Tennessee.

They slipped from the reservoir to Mr. Swenson's house. Dawn was coming, but no one seemed to be moving around the house, and no lights were on inside. Of course, Hank doubted anyone had gotten much sleep that night. Instead of going to the main house, Hank led Dog to the barn that held Mr. Swenson's contraptions. Hank took hold of the large handle on the door and turned it as quietly as he could.

It squeaked. Hank froze. He glanced at the house but didn't see anyone moving. He waited a little longer, just to be sure, before slipping into the barn. He shouldn't have been able to see, but he could make out the shapes of all the contraptions. A perk of the ley line energy inside him.

Hank made his way to one of the last stalls. It was still there: the motorcycle with the side car. A truck parked in the next stall was covered by blankets. He pulled off two of the heavy wool blankets and shoved them into the side car. He pushed the motorcycle from the stall, through the barn, and into the early morning air.

He closed the barn door and shoved the motorcycle forward. Gravel popped and cracked under the wheels. He started down the lane. He'd walk it down the road a mile before starting it up. He figured it couldn't be that much different than driving a truck.

They'd pushed the motorcycle a few hundred yards when Dog froze, his ears pointing.

"What is it?" Hank whispered.

Dog stood still, not barking a word.

Hank scanned the tree line and even the sky, looking for what Dog had sensed. If it was someone from the encampment, they might tell Stin where Hank was going, but what if it was one of the brotherhood? He pulled at the ley line energy and prepared to strike.

"Is someone there?"

"Hank?" a voice said from the tree line.

It was Lina. Dog bounded forward, tail wagging, but Hank's heart took a fast dive.

He cleared his throat. "Lina? What are you doing out here?" He shook his head. She had to be hurting.

Hank took six quick steps. Lina sat on the ground against a tree, her knees pulled to her chest.

"What am I doing out here? What are you doing here?" She didn't wait for a response. She stood and hugged him tightly. "We thought you were dead," she whispered in his ear.

Dead. Mrs. Nieves came to his mind. He pulled Lina tighter. "I heard about your mom. I'm so sorry. I didn't mean for any of this to happen."

Lina pulled back and looked at him, her eyes filling with tears. "This isn't your fault." She looked at the motorcycle and then back at him. "You're leaving us?" It sounded more like a statement than a question.

"I can't risk losing anyone else. I have to do this alone."

"That's foolish!" she said, raising her voice.

"Shh! I don't want anyone to know I'm here. Please, you can't tell them."

"I'm not going to tell them. Besides, I'm not even sure what it is you're doing. But I do know one thing: This wasn't your fault. What happened in Charleston wasn't your fault. You have to believe me, Hank."

Hank looked at the ground. Even coming from Lina, how could he accept that? He was the reason Ms. Cabot and her thugs had come to the encampment. He was the only one who could stop them, even if it meant sacrificing himself.

Lina lifted his chin with a delicate touch. "I know that look. Please, Hank."

His throat tightened, and he looked away. "I can't stay. The brotherhood found something in Tennessee. If I can get there, maybe I can get them to turn my parents back," he said and pushed the motorcycle forward.

Lina stepped out of his way. "I won't tell them. But wherever you're going, are you planning on pushing that the entire way? Seems like it'll take a lot longer."

"I'm just pushing it down the road so no one hears the engine when I start it."

"So you can start it? You can drive it?"

Hank stopped and looked at the motorcycle. There were levers and switches that he'd never noticed in the truck. He looked at the pedal on the right side. "Just like the truck. All I have to do is start it and push on that gas pedal," he said pointing down. He'd tried to sound as confident as possible.

"That's where you shift gears, not give it gas," she said as she walked next to him. "Let me go with you. I can drive it."

Hank thought about it for a moment. "No. I can't risk what happened to your mom happening to you. I couldn't live with myself."

Lina grabbed his arm and spun him around. She pushed a finger into his chest. "Now, you listen to me because it's the last time I'll say this. You didn't kill my mom." Her words spilled out with shaky conviction. "It's not your fault she died. It was that man who killed her. Elmer Grossman." She said his name like it had a vile taste. "He did it." She looked at him, as if she were letting her words sink in. "Now, are you walking, or am I driving?

Hank couldn't hold back the smile. "Driving."

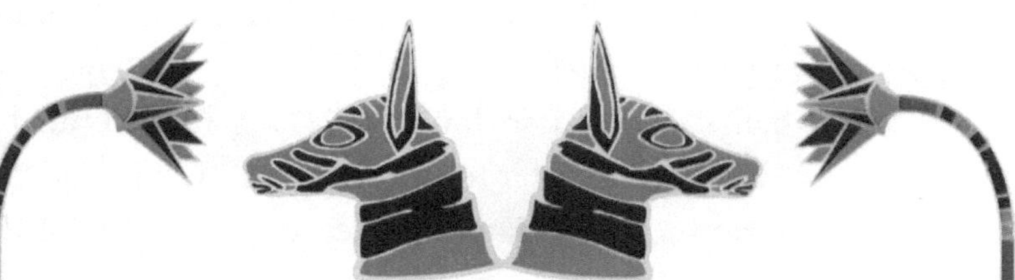

19

THE OPEN ROAD

November 10, 1933, 50 miles west of Fruitland, North Carolina

The motorcycle ran like a charm. Hank wouldn't have expected anything less from one of Mr. Swenson's contraptions. They'd pushed it on foot for about a mile before starting it up and heading west. Lina drove with Hank riding behind her. This was the first time he'd ridden on a motorcycle.

Knowing how fast Mr. Swenson said the motorcycle would drive and experiencing it were wildly different feelings. Hank held onto the sides of the machine as the wind whipped past him. *Don't fall off.* Maybe he should have risked taking a car or a truck. He glanced at Dog sitting in the sidecar, his tongue hanging from his mouth, flapping in the wind. He looked like he was in heaven. Hank relaxed his death grip and took a deep breath. A smile crept across his face.

They'd been on the road for two hours now, and the sun had just crested over the mountains, bathing the road in light. The motorcycle sported an olive green paint job with thin red stripes on the edges. It gleamed in the sun.

The dirt road flew beneath them as the miles rolled by. Looking across the landscape, Hank watched three deer dart from the tree line. It seemed like the motorcycle's roar brought out all kinds of wildlife. Some would dart back into

the trees, but the others, like the deer, stared as the contraption disrupted the peace and quiet.

The exhaust rumbled so loud that Hank had to put his mouth right at Lina's ear in order to talk with her. "Where did you learn to drive a motorcycle?" Hank shouted over the roar of the engine.

Lina twisted her head just a little to respond, but kept her eyes on the road. "The last circus we were traveling with had a daredevil. Part of his act included jumping his motorcycle across dangerous things. I loved watching him perform. Finally, I got the courage to ask him to teach me."

"Was it really that scary to ask?"

"My mom wanted me to follow in her footsteps, become a fortune teller. I wanted to become anything else. A trapeze artist. Daredevil. Knife thrower. Anything. But whenever I'd bring it up, she would say no. So, I'd sneak out and ask the other carnies to teach me."

"Well, I'm glad you did. I'd never have been able to get this thing started, let alone drive it," Hank shouted. He wished he'd had a circus nearby his old house so he could have learned such exciting things. "I think it's so cool what you've learned to do."

"Really, it's not all that helpful. I wish I could turn invisible."

"You can't?" Hank had always assumed Lina was just like him. Well, almost.

"Nope. I don't even know if I can see you when you turn invisible."

"I've never done it around you?"

"Not once."

Hank thought back for a moment. Surely he'd gone invisible around her. It still happened around his family and with others from the encampment. But then again, he'd always wanted Lina to see him.

Dog barked.

"Yeah," Hank said.

"Yeah, what?" Lina shouted back.

"So, you can't understand Dog either?"

She chuckled and looked at Dog. "I can understand you, right, boy?"

Dog smiled at her, his tongue still lolling out to one side.

She smiled back. "I just can't understand what you're saying," Lina said.

Dog whined.

"Yeah." Hank said in agreement. "For some reason, I thought everyone at the encampment could understand Dog."

Lina shook her head. "Not many people at the encampment can truly understand Dog." She paused for a moment. "Or Nobo. Although that might be okay. For some reason, I get the feeling he swears a lot."

Hank laughed. "He doesn't have a lot of good things to say, that's for sure."

Up ahead, Hank could see the outskirts of a little town.

"We should stop to get breakfast and fuel for the motorcycle. Who knows how long it'll be before we get another chance?" Hank said.

Lina slowed as they entered the little town. It took a few minutes, but they found a small roadside cafe where they bought some box lunches of chicken, rolls, and fruit cups. They filled the motorcycle's tank at a gas station, and Hank went inside to pay. He'd taken the rest of the money from his dad's wallet. He'd pay it back when this was all done.

The attendant gave Hank an odd glance. Hank tried to be calm and gave the man a smile as he handed him the money. The man didn't return the smile, just made the change and handed it back.

As soon as Hank closed his fist around the change, he walked out. "We should go. Get out of town before we eat."

"Why?" Lina said.

Hank tilted his head back toward the attendant, who now

stared at them through the window. Lina looked over at the man and waved.

"Yeah, let's go," she said, hopping on the motorcycle. With a swift plunge of her foot on the kick starter, she brought it roaring to life.

Dog looked up from the sidecar just as Hank swung his leg over the seat. He'd barely wrapped his arms around Lina when she rotated the throttle. The motorcycle shot forward, sending Dog sliding back in his seat.

Hank looked over his shoulder to see the man run outside. He yelled something, but the engine drowned out his words.

"You're crazy!" Hank shouted to Lina.

"Thank you."

Dog barked twice.

"If you do, make sure you don't do it in the sidecar. I don't want to clean it up," Hank replied.

They drove out of the little town and back onto the dirt road. They traveled another thirty miles before they felt it was safe to stop and eat. Lina pointed out a grassy meadow with a stream running by.

Lina stretched, lifting her arms high in the air. "Do you think that guy knew us?"

Hank scratched Dog behind the ears. "Go on," he said to Dog.

Dog raced into the nearby woods.

Hank turned to Lina. "I don't think so. He probably just thought we were truants or maybe thieves."

"Well, he would be right about the truants. I haven't been inside a school since..." she looked into the blue sky, like her history was stored in the clouds. "Shoot, since I was eight," she said, looking at Hank. "We'd stopped in Florida for the winter, and me and a few of the other kids were allowed to go to school. Just a little one-room school house, and there must have been fifty kids. We were a rowdy bunch, running around, talking, laughing.

It didn't last long before the teacher asked us not to come back." She giggled at the memory, but only for a moment, as sadness washed over her face.

"What is it?" Hank asked.

"When the teacher kicked us all out, my mom marched to the school and told her to let us back in. When the teacher refused, my mom said she'd put a gypsy curse on her if she didn't," Lina said and sniffed. "The next day the teacher came to our tents and asked us to please come back."

Hank could see the tears forming in her eyes. They pooled in the corners and slipped down her cheeks.

"She was always there to help me," she said. Her tears increased, and through the sobs, she said, "I don't know what I'm going to do."

Hank put a hand on her arm. "She was amazing, and I know there's nothing that can replace her. I'm here for you, though." They were the only words Hank could think to say.

Lina wiped the tears from her eyes and smiled at him. "I know. And I'm here for you. I don't want you to lose your parents, too." She pulled two of the box lunches from the side car and handed one to Hank. They sat. The grass meadow was a pleasant break from the vibration of the motorcycle. Hank's ribs, still injured, had been telling him all day to stop moving, but with the ley line energy coursing through his body, it was easy enough to ignore them.

Hank opened the box and dug in. It was like he hadn't eaten in days. Then again, when was the last time he'd eaten? A few moments later, he was wiping his mouth with the back of his hand.

"You finished that already?" Lina asked.

His face grew hot. He gave her a sheepish smile and looked away.

"You've got a healthy appetite, Hank."

He laid the empty box on the ground and tried to think of

something to change the subject. "Hey, so, you said you'd never seen me turn invisible." Hank stood up. "I bet you'll see me."

She set her lunch down and watched Hank expectantly. He cleared his mind and went invisible.

"See? You can still see me, right?"

She was grinning from ear to ear. "I can't! That's amazing! You're completely gone. I can't even see your clothes. Does that mean you can make other things invisible?"

It was something Hank had wondered too, but for him, everything looked the same, and he couldn't tell. He picked up his empty lunch box.

Lina clapped her hands together. "You are amazing, Hank Hudson!"

The warmth he felt in his face spread across his body.

"Here. Catch this," she said as she pulled out a smooth skipping stone from her pocket and tossed it to him.

Hank dropped the empty box and caught the rock.

"It's like I threw it into a hole. It's just gone. I wonder if–" she stopped herself mid-sentence and walked over to Hank. "Make me invisible."

"I don't know if it'll work that way," Hank said.

"Well, at least try," she said, putting her hands on her hips.

Hank stepped forward and reached out a hand. She looked at it but didn't take it.

"Does it hurt?"

"Not at all."

She put her hand in his. A swarm of butterflies invaded Hank's stomach. He smiled at Lina, but she frowned.

"You're visible again," she said, looking Hank in the eyes.

Hank grinned. "No, I think it worked. This is how it looks from my side," Hank said, dropping the volume of his voice. He stared into her eyes. They looked golden in the sunlight.

"I don't know. To me, we look pretty visible," Lina said in almost a whisper.

Dog bounded out of the woods and barked. Hank looked at him and then back at Lina. He let his hand go slack, and they both took a step back, blushing.

Dog whined. Hank wasn't positive, but he thought he saw Dog roll his eyes.

The trio set off on the road again. They passed three more little towns with boarded up windows on several buildings. Hank hadn't noticed very many people. It was like the towns were struggling each day to stay alive.

They kept the motorcycle off the main roads and tried not to make eye contact when they had to drive through a town.

The midday sun had passed overhead and now slipped closer and closer to dusk. Old trees lined the dirt road and cast long shadows across them as they drove. Dog slept in the sidecar, curled up on the seat. The knapsack of geodes and their remaining box lunches sat on the floor of the sidecar.

Hank absently watched the passing trees. Neither he nor Lina had said more than fifteen words to each other since being invisible. Every few minutes his mom and dad trailed across his mind. He wondered how she was holding up.

There has to be a way to reverse it. They hit a large bump that brought Hank back to the present. "What did we just hit?" he shouted.

Lina gave him a quick glance. She looked confused. "We didn't hit anything!"

"You didn't feel that just now?"

"No," she said.

Hank looked over his shoulder. The road was empty. He glanced at the sidecar. Dog was wide awake with a concerned look on his face.

"Did you feel that?"

Dog barked.

"Stop," Hank shouted.

"What?"

"Stop the motorcycle. I need to check something."

Lina stopped the machine and Hank pulled out Adam's journal. He flipped furiously through the pages until he found the one he wanted. The ley line map.

"We need to go back."

She slowed down and looked at him again. "Why?"

"Adam marked a crossing nearby here, and I think we just went through it. And it's a big one."

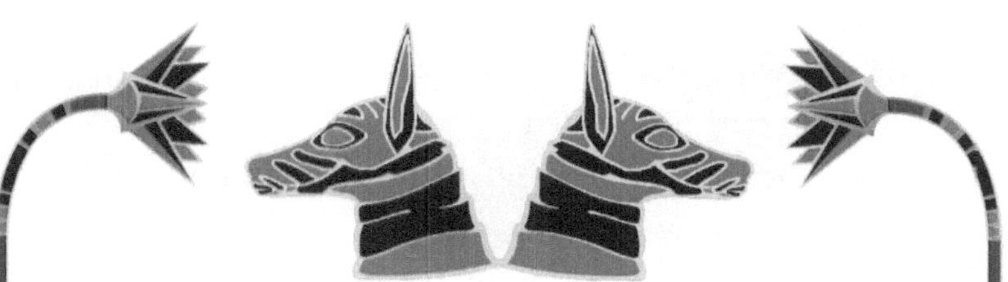

20

WOODBURY, TENNESSEE

Lina turned the motorcycle around and idled it along the road, as if she was afraid of going too fast and missing the ley line.

"It should be just up there," Hank said, pointing a hundred yards away. Lina gave the motorcycle a little more gas.

When they'd passed through it a moment ago, Hank had felt a jolt, like something moved him from the inside. With that kind of power, he knew he wouldn't miss it.

"I think this is it. Slow down."

Lina did as he said. They moved through the spot where Hank pointed, but he felt nothing.

"Maybe just a little farther," he said.

She drove another five feet.

Nothing.

Another ten feet.

Still nothing.

Another fifteen feet.

"Stop here!" Immense energy rocked Hank. He grabbed Lina so he wouldn't fall off the motorcycle.

"What's wrong? Are we there? I don't feel anything," she said and stopped the bike.

"Yeah, this is it. Pull over."

She maneuvered them off the road.

Hank swung his leg over the seat and swayed.

"Watch out!" she yelled.

She reached out her hand. Hank grabbed it just before he tumbled all the way over.

"What's wrong?" Lina asked.

Hank took in a deep breath and stood up. "It's the line. It's making me feel like everything's moving." He closed his eyes and concentrated on the energy. It wasn't filling him up. Only a crossing of two or more ley lines could do that, but he felt something new. Not only could he tell the direction the energy flowed, but he could also feel it flowing into another ley line. He pointed north. "We need to follow it. That way."

Hank moved to walk in the direction he'd pointed but slipped and fell. "Ouch!" he cried as his head hit the hard ground.

"Hank!" Lina was by his side in a flash, helping him up. "Your face!"

"What's wrong with it?" His ribs were already bad enough. Since he wasn't letting them heal properly, they looked black and blue. He didn't want his face to join that club.

"It's really red." She looked more closely. "Not bleeding, but I'll bet for sure it'll swell," Lina said. "How do you feel?"

"I'm okay. Just trying to get my balance. It's a little like being on a rocking boat." He looked at her and rubbed his head. "You don't feel it at all?"

She paused for a moment, her face seeming to concentrate. She shook her head. Hank looked at Dog, who'd already moved out of the ley line.

Dog barked.

"Good idea," Hank said, moving out as well. He shook his head and stood up straight. The motion he'd felt left as soon as he'd moved out, but he could still feel the power flowing by. They could walk alongside it to the crossing.

"Lina, can you grab my knapsack from the sidecar?"

She did so and handed it to him.

They hiked up a nearby hill, staying close enough to the ley line to know where it traveled, but far enough away to keep Hank and Dog from losing their balance and tumbling down the hill.

As they crested the top of the hillside, only a sliver of sun remained. It cast purple and magenta hues across the clouds.

"It's beautiful," Lina said.

The three of them stood still for a moment and took in the last of the sun's painting.

"We'll have to be extra careful going back down in the dark," Hank said as they continued along the edge of the ley line. His own vision at night continued to improve, but he didn't want Lina to fall and hurt herself.

As they moved through the trees and brush, Hank paused to concentrate on the energy. "We're close. The other line is just up ahead. It's faint right now, but we'll find the crossing soon."

Every step they took, the power grew stronger. He wanted to run ahead but didn't want to leave Lina alone to traipse through the woods in the early evening. He took each step with care. As he led them deeper in the woods, he pointed out every possible snare that waited to grab an unsuspecting ankle.

"Are we almost there?" Lina asked.

"Just ahead."

They walked through a thicket of trees and directly into the other line. Warmth poured over Hank.

Dog barked twice.

Hank smiled. "Maybe."

"What'd he say?"

"He wanted to know if we could stay in the heat stream for the night."

"Heat stream?"

Hank drew a line with his hand in the air. "This ley line is warm. Some are cold. Some are weird like the one we followed.

One made Dog float," he said.

Lina looked at Dog and giggled. Dog rolled around in the warm ley line, a happy expression splitting his face.

"Let's see what this does," Hank said as he dropped his knapsack. He didn't want the geodes to charge with a worthless power. He minced toward the crossing and took the final step in.

ARGHH! Hank grabbed his damaged ribs.

"Hank!" Lina shouted. She ran for him.

"Don't—come—in—here!" Hank didn't know if not feeling the lines would protect her from what was happening, but he didn't want to find out. He tried to take a step, but the pain in his ribs pulled him down. He fell to his knees. It felt like his ribs were twisted in place, and his face pulled back inside his skull. Hank pulled up his shirt.

"What's happening?" Lina said, her voice filled with panic.

Hank looked at his ribs. It wasn't just a feeling. They were moving. Not much, but enough for him to feel it. Then the twisting stopped. He looked again. The bruises on his ribs faded. The pain subsided. He twisted his body and felt his face. Both were fine.

"It healed me. It heals people!" Hank said with excitement. "Toss me a couple of geodes."

"Coming right up!" Lina said as she opened the knapsack and tossed them to him.

Hank caught one in each hand. "If this could heal me, I think it could make my parents young again!" Hank looked up from the geodes. Lina stared at the ground. Hank could see her shaking with tears. He dropped the geodes and went to her side.

"What's wrong?" he said as he put a hand on her arm.

"We keep discovering all this stuff. If we'd had this just a couple of days earlier maybe my mom—" she couldn't finish the sentence, as more tears came.

Hank hugged her and Dog came up to her side, nuzzling his nose into her dangling hand.

"I'm sorry, Lina. I shouldn't have said anything about my parents."

She sniffed. "It's not that, Hank. I want your parents to be okay. I just wish my mom could be okay too."

Hank hugged her tighter as she cried. *Maybe we can find something.*

Lina sniffled. "Okay, we better get back to the road."

Hank let her go, and she wiped her eyes. The moon shined bright across the woods. In the dark it would take them longer, but they'd make it down okay.

They worked their way through the dark woods in silence. Hank wanted to tell her everything would be okay, but what did he know about things being okay? He had to say something.

"Lina, you were saying earlier about the trapeze. Did you learn how to do any of that?"

Lina stopped mid-stride.

Maybe talking about the circus was the wrong choice. He didn't want to make her hurt or start crying again. She turned towards him, and Hank prepared himself to comfort her.

She smiled. "I did. It was my favorite thing to do. I learned how to walk the high wire, swing from the trapeze, climb the silk ropes." She paused, and her smile widened. "I even did a somersault mid-air and caught hold of the other flyer. It's like being a bird." She giggled. "Or maybe a flying squirrel."

Hank would love to see a trapeze show, but the thought of being the one flying through the air, trying to catch hold of someone else, gave him a shiver. He could imagine himself failing to grab hold and landing on the ground with a splat.

"Can you still do it?" Hank asked.

"I'd be a little nervous about flying somersaults, but I practice my tumbling, climbing, and tight rope walking as much as I can." She opened her mouth like she was about to say something else, but paused.

Hank didn't press her about what she didn't say "That's

really cool. You'll have to show me sometime. But no way you're getting me up on a trapeze!"

Lina laughed. "Okay, but I think you'd be pretty cool flying through the air."

Dog barked.

"I would not look like an ostrich trying to fly," Hank said, his voice taking on a tone of annoyance.

Dog barked again.

"I do too have a sense of humor."

When they reached the motorcycle, Lina climbed on and started it. Dog jumped into the sidecar, but Hank stood gazing at the geode in his hand.

"Come on. We can get back to Columbus by tomorrow night," Lina said.

Hank continued to look at the geode. "What if it doesn't help them?"

"Why wouldn't it? It healed you."

"But if we kept going, we could grab Cabot. Even if this didn't work, she'd know how to turn them back."

"Are you sure?"

Dog barked twice.

"I'm not sure about anything. That's why I think we should keep going."

"Okay. I can drive for a couple more hours, but then we'll need to find a spot to camp for the night."

Lina had been driving all day. She must have been exhausted. "Let's camp here tonight."

Lina killed the engine.

The next morning as Hank opened his eyes, he looked around the little camp they'd made. The motorcycle gleamed in the morning sunlight. Dog wasn't beside him, and Lina wasn't where she'd gone to sleep either. A sense of panic ripped through Hank's body. He threw the wool blanket off and jumped up.

"Dog! Lina!"

No answer.

"Where are you guys?" Hank said as he took large strides around the camp. *Where are they?* Thoughts of Apeps, Max, Ms. Cabot, and Mr. Grey flew through his head. Had they found them? Was this their next plan in getting Hank to give himself up?

A bark in the distance stopped him. "Dog?" he called as he ran in the direction of the sound. Fifty yards ahead, Hank came to a stop. Dog was sitting still, looking up.

"What's going on? Where's Lina."

Dog barked, not moving his head.

Hank looked up.

"Morning, sleepyhead. We didn't want to wake you," Lina said. She hung from a branch that was twenty or more feet above the ground.

Hank's fear didn't leave, but it changed from a kidnapping to a broken spine. "Lina, get down. You'll hurt yourself."

Lina laughed. "You said you wanted to see. And don't worry. I'm not going to hurt myself. I'm trained to do this." With the last word from her mouth, she swung her body back and kicked her legs off the branch.

Hank lurched forward to catch her as she fell through the air.

But she didn't hit.

Lina reached out a hand and swung herself onto another branch. She stood on it and leapt into the air, catching another. Three more leaps, a swinging turn, and two spins finally landed her on the ground.

She stood tall, throwing her hands skyward in a V shape. "Tada!"

Dog howled in approval.

Hank stood speechless.

"This is the part where you clap," Lina said with a smirk.

Hank brought his hands together. "That was incredible!

Scary as all get out, but incredible."

"Want to learn a couple moves?"

Hank looked between her and the tree. "I'm okay."

Lina laughed. "That took me a couple of years to learn. How about a cartwheel?"

Hank thought for a moment. "Actually, do you think you could teach me to drive the motorcycle?"

She smiled wide.

The motorcycle lurched forward and died. Again.

They'd been at it for almost an hour. Hank had had a couple of good tries but kept stalling it.

"You've got to ease the clutch out," Lina said.

Hank kick-started it back to life and tried again. He turned the handle to give it some gas and let out the clutch. It lurched, but this time they were moving forward.

"There you go. Now, clutch, lift your foot, and shift the gear up."

Hank had to think. The engine whined, begging to switch gears. Hank did and she said, and this time, the motorcycle shifted with a bump.

"Better," Lina said with encouragement.

Dog had dropped to the bottom of the sidecar.

"Dog, you're missing a great view," Hank said.

Dog barked.

"Scaredy-Cat."

"Be nice. If there was room, I'd be down there too," Lina said, poking a finger into Hank's side.

Hank laughed and shifted through the next gear. It bumped again, but only a little. He smiled and not just with his mouth. His whole body seemed to be smiling. He shifted into the next gear.

"Hey, that was great. I think you've got it!"

He looked in the rear-view mirror and could see the trail of dust puffing up in the wake of the motorcycle. Hank shifted into the top gear.

"You've got it!" Lina shouted.

Those words were the icing on the cake.

"Did you want to switch?" Hank called back over his shoulder.

"No way. I'm tired of driving. You've got this."

Hank gave the bike more gas, and they zoomed down the dirt road.

They drove for two more hours. A town was just on the horizon. Dog was asleep, and Lina held Hank lightly around the waist, her face on his back. She must have been asleep too. He'd let them rest a little longer.

The town grew in focus and size as they neared it. Hank slowed as he passed a sign:

Welcome to Woodbury, Tennessee

This will all be over soon.

21

A CACHE OF POWER

Hank drove the motorcycle at a crawl through the paved streets. This was the first town that really seemed to be alive, no doubt injected with life from Ms. Cabot's secret army. There were TVA vehicles parked all over. Workers walked the streets, gathering supplies and loading them into their trucks.

Lina stirred. "Where are we?"

"Woodbury."

She sat up straight. "Who are all these people?"

"Men working for the Tennessee Valley Authority." Hank looked back. "And the TVA works for Ms. Cabot."

"So all these are members of the brotherhood?"

"No, I don't think so. Stin guesses that most of these men are probably just trying to make some honest money for their families, but she's using it as a way to get what she wants."

A recently built sign pointed to the right. It read:
**Entrance to Short Mountain
and Cumberland Plateau
are closed until further notice
-TVA**

Hank turned to the right. "If they don't want people up there, that's exactly where we want to go."

The road from town quickly turned from pavement to dirt and gravel. It wound back and forth through tall trees into the mountains. It would have been a great place to go sightseeing, but they weren't here to take in the beautiful scenery.

"Look over there," Lina said, pointing a finger.

Hank slowed the motorcycle to a stop.

"That looks like the direction we need to go," Hank said.

Dog sat up in the sidecar.

The road went around a bend, and Hank could see a TVA truck parked to the side. A silhouette of a man carrying a gun stood beside it. Hank didn't want to deal with anyone knowing they were here. His mind flashed back to Idaho.

"I've got an idea," Hank said as he slid off the motorcycle. "You drive." Hank sat on the back of the side car, holding tight to the metal rack and letting his feet dangle off the end. He cleared his mind and went invisible.

"What should I do?" Lina asked.

"Distract him."

Lina drove a bit slower than necessary. The motorcycle followed the dirt and gravel road, stopping by the trucks. There were three of them, all parked end-to-end. The thin man with the gun had already stepped into the road, a hand in the air, his rifle by his side.

"You can't be up here," the man said.

Lina gave him an "I'm sorry" smile. "Goodness, I'm so turned around. I thought this was the cutoff road."

Dog whined.

"Cutoff road to where?"

"Um," she stuttered. "You know, the cutoff road."

The man lifted the rifle, but before he had it halfway up, he shook and contorted. Hank appeared as the man fell like a sack of rocks.

"The cutoff road?"

"What? It was all I could think of," Lina said, shrugging

her shoulders.

"Park the motorcycle, and let's see if there's something to tie him up with."

They dug through the trucks. There were empty crates with bold letters that read Costa Rica. There were tools and a basket of food.

"Here's some," Lina said, holding three coils of rope she'd found in a truck.

They used one on the man, and Lina slung the others over her shoulder. She groaned as she lifted the man's legs. Hank held the man by his shoulders. For as thin as the man was, he was heavy.

With a couple of tries, they lifted him into the back of the truck, bound and gagged.

"How long will he be out?"

"I don't know. A few more minutes at least," Hank said. He swung the knapsack from his back and handed Lina two of the geodes filled with the reservoir ley line energy. "You remember how to use these?"

"Pull up an emotion, and let it fly," she said, taking the stones.

"If you put the geode directly on someone, it will knock them out for sure."

She nodded.

Hank looked around. No trail or side road led into the woods, but Hank spotted some matted brush and guessed the other TVA men had gone on foot into the woods.

"You two stay here. I'll scout ahead and see if I can find where they are."

Lina grabbed his hand. "Be safe."

"I will," Hank said, he turned himself invisible and crept into the tree line. He took each step with care. His heart pumped faster, and his palms went clammy. *Almost done.*

After moving fifty yards into the woods, Hank heard

men talking to each other. Hank froze and glanced towards the direction of the voices. Several men were working. Some were digging while others were pulling on a rope that must have been as big as Hank's fist.

Hank snuck closer.

"Steady on the rope," one man said.

Hank wasn't positive, but the man speaking looked like one of the men from the ambush in Charleston. He gave orders to six more men pulling a rope, which connected around a set of block and tackle attached to an eight-foot tripod. At the end of the rope swung a massive stone, almost as big as Misha. Hank could see the six men were struggling to pull the rope that lifted the stone. Another man pivoted the tripod. *How many are there? And where's Cabot?* He counted ten men but no sign of Cabot.

The stone arced in a wide half-circle away from the hole.

They must have been excavating. Hank's grandma had sent his family a subscription to National Geographic. She always wrote to see if he'd read about the archaeologists digging at sites in Egypt. Hank would have read the articles even if his grandma didn't write, but what always drew his interest were the pictures. Many of the same tools in the photos were here. *Are they just getting that rock out of the way?*

Hank took two cautious steps forward.

One of the men holding the rope slipped. He let go of the rope and fell to the ground.

"I said, careful!" the man giving orders shouted. He threw down his gloves and ran his fingers through his black hair.

The sixth man tried to get up quickly. The other five tried to hold the rock. They couldn't. The rope spun forward through the block and tackle as the rock crashed down.

"Look out!" someone shouted.

CRACK!

The stone split in two. The men gazed at the stone in awe. Hank gawked at it too, opened mouthed. It wasn't just any old rock. *It's a geode.*

The light hit the crystals inside and reflected across the gathered men. He'd never have imagined a geode could be so large. *How much energy could you store in that?*

"You idiots!" the black-haired man said.

"What happened?" a younger male voice asked.

The voice sounded hollow. It came from inside the hole, where the men had lifted the stone. A hand emerged from the hole and placed a crystal prism on the ground, like it was putting a baby down for a nap. The prism was at least the size of a football.

"It's bad, sir," the black-haired man said. His voice had gone from gruff to apologetic.

"Give me a hand with these artifacts," the voice from the hole said.

Several men jumped at once to help. The hand appeared again and again, handing things to the gathered men each time. They lifted smaller geodes, like the ones in Hank's knapsack. Then came an ancient-looking book.

Hank's heart beat faster. *It's not just a dig site. It's a treasure cache, just like Treasure Island. Someone buried that stuff here.* A smile parted his lips.

The hands emerged again. "Pull me up," the voice said.

Men grabbed each hand and pulled. Hank's eyes widened as his smile dropped away. Max was being pulled from the hole.

Hank's stomach knotted. He crept back to Lina and Dog.

"You look terrible. What's going on?" Lina asked as she rushed to his side.

Dog barked.

"I'm okay. It's a treasure trove. Even a huge geode. It's just..." Hank paused a moment. "He's here."

"Who?"

"Max. The boy who attacked my parents."

"That's good, right? If he turned your parents old, he should know how to make them young."

"Maybe, but he'll be able to spot me even if I'm invisible to everyone else."

"How?"

"He's like me."

"Then we'll need to be extra careful," Lina said.

Hank looked back into the woods. They'd come this far, and even if Ms. Cabot wasn't there, they might be able to get Max. Hank wrung his hands and looked at Lina. Confidence spread across her face. *Mrs. Nieves.* He'd left to make sure no one else would get hurt. What was he doing?

Hank shook his head. "No, it's too risky for you to go."

"No. We do this together. The three of us."

Hank squeezed the bridge of his nose. "I don't want to put you in—"

"Hank, I'm in this. My choice, not yours."

Hank took a deep breath. "Okay." He thought for a moment. "We can't get the giant geode, but we might have a shot of grabbing some of the smaller stuff. Maybe grab Max." Hank looked at the trucks. They could load their collection in one of those. "I can drive a truck, and you can drive the motorcycle," he said.

"But we have to get the stuff first," Lina said.

"Right. We need a good plan," Hank said as he looked at Dog and then the rope slung over Lina's shoulder.

After discussing it for a few more minutes, they split up and made their way to the treasure cache.

Hank peered through the branches. Max was nowhere to be seen. There were four men with rifles on the perimeter. They looked bored. The one closest to Hank seemed to be counting pieces of bark on a tree.

The men who'd dropped the geode were now loading up the halves onto an over-sized cart. It would take them at least an hour to move it through the woods.

Hank smiled. *This just might work.*

He moved to the guard counting bark on a tree. The man didn't turn as Hank gave him a jolt of energy, causing him to slump to the ground. Hank tied his hands and feet and put a rag in his mouth. Another guard stood on the opposite side.

Above him, Lina moved with stealth and grace. She lowered herself from the rope. It reminded Hank of a spider climbing down its thread. If he'd blinked, he would have missed it. Lina shocked the man with the geode to the ground and tied him up.

There wasn't enough rope to tie up the other two guards. They'd simply have to knock them out and move quickly to get what they'd came for. Hank knocked out the last guard just as Dog bolted from the tree line, barking at the workers and wagging his tail.

"Look," one of the workers said.

"How'd you get out here, boy? Are you lost?" The workers stopped what they were doing and formed a circle around Dog. One of the men knelt and began to pet him.

"Someone get a stick. I bet you like to play fetch."

Hank padded his way out of the tree line and toward the cart. It was half full of treasures. The book he'd seen Max hand up sat on the nearest edge. Hank picked it up. It was bound in heavy leather with large brass clasps securing the pages shut. Carved in the leather were markings. *Egyptian?* Hank couldn't be certain. He placed the large book into his empty knapsack.

Dog barked.

"You do like to play fetch! Get the stick!" one of the men said.

Hank smiled. He could only imagine how much fun Dog was having with his part of the plan. He looked again at the treasures. The prism crystal sat just out of reach. Hank hoisted his body onto the side of the cart and leaned in. He passed over some of the geodes. *They aren't empty.*

The ley line energy contained in the geodes called to Hank. It was like nothing he'd felt before. *Power.* It continually repeated in his mind. He spied one particular geode. It had been split open to expose deep purple crystals. He reached for it.

"What in the world are you doing?" Max called.

Hank froze and looked up. There was Max, glaring at the workers playing with Dog. Max's left eye was black and blue with bruises. A part of Hank hoped they were from when he'd hit him.

The men separated their circle as Max approached. Dog sat panting in the center.

"It's a lost dog, boss," one of the men said.

"We're just taking a break," another man tried to explain.

"Can we keep him?" a third man asked. That must have been exactly what Hank had sounded like to his parents.

"No, we can't keep him. Get out of here, you mangy mutt!" Max went to kick Dog, but Dog rolled to the side and jumped under one of the men's legs.

"Get him out of here and get back to work!"

All the men moved to grab Dog at once. A man reached for Dog and fell as Dog slipped through his legs. One dove.

"I've got him boss!" another man said, running into the diving man.

Dog turned sharply in front of a tree. The man chasing him didn't turn so smoothly. He hit the tree with a thud and crumpled to the ground.

The men were still trying to get Dog, and Dog led them on a merry game of chase, weaving in and out of the trees. Hank couldn't help watching the show.

Fury crossed Max's face. "Will you stop it!"

Hank watched as Max scanned the perimeter.

"Where's Nelson and Carter?" Max asked.

Hank knew he was looking for the unseen. Looking for him.

Max turned towards the cart just as Lina swung down from a rope tied to a tree. It was like watching Tarzan swing through the jungle. She kicked Max full force with both feet. He flew backward, landing next to the cart.

Hank looked down at him just as Max opened his eyes. "Looking for me?" Hank said with a grin.

Max got to his feet as Hank swung from the cart, his right fist cocked back. Hank crashed into Max, but Max turned Hank's momentum against him. The older boy lifted his legs, pushing them into Hank's stomach. Max rolled back and Hank became airborne.

Hank stood and pulled at the ley line energy. He didn't have much left for throwing behind his emotions. He'd need to make it count.

Max reached into the cart and pulled out a geode just as Hank fired off a blast of energy. It struck Max and split around him. The divided energy smashed into the trees, showering them with sparks and embers.

Hank pulled up more energy and got ready to charge.

"You can't do anything to me, Anubis," Max said, twisting the ball of his foot into the ground and waving the geode at Hank.

Hank let go of the energy and stood, relaxed. Max squinted at him, a confused look on his face.

"Maybe I can't. But she can," Hank said, as he nodded towards Lina.

Max looked over his shoulder just as Lina swung a tree branch into his stomach with the force of a baseball player hitting a home run. He crumpled over and dropped the geode. Hank was there in three steps. He scooped it up and placed it in his knapsack, then knelt by Max.

"Sorry about your right eye," Hank said.

"It's my left," Max said, just as recognition crossed his face.

Hank punched him with a little ley line energy.

"Grab the prism from the cart," Hank said.

Lina snatched it. Hank had the knapsack open, and she placed the foot-long crystal inside.

"We couldn't catch the dog," a voice said from behind

them.

Hank and Lina looked over their shoulders. The group of workers were back.

"What's going on?" one of the men shouted.

"Hey! Carter is tied up over here!" another voice called out.

A gunshot ripped through the woods and hit the cart just above Lina's head. Hank darted a glance toward the noise. One of the perimeter guards stood, cocking his bolt action rifle for another shot. Hank grabbed Lina's hand and moved to run.

"What about bringing Max?"

"Forget about him. We need to not be dead!"

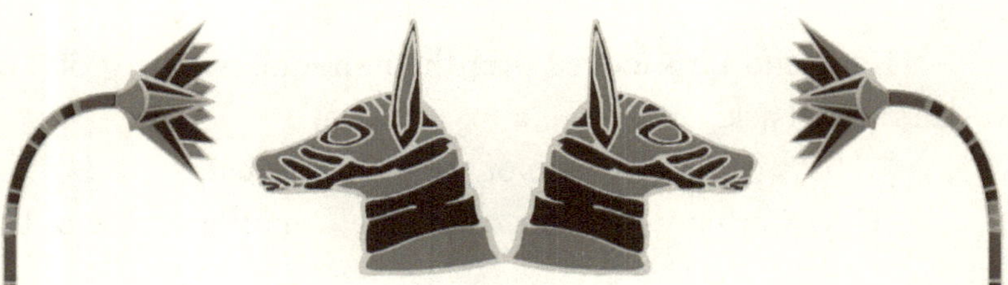

22

CAPTURED BY THE INVISIBLE BOY

"Dog, run!" Hank shouted. He took hold of Lina's hand and said, "Here goes nothing." He turned himself invisible and hoped Lina had turned too.

They dashed for the tree line, heading back to the motorcycle. Sporadic gunfire flew several yards to the left and the right of them.

"Don't just spray the forest with bullets! Give me that gun."

Hank looked back. Max was up and taking aim at them with a rifle.

CRACK!

The sound of the bullet ripped through the trees.

Hank pulled Lina down, and they scrambled to take cover behind a large tree.

"He's up!" Lina shouted.

"I know. He almost hit us that time. What now?"

Lina looked up.

"No, I can't do what you do. You go, I'll get him to shoot at me. Take the bag," Hank said, his voice moving in staccato over his words.

She pushed the knapsack back at him. "We're all getting out of here! You have to trust me. Just follow where I go," she said as she sprung up and grabbed a branch. She

was already six feet up the tree before Hank had climbed the first rung.

"Fan out and watch for any movement," Max shouted at the other workers.

Hank reached for another branch. Lina shook her head at him.

"Not that one. Grab the higher one," Lina said in a whisper.

Hank looked at the branch she wanted him to take. He'd have to jump to get it. He made to jump and stopped himself.

"Hurry," Lina mouthed.

Footsteps were crunching through the woods. They'd be at the tree soon. It was now or never. His gut wound tight.

With one jump, he caught the branch. Lina hoisted him up and led him from one tree to another. They were moving higher and higher in the trees. The first of the workers passed far underneath them. The man scanned from side to side, not up.

Lina motioned for Hank to follow as she moved from a limb and into another tree.

"There they are!" Max shouted. "They're in the trees!"

Lina swung around the trunk and Hank followed as two bullets splintered the spot where they'd been standing.

"Look out!" one of the men shouted.

Other men were screaming and running in their direction.

Hank could hear growls. "Dog?"

"Wolf! It's a wolf!" one of the men said as he ran away towards the dig site.

Hank swung his head out for a moment and saw a great white wolf tackle one the workers.

Nobo growled.

"He has such a filthy mouth," Hank said.

WIZ! A bullet from Max's gun flew past. Hank yanked his head back.

"Are you okay?" Lina asked.

Hank felt his face and nodded.

Lina looked down. "If that's Nobo, then Volk must be here too!" Lina exclaimed.

Hank looked to see Dog run under the tree, followed by Misha, barreling through the forest like a bear on the attack. Branches splintered and flew into the air as he crashed through them. The man Misha chased didn't stand a chance.

Misha picked him up and spun him in the air. Round and round he went, like a propeller on an airplane. When Misha finally set him down, the man took two shaky steps and doubled over, vomiting.

"Eww," Lina said.

Hank smiled and looked for Stin. He still didn't see him. Nobo and Dog rounded up a few of the remaining men, and Volk had made his way into the fray. The lengthy Russian knocked out a guard with a quick blast from his geode.

Hank swung his body around the tree. He spied Max at a dead sprint for the cart. Lina poked her head out from the other side.

"He's going for more weapons!" Hank shouted. No one seemed to hear him.

"Wait," Lina said and pointed. "I don't think he's going anywhere."

Hank followed Lina's finger. *Stin.* The hobo stepped out from behind a tree, grabbing Max's gun in one hand and his shirt collar in the other.

Lina exhaled a sigh of relief.

Volk and Misha tied up the other men while Stin tied up Max.

Nobo and Dog trotted underneath the tree. Hank hadn't realized that he'd been sitting still, staring at the action below.

Nobo howled at Hank and Lina. Hank could feel his face

getting warmer at his taunts.

Dog continued the playground song right along with Nobo.

Lina looked at them and then at Hank. "Just what are they saying?" she asked, her tone concerned.

"I think it's just better if you don't—"

Hank was cut off by Volk finishing the playground rhyme, singing, "K-I-S-S-I-N-G!"

"That's what they were saying?" Lina said, her voice filled with embarrassment.

Hank swung around the tree in an attempt to hide his face. He was sure it must be the color of a fire engine by now.

"You two planning on staying up there all day?" Stin asked.

Hank looked down. Stin was smiling from ear to ear with Max tied up at his feet. Lina scrambled down the tree in less than a minute. Hank took considerably more time to get down.

Stin put Mr. Swenson's truck in gear and leaned out the window. "We'll get a message to the TVA and let them know you're here," Stin said to the tied up workers.

The truck crawled down the dirt road. This was another of Mr. Swenson's modified contraptions.

It wasn't as big as the truck they took to Idaho, but it had two rows of seats and an extended bed. They'd loaded the motorcycle along with all the geodes and artifacts, into the bed. Crammed in the backseat were Misha, Lina, Dog and Hank. In the front were Stin, Nobo, and Volk, with Max squished between them.

"This is a big mistake," Max said.

Lina leaned forward. "No, the mistake was your brotherhood killing my mom!" She pulled her fist back to punch Max, but Hank caught hold of her wrist.

Max fell silent.

Stin looked over his shoulder at Hank. "What were you thinking?"

Hank sat silent.

"Everyone was going crazy trying to find you. It was your dad who finally mentioned Woodbury. I'm just glad we got here in time."

Hank nodded. "Thanks."

They bounced through a series of ruts. Misha smashed into Hank's shoulder, which knocked him into Lina, who knocked into Dog. Dog let out a whimper.

"Sorry," Misha said.

Dog barked.

Hank glanced at Max with a grin.

"I can understand you, even if you are just a mangy mutt," Max said over his shoulder.

Dog whined.

"So, you're just like Hank," Lina said.

Max scoffed. "I may be an Anubis, but I'm not a vessel." He looked over his shoulder and sneered at Hank. "I'm also not an idiot. I'm just traveling with idiots."

This time it was Lina stopping Hank from punching Max.

"Anubis?" Misha asked. "What's an Anubis?"

Max gaped at him. "Are you serious? You really are a bunch of idiots. You've got no idea what you are."

"Well, if we're such idiots, why don't you educate us," Stin said.

Max sat in silence. Several moments passed, and Stin looked at him. "Finally. Maybe we can make the rest of this trip with some peace and quiet," Stin said.

"But, what's an Anubis?" Misha asked, sounding like a kid wanting an answer to a complicated riddle.

"Read a book, you oaf," Max said. He closed his eyes, his face painted with a calm expression.

Misha looked at his hands and then out the window. "Just because I'm strong doesn't mean I can't read."

Hank looked at Misha. He'd never seen his friend look so wounded. "Just who do you think you are, Max? Do you think just because you know something we don't, that makes you better than us?" Hank didn't wait for Max to answer. "It doesn't. And besides, we know a lot."

"Yeah, right," Max said.

"We know heaps of stuff, and we're learning more all the time. So don't sit there pretending to be better than us."

Max opened his eyes and looked at Hank. "Whatever you think you know, it's still a fraction of what you should. I'm sure each of you has developed the powers of their Anubis type. But so far, you seem to be the only one crossing types, Hank."

Hank tilted his head to the side. He was about to ask, "What are types?" but stopped himself.

"Your ability to become invisible. It's an easy power for a specter to gain, not so for a vessel," Max said. As he continued to look at Hank, his face softened just for a moment. "You should have gone with her, Hank. You still can. She can help you reach your potential. Make you into a useful tool."

The thought of that night when Ms. Cabot had taken them to the cove made his stomach turn. He clenched his fist, pulling up the emotion from the memory of that night and combining it with the ley line energy. "You're telling me that if I had gone, this wouldn't have happened?" He placed his hand on Max's shoulder and gave him a light shock powered by the memory of his parents screaming as they aged.

Max jolted and let out a whine. "Why would you do that?" he asked, his teeth clenched tight.

Hank pulled up the memory of the first Apep attack and shocked Max with it.

"Stop it!" Max said, his jaw set tight.

Hank didn't stop. He brought up more memories: returning to find the encampment sacked, his sister's anger, the Apep's attempts to possess him, his mom and dad not knowing him, and learning Mrs. Nieves was dead.

With each quick pulse of power, Max's jaw tightened. Sweat poured from his face. Hank stopped and sat back. No one said a word for a long moment.

Max looked back at Hank. "Why would you want me to see all that?"

"Just thought you should see it from my point of view," Hank said. He looked out the window. In the reflection, he could see Max stare at him.

23

LIAR'S DEAL

November 14, 1933, Columbus, North Carolina

It hadn't taken much time before Hank fell asleep. He'd actually slept almost the entire way back, except for the bathroom breaks. In fact, Stin told Hank that everyone but Max and Stin had been fast asleep for the entire ride back to Columbus.

As soon as the truck came to a stop, Hank jumped out and made a beeline for his parents. He walked into the little bedroom where he found them sleeping. He still couldn't get over how old they looked. Would he look that wrinkled when he got older?

The twins sat at the foot of the bed, reading. Thomas was there too, snoring in the only chair in the room. Sarah sat on the floor and glared at Hank.

"I take it they found you," she whispered. "Out there putting everyone else at risk, no doubt." She stood up and knocked past him as she left the room.

Hank stood still, open mouthed.

"She's still really mad," Kyle said.

"I can see that," Hank said. "Hopefully she won't be for long." He set the knapsack down and pulled out the healing geode.

"What's that?" Kathy asked, pointing at the stone.

"Something that will make them better," Hank said. He placed it against his dad's arm.

His dad groaned as all of his limbs contorted. His eyes went wide and then closed tight. Tears ran from the corners down his wrinkled cheeks.

ARGH! Hank's dad screamed in pain.

Kyle screamed and jumped from the bed. "You're hurting him!"

Their mom opened her eyes, a confused look on her face. "What's going on?" she asked.

Hank could see small movements under his dad's skin. *I think it's working.* "It's going to heal him." He continued pressing the geode against his dad's arm.

His dad tightened his jaw.

Kathy edged closer. "He doesn't look like he's getting younger."

"It's gotta work," Hank mumbled.

His dad relaxed. Every wrinkle and white hair was still in place.

"No!" Hank shouted. *Stupid thing!* He tightened his fist around the geode, ready to throw it against the wall.

His dad opened his eyes and sat up. He wiggled his fingers and rotated his shoulders. An excited grin crossed his face. "Wow! I feel great." He looked at his hands. The excitement on his face slid away. "Oh, but I'm still old."

Where's Max? Hank made to leave the room.

"What about Mom? I mean, Mrs. Hudson?" Kathy asked.

"Here." He tossed the geode to Kathy. "Just hold it against her. It'll hurt for a moment, but it should heal any pain she has." He turned and marched from the house and into the yard.

Hank spotted Stin by one of the out-buildings.

"Is he in there?" Hank asked.

"Who?"

"Max," Hank said. "I need to talk with him about my parents."

Stin turned the key and opened the door.

Hank stepped inside. A strange feeling crossed though him. This was the same room where Julie and Steve would lock him up at night. Max sat on the lower bunk bed.

"Why can't I make my parents young again?"

"Nice to see you again too," Max said.

"I'm serious. How do I turn them back? I just tried using a healing ley line on my dad, and all it did was loosen his joints."

Max rolled his eyes. "What did you expect it to do? Old age isn't an injury." He looked at the top bunk. "Some ley lines heal the body. Others heal the mind. Neither of them heal age, idiot."

"That's it!" Hank yelled as he tackled Max.

Max grunted on impact and then fought back.

"Stop it!" Stin said as he stepped in and pulled Hank away.

Max jumped up and tried to charge Hank. Stin took most of the hit, but he didn't go down.

"I said, stop it!" Stin yelled as he pushed Max onto the bed. Stin hauled Hank from the room and locked the door.

"I'm not done with him," Hank said.

"Yes, you are. He's our prisoner, not your punching bag."

"But he knows how to make my parents young!"

"Hank, we don't know that. Give us some time, and we'll find out everything he knows."

Hank kicked a rock. It bounced across the yard and stopped in front of Julie. She made a beeline for Stin. By how fast she moved and her flushed red cheeks, Hank thought she looked part locomotive.

"Stin! What do you think you're doing?" she called.

"Locking up the prisoner."

"He's not a prisoner. He's just a boy," she said. She parked herself in front of them, arms crossed.

"That's funny coming from you. If he's just a boy, what was I when you locked me up? Just a slave?" Hank said, finding another place to direct his anger.

The color in her face washed away. "That's not what—"

"No." Hank held up his hand, stopping her. "Dog! Nobo!"

he called.

They bounded up from the main house.

"No one is to let him out but Stin or me? Got it?"

They barked and howled their understanding.

"I don't want another incident like what happened at the reservoir," he said to Julie as he pushed past her.

Stin followed. When they were out of Julie's earshot, he said, "I can understand you're angry—"

"No, Stin. I'm more than angry. You want to know who was really responsible for Mrs. Nieves getting shot? Her," he said, pointing at Julie. "Ever since she and her husband joined us, things have been going wrong. Now, she wants to let the prisoner out. Let the guy out who attacked my parents! Don't stick up for her. She's a liar." Hank clenched his fists tighter and stormed into the main house.

Gathered around the small table were Mr. Swenson, Kiska, Volk, Misha, Lina, three of the men from the Charleston raid, and Steve. The twins were in the hall, listening.

"Really? He's here?" Hank shouted, pointing at Steve.

Stin put an arm on Hank's shoulders. Hank pulled away and glared at Steve. "You know what his lying wife just tried to do?"

"Hank, stop it," Stin said.

"No. Julie was just out there trying to let Max out. We can't trust either of them!" Hank slammed his fist onto the table like a physical exclamation point.

"Hank!" Stin shouted. "You need to go cool off."

Pain crossed Hank's heart. He spun to face Stin. "What? You're taking their side?"

"I'm not taking their side. I'm just saying you're not thinking clearly. You need to calm down."

Hank balled his fists. The ley line energy swam up to meet his need.

"Little Fish," Misha pleaded.

Hank looked at him and let go of the energy. This wasn't a fight he could win, and, thinking about the last time he'd attacked

Stin, this wasn't a fight he wanted to win.

"Let's take a walk," Misha suggested.

Julie entered the room and stood behind her husband.

Hank took a deep breath and let it out in a slow stream. "No. I want to stay. I promise no more outbursts. I'm sorry." He sat by Misha, wiped his eyes, and took several deep breaths. He glanced at Julie and Steve and then around the table. How could they sit there and listen to the lies? Why couldn't anyone see the truth about Julie and Steve?

Stin cleared his throat. He stood at the head of the table and looked everyone over.

"First of all, don't you two ever do anything like that again," Stin said, pointing at Hank and Lina. "You could have been killed. And I understand that you wanted to keep everyone safe, but you need to know we're all in this together. To the end."

The back door opened again. Max stepped in and said, "Nice sentiment, but will your merry little band really hold strong when put to the test?"

Hank sprung up, pulling ley line energy into both hands. One hand pointed at Max and the other at Julie. "You let him out?" Hank yelled.

Stin spun, pulled out a geode, and trained it on Max.

"No, I didn't," Julie said.

"Hank, stop it," Steve said as he sprung from his chair, both arms extended as he tried to shield his wife.

Hank kept a hand pointed at them and looked at Max. "Where's Dog and Nobo? What'd you do to them?"

Max lifted his hands in the air. His face seemed just as serenely calm as it had been in the truck. "They're both asleep. Doggie dreams are so much more pleasant than people dreams." Max smiled. "And she didn't let me out. I simply picked the lock." He reached into his pocket, pulled out a lock pick kit, and tossed it to Stin. "Sorry to have borrowed that without asking."

Stin looked embarrassed as he placed the kit back in his coat.

Hank looked at Stin, then Julie, then back to Max as

mistrust rocked through his body. "What do you mean, they're asleep? Did you knock them out? Are they hurt?"

"I know you don't believe me, but I don't like hurting any living thing. They're just asleep. It's what I do."

Hank gave him a puzzled look.

"I'm an Anubis guide. Why don't you put your hands down, and we can all talk. I assume this little meeting is all about how to get me to spill the beans, right?"

No one said anything. Hank still held his hand up, ready to strike if necessary.

"I'll take that as a yes." Max took a timid step forward.

Hank's hand crackled with energy, adding a glow to the room. Max stepped back.

"Hank, I'm unarmed. I don't want to be tortured. I've been thinking a lot on the ride here. What you showed me, what the brotherhood and the Apep have done to you and your friends—I don't understand it. That's not what we're about."

"Tell that to Elmer Grossman," Lina said.

Disappointment replaced the calm on Max's face. "I'm sorry. The brotherhood was instructed to remove you, not kill anyone."

"And what about my parents and me? You were instructed to kill us."

"Yes. Not something I wanted to do, but we can't risk you becoming a vessel for the Apeps."

"My parents aren't vessels."

Max looked down. "I'm sorry for that, but she ordered me. I can't disobey her. I won't be a broken tool."

Broken tool?

"Sure," Lina spat.

"I'm willing to talk. I think you'll see we want the same things."

Hank rolled his eyes. "He's another liar."

"Volk, do you have any more of your truth telling energy?" Stin asked.

"Nyet, we used it all at the prison. I'd have to travel to

Mount Odin in Canada just to get more."

Max snorted. "You still can't split the ley lines?"

"That's not even possible!" Volk snapped.

"It is, if you have the right tools and knowledge," Max said, and then added, "Which obviously, you don't."

Volk stood, fist clenched and moved to punch Max. Stin stepped in his way.

"No!" Stin looked at Hank. "No one is punching or shooting anyone today. Calm down. I don't see what other choice we have."

Hank dropped the energy and sat. Without an invitation, Max took Volk's empty seat. Volk shook his head and left the room.

"I don't know where to start," Stin said. "How about with Dog and Nobo? What did you mean, it's what you do?"

"I'm a guide. I help people make their way through the physical world and the dream world. Part of that is putting them to sleep."

"So, you can make people fall asleep?" Lina asked. "So, why didn't you make Hank and I pass out in Tennessee?"

"That's not how it works. The person needs to be at rest. Sitting or lying down works best, but if they're standing still with a resting heart beat, I could put them to sleep. So, with all your running around and excitement, I couldn't help you find sleep. But on the way back from Tennessee, I had no problem."

"You did that to us?" Lina shouted.

"I did. I wanted to see if the memories Hank showed me were accurate."

Hank heard the twins whisper, "Cool!" to each other, but Hank didn't think it was cool. He shifted in his chair. "You don't have the right to go poking around in people's dreams."

"Seeing your memories and dreams is the only reason we're talking now, and I'm not halfway back to the brotherhood."

A hush fell over the room. Max could have slipped away twice, but he stayed. Hank narrowed his eyes. What sort of game was he playing?

"So, you're a guide, and Hank is a vessel. What other types are there?" Stin asked.

Max rolled his eyes. "This is what you want to know? It's like grade school in the brotherhood all over again."

"You mentioned specters too," Lina said.

Max let out a huff. "At least someone listens. Yes. Specters, guides, vessels, and guardians."

"And why do they call us Anubis?"

Max wiped his face, clearly annoyed.

Volk returned to the room. He carried a wooden crate with some of the items they'd taken in Tennessee.

"That book," Max said and pointed to Volk. "It has the answers you want—the method for splitting ley line crossings, how to change what power is extracted, and all about what it means to be an Anubis."

Volk pulled out the ancient tome. "No one could read this," he said, flipping through the pages. He tossed the book to Stin.

"Hey, easy. That's thousands of years old. It's one of only two copies we've been able to find," Max shouted.

Hank smiled to himself. *Finally, something you care about.*

Volk set the crate on the table and pulled out the prism with both hands. "And what about this? Is it another tool you need for the Apep?"

Max sat silent.

"What about the giant geode in the truck? What's it for?"

Still, Max didn't say a word. He stared at the book.

Volk huffed, and moved next to Max. He grabbed him by the collar and brought his fist back. "You said you'd talk! Do I need to use motivation?"

Max stared at Volk with defiant eyes, as if he was saying, "Do it."

Volk clenched his fist tighter. "Fine. We'll do it my way."

"Volk! Stop!" Hank stood. "Let him go."

Julie smiled at Hank. He ignored her.

"Why?" Volk asked.

"Because I said so. Now, everyone out. Let me talk with

him."

Protests came from around the table, but Stin and Misha herded everyone from the room. Volk shouted back, "I'll be waiting out here for my turn with the rat."

When it was just the two of them, Hank pulled the book close and looked through the pages. "Egyptian hieroglyphs, right?"

Max nodded.

"That's what I thought. My grandma always sends us articles about ancient Egypt." He examined the cover. "It's an important book." Hank closed it and looked at Max. "We both want something. I just want my parents back."

"Why? So they can forget about you? Leave you again? They always leave!" Max's face flushed red, and he clenched his fists.

"Family. That's what the brotherhood is to you, isn't it? I know what that feels like, finally finding the place you belong." He pushed the book across the table to Max. "But what the brotherhood is doing... It's wrong. It's dangerous for all of us. Helping the Apep to gain its full power...Well, that's just crazy."

Max snapped his head from the book to Hank. "Again, we're not helping the Apep gain its power back. We're trying to destroy it. The brotherhood has served the Apeps in the past, but they were also the ones to lock them away the first time. We're doing the right thing, Hank. For all people. What do you think that giant geode is for?"

Hank shrugged.

"Trapping them. They're an enormous amount of energy. It will take geodes and crystals large enough to hold all that energy. That's why they want you. You're a vessel. You could hold all seven of them," Max said, and then added, "Forever."

A chill crawled up Hank's back. He looked at Max and wished he'd had Volk's truth energy. It was a tall order to believe a group like the brotherhood, Ms. Cabot, and Mr. Grey would stop at capturing the Apeps.

Max exhaled. "I'd planned on escaping by putting you all to sleep in the truck, but when you showed me what had happened,

I needed to help you see why. We want you to be with us. You're all powerful. We need good tools like you."

Hank looked at Max. In many ways they were alike. They both wanted a place to belong.

"So, let's make a deal. You help me get my parents back to normal, and I give you the book."

Max looked at the book and then at Hank. "I don't..." he hesitated. "I really don't know how to turn them back."

"You're the one that made them old!"

"Yeah, but it's not like I made the staff. Ms. Cabot taught me how to use it."

"What about in the book? Maybe you can find a place where it says how to do it."

Max turned the pages as gently as if he were doing surgery. "Maybe. But you'll still need a translator. I can only read bits and pieces."

Hank huffed. "But, if there's a way to make them old, there has to be a way to make them young, right?"

"Ms. Cabot."

"What?" Hank asked.

"Ms. Cabot. She made the staff of aging. She'd be the one to know how to reverse it."

Just the thought of seeing her again turned Hank's stomach, but if it meant getting his parents back, he'd do it.

"Where is she?"

Max sat silent, looking at the book. Hank reached over and pulled the book from him.

"Where is she, Max?"

Max still didn't say a word. His eyes flitted to the book.

Hank pulled up the ley line energy and created a shield, just larger than his fist. He brought it close to the book. "What do you think will happen? Think I can push the shield right through the book?"

"No! You do that and you lose out on knowing too!"

"I don't care about guides, vessels, Apeps, ley line splitting, or what it means to be an Anubis. I just care about my family, and

I want my parents back." He inched his fist closer to the book. Its cover caught the glow of the energy shield.

"Fine! I'll tell you where she is," Max said.

"No, you're going to take me to her." Hank let go of the shield and slid the book back to Max.

24

COSTA RICA

Max walked out the back door with Hank a step behind him. All eyes were on them the moment the door opened. Everyone looked like they were holding their breath and waiting for bad news. Everyone except Volk.

"Why is he holding the book?" Volk asked.

Hank looked at him. "It's part of the deal we made."

"Deal?" Volk asked.

Murmurs ran through the group.

"Yeah. I made a deal with him. He gets us to Costa Rica—"

"Costa Rica?" Volk shouted.

"Please, Volk. I can do this faster without you butting in every other word," Hank said.

Volk closed his mouth and glared. Hank held the glare for a moment and looked back at the rest of the group. He wouldn't be intimidated by Volk. Not this time.

"Like I was saying, we took Max from one of two cache sites. He led the expedition in Tennessee, and Ms. Cabot left at the same time to lead another expedition to Costa Rica. She's going to end up with another gigantic geode. Big enough to trap an Apep."

"Can you even do that?" Misha asked.

"How would you trap it?" Kiska added.

"Yes, you can. Max told me that's what the brotherhood did before. It's their plan again. They mean to capture the Apeps."

"Lies!" Volk shouted. "Those are all lies! You can't believe a word that comes out of that trickster's mouth!" Volk pushed his way forward.

"Volk, you're right. I don't trust the brotherhood. I don't believe they want to trap the Apeps, but I believe that Ms. Cabot is in Costa Rica. I believe she's the only chance I have at making my parents whole again." He took a step forward with his fist clenched in determination. "I believe this is what I was made to do. Stop the Apeps. And you can either come with me or stay behind. I don't really care which."

Volk took a step back. His eyes narrowed as he looked at Hank. Hank didn't flinch as he kept his gaze.

After a moment, Stin spoke. "Hank, you know this is most likely another trap."

"Yeah..." he paused and looked at Max. "It probably is. That's why we need to be ready." He paused again and looked over the group. "That's also why I'm not asking anyone to go. You don't have to be put in harm's way because of me."

"We won't be able to take too many people. The Loon will need to be as light as possible if we're going to Costa Rica," Volk said and added as an afterthought, "For the best use of fuel."

Hank wanted to smile but kept it to himself.

"You heard the young man," Stin said. "Who's going with us?"

Every hand in the group shot up.

Hank gently opened the door to his parents' room and peaked his head inside. The bed-spread that covered them gently rose and fell. They were asleep. Hank moved to close the door. His mom stirred.

"Wait," his mom called in a whisper. "Please come in."

Hank moved to the side of her bed. She tilted her head and examined him. A tear formed in her eye. "I don't know how it's possible, but you really are our son, aren't you?"

Hank nodded.

"And Joseph, Sarah, Mary, Thomas, Kyle, Kathy, Helen, and William—they're ours too?"

"Yes."

His mom's tears increased.

"Don't cry. It's okay. I'm going to get you back to normal."

She shook her head and wiped her eyes. "That's not why I'm crying. I can feel you're my children, but I can't remember anything about you. Not when you were born, not your first step, your first word—it's all just—"

Hank took her hand and gave it a gentle squeeze. She pulled him close and hugged him, her bony arms pulling tight around him. "In spite of it, I still love you so much," she said as her tears washed down his face and mixed with his own.

"I love you too, Mom. I'll be back soon," he said and pulled from her embrace.

She blew him a kiss as he walked from the room. He closed the door with care and walked into the kitchen. Stin leaned against the sink.

"You okay?" he asked.

"I am," Hank said and wiped his eyes.

"You don't have to do this, Hank. You should stay here and take care of your family."

"And who's going to take care of my other family?"

"Other family?" Stin asked with a raised eyebrow.

"You guys. You're my family too, and family helps family, no matter what."

Stin smiled and nodded.

Hank, Stin, and Dog were the last to arrive at the little landing strip. The Loon gleamed in the setting sun. Over to one side, Hank saw Mr. and Mrs. Swenson. Volk poked his head out the cockpit window. "About time! Get on and help the others get everything secured."

Inside, Max had been tied to a chair. His expression was just as bored as ever. Misha tied down the crates containing the geodes they'd collected from before and the ones they'd retrieved in Tennessee. Julie secured the water jugs and food. When she saw Hank, she smiled.

"What's she doing here?" Hank whispered to Stin.

"We need another Anubis," Stin said.

Hearing the word come from Stin's mouth seemed odd and out of place. Hank nodded. He knew it wouldn't do any good to argue with him. Hank knelt by Dog as Stin went to help Misha.

"You and Nobo keep a good eye on her, okay? I still think she's working with Max and Ms. Cabot."

Dog barked.

A heated conversation drifted in. Hank turned to see Mr. and Mrs. Swenson standing outside the door. Mr. Swenson held a suitcase in one hand. Mrs. Swenson had a handkerchief to her eye.

"Don't go. You've done more than your share," she said to her husband.

"They need me."

"I need you! You already left me for one war."

"And I came back," Mr. Swenson said.

"It's not about coming back. Do you know how many times I worried about you? How many times my heart broke when I'd hear of more people dying and not hear from you?"

"And if I hadn't been there, more would have died. I need to help Hank on this path."

"Hank is on his own path. You need to be here on our path. I'm begging you, Albert. I'm begging you with everything I have. Don't go."

Mr. Swenson pulled her into his arms. "I'm coming back." He kissed his wife and climbed into the plane.

Hank looked away, trying to act like he hadn't been eavesdropping. Mr. Swenson didn't say a word. Hank relaxed and went to sit down. He heard a bumping. He looked beside him at a metal set of doors. The bumping sounded again. It came from behind the metal doors. "Not this time!" Hank hollered at the twins as he opened the doors.

Kyle and Kathy were huddled on the bottom shelf, a blanket doing a poor job of concealing them. Hank pulled it off.

"Come on, Hank. We want to go too," Kyle said.

"Look," Kathy said, pointing to where they were sitting. "We're not taking up any space."

"And you'll take up even less when you've gone back to the house," Hank said.

Dog barked.

"We can to protect ourselves," Kathy said, looking at Dog.

Hank didn't listen to her and helped them both out of their hiding place. Just as he ushered them out of The Loon, Mrs. Swenson approached. "You two! What am I going to do with you?" she asked as she grabbed both twins, one under each arm.

"Thanks, Mrs. Swenson," Hank said.

She didn't respond as she walked away with the twins. Kyle and Kathy gave him a sour expression. *It's for your own good.*

"Anymore stowaways?" Volk called back.

Hank shut and latched the door where the twins had been. "Looks like we're all clear," he said.

"Then let's get going," Volk said.

The Loon roared to life. Hank sat beside Dog. At least this time, he wouldn't have his ribs hurting with every bump. The engines increased in power, and The Loon taxied onto the narrow, dirt runway. It jolted forward as the engines whined. The force of the acceleration sent Dog and Hank sliding against a crate. A moment later, they were airborne.

The flight was uneventful. They landed in Cuba to refuel. Volk had been upset that his calculations were off by ten gallons. Stin had just shaken his head and paid the extra cost. The second leg of the journey had taken them through the night.

Hank awoke and peered out the window to watch the sun climb over the Caribbean Sea. It splashed bright color across the blue water. He thought of the sunset in Tennessee, and he wished Lina could be here to see this with him. Stin had put his foot down and wouldn't let her come. Hank understood. He didn't want to risk her getting hurt either, but he still missed her.

The blue water quickly changed to green and brown fields.

"Welcome to Costa Rica!" Volk shouted.

They flew for another thirty minutes before Volk spoke again. "Get ready to land!"

Hank smiled. It was the best thing he'd heard all day.

Hank's nerves twisted. Some of it felt like excitement, but most of it felt like dread.

The Loon descended towards Costa Rica below. A few white puffy clouds rushed up to meet them. They were going on Max's directions, but he only knew the general location of Ms. Cabot's expedition: the Arenal volcano. The plan called for Volk to circle the area and try to find a suitable place to land.

Hank looked out of the window again. Jungle. Miles and miles of jungle spread across the landscape traveling beneath them. "I don't see any place to land," Hank said to no one in particular.

The ground was getting closer and closer. "Volk, what are you doing?"

Volk didn't respond. Hank's heart beat faster. It looked like they were about to crash. The tops of the trees were just feet below them. "Hold on to something!" Hank called to the others as he reached up and took hold of a strap, trying to find something to brace himself with for impact.

The Loon dropped faster. Hank closed his eyes and waited. Nothing.

They should have hit the trees by now, but they were still descending. Hank shot a look out the window again. The jungle had turned to blue water, and the Loon slowed and skipped across it for a perfect landing. Hank let out a sigh of relief.

It took several minutes to find a suitable place to park along the shore. Hank unlatched and opened the door. The warm air rushed to greet him. He sniffed at it. *Flowers.* Not as sweet as the ones from home, but they were pleasant. He scanned the area. There wasn't an inch of space that didn't look green. Colorful birds flew overhead.

Hank continued to admire the scene. He took a deep

breath and pulled his shoulders back. This is what it meant to be an adventurer.

"Hurry up," Volk said.

Hank looked back and saw he was holding everyone up from getting off the plane. "Sorry," he said and exited.

They all helped in unloading the gear while Max watched from his secured chair.

"I really feel like we should be making him do this," Hank said.

Stin chuckled.

Misha went in for the last crate while Volk untied Max. Volk led him out of the plane.

"So, where do we go?" Volk asked.

Max looked around, up at the volcano, and across the lake. Finally, he looked at Volk and shrugged. "I haven't got a clue."

"I thought you were supposed to be a guide or something," Hank said.

Max looked away.

"You can guide us, can't you!?" Hank exclaimed.

"Excuse me," Misha said from the plane.

"It doesn't work like that. I don't know where Ms. Cabot is exactly," Max said.

"Hey!" Misha called again.

"So how does it work?" Hank challenged.

All eyes were on the two boys.

"Someone!" Misha said again, this time raising his voice.

"What!" both Hank and Max shouted.

"We have small problem," Misha said.

They all looked over at Misha.

"What's wrong?" Stin asked.

Misha stepped to one side to reveal a girl with dark hair and dark eyes.

"Lina!" Hank shouted.

She gave a smile and a little wave.

"Not again!" Mr. Swenson threw down his hat.

"How in the world did you—" Hank started to say.

Volk cut him off. "You're the reason it took an extra ten gallons to get to Cuba!"

"First the twins. What if all three of you had made it here?" Julie asked.

"They were actually my cover. I guessed you'd look for them to stowaway again, so I asked them to get caught," Lina said. She looked down as her face turned crimson.

"I don't think it's safe to have her here," Mr. Swenson said.

"Can we go back to America now? I'm having second thoughts about this," Max said and added. "You can keep the book."

Hank spun back to him. "We have a deal, and I know you can help us find her. Your second thoughts or Lina's appearance doesn't change anything. We're going forward."

No one countered Hank.

"And besides, she's really good in a fight," Hank said.

She smiled and stepped down from the plane to join them.

"Fine. Let's just take all the kids into the jungle. I'm sure that's safe," Mr. Swenson said, and he threw a knapsack over his shoulders.

Stin chuckled, but stopped when Mr. Swenson glared at him.

"Don't start with me, shadow-man. I'm not in the mood."

Everyone grabbed a knapsack except for Max and Lina.

"Okay, Max. Where are we going?" Hank asked.

Max rolled his eyes at Hank. "This isn't a good idea."

"Just guide."

Max closed his eyes for several long moments and then pointed northeast towards the volcano. "About two miles in, we'll find a small village. There should be a man who knows something."

"Something like what? Like where Ms. Cabot is?" Hank demanded.

"Just something that will lead us to her. It's not an exact science. I can't always see every point along the path. Right now, I can see we need to go that direction. That's how it works," Max said, his tone irritated.

"Lead the way, guide," Stin said as he patted Max on the

back.

If Hank had thought the trees and brush were hard to walk though in Tennessee, Costa Rica was almost impossible. Every step required them to move over, under, or around something. It took hours to reach the village, but it was like an oasis in the desert. Hank looked back at everyone in the group. They were all sweating profusely, except for Stin, who hadn't even taken off his overcoat.

"Water!" Lina exclaimed as she pointed to a large drum of fresh water that stood a few feet away. "Everyone give me your canteens. I'll fill them."

They handed them over to Lina, and she went to the drum.

Hank looked at the ground. "Nothing to trip on!"

"Also no one to trip on, either," Mr. Swenson said.

Hank looked across the small village. He didn't notice anyone. Not even people talking or children laughing. It felt odd.

"Where's this man who's going to help us, *guide*?" Hank said the last word with a touch of disdain.

"There," Max pointed at a man sitting on a log.

The man looked ancient, and he sat very still. Hank wasn't sure the man was even awake.

"Hello," Hank said.

"I'm sure he can't understand you," Mr. Swenson said.

The old man stood, turned slowly, and motioned them to come. Hank moved to join the man, but Max caught his arm.

"What?" Hank asked.

Max looked at him, then at the old man, and back to Hank.

"What, Max?"

Max let go. "Nothing."

Hank stepped close to the old man by the fire. The man had torn garments, no shoes, and dirt on everything. The only thing that seemed to be untouched by the dirt was a gold ring the old man wore on his right pinky. The old man smiled. There was something familiar about his eyes.

"I waiting you to come," the old man said in broken

English.

"Waiting for us?"

The old man nodded. "I take all you up," the old man said and pointed in the direction of the volcano.

The old man stood, picked up a walking stick, and plodded across the village towards the jungle.

Hank looked back at Max. "Is this how it works?"

"Yep."

"Excuse me, sir. Where is everyone?" Lina asked.

"Gone work." The old man said and shuffled away.

They all followed after the old man. He wasn't fast, but he moved them to a small path that made it much easier to walk.

"Where do you think he's taking us?" Lina whispered to Hank.

"Up! Go to cold path," the man called back.

Hank and Lina exchanged glances.

"How can he hear us?" Lina mouthed.

"Good ears," the old man called back.

He continued to lead them up the winding path for at least two hours. The man never stopped, and not a bead of sweat dripped from his face. In that way, the old man reminded Hank of Stin. Finally, when Hank's legs felt like they couldn't take another step, the old man stopped.

"Here," he said and pointed behind him. "Cold path."

Hank approached it, followed behind by Nobo and Julie. He could feel that what the old man called the cold path was a ley line. The power felt weak. *Not weak. Drained.* He took a tentative step forward. The ley line felt as cold as the stream on the road to Fruitland. It ran across the path and into the jungle. Hank took a moment and felt it closely.

"It's flowing that way," Hank said and pointed north.

"Let's see where it goes," Julie said.

"Do you want to guide us up the ley line?" Hank asked the old man.

He shook his head and walked down the path.

"That's it?" Volk said to Max.

"Looks like he's done," Max said.

"Thanks," Hank called to the old man. "Well, let's see

where this goes." He stepped into the jungle with Julie behind him. Hank didn't like her so close, but his main thoughts were on the ley line. What was draining it?

He'd only walked about a hundred yards when the jungle opened up. A large rock slab extended twenty-five feet, and then it went back to jungle. He stepped onto the slab of rock. It was nice to have a break from the jungle terrain. He'd taken five steps when the ground under his feet seemed to give way.

CRACK!

He looked down. Fissures along the rock slab ran under his feet. He looked at the others. "Get back!" The rock slab under his feet split.

CRACK!

The rock broke into pieces. Hank tried to jump back, but he was in a free fall. He looked up to see Julie and Nobo falling too. He hit the ground below with another crack. He screamed in pain and reached for his leg. His pants were torn, and he could feel his leg bone poking out.

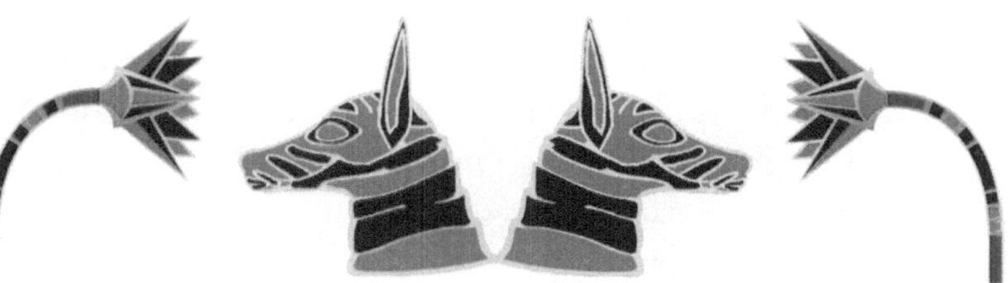

25

TRAITOR

The only light Hank could see spilled from the opening where they'd fallen. The cold rock under his body hadn't been forgiving. He clenched his teeth against the pain from his leg, and warm liquid pooled around his hand. *Blood.* Hank tried to ignore it and stand. He planted his hand and pushed, keeping as much weight off his leg as possible.

Whimpers echoed through the cavern.

"Nobo?" Hank called.

Nobo howled.

"I'll be right there!" he said and took a fast step on his broken leg. He screamed again and collapsed on the ground.

"Hank! Are you there?" Stin yelled from the opening.

"I'm here, but hurt pretty bad."

"What about Nobo and Julie?" Stin asked.

"Nobo's hurt too. I haven't found Julie yet," Hank said.

"Hank, do you have one of the healing geodes?" Lina called.

How could he have forgotten? He pulled the knapsack from his back and opened it. "I'm checking!" He dug through it, grabbing each geode and feeling for what energy it held. *No. No. No.* It had to be here. He dumped the contents on his lap. His canteen clattered to the ground.

Nobo howled again.

"Hold on. I'll be right there," Hank said. Lightheadedness spilled over him. He blinked and shook his head to clear it.

A tingle of the healing energy flitted across his fingers. "I've got one!" he exclaimed. He picked up the stone. As soon as his skin touched the rough geode, the ley line energy poured through his body. The pain he felt when he crashed and broke his leg paled in comparison to the cure.

He screamed as his leg bone fused together and the torn skin pulled tight and reformed. After a few moments, the pain subsided. He scrambled to his feet and rushed to where he could hear Nobo calling out in pain.

Nobo's white fur was patched with dark spots that Hank guessed were soaked blood. He touched Nobo on the head. The wolf recoiled and whimpered.

"Hold on," Hank said as he lifted the geode to Nobo's body. "This is going to hurt a lot."

Nobo growled.

"Swearing about it won't make it hurt less," Hank said and pressed the geode against him.

Nobo's body convulsed, and his howls echoed through the cavern.

"Nobo!" Volk cried from above.

Hank had never heard even the slightest tinge of fear in Volk's voice, but now, his tone was laced with broken shards of it. Hank kept the geode pressed firmly against Nobo's coat until he'd stopped convulsing.

"Better?"

The wolf put a massive paw on Hank's lap and licked his face. Hank smiled and scratched behind Nobo's ears.

"Nobo! Are you okay?" Volk called, still on edge.

Nobo howled and jumped off Hank, tail raised high in the air.

"Well, that was short-lived," Hank said.

A few yards away, Julie coughed. Hank went to her side. Even in the dim light, Hank could see she was hurt badly. Her body twisted in a way Hank knew wasn't normal. He knelt by her. Her breathing was shallow, and her eyes were closed. Hank knew if he didn't help her now, she probably wouldn't make it.

He moved the geode toward her and stopped an inch from her skin. He could feel that the energy from the geode was almost gone. If he used it on Julie, there would be none left for other injuries. He could stand up and walk away. No one would ever know he'd left her, and besides, she was a traitor, right? She'd been the one to tell Ms. Cabot about Charleston, right?

Julie coughed again, choking. Hank squeezed the geode tighter. The truth was, he didn't know if it was her, and no matter what she might have done to him in the past, it didn't make her a traitor. He pressed the geode against her, hard.

She didn't move.

"Come on. You aren't dying here. I won't let you!" Hank screamed. Fear crept though his body. *I took too long. Now she's dead.*

She stiffened, her eyes opening wide as she screamed. There were pops and cracks as her body straightened back to normal. She closed her eyes and rested her head on the ground.

"Thank you, Hank," she said, her voice quiet.

Hank tossed the empty geode into the knapsack and put the rest of the contents away.

"Hank, we're going to find a way to get you out of there," Stin called down.

"That'll take too long. We could miss our chance!" Hank shouted back.

There were murmurs from above, and then Max spoke. "Hank, you can reach an exit. It's to the northwest through the cavern. About four hundred yards."

"How do you know that?" Hank asked.

"Because that's how being a guide works."

Hank hesitated. Going deeper into the cavern could get them stuck, or worse. He imagined another cave-in, but this time without the ley line power.

"He might be right," Julie said. "I can feel air moving this direction."

He looked at Julie. She'd turned a flashlight on. The beam cast an odd outline around her body. The idea of following Julie down a dark path guided by Max made his stomach turn.

Nobo must have sensed his hesitation because a moment later, he sat in front of Hank and put a paw out like he was asking to shake. Hank took the paw.

Nobo gave a short whine and then padded towards Julie.

"We'll see you on the other side," Hank called to the group above. He stepped over to Julie, who took the lead. It didn't take long before the cavern seemed to swallow them up. Hank looked back. He could no longer see the light from the hole.

The ceiling of the cavern stood twenty or more feet above them with long stalactites forming in narrow columns. As they moved deeper, the only sound Hank could hear was boot leather hitting rock and the occasional drip of water from the stalactites.

Julie stopped. "Do you see that?"

Hank peered over her shoulder. "Is that what I think it is?"

She lifted the light from the floor of the cavern to the roof. Every inch in between reflected the flashlight beam in a mix of color. It was the largest geode Hank had ever seen.

Nobo yapped.

"It must have formed in here," Hank said.

Nobo howled and bounded to the geode.

"How could anyone put it in here?" Hank asked.

Julie marched to the base of the geode and examined it. "It's not attached to rock bed. And look over there." She pointed the light to where Nobo pawed at something.

Hank glanced over and did a double take. The cave wall was lined with shelves made of stone, and on each shelf were rows of geodes, full crystals, prisms, and more.

CLUNK!

Nobo howled.

"What did you find?" Hank asked.

Nobo howled again.

Hank picked up what Nobo had pawed off one of the

shelves. The cold feel of steel hit Hank's hands as he picked up the object. It must have weighed close to ten pounds. Julie pointed her light at him. He held the ornamental head of a dog. He held it into the light for a better look. It gleamed with silver and gold. He turned it around in his hands and stopped.

"It's a mask," Hank said as he held it up and observed two slits wide enough for eyes. The sides also had a seam and two clasps. He unfastened them, and the dog-headed mask split into two halves.

"Is this the cache that Ms. Cabot was looking for?" Hank asked.

Julie didn't respond. Her light moved from Hank and the mask. He started to put it in his knapsack, but stopped as Nobo began to growl.

"What's wrong?" Hank asked as he looked up. Julie stared at him, her hand extended with a geode pointed at him. Hank's blood went cold. How could he have let his guard down? "What are you—"

He didn't get a chance to finish his sentence as Julie yelled, "Get down" and fired a blast of ley line energy. Hank dropped as Nobo sprung over him, following the flash of energy.

A man screamed.

Hank rolled over to see the screaming man fall to the ground in the flash of the blast and Nobo's body colliding into a second man. A hand wrapped around his arm. It was Julie helping him up. Hank stepped closer to the men, both unconscious. Hank expected to see men in rags, like the old man, but these men were in work clothes and leather boots.

Julie searched one of the men's pants pockets. She pulled out a wallet. "American. I'd guess Cabot's men. They're probably here to collect the goods."

Hank didn't say a word, staring at her.

"What's wrong?"

"I can't believe it. You saved me. You could have let them attack me and you didn't."

"Of course, I didn't, Hank. Why would I ever want anyone

to hurt you?"

"But you're working for them! You were the one who warned her about us coming to Charleston."

She scoffed. "Sorry, Hank. I'm not your spy." She stood.

Nobo sniffed her and then snorted.

"You don't have to believe me, either, you arrogant four-legged chicken killer."

Nobo whined.

"Poor, baby," she said. "Come on. Let's get out of here before more of them show up."

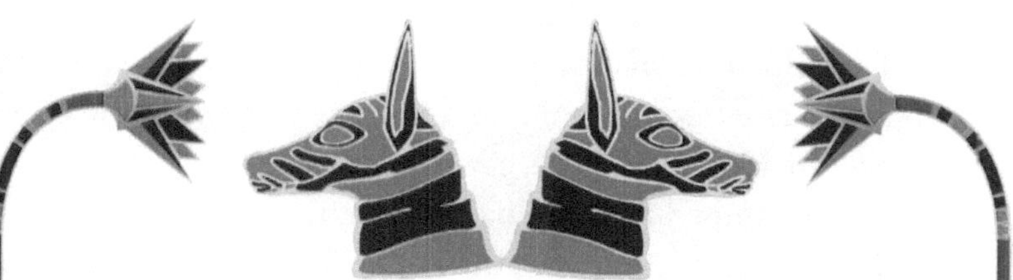

26
BROKEN TOOLS

Dim light spilled into the cavern from the mouth opening. They'd found the exit without running into any more of Ms. Cabot's men.

"Finally, we can get out," Julie said.

Hank's stomach twisted into a knot. "I don't think we're out of it yet," Hank said as he observed men moving near a truck at the mouth of the cavern. Hank pulled up the ley line energy, getting ready to blast his way out.

Julie lifted her geode. "Let's go on the count of three," she said. "One—"

Nobo howled and sprung forward into a sprint.

"Wait!" Hank called after him. One of the men stopped and turned, just as Nobo sprung on his back legs and collided with him. Hank expected to hear a scream, but instead it was a familiar voice.

"Nobo!" Volk cried in excitement.

The knot in Hank's stomach loosened, and Julie dropped her arm.

"Come on," she said.

They tromped from the cavern and rejoined their friends. Misha, Mr. Swenson, Volk, and Lina excitedly greeted them. Max stood off to one side, a sullen expression on his face.

"Where's Dog and Stin?" Hank asked.

"He helped us take care of these guys," Volk said, pointing behind him to five tied-up men, "and then he and Dog went ahead to scout the area."

Misha climbed into the back of the truck.

"The cavern is the cache they're looking for. We ran into a couple more of Cabot's men, but Julie and Nobo made short work of them."

"What's in there?" Mr. Swenson asked, pointing into the cavern.

"It's incredible." Hank held up the mask. "We found this, and there's a geode that must be close to twenty feet tall," Hank exclaimed.

Max moved closer.

Mr. Swenson took the mask from Hank and examined it. "What do you think this is for?"

"I don't know—" Hank started.

"It's an Anubis mask," Max said. He pointed to the insets around the crown. "You can put stones of different powers into each spot."

Misha poked his head out of the truck window. "There's enough dynamite in here to blow a hole in the moon," he said.

Hank turned at the sound of approaching footsteps. It was Stin and Dog coming out of the jungle. Dog sprinted forward and hit Hank hard. He tumbled backwards as Dog licked every inch of Hank's face. "I'm glad to see you too, buddy!"

Stin offered Hank a hand and helped him up. "We might need that dynamite. You remember all the derrick equipment at the reservoir?"

"Yeah," Hank said.

"Well, they've built one here," Stin said.

Max jumped up and joined the group. "They've finished the apparatus?"

"The what?" Misha asked.

Max ignored him. "It's operational?"

"It's pumping, so I guess it is," Stin said. "What is it?"

"It's draining the ley lines," Hank said.

Max spun and looked at him. "That's not what it does. Ms. Cabot said—"

Hank cut him off, "It doesn't matter what she told you. I felt it when we were in the cold stream. The ley line is being drained."

Max clenched his fists. "Don't you call her a liar!"

"I'll call her whatever I want. She's a liar, a killer, and she's tricked you into believing she's some kind of saint," Hank shot back.

Max swung a right hook. Hank wasn't expecting it. It landed square on his jaw, knocking him onto the ground. Stin grabbed Max by the shoulders and stopped him.

"Take it back! Take it all back! You don't know anything about her. She saved me. Took me off the street. Protected me when no one else would. You don't know anything!"

Hank sat up and rubbed his jaw. Stars danced across his vision, but he focused on Max. "I'm sorry, Max. I'm sorry you've put your trust in a woman that would willingly kill a boy just for disagreeing with her."

Max tried to fight his way out of Stin's grasp but couldn't. "You don't understand! She sees the big picture. If we don't protect you, the Apeps will take you. Then we're all doomed."

"I think we're doomed if she goes through with whatever she's built up there," Hank said and stood.

"I have to agree with Hank. Whatever this apparatus is, I'm sure it's not good for us," Stin said.

Misha climbed from the truck, his arms filled with sticks of dynamite. "Let's blow it sky high, get Cabot to tell Hank how to save his parents, and get out of here. The heat is killing me."

Max's eyes widened in shock. "You can't do that. With the apparatus in operation, you could damage the ley lines."

"Maybe," Stin said. "But it's a risk we'll have to take."

Stin led them through the jungle for a half mile to where he'd seen the derrick. Like the village, the jungle here had been cut away to create a clearing. The derrick stood three stories tall in the center. Its massive arm pumped up and down in a slow, methodical rhythm.

"Three platforms. I wonder what they're for?" Hank asked.

"Not sure," Stin said.

The pull of the ley lines tugged at Hank. He could feel seven crossing under the derrick, and with each pump, the ley lines lost a fraction of energy.

Hank counted only three men. Maybe the rest were all tied up at the cavern.

"Ready?" Stin asked Hank.

"Let's go," Hank replied as he went invisible.

They stalked into the clearing. There were a series of large wall tents on the left side of the derrick like ones he'd seen in the magazines his grandma sent him from her expeditions. On the right side of the derrick, there was a large, fenced-off area with what looked like piles of trees from the jungle.

Hank could feel the ley lines much stronger now. Some of them were like the ones in Idaho, running under the ground. Two were above ground.

Stin and Hank slipped against the metal footings of the derrick. At the base, it was at least three times as wide as Mr. Swenson's Mack truck. "Do we have enough dynamite?" Hank whispered.

"Put it on the legs down here. I'll climb up the rigging and place some up top."

"What about a fuse?" Hank asked, thinking about the twins' fireworks.

Stin pulled out a geode and smiled. "I think a blast from this ought to set it off."

Hank smiled back and moved to place the first stick. Stin took the stairs two at a time to the first platform. Hank moved to the next leg and placed two more sticks of dynamite while Stin wedged one of the sticks into the metal rigging on the top platform and walked to the other side.

Hank placed the dynamite on the third leg and moved

towards the opposite side. He walked through the center of the derrick, passing the heavy metal pumping rod. He stopped like he'd hit a wall. He closed his eyes and took a sharp breath. The ley line energy poured into him. It was powerful and seemed to revitalize him, similar to the Fruitland crossing but with something Hank could only describe as zest. He opened his eyes and saw Stin place his last stick.

Hank hurried from the center and started on the last leg as Stin climbed down from above. *Almost done.*

Stin knelt beside him. "There's a prism just like the one we took from Tennessee mounted on the top platform."

Hank looked at him. "What's this thing built to do?"

"I don't know. Maybe it splits the lines like Max was saying."

"I doubt it," Hank said.

Yelling came from the wall tents. Hank put the last stick in place and looked up to see what the commotion was about. One of the tent doors flew open, and Ms. Cabot walked out. She looked like she'd stepped out of one of the expedition photos. She had a pith hat on her head, and her jacket and pants were both khaki. The pants flared just above where they were tucked into her boots.

"Why aren't they back yet?" she yelled into the clearing.

An older man, dressed the same as Ms. Cabot, teetered behind her. He was a full head shorter than she. He took off his own pith hat and held it in his hands. "Dear, I'm sure it's taking them time to retrieve all the artifacts."

She spun to face the little man and slapped him. "Father, when I want your thoughts, I'll ask for them." She turned back to the clearing. The three men all stared at her. "You there," she said to the closest. "Get down to the cavern and see what's taking so long. I want them here in less than thirty minutes."

The man turned and ran into the jungle.

"I think that's our cue to exit," Stin said to Hank.

Ms. Cabot continued. "You two. Get those workers out here, and put the crystal piping into place."

The other two men ran to the fenced-off area with the

trees. Stin and Hank were almost back to the jungle when Hank heard a crack. He looked back to see one of the two men with a whip in his hand.

Those aren't trees. "They're shelters," Hank said.

"What?" Stin said.

"Look at all the people."

The two men were herding a gaggle of women, men, and children from the fenced-off area toward the derrick. "Come on. Get those crates unloaded!" one of the men shouted.

The workers looked exhausted.

Stin raised his geode.

"They're too close," Hank said. "We can't risk—"

"We're not getting another chance at this, Hank," Stin said.

Hank yanked Stin's arm just as yelling came from the tree line.

"Ms. Cabot! Ms. Cabot!" Max cried as he ran from the jungle's edge. "They're going to blow it up!"

Hank started to sprint, but instead of running, he seemed to zoom across the clearing. *The ley lines.* He tackled Max with enough force that it sent them rolling across the ground.

"Guards! Everyone get out here!" Ms. Cabot yelled.

Hank looked up from the ground just in time to see eight armed men running out from another wall tent. He'd have to act fast if he had any hope of saving his parents. Hank stood and snatched the back of Max's collar, coaxing him to a standing position.

"I want to make a deal with you!" Hank yelled at Ms. Cabot. He marched Max forward until they were ten feet from her and her armed guards, each with his rifle pointed directly at Hank.

"Are you offering me your services, Vessel?" she asked with a hopeful expression.

"No, I'm offering to return your Anubis in exchange for making my parents whole again."

She scoffed. "Why in the world would I want to do that?"

Hank looked at Max and then back at Ms. Cabot. "He's part of your brotherhood. He's your family."

This time she laughed out loud. "Him? A part of my family? He's nothing more to me than a tool. With his failure in Tennessee and him leading you here, I can confidently say he's a broken tool. I have no use for broken tools."

"But he's your Anubis," Hank said, defending Max.

"I can always find another Anubis in search of a home," she said mockingly to Max.

Max rushed forward and threw himself at her feet. "No, please, ma'am. I'm not a broken tool. I'm still useful to you. Look. I've brought him here to you, and I can get you the Tome of Thoth."

She bent down and lifted his chin. "You are worthless," she said in a cool, solemn voice. She stood again.

Max sniffed and got to his knees. "Please, I'm begging you."

"I've no use for beggars!" she said and slapped him across the face.

A splash of energy lit up the clearing as Hank let loose a quick attack of the ley line energy. Ms. Cabot's eyes said she hadn't seen that coming as the energy hit her squarely in the chest, knocking her back into two of her guards.

The other guards shouted and readied to shoot at Hank.

He didn't think. It was time for action. He sprung forward with the same veracious speed he'd used to tackle Max. Bullets nipped at where he'd been as he grabbed Max and pulled him to the side, dodging another bullet.

More flashes of energy lit up the clearing. Hank and the guards looked up to see Julie, Volk, Stin, Misha, Lina, and Mr. Swenson charging across the clearing, firing blasts of ley line energy at the guards.

"Hank! Hurry. We've got to get out of here," Stin called.

He couldn't leave yet. Hank scanned the clearing for Ms. Cabot. "Max, catch up with the others," he said and gave him a push to move.

Max staggered off, and Hank continued his search for Ms. Cabot. He saw Mr. Swenson and Lina helping to remove the workers from the area. The man with the whip lay unconscious near Lina's feet. Hank scanned again.

"There you are!" he yelled. Ms. Cabot's father helped her up. Hank zipped beside them.

"What have you done?" Ms. Cabot screamed at her father.

"I had to call him," her father said, then added in a panic, "We serve him!"

"Am I interrupting?" Hank said.

"You insolent little brat! Do I need to teach you another lesson in power?" she asked as she lifted her hand with the ring that had drained him before.

"You'd have to catch me first," Hank said.

She lunged forward, and Hank zoomed to the left, kicking up a cloud of dirt.

"Tell me how to make my parents young again!"

"You short-sighted brat!" She spun around in a vain attempt to follow his movements. "It can't be undone!"

"Liar!" Hank spat back. He pulled at the ley line energy, ready to strike her.

"Hank!" Stin called. "It's coming!"

Hank shot a quick glance to Stin. He hadn't noticed the sudden darkening of the sky, but now, he could feel the crushing weight. An Apep was here. He looked back at Ms. Cabot just as she reached out with her ringed hand.

Her touch burned his arm as it began to suck the power from him. Hank kicked back with all of his might and wrenched his arm from her grasp.

"You got a little, but not enough to stop me." He zipped to the left, then to the right, and then behind her. She tried to keep up, but it was no use. Hank was like a bullet.

He pulled up the ley line energy and blasted her. She flew through the air and smashed into the derrick. He zoomed next to her crumpled body. Hank reached down and yanked the ring from her finger, tossing it aside. "How do I turn them back?" he yelled into her ear.

She didn't answer, didn't stir. *Knocked her out.* He turned to catch up with Stin.

The Apep hit full force into Hank's chest. He screamed as pain tore through his body. He pushed himself against the Apep as they cruised across the clearing.

"I've been waiting for a chance to meet you, Hank Hudson. I understand your parents have aged. Time moves so quickly," the Apep hissed in his ear.

"And I want them back!" Hank shouted as he shot energy into the Apep.

27

RUNNING WITH THE APEP

The shock from Hank's energy blast seemed to irritate more than injure the Apep. It hissed and dropped him to the ground. Hank hit the dirt with a thud, rolled twice, and sprung to his feet, ready for the Apep to strike again.

The Apep seemed to turn inside itself and immediately lashed out at Hank.

"You're too slow!" Hank said, dodging the Apep's main attack. A moment later, he tightened his muscles as a tendril from the darkness swung wide to hit him in the back.

They'd only made contact for a second, but it was enough for the Apep to speak to Hank. "Your speed won't help your parents. Only giving yourself to me will allow you the power to save them."

In his mind, Hank saw a flash of his parents growing young, and then it was gone. He gained his footing and zoomed to the edge of the clearing, the Apep nipping at his heels. Three blasts of energy lit up the jungle as Hank brought the Apep past Stin, Misha, and Volk.

It fell back and circled around the derrick, climbing higher and higher. Hank zipped after him up the stairs, firing blast after blast of energy. Each one caused the Apep to shriek but not to shrink. *Why isn't this working?* He was

 230 

hitting it with the anger from his memories. He'd expected it to have the same effect it did when he'd used it on Stin.

Hank reached the top and realized he had nowhere left to turn. He skidded across the platform and passed the prism, trying to turn with enough time to run down the stairs.

He wasn't fast enough.

The Apep sent six tendrils of darkness around him like a massive hand scooping him up. Pain ripped through Hank's body.

"See, Vessel? You can't beat me. Your only choice is to yield and let me in," the Apep hissed.

"No!" Hank grunted through the pain.

"I will show you what will happen if you don't," the Apep hissed.

Hank's view of the clearing suddenly shifted. Instead of seeing his friends fighting Ms. Cabot and her men, and Lina and Mr. Swenson rescuing the workers, he saw the jungle in flames. His friends were still there, but now, they were in crumpled piles, like rag dolls. And then, he spotted Dog, dragging himself forward before collapsing.

The vision of the jungle floor faded to inky black streaks and was replaced with an aerial view of the Dubois home. Like the destruction in the jungle, the home too was ablaze. His brothers and sisters, his mom and dad, and everyone from the encampment were dead. Their bodies were strewn across the yard, crumpled and broken.

"I see your heart. I see your desires. I will destroy them all. I will lay waste to everything you hold dear, Hank Hudson. There is no end to my power, and I will use it to hunt down and destroy everything and everyone who has ever been important to you," the Apep hissed.

Its slick voice struck fear deep into Hank's heart. He wanted to cry out. He wanted to fight the Apep, but at that moment, seeing his friends and family lying dead, all he could do was cry. He couldn't fight against this, could he? How could anyone fight against this?

"Hank! Hank!" a voice called from below.

It was Lina.

Dog barked again and again.

Hank opened his eyes, the vision of destruction now gone. There was Lina, shooting the Apep as Dog rushed up the stairs. Stin and Volk joined the attack.

These were the people who could fight this evil. "No! You won't take them or anyone I love. I won't let you!" Hank screamed as he pulled up the ley line energy. His parents were at the forefront of his memories. He thought of them growing old in the cavern, thought of them no longer remembering who he was, and finally, he thought of his mother's farewell. He'd felt an overabundance of love in that moment. Hank used that last memory and the emotion it brought and combined it with the remaining ley line energy he had from Fruitland.

The energy flashed white and fired in each direction the Apep held him. It dropped its grip and let out an enormous shriek of pain that cracked across the sky like a thunder clap. The Apep lurched away from Hank.

Dog barked and licked Hank's face.

"I'll be fine," he said.

Lina was by his side. "Come on, Hank," she said as she helped him up.

The Apep had retreated, stopping just above the jungle.

"It still wasn't enough. I used everything I had, and it still didn't work. If I only had a little more energy," Hank said, defeat in his tone.

"We've got another plan," Lina said as they hurried down the stairs of the derrick.

When they reached the bottom, Stin clasped Hank's shoulder and spoke quickly. "You need to keep that thing occupied for a little longer."

"What are you planning to do?" Hank asked.

"Capture it."

Hank looked doubtful. "How?"

"That geode you saw. Misha went to get it."

"Misha's strong, but can he really carry it back?" Hank

asked.

"Max placed strength geodes in the Anubis mask," Stin said, and then added, "Max says we can divide the ley lines on top of the derrick, and with the geode, create a way to trap the Apep," Stin said.

"And you believe him?"

"I do," Stin said.

His words were enough for Hank. "Okay. I need some Fruitland energy."

Stin pulled two geodes from his coat pockets and handed them to Hank. "Ready?"

Hank concentrated and absorbed the energy from the geodes. There wasn't enough energy in the stones for half the blast he'd given the Apep before, but hopefully it'd be enough to buy them some time.

"Almost," he said and stepped into the center of the ley line crossing. His body filled with the zest, and he tore off in the direction of the Apep.

"We're not finished yet!" Hank shouted as he zoomed underneath the dark mass. He fired a quick blast at it. The energy wasn't enough to do any damage but hopefully enough to pick a fight.

It worked.

The Apep circled downward in a quick spin.

Hank zoomed from his position just as the Apep crashed into the ground and vanished.

"You want to play the invisibility game? We can do that," Hank said and went invisible. The Apep wouldn't see Hank, but Hank had an idea about spotting the Apep. He could feel the crushing weight of it. He stilled his mind and concentrated on all the energy flowing through the area. The seven ley lines were the easiest to feel. He could feel the energy in geodes around the clearing calling to him, and then he found what he was looking for.

Like a wave, Hank felt the Apep rolling across the clearing on a direct path to Dog.

Hank zipped around the derrick and scooped Dog into his arms just as the Apep materialized and struck.

Dog barked.

"Catch up with the others," Hank said as he set Dog on the ground and spun back to face the Apep. He went visible so the Apep could see him.

"Seems like your invisibility isn't as good as mine," Hank said with a smirk.

The Apep lashed out at Hank. This time, it was too fast, and Hank was too close to dodge. It smashed him in the chest, throwing him through the air.

Hank crashed into one of the wall tents. It was like he'd dropped into a pool of white water. The fabric of the tent collapsed on top of him. He was frantic and began pushing and pulling at the fabric to get free, but it only seemed to tangle him more.

The Apep picked up both him and the tent. The pain of being in the Apep's grasp was worse than ever.

"You dare mock me!" the Apep hissed.

Hank screamed as the Apep squeezed tighter.

The Apep tossed Hank and the tent into the air and then the pain vanished. The white fabric surrounding Hank sloughed from his body like a snake shedding its skin. He glimpsed something crashing through the jungle as the Apep caught him in its tendrils of pain.

"I am a god of this world, and I will not be mocked by a mortal bug!" the Apep hissed. "I have no need for your insolence!"

It squeezed tighter around Hank. Every muscle in his body tensed at the pain. He wanted to close his eyes but forced them open. *How much longer, Stin?* The Apep carried Hank higher. *There!* Hank spotted what was crashing through the jungle: Misha's body with the head of a dog, carrying the twenty foot geode. He spotted Volk and Max on the derrick platform. White light poured from around them.

"You are not worthy to be my vessel!"

"Good—that's—something—we—can—both—agree—on!" Hank said in gasps.

"Enough! Your life is forfeit! Everyone you love is now forfeit!" the Apep screamed in Hank's mind and increased the pain as he dove through the sky towards the ground.

"Not—if—I—have—any—life—left!" Hank shot back in pain. He ran through his mind, pulling every memory he had of love. He thought of his parents, his siblings, Dog, Stin, Misha, Kiska, the Swensons, Mrs. Nieves and Lina. He pulled at the remaining Fruitland energy and formed a shield. It pushed against the Apep.

"You bug! You brat!" the Apep hissed as the energy smashed into it. "I—won't—"

Hank pushed hard with the shield.

The Apep shrieked in pain, releasing Hank thirty feet above the ground. Misha dropped the geode and dove forward. It seemed that everything slowed. Hank saw Misha stretch out to catch him, felt his body smash into Misha's, heard the crack and pop in Misha's back, and finally Misha's cry of pain.

"Misha!" Hank yelled as he looked at his friend in the Anubis mask.

"Go. It's just my back."

Hank hesitated.

"Go, Little Fish! Go!" Misha said, his voice muffled by the mask.

"I'll be back to help you," Hank said and zipped away from Misha.

The weight of the Apep crushed him. It would grab him in another second.

"Hank! Up here!" Volk called from the derrick platform.

Hank zoomed up the steps. Volk and Max pushed against a metal pipe as big as a rowboat oar. Sweat poured from their faces. The pipe was in a sprocket that rested under the prism. Hank could see how much effort they were putting into holding the prism in place.

Ley line energy spilled from the prism and dissipated into the air. "Grab the prism and take the energy!" Max called.

Hank looked between Max and Volk.

The Apep screamed as it ripped through the air, aiming directly at Hank.

Hank nodded at Max and put a hand on top of the prism. New ley line energy flowed through his body. His skin pricked. He braced himself, and then the Apep hit him, but instead of getting knocked back, Hank stood still. A new energy filled him.

He looked down to see the Apep entering his body. Hank expected the pain. He expected the Apep to take control of him.

"What are you doing?" the Apep hissed.

Hank could feel the new ley line energy latch on to the Apep and pull it into Hank's body. *Max, what did you do to* me? Fear flashed across Hank's mind. Had Max tricked him into being the Apep's vessel? The thought was clear in his mind until he realized he wasn't in pain.

Hank looked to his left and saw the geode. The ley line energy seemed to whisper in his ear what he had to do. He held the Apep inside him. The ley line energy he'd absorbed created a barrier between him and the Apep, but he could feel the immense power of the being. What if he could control it? This could be what his parents needed. *No.* He knew he'd never make his parents whole with a dark power.

He stretched out his other arm and pointed at the massive geode.

"Do not dare!" the Apep screamed at him in his mind.

"I do dare," Hank said and released the new ley line energy and the Apep. He'd become a conduit for the energy to transfer it from his body to the giant geode.

"What have you done, Anubis? I will return and will destroy you!" the Apep screamed in his mind as the last trace of it left his body.

The darkness in the sky vanished. Below, everyone stared in disbelief.

"What have you done?" Ms. Cabot screeched.

Hank wasn't about to let her leave. He zoomed down the stairs just as her father took hold of her hand. "We have to go, dear," her father said. They turned to light and shot into the sky.

"No! Come back! I need to know how to make my parents young!" Hank screamed into the air. The light flew across the sky, just like a shooting star, and then was gone.

Hank dropped to his knees. He'd won the fight but lost the prize. He looked at the earth. He could feel several eyes on him. *What now?* The workers of the brotherhood were staring at him. He stood and flexed both hands in front of him. "Did you just see what I did to your master? Who's next?" he challenged.

The men looked at him and then at each other. They dropped their guns and ran into the jungle.

"I guess they don't want to cross paths with the destroyer of Apeps," Stin said, his voice exhausted.

Hank looked at him and gave a half smile. He looked at the others. Everyone was giving him nods and smiles. Everyone but Misha. *Where was Misha?*

"Misha!" Hank said as he zoomed to Misha's side.

"I'll...be...fine...Little Fish," Misha said, his words coming out weakly between gasps.

"Someone give me a healing stone," Hank called as he reached back and unclasped the mask.

Misha gave him a weak smile and closed his eyes.

"Hurry. Someone give me a stone!" Hank shouted.

No one did. There must be someone who could help him. Everyone's eyes were on the ground. Stin shook his head.

"No!" Hank shouted. Why did he use the healing energy on himself? "Come on. Someone get that truck. We can get him to a hospital!"

Misha gurgled, his breath shallow.

Stin stood behind Hank and put a hand on his shoulder. "I'm sorry."

"No!" Hank ran to Mr. Swenson. "You have to help him," Hank said between sobs.

Mr. Swenson's expression softened. "Hank, if there was anything I could do to save Misha, I would."

It was like a monster grabbed Hank's heart and ripped it from his chest. Misha gasped and fell silent. In two steps, Hank fell by the strongman's side. "Don't be dead. You can't be dead!"

Misha didn't move. Hank didn't know a heart could be torn out of his chest twice. He threw his arms around Misha's lifeless body. His parent's were senile, Mrs. Nieves was dead, and now Misha.

"Guardian," a voice said from the edge of the jungle. The old man from the village plodded forward.

"We don't need a guardian to watch him!" Hank shouted.

"No. Guardian saves friend. You vessel." He pointed to Hank. "Him guide." He pointed to Max. He looked at Volk, Stin, and then Mr. Swenson. "Who guardian?"

Even if the words hadn't been in broken English, Hank wouldn't have understood what the man was trying to say.

Max jumped up. "Guardian! One of you is a guardian. You can save him," Max said.

"What are you talking about?" Stin asked.

"Hank's a vessel. He can store energy. I'm a guide. I can see where people need to go. Guardian's can save people, but..." Max's eyes fell on Misha.

"But what?" Hank asked.

"But with Misha gone, it'll mean life for life."

Stin dropped to Misha's side. "How? How does it work?"

"I've never worked with a Guardian. I guess you put your hands on him," Max said.

Stin reached out to place a hand on Misha's forehead and another on his chest. Would this work? If it did work, then Stin would be dead. How could Hank ask him to do that?

"Move out of the way. He's my brother," Volk said and shoved Stin away. "If anyone should trade places, it should be me!"

"No!" Mr. Swenson's voice boomed across the clearing.

Volk moved away from Misha's body, and Mr. Swenson knelt. His withered hands took hold of Misha's face. Mr. Swenson inhaled a sharp breath.

"No, he wouldn't want you to do this. Not if it means—" Hank tried to say it as a huge lump gathered in his throat.

"Trading my old life for his? A trade I'd make any day," Mr. Swenson said.

Misha took a quick breath. Mr. Swenson took his hands away from Misha's face. Misha's eyes fluttered open.

"Tell my wife I'm sorry I couldn't keep my promise," Mr. Swenson said and collapsed to the ground.

28

ALLIES AND SPIES

They wrapped Mr. Swenson's body in one of the canvas wall tents. Dog and Nobo stood watch over the body as Misha and Julie built a makeshift casket out of discarded wooden crates.

"We should take him home now," Hank said.

Stin shook his head. "He wouldn't have that. You know he'd want us to take care of this first."

"I just—" A lump lodged in Hank's throat. He hadn't been able to clear the lump since Mr. Swenson sacrificed himself for Misha. "I just want to know when this will be over."

"I know, but it will never be over unless we slog our way through the muck."

Hank wiped his eyes. "But why does the slog need to be so hard?"

Stin gave a half smile. "I used to ask Adam that almost every day when we were in Argonne. He'd say something like 'Everyone knew what they were called to do, but few did it.'" Stin turned and looked to where Dog and Nobo stood guard. "I know it feels hard, and it's going to continue to be hard, but it won't be impossible. Look at the ones who stand beside us. They're here because they know what they need to do. That's who Mr. Swenson was. A man who knew what

he was supposed to do and did it."

Hank nodded through his tears.

He left Stin to help finish the casket. When they finished, they joined the others, and with the help of the people from the village, they tore down the prism assembly and loaded the artifacts and the giant geode into trucks.

Hank had placed a hand on the geode and could feel the Apep. Its anger was still hot.

"It has room," Hank said. "It's less than half full. We could hold another Apep."

"Or, we could avoid them," Julie said. "Do you really want to carry that thing around filled with monsters?" she added.

That was a frightening thought. "Maybe we can destroy them."

"I don't know if that's possible," Max said. "One of the first principles I was taught about energy was that it couldn't be made or destroyed."

"Well, then, we'll have to find a safe place to store it," Stin said.

Hank nodded. He held his hand out to Max, who looked at it. "I'm sorry, Max. I know what it feels like to be alone."

Max took Hank's hand. "Sure," he said, not making eye contact with Hank.

"Listen. It's up to you, but if you want to stay with us, you can." Max didn't look up, so Hank added, "Or if you want to go, that's fine too."

Max nodded. "Yeah, maybe I'll stay for a bit."

Hank then approached Stin.

"That was big of you," Stin said.

"He and I are a lot more alike than I thought. I think he's the kind of person who knows where he's supposed to be and goes there," Hank said.

"I hope so. He'd be a huge asset." Stin looked over the

items in the back of the truck. "We'll need a guide to figure all this out."

"Yes," Volk said as he joined them. "This brotherhood has centuries of knowledge. We need to learn everything we can if we have a chance at winning this war."

Hank looked up at him with surprise. "Were you not here a few hours ago? We totally whooped that Apep."

Volk scoffed. "If by 'whooped' you mean flying through the air while that beast tried to kill you, then yes, we 'whooped' it."

"We beat him, though."

"The other's won't be nearly so naive. Ms. Cabot will tell them what happened here. They'll be expecting us."

Hank hadn't thought of that. He didn't know what to say.

Misha came to his rescue. "But, we'll learn what to do and with the little fish with us, we'll beat them all."

Lina joined to the group. "And, if we can find someone to read that book, we should have all sorts of..."She paused like she was looking for the right word. "Recipes to make stronger power."

"The Egyptian recipe book. I like that," Stin said.

That caused a good laugh through the group of weary fighters.

They stopped as the old man from the village approached them.

Stin put out his hand, and the old man shook it. "Thank you, sir. We never got your name. I'm Stin."

"Dusky," the old man said, emphasizing the second syllable so it sounded like Dus-Kay.

"Well, sir, we couldn't have done this without your help. I think we're all loaded up, and we'll be out of your way," Stin said.

"I go," Dusky said.

"Okay. Have a safe journey back to your village," Stin said.

"No. I go with you," Dusky said and pointed at the truck.

Hank and Stin exchanged puzzled looks. "You don't have to do that, sir," Stin said.

"I help you fight dark monster. I know about things in cave," Dusky said.

"Won't your village need you here?" Hank asked.

Dusky shook his head. "More important," he said and pointed to Hank. "Help parents."

Hank's eyes widened, and he nodded his head. "Yeah, maybe you should go with us."

The flight back to Columbus was solemn. Volk flew the plane. Hank, Lina, Max, Dog, Misha, Nobo, and Dusky rode in the back with Mr. Swenson's casket beside them. Now, they were the guardians escorting their fallen brother-in-arms.

Hank had tried to think of what to say when he saw Mrs. Swenson. He didn't have the words. How could he explain the sacrifice? How could she ever understand what Mr. Swenson had done? Hank gave up and thought about Stin.

With the amount of artifacts they'd recovered and the size of the geode prison, Stin and Julie volunteered to travel with it by boat. They'd be an extra week at least before joining them.

Hank had wanted to ask Dusky everything he knew about the artifacts and how to turn his parents young again, but this was not the time. Besides, as soon as the plane took off, the old man had fallen asleep and didn't wake until they had arrived in North Carolina.

When they landed, Mrs. Swenson greeted them with open arms until she saw the looks on their faces.

"Where's Albert?"

No one answered.

"Where's my Albert?" Mrs. Swenson asked again, her voice cracking.

Hank stepped forward. "Ma'am—"

He couldn't finish as Misha moved in front of Mrs. Swenson. He fell to his knees.

"He saved my life. Gave his so I could live. I'm so sorry. I would never have asked him to. I don't know how I can ever make up for your loss."

Mrs. Swenson's tears flowed. She pushed past Misha and moved to the plane. Hank followed behind her.

"You don't have to go in there," Hank said.

She pulled herself inside and went to Mr. Swenson's casket. Hank followed. Only the two of them were in the plane.

"Please, Mrs. Swenson. Come with us," Hank said.

She didn't look at him. She placed a hand on the casket and shook. Her knees buckled, and she collapsed on top of it. "No! No! I told him not to go! They promised."

Hank went to her side. "I'm so sorry, ma'am."

She looked at Hank and recoiled. "No! They promised me he'd be safe, that we would have our home back. And now he's gone—" her words caught in a sob. "And you're still here. It's not fair! It's not fair! I gave them the ring and you for him, and you're here, and he's gone! All I wanted was my family back..." Her sobs increased as she squeezed tighter to the casket.

Hank looked at her in disbelief. He didn't understand the words she was saying. "You?"

Mrs. Swenson didn't respond.

"It was you? You told them about Charleston?"

Mrs. Swenson continued to sob. Hank's heart twisted like a corkscrew. He shuffled across the plane floor. His body felt like he'd just taken the full force of an Apep attack. His legs wavered. Before he could step out, he fell.

Lina rushed to his side. "Hank, are you okay?"

She helped him to his feet.

"Let's go the house," Hank said.

"What about Mrs. Swenson?"

"I think we should let her grieve in private," Hank said.

A warm meal waited them at the Dubois house. Hank left the others feasting in the kitchen and went to his parents' bedroom. He knocked on the door.

"Come in," his mother said.

Hank opened it. His parents were sitting on the bed. They stopped playing cards as Hank entered.

"Hank Hudson. So good to see you, young man," his dad said.

His mom looked at her husband and then to Hank. "It is good to see you. Did you have a nice trip?"

"I'm sorry. I didn't find a way to help you yet."

His dad's cheerful expression fell away.

"That's okay," his mom said. "You'll find it. I know you will."

"I will. I won't ever stop until I find a way to turn you back."

They smiled, and Hank left them. As he walked into the kitchen, Sarah stood by the door, her eyes moist like she'd been crying. She looked at Hank and ran to him, throwing her arms around him. "You're okay. They told me what you did. I'm sorry for saying all those mean things. I just—"

"I know," Hank said. He hugged her back, and she moved to the stove. He looked out the window. Dusky sat under a tree, legs crossed, staring at the sky.

"Don't you want to eat?" Sarah asked.

"I will in a bit. There's something I need to do first," Hank said and went outside.

Dusky continued looking up as Hank approached.

"Excuse me, sir?" Hank said. "I don't want to bother you, but you said something about my parents. They were turned old. Do you know how to turn them back?"

Dusky still stared upward. "One way."

"How?" Hank asked.

"A pool."

"Where is it?"

"I guide you there."

Hank's heart beat faster. He wanted to shout in excitement but did his best to keep his cool. "When can we go? I'm ready now."

"You not ready. Dangerous path."

"But with everyone, we could—"

"Only you and me," Dusky said, cutting him off.

"Hank!" Max shouted from the house.

Hank looked back. He didn't want to be interrupted.

Max stepped down and joined them. "It's your mom. She's ... uh ...calling for you."

Hank looked at Dusky and then the house. "I'll be right back, Dusky." Hank left them to go inside.

Max watched Hank go in and shut the door before turning to Dusky. He looked at the old man, and the old man smiled. Max squatted so they were eye to eye. He stared at him for a long moment, his heart beating faster.

Dusky didn't blink.

Finally, Max spoke. "Did she send you? Does she want you to bring me back home?" ."

Dusky's face didn't change.

"It's a good disguise, But I know who you are, Mr. Grey, you can't change your eyes. It's you."

Dusky gave him a quizzical look. "No, I Dusky. I help."

"Please Mr. Grey, if I can make it up to her, I want to go home."

Dusky didn't say a word.

"Fine, be that way. But I'm watching you," he said through gritted teeth.

A sliver of a smile crept across Dusky's lips.

PUBLISHERS ENDNOTES

We hope you enjoyed Hank Hudson and the Anubis. If you did, we'd ask you to share it. In today's book world, small presses like ours rely on fans like you sharing the love of our stories. You can do this by telling your friends and family and posting reviews to websites like Amazon and Goodreads.

We couldn't continue without your support and to say thank you we want to give you the next book for free. All you need to do is post an honest review of this book to Amazon and send us the link and we will send you an autograph copy of this book for free.

You can email your link to:
RIP@RavenInternationalPublishing.com

Thanks so much, we can't do this without you!

WHAT WAS I THINKING?

NOTES FROM THE AUTHOR

Stories come to me from all kinds of places. The first ideas for the world Hank Hudson appeared in my mind when I was working up in West Yellowstone back in 1993.

In that little town, there was a shop that sold gems, crystals of various sizes and colors, and huge geodes. In fact, one of these geodes stood over 6 feet tall. The man who owned the shop believed there was power in these crystals.

Now I wasn't exactly sure if the crystals held any real power, but I certainly loved the idea.

I started having these daydreams about how cool it would be if you could have one of these crystals and hold it in your hand and it would grant you a superpower.

The world of Hank Hudson wasn't created at that time, but the seed was planted. A seed that grew for almost 15 years before the next piece of the Hank Hudson world entered my imagination.

When I returned from the Iraq War, I took a job at the Minidoka Wildlife Refuge. I spent the entire summer on the back of a four-wheeler spraying weeds. Every day was long and hot as I drove across the Idaho desert. Occasionally I would find sites in the middle of nowhere that had been built by men from the Civilian Conservation Corps, an organization much like the Tennessee Valley Authority.

I want you to understand when I say that I found sites in the middle of nowhere I really mean it. I'd be 30 miles from the nearest road or trail and find a portion of a wall, a chimney or some other structure that had no business being there.

And then there was the day I saw the wolf.

I drove out from under a Russian-olive tree when I saw several rocks. Rocks by themselves are not interesting but these rocks seemed to have been placed for a purpose, and not like the

249

random rock wall I'd found a month earlier. These rocks were placed in a circular fashion spiraling around and into four rocks that held the center.

It was so odd that I got off of my four-wheeler and walked to the center of the circle to take a short video of the rocks.

These rocks certainly didn't come anywhere near the splendor and mystery of Stonehenge, but my writer's mind was already thinking along those lines.

"What if the refuge is here to keep people away from this place?"

"What if this is an important ley line and Roosevelt needed to keep it safe for his personal power?"

"What an incredible story this could become!"

As my mind continued to spiral on its own, I went to look across my stone circle again and then I saw him.

He was standing in the shade of a nearby Russian-olive, and he was close. So close I could easily have struck him with a stone (and if you'd ever seen me throw you'd immediately understand just how incredibly close he had to be for me to claim such a feat).

He stood there panting looking right at me. His fur was gray-white, and he stood slightly taller than a coyote but smaller than most wolves I'd seen. Add to the fact that there are not supposed to be wolves in the area I wanted to call him a coyote but he didn't act or look like any coyote I'd ever seen.

True, coyotes will stop and look at you before running off; that is if they are at a distance. Coyotes also don't hang around when four-wheelers are involved; they scatter fast and disappear into the sagebrush.

He was not scattering, nor running. This animal just watched me as if my presence didn't bother him in the least; as if he'd been expecting me.

The wolf finally turned and padded off. At this point I thought my animal encounter was through and once again, I would be relegated to the title of Weed Killer, but I noticed him 50 yards up a small trail looking back at me.

Perhaps I wanted to see where this wolf was going. Perhaps I was simply looking for something to take me away from the weeds. Perhaps it was something else; something that I just knew had to be done. Whatever the reason might have been I felt the overwhelming sensation that he wanted me to follow him.

I sat back down on my four-wheeler and pushed my right thumb against the throttle and navigated up the lightly worn trail that the wolf had taken. As it was a single track trail, I needed to turn more often to avoid the sage brush. The small scrub plant gave excellent concealment for all of the roaming desert animals. But I never lost sight of my guide.

He would trot ahead for some distance and then stop and turn back as if to make sure I was still following him.

After several hundred yards on the light trail, he took a quick left under a large sage brush. I stopped the four-wheeler and scanned the area trying to see where he'd gone.

Worry crept through my mind that I'd lost him.

I drove forward at a crawl searching close than far out; letting my eyes do zigzag patterns across the desert. And just as fast as I had lost him I saw him again. He was much farther away, almost 100 yards; silhouetted on a nearby rise. He had to have moved with incredible speed to appear that far away so quickly.

I drove the four-wheeler toward him, and he stayed almost motionless.

I had no idea where I was going or why he was leading me, but I knew that he was leading me. As I neared the crest of the rise where he stood, he padded off again this time to the right.

He was climbing a hill that gently rose above the desert floor and formed a plateau. He'd made it up easily, but my going was slightly slower. I eased the four-wheeler forward, climbing over basketball-sized rocks that jutted from the earth. I had to move slowly or risk puncturing a tire.

When I reached the top of the small plateau, I was alone. I sat there wondering why he had brought me here to this place at this time.

I looked in every direction, but there was no sign of the wolf. There was, however, a large pile of rocks.

As I have said before seeing a pile of rocks in this desert was nothing new, but I couldn't help wonder why anyone would hike rocks up on top of a hill to pile them. And then a sudden thought occurred to me:

"What if there was something hidden under the rocks?"

I felt very strongly that this was why the wolf had guided me here.

I swung my left leg over the seat of the four-wheeler and stepped on the ground. I took three steps toward the pile of rocks and stopped. Two children and a tour in Iraq have made me a cautious man.

The summer sun beat down, and the pile of rocks could be the perfect shady place for a bull snake or even a rattlesnake. Being bit by the former would hurt but give me a good story to share, but a bite from the latter would earn me a trip to the emergency room if I was lucky, or earn me a spot as the main dish at a coyote family reunion if I wasn't.

I turned off the four-wheeler engine so I would hear any movement or rattles. On the front of the four-wheeler was a metal basket that carried a fire extinguisher, emergency eye wash, and a machete for cutting the heads off of weeds.

I picked up the machete; if it worked on the head of weeds it might work on the head of a snake.

I crept towrd the pile of rocks. They were stacked over three feet high, which ruled out any natural occurrence unless it was the poop of some yet undiscovered rock monster.

I reached carefully with my left hand and picked up the first rock while my right hand was ready to strike with the machete. There was nothing under it but more rock.

Even with the porous nature of the rock, it was lighter than I had expected. I tossed it to the side and picked up another in the same manner. It didn't take long to clear the pile down toward the plateau's floor.

I noticed something peculiar. There was a relatively flat rock resting on the top of several others that were sunk into the ground. I looked to the left and the right of these partly buried stones, and it appeared they were butted up against each other like someone had made a box out of them.

I took a moment as my mind ran through the possibilities of what could be inside.

"Treasure?"

"Artifacts?"

"Forgotten truths and mystic ways written for me to find?"

I reached my left hand out and grasped the flat stone lid. I could feel the porous holes on my fingers as I lifted it up to reveal what hid beneath.

I could hardly believe my eyes. The wolf, my spirit guide, had led me to this. Not treasure or artifacts or even forgotten wisdom rested in the stone made strongbox. No, he had led me here to find a great pile of mouse doo-doo.

"Just kidding Harry you're not a wizard."

"Sorry, Luke you but ignore your feelings and use that computer."

"Actually, Bilbo I think you should sit this one out."

To be fair, there might have been ancient records there at one time, as I could see the mice had made a nice nest out of bits of paper.

I may not have found a treasure that day but that one event in my life gave the fertile soil needed to grow Hank Hudson and the Anubis.

I hope you enjoyed the book if you did please share with all your family and friends. Also please send me an email and tell me what your favorite part was.

Look forward to talking to you soon,

Clark Chamberlain

clark@RIPub.com

FIND MORE ADVENTURES AT
RAVEN INTERNATIONAL PUBLISHING

WWW.RAVENINTERNATIONALPUBLISHING.COM

KEEP UP TO DATE WITH ALL OF
CLARK'S WRITING, ARTWORK AND TEACHING

WWW.CLARK-CHAMBERLAIN.COM